WHEN FLESH BECOMES WORD

WHEN FLESH BECOMES WORD

An Anthology of Early Eighteenth-Century

Libertine Literature

EDITED BY

Bradford K. Mudge

OXFORD

UNIVERSITY PRESS

2004

OXFORD

UNIVERSITY PRESS

Oxford   New York
Auckland   Bangkok   Buenos Aires   Cape Town   Chennai
Dar es Salaam   Delhi   Hong Kong   Istanbul   Karachi   Kolkata
Kuala Lumpur   Madrid   Melbourne   Mexico City   Mumbai   Nairobi
São Paolo   Shanghai   Taipei   Tokyo   Toronto

Copyright © 2004 by Oxford University Press, Inc.

Published by Oxford University Press, Inc.
198 Madison Avenue, New York, New York 10016

www.oup.com

Oxford is a registered trademark of Oxford University Press

Library of Congress Cataloging-in-Publication Data
When flesh becomes word : an anthology of early eighteenth-century libertine literature /
edited by Bradford K. Mudge.
p. cm.
Includes bibliographical references and index.
ISBN 0-19-516187-4; 0-19-516188-2 (pbk.)
1. Erotic literature, English.   2. English literature—18th century.   3. Litertinism—
Literary collections.   I. Mudge, Bradford Keyes.
PR111.E74W47 2004
820.8'03538'09033—dc21   2003008550

1   3   5   7   9   8   6   4   2

Printed in the United States of America
on acid-free paper

PREFACE

In the spring of 1987, Catherine MacKinnon lectured at the University of Colorado.[1] Her subject was feminism and pornography, and she spoke with great passion and intelligence. Pornography, she argued, is the epitome of patriarchal oppression. It is not the distant cousin of literary fiction or cinematic fantasy, deserving protection or analysis; it is instead its own kind of sexual violence, a text that acquires psychological and political reality when it facilitates the orgasm of its user. That "pleasure" may appear solitary and victimless, but because objectification is its means, oppression is its end. Pornography, MacKinnon continued, is an industry that hurts women twice: first in its production, where it exploits and humiliates (*Deep Throat* serves as the rule, not the exception), and then again in its consumption, where it structures the death of female subjectivity as the precondition of male satisfaction. The First Amendment is thus irrelevant. Pornography is neither "free" nor "speech." Pornography is a crime whose violence is invisible precisely because it is seamlessly consistent with the patriarchy that produced it. Sex is to feminism, MacKinnon concluded, what labor is to Marxism: that which is most one's own, and most taken away. Predictably, perhaps, the question-and-answer session after that lecture was as heated and contentious and ill mannered as any I have heard before or since.

For a young assistant professor finishing a traditional biography of an early nineteenth-century woman of letters, this lecture came as a rude awakening. I was more than intrigued and profoundly perplexed. No stranger to feminist thought and politically sympathetic, I was certainly not offended by MacKinnon's indictment. Nor did I have a personal stake in the argument: pornography had not played a large role in my youth, and there was certainly no room for it at the time in my politically correct universe. Nevertheless, I was disoriented. Like a traveler on a well-known journey who suddenly arrives at an unexpected destination, I had followed the argument to troubling conclusions. Somewhere along the line, pornography had relinquished its status as text and had become a sexual act, and that act had in turn been transformed from private and prurient into public and commonplace. No longer a cultural aberration, an unwanted waste product of the modern marketplace, pornography became constitutive of and not incidental to patriarchal expression. The crisis was thus systemic, and there was more than enough complicity to go around. If these arguments were not disturbing enough, there was the animosity exhibited during the questions and answers. While I was doing my bit for cultural diversity by adding minor women writers to the canon, my colleagues had moved on to scrutinizing the politics of the bedroom with murderous intensity. Academic life—at least when it came to feminism and pornography—appeared anything but safe.

Doing what academics always do under such circumstances, I began to read, and I soon read enough on the subject to be even more confused. MacKinnon expanded the definition of "objectification" past the fashion ads and girly magazines to describe the routine projections of male sexual psychology. Andrea Dworkin upped the ante and argued that within patriarchy even so-called normal sex was rape, while Susanne Kappeler contended that representation itself was inherently pornographic.[2] Then there were the women on the other side, the "prosex feminists": among them Annie Sprinkle, the performance artist, Candida Royalle, the filmmaker, Susie Bright, the journalist and author, Pat Califia, the gay activist and writer, and Camille Paglia, the literary critic and historian.[3] They argued against censorship and for a celebration of women's sexual agency. The fact that the pornography industry has traditionally been run by men with men's interests in mind hardly precludes a whole host of other "feminist" possibilities. Sprinkle celebrated sex as crucial to political liberation; Royalle made films that championed nonhierarchal pleasuring; Bright wrote self-help columns for the sexually adventurous; Califia validated lesbian sadomasochism; and Paglia managed to point out everything that was wrongheaded about white, middle-class, academic feminism. In these capable hands, pornography was transformed from an oppressive genre into an exciting possibility.

The next step was to perpetrate my confusion on others. My partner in crime was a colleague in the History Department with whom each fall I taught "Introduction to Feminist Thought." A historical survey of British and American feminism from 1700 to the present, the course, we reasoned, could easily accommodate a small section on the pornography debate. The first year there was a shouting match, the second we almost came to blows. While consensus could be reached when the subject was Mary Wollstonecraft or Elizabeth Cady Stanton or Charlotte Perkins Gilman, something about pornography caused normally reasonable people to indulge in vituperation. Amid the turmoil, however, one request was heard loud and clear: "Please provide a historical context for this debate!" We took that request seriously, and aided by Walter Kendrick's splendid history *The Secret Museum: Pornography in Modern Culture* (1987) and Peter Wagner's encyclopedic study *Eros Revived: Erotica of the Enlightenment in England and America* (1988), we began, slowly at first, to situate the contemporary feminist debate about pornography within a larger understanding of its relatively recent appearance in the modern cultural marketplace. Crucial to this process, we found, was Kendrick's observation that "pornography" names a debate, not a thing: pornography, he argues, is a controversy about where to place the boundary between legitimate and illegitimate cultural artifacts, not an unchanging category of stylistically similar, generically consistent objects. So defined, acrimonious debate about what pornography "is" yields to a more reasoned historical inquiry about how such objects function at any given moment in their cultural environment. Similarly important was Kendrick's observation that "pornography," emerged from the older and more inclusive discursive category: the "obscene." Although societies since the beginning of time have policed "obscenity"—those materials or behaviors that for whatever reason offend the powers that be—"pornography," the graphic depiction of sexual acts intended to arouse its audience, is exclusively the invention of modern culture.

Over the next decade, thanks to those insistent students, my scholarly activities became more and more preoccupied with the subject. Specifically, I began thinking about the rise of pornography in Britain in relation to the evolution of the eighteenth-century novel. A controversial subliterary genre, the novel sparked a debate about legitimate and illegitimate readerly pleasures that was similar to debates in the twentieth century about film, television, and music. In the eighteenth century, however, the debate about the novel was curiously intertwined with two other controversies: that over the masquerade and that over prostitution. The former was largely about the dangers of fiction, but never strayed far from women's peculiar contributions; the latter was largely about the dangers of predatory women, but never strayed far from crucial roles played by fiction. Taken together, these controversies offered an opportunity to rethink women's curious centrality in the evolving relationship between literature and pornography. Key to this study was the recognition that prior to 1800, "pornography" did not yet exist as a clearly defined discursive category. Rather it was intermixed and intertwined with other genres, out of which, over the century, it emerged into a more conventionally stable form. As a result, my inquiry considered material not frequently examined by traditional literary criticism. In addition to a wide selection of novels—sensational romances and scandal fictions chief among them—I looked at sermons and political tracts, medical literature and travelogues, whore dialogues and bawdy poems, divorce proceedings and criminal biographies. Prior to 1750, the cultural marketplace in England seemed an intriguing maelstrom, a kind of primordial stew out of which the stable categories of modernity would later emerge. Driven by that perplexity bestowed originally by MacKinnon's lecture and bolstered time and time again by the enthusiasm and support of my students, I tried to make sense of this complex process.[4]

This book extends the focus of my earlier work by reproducing the major (and several minor) texts of the "prepornographic" era in Britain. I have tried in seven chapters to provide a representative sampling of the wide variety of material available to the "curious" reader of the early eighteenth century. Chief among these are the three English translations of the early classics of prepornography: *L'Ecole des filles*, by Michel Millot (1655); Nicolas Chorier's *Satyra sotadica* (1660); and *Venus dans le cloître*, by Jean Barrin (1683). The first became *The School of Venus* (1680), the second *A Dialogue Between a Married Lady and a Maid* (1740), and the third *Venus in the Cloister* (1725). Although very different in tone and subject matter, all three are "whore dialogues," dramatic conversations between an older, experienced woman and a younger, inexperienced maid. Direct descendants of Pietro Aretino's *Ragionamenti* (1536), these three dialogues were translated into a variety of languages and frequently reprinted. Print runs, however, were very small and circulation limited because prosecution was always a concern. *The School of Venus*, for example, went to court in 1688, *Venus in the Cloister* in 1725. *A Dialogue Between a Married Lady and a Maid*, a slightly toned-down abridgment of the original, escaped prosecution.

In addition to the whore dialogues, this anthology includes bawdy poetry, a salacious medical treatise, an obscene travelogue, and a criminal biography. Thus, while experts in the field should be pleased to have the three "classics" printed together for the first time and in their entirety, newcomers will find the diversity of contents a useful introduction to very different ways ideas about sex and sexuality found expression.

Needless to say, because the subject matter was, and still can be, considered offensive, these texts have been both rare and restricted. Many originals no doubt suffered a fate similar to Samuel Pepys's copy of *L'Ecole des filles*, which was burned to protect the reputation of its owner.[5] Those copies that did survive were often housed in special collections that, until recently, permitted only limited access. In the last ten years, however, scholars doing work in this area—historians, literary critics, sociologists, genderologists, and medical historians—have become increasingly reliant on material that remains very difficult to procure, and it is hoped that this edition will facilitate their inquiries and those of their students.[6] It is also hoped that this collection will prove of interest to the general reader who is curious about the "libertine literature" of the early eighteenth century.

To that end, editorial interventions have been kept to a minimum and located unobtrusively in the notes.

Although this edition follows quite logically from my earlier work, the impetus for its creation is not entirely mine. Graduate students in a research methods class eagerly transcribed *Venus in the Cloister* as a way to sharpen their knowledge of textual criticism and then, enthusiastic about justifying the ways of Edmund Curll to man, planned an edition that would appeal to the modern reader. Four of those students—Tracy Hindman, John Lyons, Brett Keniston, and Ketievia Segovia—decided to pursue the idea and make it real. In the spring of 2002, they revised the original plan to include other texts and then traveled with me to London where they selected and transcribed much of the material included here. For all of their various labors—in particular, for Tracy's careful transcriptions, John's passion for all things Curllish, Brett's work on Latin and Greek passages, and Ket's masterful computer organization—many, many thanks. Thanks go as well to my dean, Jim Smith, for his continued support, and to my colleagues Nancy Ciccone, Bruce Ferguson, Marjorie Levine-Clark, Elihu Pearlman, and John Stevenson, for their assistance when I was in over my head. Special thanks to John O'Neill of Hamilton College for his help with an obscure poem and to my good friends Gary Watson and Grit Eichler for all their assistance with the Bayerischer Staatsbibliothek in Munich. I was especially fortunate to have an excellent editor, Elissa Morris. Thank you for your enthusiasm and patience.

Finally, I am grateful to my family for their support and patience and, in particular, for their willingness to endure my annual trips to England and for their continued good humor in the face of all those arched eyebrows whenever the topic of conversation turns to my area of academic interest.

CONTENTS

LIST OF ILLUSTRATIONS

A NOTE ON THE TEXTS

Material of this nature, I believe, requires a different editorial approach from what would be traditionally employed in service of more properly "literary" texts. Because these works generally occupied a marginal position in the cultural scheme of things, their processes of production—the composition or translation, the typesetting, the printing, the proofreading, and the binding—were often hurried, the niceties of style and punctuation and orthography giving way in favor of a speedy delivery of sensational or obscene content. Thus, the three works with the most graphic depictions of sexual activity—*The School of Venus* (1680), *Venus in the Cloister* (1725), and *A Dialogue Between a Married Lady and a Maid* (1740) —are also the three works seemingly most in need of editorial assistance. An editor bent on restoration would have a huge job modernizing and/or normalizing spelling and punctuation, in the end creating a text more easily read by a modern audience but not in any way faithful in flavor to the original. For other works in this collection, like John Marten's *Gonosologium Novum* (1709) or Henry Fielding's narrative *The Female Husband* (1746), both of which claimed legitimacy elsewhere, Marten from medicine and Fielding from law, the texts appear to have been produced with diligence and care. Still others, like Thomas Stretzer's work *A New Description of Merryland* (1741), take their place somewhere in between the two extremes.

Although tempted by the cleanliness of restoration, I have chosen— on the basis of the unique situation of the three "whore dialogues"—to preserve the eccentricities of the originals and follow what I call a "consistently inconsistent" editorial method. The latter does not make orthography consistent throughout, or systematize punctuation—possessives or comma splices, say—according to modern practice. Instead, such a method allows the same word variant spellings within the same text ("scholar" and "schollar," "show" and "shew," for example) and permits what today we would consider an overly enthusiastic use of commas, frequently to the extent of run-on sentences and comma splices. In so doing, I have tried to preserve the hasty, rough, and at times breathless qualities of the original, while trusting the reader to acclimate to the variant spellings and unorthodox punctuation. I have also preserved the original use of italics, which, in the early eighteenth, was creative to say the least. On the other hand, I have silently corrected obvious typographical errors and added words, indicated by brackets, where they appear to have been omitted accidentally. Similarly, questions marks have been added where their omission seems odd and off-putting, and spellings have been corrected when the original threatens undue confusion for the modern reader. On rare occasions, particularly devious run-ons have been untangled with the odd semicolon or period. These editorial alterations, however, are relatively few, and these texts appear here in much the same dress as they appeared more than 250 years ago.

Notes in the original texts appear as footnotes at the bottom of the page, my notes as endnotes. I have defined words where the usage is archaic or slang; translated passages when necessary; and provided citations whenever possible. I have also tried to identify people, places, and things unfamiliar to the modern reader. On occasion, I direct the curious reader to appropriate secondary sources. Striking the proper balance between the useful and the unobtrusive is an art, not a science, and I apologize in advance for those inevitable moments of editorial disequilibrium. The works reprinted here are fascinating and complex—unusual to say the very least—and it is my hope that they will speak for themselves, regardless of the strengths or weaknesses of my editorial interventions.

The first work in this collection, *The School of Venus* (1680), is the earliest English translation of *L'Ecole des filles* (1655), which is generally attributed to Michel Millot. The translation changes the names of the original protagonists—Susanne, Fanchon, and Robinet—to Katy, Frances, and Roger but otherwise remains faithful to the original. Like the French, it appears in two dialogues. Unlike the French, it contains twelve plates, or "cutts." The only copy of *The School of Venus* (1680) that I am aware of resides in the Bayerischer Staatsbibliothek in Munich. It was a reprint of this edition, I believe, that incurred the prosecution of Robert Streater and Joseph Crayle, the printer and publisher, in 1688. David Foxon's account of the matter in his very helpful study *Libertine Literature in England, 1660–1745* (1965), relies on newspaper advertisements and court records, but he is obviously unaware of the existence of the 1680 edition. He does point out that rival translations appeared again in 1744 and that their publication resulted in the prosecution of Daniel Lynch and John Stevens. We know from Pepys's account that the French original was available to British readers, and no doubt continued to be available, as a somewhat safer option, even after the translations appeared. *The School of Venus* is reprinted here in its entirety.

Chapter 2 consists of three poems: *The Pleasures of a Single Life* (1701), *The Fifteen Comforts of Cuckoldom* (1706), and *The Fifteen Plagues of a Maiden-Head* (1707). These three, all of which are to be found at the British Library, are bawdy, half-sheet octavo pamphlets. Related to the seventeenth-century ballad and to the kind of bawdy humor represented most famously in Chaucer's *Miller's Tale*, these poems were cheaply produced and cheaply consumed. Other titles of the same type include: *The Fifteen Comforts of Matrimony*, *The Fifteen Comforts of Whoring*, and *The Fifteen Comforts of a Wanton Wife*. When *The Fifteen Plagues of a Maiden-head* lent its name to a small collection of similar poems in 1707, it attracted the attention of the authorities, and James Read and Angell Carter were charged and convicted of its publication. Because, however, the obscene libel offended the community and not an individual, the case was adjourned *sine die*. The poems were then of course reprinted. A 1709 edition of the *The Pleasures of a Single Life*, annotated and also at the British Library, allowed for a more careful restoration of the 1701 edition.

John Marten's medical treatise *Gonosologium Novum, or a New System of the Secret Infirmities and Diseases, Natural, Accidental, and Venereal in Men and Women* (1709), the second half of which is reprinted here as chapter 3, was also prosecuted. It was the first time that the author—rather than the printer or publisher—was named in the case; and it was also the first time that a medical treatise was charged with an offence against civic morals. Published as an appendix to the sixth edition of Marten's work *A Treatise of all the Degrees and Symptoms of the Venereal Disease* (1708), the *Gonosologium Novum* represents a long line of medical works that combine some knowledge of anatomy with folklore, fable, and prurient curiosity. Other popular works of the period include *Aristotle's Master-piece* (1690), which was not by Aristotle, and *Onania, or, The Heinous Sin of Self-Pollution, and All its Frightful Consequences in Both Sexes* (1708). Both went through numerous editions throughout the course of the century. *Gonosologium Novum* also resides in the British Library, and I am here reprinting the second of its two chapters. That chapter has not been reprinted in its entirety: a small section toward the end has been omitted in order to facilitate the flow of the whole.

The fourth chapter, *Venus in the Cloister* (1725), is a translation by Robert Samber of Jean Barrin's 1683 *Venus dans le cloître, ou la religieuse en chemise*. Although based on an earlier English translation, this edition—published by the infamous Edmund Curll—also incurred prosecution. Expanded from the original three dialogues into five, the 1725 edition included strongly worded antiecclesiastical sentiments and several graphic scenes involving flagellation. The story of Curll's trial was told first by Ralph Straus in *The Unspeakable Curll* (1927) and then repeated by Foxon in 1965, only to be revised recently by Alexander Pettit ("Rex v. Curll: Pornography and Punishment in Court and on the Page," *Studies in the*

Literary Imagination [Spring 2001] 64: 63–75). Curll's trial is important, first because the bookseller was the foremost purveyor of libertine literature in the early eighteenth century and also because the prosecution set the standard for English obscene libel law for the next two hundred years. Both Foxon and Pettit identify the first edition of *Venus* as appearing in October 1724 and lament the disappearance of January 1725 reprint. The copy text for this edition of *Venus in the Cloister* is dated 1725, and it is part of the Private Case Collection at the British Library. It is reprinted here in its entirety.

A *Dialogue Between a Married Lady and a Maid* (1740) is an abridged translation of Nicolas Chorier's work *Aloisiae Sigeae Toletanae Satyra Sotadica de arcanis Amoris et Veneris* (1660). The original, in keeping with the common practice among "curious" works of providing misleading information on the title page, purports to be a translation from the Dutch of a Spanish work by Luisa Segea of Toledo. The first French translation, *L'Academie des dames*, appeared in 1680 and, like the original, has seven dialogues. It was also translated into English about the same time. When Streater and Crayle are prosecuted in 1688, *A Dialogue between a Marridd Lady & a Maide* is mentioned in the record. The earliest surviving English translation is that which is reprinted here, the edition of 1740, now at the British Library. Abridged to three dialogues from the original seven, the 1740 edition omits the second and most of the third dialogue, which concern sex between women, but retains the Tullia's advice for the wedding night, which is Chorier's fourth dialogue, and the account of the actual wedding night, which is from the fifth dialogue. As Foxon points out, the abridgement foregrounds sex as a rite of marriage, in effect transforming the original libertine guide into a risque marriage manual. The entire abridgement is reprinted here.

The sixth chapter, *A New Description of Merryland* (1741), is an obscene travelogue that figures female genitalia as a distant and exotic land. A popular subgenre of libertine literature, *Merryland* traces its roots to Charles Cotton's *Erotopolis. The Present State of Betty-land* (1684). Thomas Stretzer, the author of *A New Description*, was also responsible for both *The Natural History of the Arbor Vitae, or Tree of Life* (1732), which combines botany and erotica in an effort to satirize the scientific enthusiasms of the day, and *Merryland Display'd: or plagiarism, ignorance, and impudence, detected. Being observations, on a pamphlet intitled A new description of Merryland* (1741), which purports to refute the earlier work. Edmund Curll, in a characteristic attempt to corner the market, was responsible for printing both *A New Description* and *Merryland Display'd*. The former, according to Wagner, went through seven editions in 1741 alone, although I suspect Curll may have initiated the printing with the "fifth" edition. Similar titles of the same type include: *The Natural History of the Frutex Vulvaria or the Flowering Shrub* (1732) and *Teague-root Display'd: Being Some Useful and Important Discoveries Tending to Illustrate the Doctrine of Electricity, in a Letter from Paddy Strong-Cock to W— W———N* (1746). *A New Description of Merryland* is currently part of the Private Case Collection at the British Library, and it is reprinted here in its entirety.

Henry Fielding's narrative *The Female Husband: or the Surprising History of Mrs. Mary, alias Mr. George Hamilton* (1746) represents another popular subgenre of libertine literature, the "rogue biography." Related in kind to the *Old Bailey Session Papers* and the *Accounts from Tyburn*, which sensationalized both the crimes and the executions of notorious criminals, and to the ever popular accounts of divorce proceedings, *The Female Husband* follows the career of "Molly Hamilton," a cross-dressing lesbian who is eventually captured and prosecuted for deceiving other women. Horrified by, but clearly fascinated with, lesbian transgressions, *The Female Husband* is particularly attentive to the unnatural acts of the transgendered. It too resides at the British Library and is reprinted here in its entirety.

When I saw them I had the same kind of impulse which made Guilio Romano do the original paintings, and . . . I scribbled off the sonnets which you find underneath each one. The sensual thoughts which they call to mind I dedicate to you, saying a fig for hypocrites. I am all out of patience with their scurvy strictures and their dirty-minded laws which forbid the eyes to see the very things which delight them most.

— PIETRO ARETINO, *Letters*

Love hath this excellency in it, that it intirely satisfyeth every body, according to their apprehensions, the most ignorant receiving pleasure though they know not what to call it; hence it comes, that the more expert and refined wits have a double share of its delights, in the soft and sweet imaginations of the mind.

—MICHAEL MILLOT, *The School of Venus*

INTRODUCTION

British Libertine Literature before *Fanny Hill* (1749)

When James Boswell met John Cleland in April 1779, the author of *The Memoirs of a Woman of Pleasure* (1749) was nearly seventy. "Found him," Boswell writes, "in an old house in the Savoy, just by the waterside. A coarse, ugly old man for his servant. His room, filled with books in confusion and dust was like Dupont's and old Lady Eglinton's, at least old ideas were suggested to me as if I were in a castle. He was drinking tea and eating biscuits. I joined him. He had a rough cap like Rousseau, and his eyes were black and piercing."[1] Life had not been easy for Cleland. After a brief stint at the elite Westminster School and an almost successful career in the East India Company, he had returned to London and debtors' prison. There, in late 1748 and early 1749, he had published *The Memoirs of a Woman of Pleasure*, better known today as *Fanny Hill*. The book became an underground bestseller, translated and reprinted over and over again throughout his lifetime and after. Yet, predictably perhaps, *Fanny Hill* brought its author only shame. The money went into other hands, and Cleland was forced to scramble. He wrote novels, plays, and poetry; he wrote medical treatises, linguistic studies, and political tracts; he knew many of the famous figures of his day, including Pope, Garrick, Sterne, and Smollett. But he would never achieve success. He quarreled with Garrick, who refused to produce his plays, and with Sterne, whose work, amazingly, Cleland thought too bawdy, too crude. When Boswell found him in 1779, Cleland had little to show for his long years of literary labor. "A sly, old malcontent" was how Boswell put it, and the image of the castle, together with the dust and confusion of the room, only confirm Cleland's isolation and embitterment. The author of the most famous "pornographic" novel in the English language, arguably the most famous "pornographic" novel of all time, seemed destined for obscurity.

Obscurity, however, was not to be Cleland's fate. Once illegal in both Britain and the United States, *Fanny Hill* is now routinely taught in university literature courses. All of his other works have long since disappeared, and the one novel he most regretted now keeps his memory alive. Is, however, "pornographic" the correct adjective to describe Cleland's masterwork? For the casual, modern reader, the answer is unequivocally "yes." For what could be more conventionally "pornographic" than Fanny's story of her sexual adventures, beginning with her arrival in London from the country, moving to her early lesbian experiences, then her defloration by her lover Charles, her brief stint as mistress, her longer career as whore, then her happy reunion with her beloved and her subsequent apotheosis as wife and mother. Although genitals hide behind metaphor, the scenes are nevertheless both graphic and calculatingly arousing. Fanny's goal, she tells us, is to represent the "stark, naked truth" of human pleasure, and if her diction is closer to Ovid than Larry Flynt, she is no less effective for it. And, as we might expect, each episode is slightly more risqué than the one before: Phoebe's gentle kisses yield first to sex for love, then sex for money, then sex for the thrill of illicit pleasure. With these escalating episodes— as evenly spaced and graphically described as they are—and with its predictable redemption-through-marriage ending, *The Memoirs of a Woman of Pleasure* appears conventional, formulaic: it appears to represent a well-established tradition of "pornographic" writing as timeless as human passion and as uncontrollable as the desire to recreate experience in paint or word. And yet, as my quotation marks suggest, the word is misleading, for it proposes a seamless continuity between modern perception and eighteenth-century intention. What if instead "pornography" is, as Walter Kendrick has argued, a distinctly modern discourse, one that comes into being at the end of the eighteenth, beginning of the nineteenth century?[2] The *Oxford English Dictionary*, he insists, confirms this view: "pornography" is an early nineteenth-century neologism whose etymology means "whore writing" or "writing by or about whores." How can we describe Cleland's *Fanny Hill* as the first great English "pornographic" novel when neither the word, nor the discursive category it names, existed during Cleland's lifetime?

This volume is proffered by way of an answer, representing as it does the variety of protopornographic writings that thrived in the English literary marketplace before Cleland's novel irrevocably changed the landscape. Although "pornography," as we have come to understand it—the graphic depiction of sexual acts intended to arouse the audience—may not have existed as a stable generic form in 1750, *Fanny Hill* unquestionably employs narrative techniques and strategies that would soon become conventional. As such, the novel marks a significant watershed in the evolution of libertine literature, and by virtue of its prescience threatens to displace the very literatures out of which it emerged. Before *Fanny Hill* erotic and/or obscene literature was intermixed and intermingled with other genres and subgenres. Whore dialogues combined lascivious passages with sex education, antiecclesiastical diatribes, and radical philosophy. Medical treatises vacillated between sound advice about sexual disorders and lurid tales from pseudo-science: in one paragraph the benefits of mercury as a cure for syphilis were carefully considered; in the next redheaded women were singled out as having particularly dangerous passions. Travelogues figured distant lands as female genitalia and punned their way shamelessly along the allegorical journey. Botanical studies transformed human genitalia into plants and had great fun parodying the contemporary enthusiasm for all things horticultural. Trial proceedings recreated the sensational events of notorious criminals and captured all of the unspeakable details from high-profile divorces. Bawdy poetry kept the seventeenth-century ballad alive and well. Sodomites and hermaphrodites were popular across the board: they appeared in the medical treatises, in the criminal literature, and in the bawdy poetry. It was the age of satire, of course, and irreverence was thick in the air. Because prosecution was always a threat and because masquerades were always amusing, duplicity was common practice. Title pages were conveniently altered either to protect author and bookseller or, more often, to fool the gullible reader. Places and dates of publication were notoriously unreliable, but so were book titles and names of authors. One might locate *The School of Venus* on the shelf and buy it furtively, only to get it home and discover that it was not the infamous translation but instead a collection of third-rate poetry. Pirated editions were of course the rule rather than the exception, and booksellers and printers often engaged in elaborate ruses in order to procure potentially lucrative material. It was a world of literary masquerades, and real passions lurked frequently beneath deceptive appearances.

The undisputed champion of unscrupulous booksellers was Edmund Curll, and for almost forty years—from roughly 1705 to 1745—he dominated the "curious book" trade. Alongside his more legitimate offerings, and there were many, one could have found an impressive selection of bawdy works. The sensational and scandalous novels of Aphra Behn, Delarivier Manley, and Eliza Haywood were all to be found on his shelves. But then again, so was the poetry of Alexander Pope, Jonathan Swift, and John Gay. Cheap editions of Chaucer's *Miller's Tale* rubbed shoulders with the plays of Shakespeare and Congreve and with the poetry of John Wilmot, Earl of Rochester. John Marten, who wrote *Gonosologium Novum* (1709; reprinted here in chapter 3), was in Curll's employ, and so was Robert Samber, who translated *Venus in the Cloister* (1725; reprinted in chapter 4). Thomas Stretzer, better known to bibliographers as "Roger Pheuquewell," wrote *A New Description of Merryland* (1741; reprinted in chapter 6) and several other works exclusively for Curll's shop. Very little in the way of opposition seemed to compromise these disreputable literary activities. Curll quarreled repeatedly and viciously with Alexander Pope, only to triumph—with the odds decidedly against him—in the end. There were also the arrests and jail terms. *Venus in the Cloister*, which was printed very carefully without mention of Curll on the title page, caused him nonetheless more than two years of trouble with the authorities: he was arrested twice in 1725 and again in 1727. Surprisingly, however, business continued, providing perhaps one of the earliest examples of what has become a modern truism about so-called obscene or pornographic works: a little legal difficulty makes for brisk sales. Thus, in the literary world of the early eighteenth century, in the world before *Fanny Hill* and modern pornography, a world where all sorts of very different books experimented with the representation of human sexuality, Edmund Curll reigned supreme. More than any of his contemporaries, Curll seemed to grasp how polymorphously perverse books could be. He delighted in finding news ways to please his readers and scandalize the status quo. His role and mission was to sell books, and his only rule was "Buyer beware."

After *Fanny Hill*, however, the world of Edmund Curll would slowly disappear. The confusing generic mishmash would sort itself out according to rules more acceptable to a modern audience. Medical treatises would continue their preoccupation with venereal disease and masturbation but would eventually learn to stick with fact and leave the longer imaginative flights to the novelists. Bawdy poetry and obscene travelogue would move into periodicals, where prose fiction would slowly gain the upper hand. Criminal accounts and trial proceedings would remain popular, but there was less pressure on writers to recreate the crime with fictionalized immediacy. After *Fanny Hill*, in other words, the novel becomes the genre of choice for those wishing to arouse an audience. Curll's deceptions and depravities—his bawdy poetry, his books on flogging and venereal disease, his treatises on hermaphrodites, his extended parodies of contemporary botany, his editions of Manley and Rochester, his trial accounts and proceedings—they would all lose their appeal and in hindsight appear a bit silly, adolescent even. By 1789, the year the Bastille fell and ten years after Boswell had tea and biscuits with John Cleland, sexual obscenity and the novel were joined at the hip. In both London and Paris, a well-funded gentleman with a taste for curious literature could find a bookseller or two who would happily satisfy his needs.

The novel, of course, played a crucial role in the cultural life of the eighteenth century, and scholars have made much of its unique influence on the nascent ideology of the modern nation-state.[3] The industrial revolution moved people into cities, increased available goods and services,

Figure Intro.1 Anonymous, *The Art and Mystery of 'Printing' Emblematically Displayed*. This illustration of Curll's print shop appeared on the front page of *The Grub Street Journal* on October 26, 1732. The two-faced figure in the middle of the triptych may be the only portrait we have of Edmund Curll.

and expanded the middle classes. With more leisure time and increasing literacy, more and more people turned to novels for entertainment. Interestingly, the novel began the century in disgrace: it was an illegitimate, sub-literary form dominated by both women writers and women readers. Aphra Behn, Delarivier Manley, and Eliza Haywood were three early novelists who borrowed freely from restoration drama and were unembarrassed to foreground sexual intrigue in their fiction. Popular and impassioned, these novels captured the attention of critics who deplored cheap sensationalism and pleaded for the refined pleasures of high literature. Before long, male authors, attracted by profit and aware of other options for prose fiction, sought to reform the genre. Samuel Richardson, among others, made the case for the novel as a didactic form capable of educating young readers. His novel *Pamela* (1740) took London by storm and replaced the scheming viragos of Behn, Manley, and Haywood with a virginal heroine capable of pushing all depraved souls to the moral high ground. Cynics, Henry Fielding and John Cleland among them, found Richardson's sanctimonious preaching hard to take and responded in kind, Fielding with *Shamela* (1741) and *Joseph Andrews* (1742) and Cleland—arguably—with *Memoirs of a Woman of Pleasure*. At stake in this midcentury debate was both the role and form of the novel—Was it to be the extended sermon of Richardson or the comic epic in prose touted by Fielding?—and the "real" nature of the men and women depicted within: Are "real" women saintlike virgins, like Pamela, or scheming whores, like Shamela? *Fanny Hill*, an underground bestseller but destined to be marginalized by two centuries of prosecution, also participated in the discussion. Cleland offered readers yet another novelistic "realism," an imaginary narrative in which characters actively pursued a "real" sexual pleasure that was in turn vicariously accessible. Although literary scholars have until very recently ignored his contribution, Cleland's novel stands at the beginning of a discourse—pornography—that has proven itself of crucial importance to the modern state.

How, then, did Cleland come to write his novel, whose significance we are still just beginning to understand? Boswell, presumably over biscuits and tea, asked the question. Cleland's response was surprising. Making no mention of his obvious financial motivations, he insisted that almost the entire manuscript was completed twenty-five years before he finally published it. It was, he claimed, a work of youth, enthusiastic and indiscreet. Of debtors' prison, of Ralph Griffiths, of the circumstances of the book's publication, not a word was spoken. More important, he also claimed that it was conceived as a challenge. He wrote it to prove to a friend that one could represent sexual pleasure without the coarseness and offensive language that characterized *L'Ecole des filles*. *Memoirs of a Woman of Pleasure* was conceived, in other words, as an aesthetic experiment, self-consciously opposed to the tradition from which it emerged. For a variety of reasons—the disturbing nature of the material, the rarity of the original texts, the restrictions imposed by research libraries—that tradition has been rendered largely invisible even to scholars of the period. This edition, then, seeks to bring to light a representative sampling of libertine literature before *Fanny Hill*. Collected here, in their entirety, are the three infamous "whore dialogues" that descended from Pietro Aretino's *Ragionamenti* (1534–36) and were translated and reprinted throughout the eighteenth century: after they moved across the English Channel, *L'Ecole des filles*, by Michel Millot (1655), Nicolas Chorier's *Satyra sotadica* (1660), and *Venus dans le cloître*, by Jean Barrin (1683), became *The School of Venus* (1680), *A Dialogue Between A Married Lady and a Maid* (1740), and *Venus in the Cloister* (1725). In addition, this anthology includes examples of bawdy poetry, salacious medical advice, obscene travelogue, and rogue biography. Fascinated both by the perplexing origins of Cleland's novel and by the image of Curll's bookshop with its diverse offerings and scandalous masquerades, I have tried to reproduce a small part of a literary world whose creative chaos and irreverent obscentiy have been irrevocably reorganized by Dewey decimals and by seemingly unbreachable generic boundaries. Conspicuously absent in this edition, however, are two important participants in that literary world: the impassioned novels of Behn, Manley, and Haywood and the obscene, irreverent poetry of Rochester. The former experimented with the ways that sexual passion could be shared by character and reader alike; the latter pushed social and political satire to new levels of obscenity. Both are well known to students of the period, both are readily available in modern editions, and both are to be remembered as ongoing presences in that literary microcosm that was Edmund Curll's bookshop.

By virtue of its diverse offerings, this edition should prove valuable to scholars, students, and general readers whose interests are not exclusively literary. Although libertine literature functioned alongside and in direct counterpoint to the more legitimate literary works of the period—eventually evolving into a discourse of illegitimate "others" against which highbrow literature would define itself—the material collected here speaks to a broad range of cultural issues. Students of prose fiction will be quick to see the dramatic experiments of the whore dialogue as important to evolving definitions of the novel, and will also note with interest the degree to which fiction insinuated itself in the supposedly nonfiction genres of medical treatise, travelogue, and criminal biography. Conversely, historians—of medicine, of sexuality and gender, of religion, of eighteenth-century British culture generally—will find the material a rich source of information about a variety of often elusive topics, among them chastity, modesty, courtship, birth control, premarital sex, marriage, fidelity, adultery, flagellation, homosexuality, and transvestism. Favorite topics of discussion include male sexual physiology, female sexual physiology, theories of sexual attraction, the acceptable and unacceptable rituals of foreplay, the nature and gradations of sexual pleasure, the appearance and importance of the maidenhead, the differences between male and female orgasm, the nature of female ejaculation, what men really want from women, what women really want from men, the need for coarse language during intercourse, the variety of desirable postures that must be tried, the justifications for adultery and premarital sex, the advantages of secrecy when conducting intrigues, the ideal female body, the ideal male body, the differences between love and lust, the irrepressible erotic imagination, and the hypocrisy of conventional ideas about sexual practice.

Although the perspectives vary from work to work and although each attempts to justify or normalize its own favorite ideas about human sexuality, the works collected here are all agreed on—indeed compelled by—the desirability of making private knowledge public. Unlike modern pornographers, whose central purpose is to arouse the audience, these works take special pains to educate as well as entertain. Whether it is Frances explaining the ways of the world to Katy or John Marten holding forth on the "secret infirmities" of the nether regions or Henry Fielding being coy about the mechanics of lesbian sex, there is an almost palpable compulsion to share forbidden information for public good. This tendency is least in evidence in *A New Description of Merryland*, where knowledge moves through a series of puns to comprise one long insider joke between well-to-do, educated men. Revealing asides about gendered behavior, however, are no less in evidence. As the preceding list suggests, a wide variety of sexual/social/political issues are addressed even as the narratives self-consciously push at the boundaries of fictional pleasure. It is not unusual, in other words, after having read a description of sexual congress, to come upon little sermons like the following from *The School of Venus*:

> [Men's] thoughts and imaginations being so intent on the pleasure they take, they can scarce speak plain, and as they breathe short, they are glad to use all the Monysyllabic words they can think of, and metaphorise as briefly as they can upon the obscane parts, what they usually called Loves Paradise and the center of delight, they now in plain English call a Cunt, which word Cunt

is very short and fit for the time it is named in, and though it
makes Women sometimes Blush to hear it named, methinks indeed they do ill, that make such a pather, to describe a Monysyllable by new words and longer ways then is necessary, as to call a
Man's Instrument according to it's name, a Prick, is it not better
than Tarsander, a Mans-Yard, Man *Thomas*, and such like tedious
demonstrations, neither proper nor concise enough in such short
sports. For the heat of love will neither give us leave or time to
run diversions, so that all we can pronounce is, come my dear
Soul, take me by the Prick, and put it into thy Cunt, which sure
is much better then to say, take me by the Gristle, which grows
at the bottom of my Belly, and put it into thy loves Paradice.[4]

The argument makes language into an analogue of the body and insists
that conversation during sex be as plain and unadorned as the lovers themselves. Euphemism, innuendo, metaphor, and polysyllabics all detract from
the naked truth of the four-letter word, and language, like the lovers who
use it, must first disrobe in order to engage in intimate conversation. This
argument, which is also, by the way, part of a justification for male vulgar-
ity during sex, serves to explain *The School of Venus* as a whole, and in particular, why the sexual activity described therein is better represented by
the ubiquitous "prick" and "cunt."

    I suspect that the preceding passage could be the very one that drove
Cleland to his novelistic experiment. He was clearly aware, as was the author of *L'Ecole des filles*, that representing human sexuality in prose fiction
called for innovative technique, but, as his comments to Boswell suggest,
obscene language was the problem not the solution. Although Fanny tells
her correspondent that her life will be told "with the same liberty that I
led it," she has no intention of dragging her story through the gutter. "Liberty" and "obscenity" are not synonymous:

> Truth! stark naked truth, is the word, and I will not so much as
> take the pains to bestow the strip of a gauze-wrapper on it, but
> paint situations as they actually rose to me in nature, careless of
> violating those laws of decency, that were never made for such
> unreserved intimacies as ours; and you have too much sense, too
> much knowledge of the *originals* themselves, to snuff prudishly,
> and out of character, at the *pictures* of them. The greatest men,
> those of the first and most leading taste, will not scruple adorn-
> ing their private closets with nudities, though, in compliance with
> vulgar prejudices they may not think them decent decorations of
> the stair-case or saloon.[5]

Through her correspondent, Fanny speaks directly to the readers, reminding them of the novelist's twofold responsibility: first, to the "truth" of nature; and second, to the "unreserved intimac[y]" between writer and reader. The first requires that the "stark naked truth" of sexual pleasure be fairly represented; the second demands that the "laws of decency" and "vulgar prejudices" of our public lives not interfere with the authenticity of "private" communication. We have, she tells us, "too much sense, too much knowledge of the *originals* themselves" to be perturbed by the "liberty" of their "*picture*." In other words, Fanny will remove the "gauze-wrapper" preferred by polite fiction, but in so doing she will honor both the intelligence of her readers and the "intimacies" of the "private closet." What follows is nothing less than a dramatically different kind of novelistic "realism."

It is no matter than Fanny is lying. All realisms do, particularly those of the novel. We know that we are not intimate correspondents sharing the private details of our lives but instead anonymous readers of a mass-marketed commodity whose central intention is to exchange pleasure for money. What matters is that we delight in the lie, that we appreciate factual fictions and public privacies. Fanny's lie is the stuff of the imagination, and it is integrally intertwined with those told by the greatest storytellers. But it is also intimately tied to other kinds of fictions, those that lived and worked outside the boundaries of the novel proper, those that risked both public disgrace and legal penalty to amuse readers with illicit pleasure. Fanny's lie would have been impossible without *The School of Venus* and *Venus in the Cloister* and *A Dialogue Between a Married Lady and a Maid*, without those whore dialogues that dared to imagine sexual pleasure as a readerly possibility as well as a corporeal experience. Those dialogues entertained, titillated, and shocked readers with graphic descriptions, but they also shared the facts of human biology and puzzled over the moral, social, and philosophic mysteries of sexual practice. Fanny's lie is also indebted to the bawdy humor of the street ballad. In keeping with the liberties permitted to satire, those ballads made fun of courtship, marriage, and adultery. *The Pleasures of a Single Life* and *The Fifteen Comforts of Cuckoldom* are extended, misogynistic jokes that turn the sanctity of marriage into the ridiculousness of incompatible self-interest. *The Plagues of a Maiden-Head* transforms chastity into disease, and the female narrator suffers because the men around her lack courage and initiative. In the world of the ballad, human sexuality is a joke and we have no choice but to laugh. We laugh as well at the adolescent humor of *A New Description of Merryland*, even as we are reminded uncomfortably of the wink-wink, nudge-nudge of an exclusive boys' club. From these works, among other things, Fanny borrows the irreverent wit that makes life so difficult for poor Mr. Norbert and keeps readers wondering about whether or not they are getting all of her jokes. Her humor, as well as that of her creator, derives from the masquerade, from impersonations, masks, and deceptions, from the relentless trickery that made Edmund Curll an almost wealthy man. All of the works here share that penchant. John Marten is alternatively the serious scientist and the scheming quack, Henry Fielding the outraged magistrate and the prurient novelist. Marten's medical treatise indulges fanciful flights of the imagination; Fielding's criminal biography tantalizes with the imagined perversions of lesbian intercourse. Fanny's lie, in other words, is not hers alone. It emerges out of and is made possible by a libertine literature whose diversity matched its irreverence, a literature whose unique contributions to early eighteenth-century British culture were lost for a time in the shadows of disreputable bookstores and ignored by purveyors of more palatable truths.

I

The School of Venus
(1680)

THE SCHOOL OF VENUS,

or,

THE LADIES DELIGHT,

Reduced into RULES of PRACTICE.

THE

ARGUMENT

In the first Dialogue.

Roger a young Gentleman being passionately in love with *Katherine* a Virgin of admirable beauty, but so extreamly simple, having always been brought up under the rigid Government of her Mother, who was Wife of a Substantial Citizen, that all his perswasions could do no good on her, by reason she understood not any thing that appertained to love, he therefore by force of presents and other allurements gains a Kins-Woman of hers named *Frances* to his Party, and she having promised *Roger* to sollicite *Katherine*, in his behalf makes her a Visit. Accordingly *Frances* who was much wiser than her Cousin, and better practised in love concerns, undertakes *Katherine* whom finding opportunly at home, she cunningly acquaints the young Girl with all the pleasures of love, and by the relation so fired her blood as she longed to be at the sport, *Frances* then strikes while the Iron was hot, and persuades *Katherine* to imbrace that opportunity, none being at home but herself and the Maid, and let Mr. *Roger* whose person she made agreeable to the young Wench, ease her of her Maidenhead, that the Girl consents to, and in the nick of time Mr. *Roger* coming to make a Visit, as *Frances* and he had before laid their design, *Frank* takes occasion to leave them alone.

In the Second Dialogue.

Katherine acquaints *Frances*, how she had lost her Maidenhead, the Variety of postures *Roger* had put her in, and how afterwards he had Swived her in various manners, besides all along in the discourse is inserted such Divine and Mysterious love Morals, as makes the Treatise very delightful and pleasant to the Readers.

THE ORTHODOX BULL,

Anathema and Indulgence.

PRIAPUS, *our most August Monarch,*[4] *thunders forth* Anathema *against all manner of Persons of either Sex, who Read or hear Read the Precepts of Love, Explained in a Book called the School of* VENUS, *without spending or at least not having some incitements of Nature which tend to Fucking, on the other side he grants a Plenary Indulgence to all those who are debilitated by being superannuated, or having some other Corporal defect, he also gives his Benediction to all those Unfortunate Pilgrims who suffer for* Venus's *cause, and have therefore undertaken the Perilous Voyage of* Sweating *and* Fluxing.

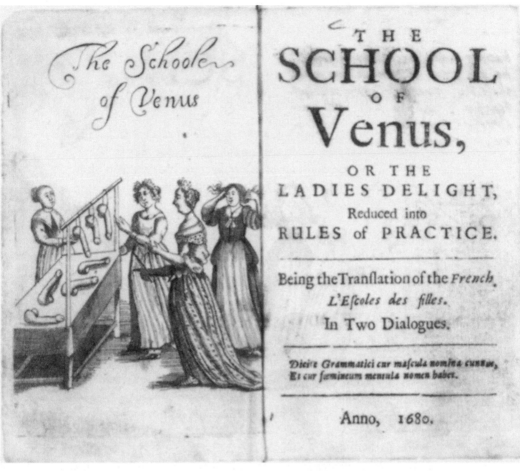

Figure 1.1   The Frontispiece and Title Page of *The School of Venus* (1680).

Dialogue the First.

Frank, Katy.

Frank. *Good Morrow,* Katy.

Katy. Oh! Good Morrow Cousin, and what good Wind blows you hither, now my Mother is from home, Lord how glad am I to see you. Is this Visit pure kindness or business?

Frank. *No business I assure you, but pure affection, I am come to chat and talk with you, 'tis wearisome being alone, and methinks, 'tis an age since last I saw you.*

Katy. You say true, and I am much obliged to you, will you please sit down, you find no body at home but me and the Maid.

Frank. *Poor Soul, what thou art at work?*

Katy. Yes.

Frank. *I think you do nothing else, you live here confined to your Chamber, as if it were a Nunnery; you never stir abroad, and seldom a man comes at thee.*

Katy. You say very true Cousin, what should I trouble my self with men; I believe none of them ever think of me, and my Mother tells me, I am not yet old enough to Marry.

Frank. *Not old enough to be Married, and a young plump Wench of Sixteen; thou art finely fitted indeed with a Mother, who ought now to take care to please thee, as formerly she did herself, what's become of Parents love and affection now adays, but this is not my business; art thou such a Fool to believe you can't enjoy a mans company without being Married?*

Katy. Why, don't I enjoy their Company and do not men come often hither?

Frank. *Who are they? I never see any.*

Katy. Lord! how strange you make it, why is there not my two Unkles, my Cousins, Mr. *Richards* and many others?

Frank. *Pish, they are your kindred! I mean others.*

Katy. Why, what make you of Mr. *Clarke,* Mr. *Wilson,* Mr. *Reynolds,* and young Mr. *Roger,* whom I ought to have named first, for he comes often and pretends he loves me, telling me a Hundred things which I understand not, and all to little purpose; for I have no more pleasure in their Company, then I have in my Mothers, or my Aunts. Indeed their cringes, congees and ceremonies,[5] make me laugh sometimes, when I speak to them, they stare upon me, as though they would eat me; and at last go away like Fools as they came; what satisfaction can one receive by such persons Company? In truth instead of being pleased with them, I am quite a weary of them.

Frank. *But, do they not tell you, you are handsome, are they not perpetually kissing and stroking thee?*

6

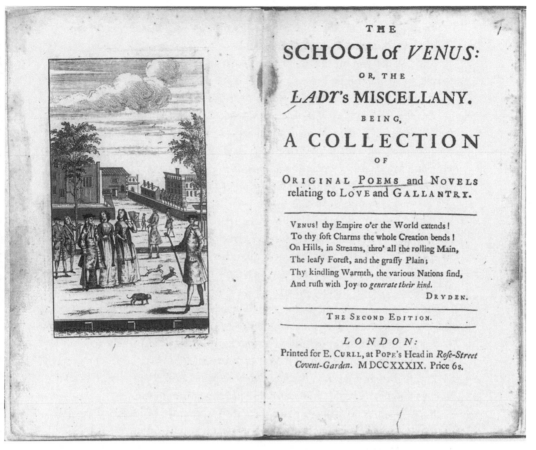

THE

SCHOOL of *VENUS*:

OR, THE

LADY's MISCELLANY.

BEING,

A COLLECTION

OF

ORIGINAL POEMS and NOVELS
relating to LOVE and GALLANTRY.

VENUS! thy Empire o'er the World extends!
To thy foft Charms the whole Creation bends!
On Hills, in Streams, thro' all the rolling Main,
The leafy Foreft, and the graffy Plain;
Thy kindling Warmth, the various Nations find,
And rufh with Joy to *generate their kind*.
DRYDEN.

THE SECOND EDITION.

LONDON:
Printed for E. CURLL, at POPE's Head in *Rofe-Street*
Covent-Garden. MDCCXXXIX. Price 6s.

Figure 1.2   The frontispiece and title page of Edmund Curll's *The School of Venus* (1739), a collection of poetry he no doubt hoped would be confused with the whore dialogue of the same title.

Katy. Why, who the Duce told you? Indeed they do little else, but commend my beauty, kissing me and feeling my Breasts, telling me a Hundred things, which they say are very pleasing to them, but for my part, they add nothing to my content.

Frank. *Why, and do you suffer them to do all this?*

Katy. Truly no, for my Mother hath forbidden me.

Frank. *Lord, what an ignorant innocent Fool art thou!*

Katy. Pray Cousin, why do you say so, is there any thing to be learned, which I do not know?

Frank. *You are so ignorant, you are to learn every thing.*

7

Katy. Sweet Cousin instruct me then.

Frank. *Yes, see, this is the fruits of being ruled by a Mother, and never mind what men say unto you.*

Katy. What can an innocent Girl learn from men, whom the world account so debauched?

Frank. *I have a great deal of reason to speak well of them; for 'tis not long since I received a great deal of pleasure from one of that Sex; my dear Rogue, they are not half so bad as thou art made to believe, and the worst is, thou art never like to be convinced, thou art so cloistered up from their intrigues and Company, that thou wilt always live in ignorance, and consequently wilt never injoy any pleasure in this World: prithee tell me, what pleasure can'st thou injoy being always confined to a Chamber with thy Mother?*

Katy. Do you ask me what pleasure, truly Cousin, I take a great deal, I eat when I am hungry, I drink when I am dry, I sleep, sing and dance, and sometimes go into the Country and take the Air with my Mother.

Frank. *This is something, but does not every body else do the like?*

Katy. Why, is there any pleasure, that is not common to every body?

Frank. *Sure enough, for there is one that you have not yet tasted of, which as much exceeds all the rest, as Wine doth fair water.*

Katy. Cousin, I confess my ignorance, in which I am likely to continue, unless you will please to explain it unto me.

Frank. *But, is it possible, that those men (especially Mr. Roger) with whom you have discoursed should not have said something of it unto you?*

Katy. No indeed Cousin han't they, if this pleasure be so great, as you say, they have not had the charity to communicate it to me.

Frank. *What do you still doubt of the sweetness of it? It is the most soveraign pleasure we poor Mortals injoy; but I admire Mr. Roger, whom all the World thinks in love, which you did hear [him] speak of it unto you; surely you do not answer his affection.*

Katy. Truly Cousin, you are much mistaken, for he himself can't deny, but when he sighs and bemoans himself in my presence, I (far from being the cause thereof) pity him, ask him what he ailes, and should be glad with all my heart if I could give him any ease.

Frank. *Oh, now I begin to understand where the shooe wrings you both, why do not you tell him (when he professeth he loves you) that you also have a kindness for him?*

Katy. Why so I would, if I thought it would do him any good, but since I know it is to no purpose, had not I better hold my peace?

Frank. *Alas Child, I can but pity thee, and thy misfortune, for if thou hadst but shewn some affection to him, he would without doubt have informed thee of this pleasure we are now talking of.*

8

Katy. Prithee Cousin, how can that be, must a Maid of necessity love a man before she can attain to this pleasure? Methinks, I may love Mr. *Roger* and many men else, and yet not enjoy any pleasure in it.

Frank. *Yes, so you may you fool you, if people only look at one another, but there must be feeling in the case too.*

Katy. Why, how many times have I touched him, and yet find no such pleasure in it?

Frank. *Yes, yes, you have touched his cloaths, but you should have handled something else.*

Katy. Dear Cousin, expound your self more clearly unto me, I understand not in the least what all this discourse tends to, tell me therefore in plain English, what must I do to attain this pleasure?

Frank. *Why then in short, 'tis this, a young Man and a Maid can without any cost or trouble give one another the greatest pleasure imaginable.*

Katy. Oh, good Cousin, what a mind have I to know what this pleasure is, and how to enjoy it!

Frank. *Be not too hasty and you shall know all, did you never see a naked man?*

Katy. I never saw a man in my life, I have seen little boyes stark naked.

Frank. *No, that will not do, the young Man must be Sixteen or Seventeen years old, and the Maid Fourteen or Fifteen.*

Katy. If they must be so big truly then I never saw any.

Frank. *Dear Cousin, I love thee too well to keep thee longer in ignorance, did you never see a man at piss and the thing with which he pisseth?*

Katy. Yes once I saw a man piss against a Wall, who held something in his hand, but I could not imagine what it was, he seeing me look at him turned himself towards me, and then the thing he had in his hand, appeared to be like a white hogs pudding of a reasonable length, which was joyned to his Body, which made me admire I had not the like.

Frank. *And so much the better you Fool, for if you had, it was not possible for you to receive the pleasure we are now a talking of. But I am just now going to tell you things which will seem a great deal more strange unto you.*

Katy. You oblige me infinitely, but pray first inform me, if this pleasure is singular, that none but a young Man and a Maid can partake thereof.

Frank. *No such matter, all People of all ranks and degrees participate therein, even from the King to the Cobler, from the Queen to the Scullion Wench, in short one half of the World Fucks the other.*[6]

Katy. This discourse is Hebrew to me, but is there no difference in this pleasure?

Frank. *Yes marry there is, Husbands and Wives take some pleasure, but they are generally cloyed with it, and therefore, sometimes the Wife, oftentimes the Hus-*

band ha's some variety by having a bit in a corner, as for example, your Father had often his pleasure of your Maid Servant Margaret, whom therefore your Mother when she perceived it, turned her away, and made such a clutter about t'other day, and yet, who knows but your Mother herself, who is yet indifferent handsome, may not have an Itching at her Tail, and have some private friend to rub it.

Katy. Of that matter I know nothing, but what mean you pray by Persons of Quality?

Frank. Oh, there is the cream of the Jest, they are young Gentlemen that fly at all game, (London is full of them) neither Maid, Wife or Widow can escape them, provided they be tolerable handsome, and that their faces (according to the Proverb) will make sauce for their Arses. Neither want these young sparks imployment, for the Town is never empty of these kind fucking Females; generally both Sexes fuck, and that so promiscuously as Incest is accounted no sin, for they put it off with a Jest, saying it makes the top of their pricks look redder, if they dip it in their own Blood.

Katy. Because I am not Married, let us talk of young Men and Maids.

Frank. Why, young Men and Maids take the most pleasure, because they are in their strength and youth, which is the season proper for these delights; but with which Sex shall I begin?

Katy. If you please let it be with the men.

Frank. Be it so then, you must therefore know, the Thing with which a Man Pisseth is called a Prick.

Katy. Oh Lord Coz, you Swear?

Frank. Pish, you are very nice, if you are minded to hear such Discourse, you must not be so Scrupulous.

Katy. I am contented, speak what you will.

Frank. I must use the very words without Mincing, Cunt, Arse, Prick, Bollocks, &c.

Katy. I am contented.

Frank. Then let me tell you, the Thing with which a Man Pisseth, is sometimes call'd a Prick, sometimes a Tarse, sometimes a Mans Yard, and other innumerable Names. It hangs down from the bottom of their Bellys like a Cows Teat, but much longer, and is about the place where the Slit of our Cunt is through which we Piss.

Katy. Oh strange!

Frank. Besides they have Two little Balls made up in a Skin something like a Purse, these we call Bollocks, they are not much unlike our Spanish Olives, and above them, which adds a great Grace to this Noble Member, Grows a sort of Downy Hair, as doth about our Cunts.

Katy. I very well apprehend what you say, but to what purpose have men all these things, sure they serve to some other use besides Pissing?

Frank. Yes marry does it, for it is this very thing which giveth a Woman the delight I all this while have been talking of. For when a Young Man hath a kindness for a Maid, he kneels down before her (when he hath gotten her alone) tells her he esteems her above all the World, and begs of her to answer his Love; if her silence continues, and she looks upon him with languishing Eyes, he usually takes courage, throws her backwards, flings up her Coats and Smock, lets fall his Breeches, opens her Legs, and thrusts his Tarse into her Cunt (which is the place through which she Pisseth) lustily therein, Rubbing it, which is the greatest pleasure imaginable.

Katy. Lord Cousin, what strange things do you tell me, but how the Duce doth he get in that thing which seems to be so limber and soft? Sure he must needs cram it in with his Fingers?

Frank. Oh, thou are an ignorant Girl indeed, when a man hath a Fucking Job to do, his Prick is not then limber, but appears quite another thing, it is half as big and as long again as it was before, it is also as stiff as a stake, and when it's standing so stiff, the skin on the Head comes back, and it appears just like a very large Heart Cherry.

Katy. So when the Man's Prick stands, he thrusts it into the Wenches Hole.

Frank. I marry does he, but it costs him some pains to thrust it in, if the Wench be straight, but that is nothing if he be a true mettel'd Blade, by little and little he will get it in though he sweat soundly for it, by doing of this Wench feels her Cunt stretch soundly, which must of necessity please her, seeing he Rubs and Tickles the Edges of it in that manner.

Katy. For my part I should think it would hurt one.

Frank. You are mistaken, indeed at first it makes ones Cunt a little sore, but after one is a little used to it, it Tickleth and Rubbeth in such manner, as it yieldeth the greatest content and pleasure in the World.

Katy. What call you the Wenches Thing?

Frank. In plain English it is called a Cunt, though they out of an affected modesty mince the word, call it a Twot, and Twenty such kind of Names. When a man thrusts his Prick into a Womans Cunt, it is called Fucking. But pray do'nt talk of such kind of thing before Company, for they will call you an immodest baudy Wench, and chide you for it.

Katy. Let me alone to keep my own Councel. But still I am not satisfied, how a man can get his great Tarse into a Wenches Cunt.

Frank. So soon as ever he hath put it a little into her Cunt Hole, he thrusts with his Arse backwards and forwards, and the Wench too is very charitable in helping him, so that between them both they soon get it up to the Head, and all the while the Man is Rigling his Arse, the Wench is extreamly delighted.

Katy. I warrant, he never holds his Arse still.

Frank. *No, he still keeps on thrusting.*

Katy. By this means I perceive he soon gets in.

Frank. *For example sake look upon me, and see how I move my Arse, just so do the men when they Fuck us, and all the time he is at it, the Woman plays with him, hugs him, and kisseth him, stroaks his Arse and Cods, calls him her Dear, her Love, her Soul, and all this while she is dying almost with pleasure, feeling his Prick thrust up so far into her Body.*

Katy. Good Cousin, you speak so feeling of this pleasure, that I have a great mind to be trying the sport, sure if it be as you say, a Young Wench cannot but love the man that gives her so much delight, but have not the men their pleasure too?

Frank. *Yes, yes, that's easily perceived, they being almost mad with delight, for when they are at the sport they cry, Dear Rogue, I dye (sighing and breathing short) saying, where am I, and such amorous words, notwithstanding the Woman's pleasure is greater than the mans, because she is not only pleased with her own Fucking, but also hath the satisfaction of perceiving her Gallant so extreamly delighted.*

Katy. You speak a great deal of Reason, sure since they have so good sport, the Wenches are loath to let the men get off of them, for my part were it my case, I should be very unwilling to let the Prick out of my Cunt, since it is the cause of such pleasure.

Frank. *Phoo, but that can't be.*

Katy. Why so?

Frank. *When one Bout is done, you must Rest a little before you begin another.*

Katy. I thought it had lasted as long as one pleased, and that there was no more in it than thrusting in the Prick.

Frank. *Therein you are mistaken, 'tis better as it is, for were it otherwise we should not be so happy.*

Katy. Pray demonstrate all this Intrigue of Fucking unto me, how they end and begin again a fresh, and what is the natural Reason why the Prick being in the Cunt, should give such delight, and why should not ones Finger yield a Wench the like pleasure.

Frank. *Listen then. A Prick hath a fine soft loose skin, which though the Wench take it in her Hand, when it is loose and lank, will soon grow stiff and be filled: 'Tis full of Nerves and Gristles, the Head of the Prick is compounded of fine Red flesh, much like a large Heart Cherry, as already I have told you, over this Head is a Cap of Skin which slips backwards when the Prick stands, underneath there is a pipe which swells like a great vain and comes to the Head of the Prick, where is a small slit or orifice; as for the Womans Cunt, I know not what it is within, but I am told it is nothing but a Prick turned inwards;[7] now when a Prick thrust into a Cunt, the cap of skin which I before spoke of, and is called the repuce slips backwards. This skin some Nations as the Jews and Turks cut off (calling it Circumcision) now as I told you, this Prick rubbing up and down in a Cunt, giveth the pleasure we have thus long discoursed of both to Man and Woman. In fine, what with rubbing and shuffing on both sides their members begin to Itch and Tickle; at last the seed comes through certain straight passages, which makes them shake their Arses faster, and the pleasure comes more and more upon them. At last the seed comes with that delight unto them, that it puts them in a Trance. The seed of the man is of a thick white clammy substance like suet, that of a Woman thinner and of a red color, mark, a woman may spend twice or thrice to a mans once, if he be any time long at it, some women have an art of holding the Tops of their Cunts, that they can let fly when they please, and will stay till the man spends, which is a Vast satisfaction to them both.*

Katy. You describe this pleasure to be so excessive, that it puts me into admiration, but after all, what do they do when they have both spent?

Frank. Then they are at ease for a little while, and the Prick which at first stood as stiffe as a Stake, comes out of the Cunt pitifully hanging down its head.

Katy. I wonder at all this, but ha'nt they a mind to t'other touch?

Frank. Yes, with playing, handling, and kissing, the Prick stands again, and then they stick it in again and have the same Sport.

Katy. But when the Prick is down, can a Wench make it stand again?

Frank. Very easily, 'tis but gently rubbing it in her hand, if thou didst but know the virtue of a Wenches hand, and how capable 'tis of giving pleasure to a man, thou wouldest not wonder at it.

Katy. Pray Cousin, since you have taken the pains to instruct me thus far, leave me not in ignorance, and therefore inform me how this matter is compleated!

Frank. In short, 'tis thus, it often happens a couple of young lovers meet in some place, where they have not the convenience to fuck; they therefore only kiss and rub their tongues in one anothers mouths, this tickleth their lips and provokes the youth so, that it makes his Prick stand, they still continuing kissing, and it not being a convenient place to fuck in, he steals his Prick into her hand, which she by rubbing gently (which is called frigging) makes the man spend in her hand.

Katy. Hey day, what must a Woman of necessity know all these things?

Frank. Yes, and a great deal more, for after a little repose they try another conclusion to please one another.

Katy. What another?

Frank. Yes, another, she begins to stroak his coddes, sliding them between her fingers, then she handles his Buttocks and Thighs, and takes him by the Prick again, which certainly is no small delight unto him; after all what will you say if she gets upon him instead of his getting upon her, which I assure you pleases the man beyond any thing?

Katy. You tell me of [a] variety of pleasures, how shall I do to remember them, how is it say you doth the Woman fuck the man?

Frank. *That is when he lyes down backward, and Woman gets a stride upon him, and riggles her Arse upon his Prick.*

Katy. That's a new way, it seems this pleasure ha's many postures.

Frank. *Yes, above a Hundred.*[8] *Have you but a little patience and I will tell you them all.*

Katy. Why is the man more pleased when the Woman Fucks him, then when he fucks her?

Frank. *Because she is so charitable to take the pains and labor upon her, which otherwise had fallen to his share.*

Katy. He is much beholding to her.

Frank. *Really so he is, for he lies under, receives the pleasure and takes no pains, whilst her eagerness at the sport makes her sweat till it drops again.*

Katy. My fancy is so extreamly raised by your very telling me how she bestirs herself, that I am almost mad to be at it.

Frank. *I have a great deal more to tell you, but let us make no more hast then good speed, for by a little and a little you will soon learn all.*

Katy. I am very well satisfied, but methinks I would fain know what makes my Cunt Itch so (especially in the night) that I cannot take any rest for tumbling and tossing. Pray can you tell me what will prevent it?

Frank. *You must get you a stiffe lusty Tarse to rub it, and must stick it into your Cunt, but if you have it not ready, you must rub your Cunt soundly with your finger, and that will give you some ease.*

Katy. How say you with my finger? I cannot imagine how that can be.

Frank. *Yes with your finger, thrusting it into your Cunt, and rubbing it thus.*

Katy. I'll be sure not to forget this way you tell me of; but did not you tell me you sometimes received a great deal of fucking pleasure?

Frank. *Yes marry did I, I have a fucking Friend in a corner, who swives me as often as I have a mind to it, and I love him extreamly for it.*

Katy. Truly he deserves it if he pleases you so much, but is your pleasure and satisfaction so great?

Frank. *I tell you, I am sometimes besides my self he pleaseth me so much.*

Katy. But how shall I get such a fucking Friend?

Frank. *Why, you must be sure to get one that loves you, and one that will not blab, but keep your Council.*

Katy. Do you know any body I could trust in an affair of this nature?

Frank. *I cannot pitch upon any whom I think fitter for your turn than Mr.* Roger, *he loves you very well, and is a handsome young Fellow, had a good* Jante mien *is neither too fat or too lean,*[9] *hath a good skin, strong and well set Limbs; besides, I am informed by those that know it, he hath a swinging Tarse and Stones, and ha's a strong back to furnish store of seed. In short, he is exactly cut out for a good Womans Man.*

Katy. I long to be dabling, but still I am afraid there is some harm in it.

Frank. *Why, you will see I am not the worse for it.*

Katy. Oh, but e'nt it a sin and a shame to boot?

Frank. *You need not be half so scrupulous, I warrant you Mr.* Roger *can farewell and not cry roast meat, neither dares he betray you for fear of losing your kindness and his own Reputation.*

Katy. But if it should be ones fortune to be Married after, [I] am afraid my Husband will not esteem or care for me, if he perceives any such matter.

Frank. *You need not take so much care beforehand, besides, when it comes to that, let me alone to tell you a way that he shall never perceive it.*

Katy. But, if I should be found out my reputation is for ever lost

Frank. *'Tis a thing some with so much privacy, that it is impossible to be known, and yet every body almost doth it; Nay if the Parents themselves perceive it, they will say nothing but put off their crackt Daughter, to one Cocks-comb or another.*

Katy. But they can't hide it from God, who sees and knows all things.

Frank. *God who sees and knows all things will say nothing, besides, I cannot think leachery a sin; I am sure if Women govern'd the world and the Church as men do, you would soon find they would account fucking so lawful, as it should not be accounted a Misdemeanor.*[10]

Katy. I wonder men should be so rigorous against a thing they love so well.

Frank. *Only for fear of giving too much liberty to the Women, who else would challenge the same liberty with them, but it is fine, we wink at one anothers faults, and do not think swiving a hainous sin, and were it not for fear of great Bellys, it were possible swiving would be much more used then now it is.*

Katy. Then you scarce think any honest?

Frank. *No really, for had not we better enjoy our pleasures, then be hard thought on for nothing, for I must confess there are some so unhappy as to be hard censured without a cause, which is the worst luck [that] can befall one; were I in those Peoples condition, if I could not stop Peoples mouths, I would deserve the worst that could be said of me, and so have something for my Money.*

Katy. You say very well, and truly I did not care how soon I parted with my Maiden-head, provided I might have my Belly full of fuck, and no body be the wiser, which I believe may easily be done, if according to your advice some discreet young Fellow be imployed in management of this secret affair.

Frank. *You cannot imagine the satisfaction you will take, when once you have gotten a fucking Friend fitted for your purpose, who as I will order it shall be wise enough to keep your secrets. How many Girles do you daily meet with, who pass for vertuous Wenches, at these you may laugh in your sleeve, for they will never think thee to be a wanton, especially if thou dost but play the Hypocrite, acting the part of a Holy Sister, frequenting the Church and condemning the lewdness of the Age, this will get thee a Reputation among all sorts of People, and by thy private fucking thou wilt attain to a kind of confidence, which is much wanting to most of our English Ladies; for few are honest now adays but some heavy witless sluts, and after all, if thou behavest thy self as I will order, 'tis a thousand to one but some wealthy Fool will stoop to thy lute, and Marry thee, after which thou mayest carry on thy designs, and order private meetings with thy fucking Friend, who will secretly swive thee, and give thee all tastes of pleasure imaginable.*

Katy. Lord Cousin, what a happy Woman are you, and what a great deal of time have I already lost, but pray tell me, how must I play my Cards, for without your assistance I shall never attain to what I so much desire?

Frank. I'll endeavor to help you out of the mire, but you must frankly tell me, which of your lovers you most esteem.

Katy. To be ingenious then, I love Mr. *Roger* best.

Frank. Then resolve to think of no body else, for my part I think him a very discreet young Gentleman.

Katy. But, I am ashamed to break the Ice and ask the least kindness of him.

Frank. Let me alone to do that, but when you have had the great pleasure of fucking, you must so order matters, that you may have frequent meetings, for when once you have tasted the forbidden fruit, your Teeth will be strangely set on edge after it.

Katy. I warrant you, you have so fired me with your Relations, that I think it seven years till I am at the sport.

Frank. The sooner you do it, the better will Mr. Roger *visit you to day.*

Katy. Cousin, I expect him every minute.

Frank. Without any more ado then, take this first opportunity, for a fairer can never present, your Mother and Father are in the Country and come not home to night, no creature in the house but the Maid, whom you may easily busie about some employment, and let me alone to do your errand to Mr. Roger, *and to tell all People that may inquire for you, that you are gone abroad. Here's a bed fit for the purpose, on which he will certainly fuck you when he comes.*

Katy. Dear Cousin, I am at my wits end, but must I let him do what he will with me?

Frank. I marry must you, he will thrust his Prick into thy Cunt, and give thee a World of delight.

Katy. Well, but what must I do then to have as much pleasure as you have?

Figure 1.3   The first illustration of *The School of Venus*.

Frank. *You fool you, I tell you he'll show you.*

Katy. Excuse my ignorance, and Cousin to pass away the time till he comes, pray tell me what your Husband doth to you when he lyes with you, for I would not willingly altogether appear a Novice, when I shall arrive to that great happiness of being fucked.

Frank. *That I will withal my heart, but you must know that the pleasure of fucking is joyned with a Thousand other indearments, which infinitely add to the perfection, one night above all the rest my Husband being on the merry pin, shewed me a very many pritty pranks, which before I knew not, and which truly were pleasant enough.*

Katy. When first he accosts you, what doth he say and do unto you?

Frank. *I will briefly tell you all, first, he comes up a private pair of stairs unto me, when all the Household is in Bed, he finds me sometimes a sleep and sometimes awake, to loose no time, he undresseth himself, comes and lyes down by me, when he begins to be warm he lays his hands on my Breasts, finding me awake, he tells me he is so weary with walking from place to place all day long, that he is scarce able to stir, still feeling and stroaking my Breasts, calling me dear Rogue, and telling me how happy he is in me; I thereupon pretending modesty say, dear heart, I am sleepy, pray let me alone, he not satisfied with that, slips his hand down to the bot-*

Figure 1.4   The second illustration of *The School of Venus*.

tom of my Belly, and handleth the heel of my Cunt, which he rubbeth with his fin-
gers, then he kisseth me, and puts his Tongue into my Mouth delicately rowling it
about, afterwards he stroaks my smooth Thighs, Cunt, Belly and Breasts, takes the
Nipples of my Breast in his Mouth, doing all he can to content himself, makes me
take off my Smock and views me all over, then he makes me grasp his stiffe Prick,
takes me in his Arms and so we rowl one over another, sometimes I am uppermost,
sometimes he, then he puts his Prick into my hand again, sometimes he thrusts it
between my Thighs, sometimes between my Buttocks, rubbing my Cunt with the
top of it, which makes me mad for horsing, then he kisseth my Eyes, Mouth and
Cunt, then calling me his Dear, his Love, his Soul, he gets upon me, thrusting his
stiffe standing Tarse into my Cunt, and to our mutual satisfaction he fucks me
stoutly.

Katy. And are not you mightily pleased at it?

Frank. How can you imagine otherwise? You may see there are more ways then one to put a Prick into a Cunt, sometimes my Husband gets upon me, sometimes I get upon him, sometimes we do it sideways, sometimes kneeling, sometimes crossways, sometimes backwards, as if I were to take a Glister,[11] sometimes Wheelbarrow, with one leg upon his shoulders, sometimes we do it on our feet, sometimes upon a stool, and when he is in Hast he throws me upon a Form, Chair or Floor, and fucks me lustily, so these ways afford several and variety of pleasures, his Prick entering my Cunt more or less, and in a different manner, according to the posture we Fuck in, in the day times he often makes me stoop down with my head almost between my Legs, throwing my Coats backwards over my Head, he considers me in that posture, and having secured the Door that we are not surprized, and makes a sign with his Finger that I stir not from that posture, then he runs at me with a standing Prick, and Fucks me briskly, and hath often protested to me he takes more pleasure this way than any other.

Katy. This last way of Fucking as are all others, (without doubt) must be extream[ly] pleasant, and now I very well comprehend all you say unto me, and since there is no more in it than downright putting a Prick into a Cunt (though in divers postures) methinks, I could find out some new ways besides those you tell me of, for you know every Bodies Fancy varies, but let us now talk of that pleasant Night you had with your Husband in which he pleased you so extreamly.

Frank. Why that was but yesterday, in this Relation I shall tell you many Love Tricks which are common to us, who dayly enjoy them, you must know I had not seen my Husband in Two days, which made me almost out of my Wits, when toward Twelve a Clock last Night I saw him steal into my Chamber, with a little Dark Lanthorn in his Hand. He brought under his Coat Sweet-meats, Wine, and such stuff to Rellish our Mouths, and Raise our Leachery.

Katy. 'Tis needless to ask you whether the Apparition pleas'd you.

Frank. He found me in my Petticoat, for I was not then a Bed, which hastily throwing up, he flung me backwards on the Bed, and with a stiff standing Tarse, Fucked me on the spot lustily, spending extreamly with Two or Three Thrusts.

Katy. Now I perceive we are most pleased when the Seed comes, and we take the most pains when we perceive it coming, and we never leave shaking our Arses till the precious Liquor comes.

Frank. After the first Fuck I went to Bed, and he undressed himself, I was no sooner laid but I fell a sleep, (for you must know nothing provokes sleep so much as Fucking) but he hugging me, and putting his Prick into my Hand, soon recovered me of my Drowsiness.

Katy. When a Mans Prick is once drawn, how long is it before it can stand again, and how often can a Man Fuck in one Night?

Figure 1.5 The third illustration of *The School of Venus*.

Frank. *You are always interrupting me! That's according to the Man you deal with, sometimes the same men are better at it than other times, some can Fuck and spend twice without Discunting, which pleaseth the Woman very much, some will Fuck Nine or Ten times in a Night, some Seven or Eight, but that is too much, Four or Five times in a Night is enough for any Reasonable Woman, those that do it Two or Three times spend more, and also receive and give more pleasure than those who do it oftener. In this case the Womans Beauty helps very much too, and makes the man Fuck a time or two extraordinary, but as in other pleasures, so in this, too much of it is for naught, and it commonly spoils young Lads and Parsons, Young Lads because they know not when they have enough, and Parsons because they think they never shall have enough, but that man that Fucks Night and Morning doth very fairly if he hold it, this is all I can say on this Subject. But you have in-terrupted me, and I know not where I left off.*

Katy. You told me as you were going to sleep, he put his standing Prick into your Hand.

Frank. *Oh, I remember now, I feeling it stiff and buxom, had no more mind to sleep, but began to Act my part as well as he, and kept touch with him. I em-braced him, and laying my heels on his Shoulders, we tumbled about and tossed all the Cloaths off, it being hot, we were so far from minding their falling, that we both stripped our selves naked, we curveted a hundred times on the Bed,[12] he still shew-ing me his lusty Tarse, which all this while he made me handle, and did with me what he would. At last he strows all the Room over with Rosebuds, and naked as*

Figure 1.6 The fourth illustration of *The School of Venus*.

I was, commanded me to gather them up, so that I turned my self in all sorts of postures, which he could easily perceive by the Candle which burned bright, that done, he rubbed himself and me all over with Jessimy Essence, and then we both went to Bed and played like Two Puppy-Dogs, afterwards, kneeling before him, he considered me all over with admiration, sometimes he commended my Belly, sometimes my Thighs and Breasts, then the Nobs of my Cunt, which he found plump and standing out, which he often stroaked, then he considered my shoulders and Buttocks, then making me lean with my hands upon the Bed, he got astride upon me, and made me carry him; at last, he got off me, and thrust his Prick into my Cunt, sliding it down my Buttocks. I had no mind to let him Fuck me at first, but he made such moan to me, that I had no heart to deny him, he said he took a great deal of pleasure in rubbing the Inside of my Cunt, which he did, often thrusting his Prick up to the Head, then suddenly plucking it out again, the noise of which, it being like to that which Bakers make when they Kneed their Dow, pleased me extreamly.

Katy. But is it possible such excessive Lewdness could please you?

Frank. *Why not when one Loves another, these things are very pleasant, and serve to pass away the time with a great deal of satisfaction.*

Katy. Proceed then if you think it convenient.

Frank. *When he was weary of Tickling and Fucking me, we went as naked as we were born to the Fire side, where when we were set down, we began to drink a Bottle of* Hypocras,[13] *and eat some Sweet-meats, all the while we were eating and Drinking, which did much Refresh us, he did nothing but make much of me, told me he dyed for love of me, and a hundred such sweet sayings, at last I took pity of him and opened my Thighs, then he shewed me his standing Prick, desiring me only to cover the Head of it with my Cunt, which I granting to him, we still eat on, sometimes putting what I was eating out of my mouth into his; at other times taking into my mouth what he was eating. Being weary of this posture we began another, and after that another, weary of this we Drank Seven or Eight brimmers of Hypocras, then being half Elevated, he shewed me all manner of Fucking wayes, and convinced me there was as much skill in keeping Time a Fucking, as there was in Musick; to be short, he shewed me all the Postures imaginable, and had we had a Room hung with Looking-Glasses to have beheld the several shapes we were in, it would have been the highest of contentment. Being now near satisfied, he shewed me and made me handle all his Members, then he felt mine. And last I desired him to make an end, took him by the Prick and led him to the Bed, and throwing my self Backwards, and pulling him upon me, having his Prick in my Hand, I guided, and he thrust it into my Cunt up to the Top, that he made the Bed crack again, I thrusting in due time every thing was in motion, his Prick being in as far as it would go, his Bollocks beat time against the Lips of my Cunt. To conclude, he told me he would give me one sound Thrust which should Tickle me to the Quick. I bid him do his worst, provided he made hast. All this while we called one another my Dear, my Heart, my Soul, my Life, Oh what will you do, pray make hast, Oh I dye, I can stay no longer, Get you gone, I can't indure it, pray make hast, pray have done quickly, you Kill me, what shall I do? And kissing me, he says, Oh, now, now, then giving me a home Thrust with his Tongue in my Mouth (I thinking my self to be in another World) I felt his Seed come Squirting up warm and comfortable into my Body. At which moment I so ordered my business, as I kept time with him, and we both spent together, it's impossible to tell you how great our pleasure was, and how mutual our satisfaction; but Cousin, had you been there, it would have made you laugh to see what variety of Faces were made in the Action.*

Katy. I must need believe what you say, since the very Relation you have given me makes me mad for Horseing, in plain English my Cunt Itcheth like Wild-Fire, but what need all these preparations, I am for downright Fucking without any more ado.

Frank. That's your Ignorance, you know not the delight there is in Husbanding this pleasure, which otherwise would be short and soon over. And now I think on it, since Mr. Roger will suddenly be here, I think it not amiss to instruct you a little more.

Katy. Yes, Pray Cousin, since we are gone so far, leave nothing Imperfect, and I shall be bound to Pray for you so long as I live.

Frank. You must know then there are a thousand delights in Love, before we come to Fucking, which must be had in their due times and places; As for exam-

Figure 1.7   The fifth illustration of *The School of Venus*.

Figure 1.8   The sixth illustration of *The School of Venus*.

ple, Kissing and Feeling are two very good pleasures, though much inferior to Fuck-
ing: Let us first speak of Kissing, there is the Kissing of our Breasts, of our Mouths,
of our Eyes, of our Face, there is also the Biting or close Kiss, with Tongue in
Mouth. These several Kisses afford different sorts of pleasures, and are very good to
pass time away. The delight of Stroaking and Feeling is as various, for every Mem-
ber affords a new kind of pleasure, a fine white hard Round Breast fills the Hand,

and makes a mans Prick stand with the very Thought of the Rest. From the Breasts we descend to the Thighs; is it not fine to stroak two smooth plump white Thighs, like two Pillars of Alabaster, then you slide your Hand from them to the Buttocks, which are full and hard, then come to a fine soft Belly, and thence to a Brave Hairy Cunt, with a plump pair of Red Lips, sticking out like a Hens Arse, now whilst the Man plays with the Womans Cunt, opening and shutting the Lips of it, with his fingers, it makes his Prick stand as stiffe as a Stake: this member has also its several pleasures, sometimes it desires to be in the Womans hand, sometimes between her Thighs and Buttocks, and sometimes between her Breasts, certainly 'tis a great deal of satisfaction for Lovers to see those they are enamoured of naked, especially if their members be proportionable, and nothing provokes leachery more than lascivious naked postures. Words cannot express the delight Lovers take to see one another naked, what satisfaction then have they, when they come to fucking, it being the quintessence of all other pleasures. A moderate Cunt is better then one too wide or too little, but of the two a little straight Cunt is better than a flabby wide one. I'll have none [of] some of these last sort of Cunts, that if a man had an [h]ell of a Prick they would scarce feel it. There is also a great deal of pleasure from the first Thrusting a Prick into a Cunt till the time of spending, and the sport be ended. First the mans rubbing his Prick up and down the Cunt hole, then the Womans kissing and embracing him with all the strength she hath, the mutual stroakings, and leacherous expressions, struglings and cringings, the rowling Eyes, sighs and short breathings, Tongue kissing and making of love moan; 'tis admirable to see the activity of the body, and the faces they make when they are tickled. And now I have told you all that belongs to these pleasures, I think you are much beholding to me, for my part I am glad I have found you so docible a Scholar, and that you hear reason so well.

Katy. Truly Cousin, there is a great deal of it, and it is pretty hard to learn it all.

Frank. Pish, I could tell you more, but I think I have told you enough for this time, but what think you of my Fucking Friend now?[14]

Katy. Truly Cousin you are happy in him, and your merit deserves no less then the pleasure you receive by him.

Frank. But I am sure you would praise him more, did you but know how secret, honest, and discreet he is, when we are in Company, he never looks upon me but with Respect, you would then by his deportment think he durst not presume to kiss my hand, yet when time and place give leave, he can change the sceen, and then there is not a loose trick, but he knows and can practice to my great satisfaction.

Katy. Hush, hush, hold your peace.

Frank. What's the matter? Do you aile any thing?

Katy. Cousin, my heart is at my Mouth, I hear Mr. *Roger* a coming.

24

Frank. So much the better, chear up, what are you afraid of, I envy you your happiness, and the pleasure you will take. Come, be couragious, and prepare your self to receive him, whilst you settle your self upon your Bed, as if you were at work; I warrant you, I'll prepare and give him his lesson, how he must carry himself towards you. In the mean time order your affairs so, that you be not surprized. God be with you.

Katy. Adieu dear Cousin, bid him use me kindly, and remember I am at your Mercy.

The end of the First Dialogue.

The Second Dialogue.

ADVERTISEMENT.

The former Dialogue having given an account of many love misteries, with the manner how to improve the delights and pleasures of Fucking. This second discourse shews the curious and pleasing ways, how a man gets a Virgins Maidenhead, *it also describes what a perfect* Beauty (*both Masculine and Feminine*) *is, and gives instructions, how a Woman must behave her self in the extasie of swiving. 'Tis not unknown to all persons, who are devoted to* Venus, *that though our* English Ladies *are the most accomplished in the world, not only for their* Angelical *and* Beautiful *faces, but also for the exact composure, of their* Shape *and* Body; *yet being bred up in a cold Northern Flegmatick* Country, *and kept under the severe, though insignificant* Government, *of an* Hypocritical Mother *or* Governess, *when they once come to be enjoyed, their* Embraces *are so cold, and they such ignorants to the misteries of swiving, as it quite dulls their lovers* Appetites, *and often makes them run after other women, which though less* Beautiful, *yet having the advantages of knowing more, and better management of their Arses, give more content and pleasure to their Gallants. This we see daily practiced, and indeed the only reason which makes many a man dote on a scurvy face is, because the woman is agreeable to his* Temper, *and understands these fucking practical* Rules *better, then a* Young *and* Beautiful Wife. *In short, I do appeal to any* Gallant, *who hath enjoyed an* Italian *or* French *woman, and commends them to the Skyes for their Accomplishments, if he would not leave the very best of them for an innocent Country* English Wench, *if she were but as well skilled in the several fucking postures, as the former are. That my dear* Country-Women (*for whom I have a particular es-*

teem) may not therefore be longer slighted, for their ignorance in the School of Venus *as I translated the first* Dialogue, *so have I finished this to the ignorant* Maid. *I am sure this must be a welcome book, but if any* Lady *be in a superior class, then is in this* School, *I beg her pardon, and humbly intreat her in another* Treatise, *to well finish, what in this I have indifferently begun. And I am so confident of the* Abilities *of the* English *this way, that I am assured, if all of this nature, with [what] our voluptuous fucksters know, were communicated to the world, we need not translate* French, *or be at the trouble to read* Aloisia, Juvenal, *or* Martial *in* Latine.[15] *But till some of them be kind, and do it favorably, accept of my endeavors.*

Dialogue the second.

Frank, Katy.

Frank. *I am glad to find you alone, and now pray tell me, how squares go with you, since last I saw you.*

Katy. I thank you heartily, Cousin, I was never better in my life, and am bound to pray for you, [in] spight of my precise Mother, who would fain make me believe Men are good for nothing, but to deceive innocent Virgins, I find the quite contrary, for my Gallant is so kind to me, that I want words to express it.

Frank. *I hope you do not repent then you have taken my councel, I am sure* Mr. Roger *will be damned before he be guilty of such a dirty action, as Babling.*

Katy. I am so far from repenting, that were it to do agen, it should be my first work. What a comfort is it to love and be beloved? I am sure I am much mended in my health, since I had the use of Man.

Frank. *You are more Airy a great deal then before, and they that live to see it, will one day find you as cunning and deep a Whore, as any in the Nation.*

Katy. Truly Cousin, I was a little shamefaced at first, but I grow every day bolder and bolder, my Fucking Friend assuring me, he will so instruct me, that I shall be fit for the embraces of a King.[16]

Frank. *He is a Man of his word, and you need not doubt what he promises, what advantage have you now over other Wenches in receiving so much pleasure, which enlivens thee, and makes thee more acceptable in company.*

Katy. I tell you what, since Mr. *Roger* has fucked me, and I know what is what, I find all my Mothers stories to be but Bug-bears, and good for nothing but to fright Children, for my part I believe we were created for fucking, and when we begin to fuck, we begin to live, and all young Peoples actions and words ought to tend thereunto. What strangely Hypocritical ignorants are they, who would hinder it, and how malicious are those old people, who would hinder it in us young people, because they cannot do it themselves. Heretofore what was I good for, but to hold down my head and sow, now nothing comes amiss to me, I can hold an argument on any subject, and that which makes me laugh is this, if my Mother chide, I answer her smartly; so that she says, I am very much mended, and she begins to have great hopes of me.

Frank. *And all this while, she is in darkness, as to your concerns.*

Katy. Sure enough, and so she shall continue as I have ordered matters.

Frank. *Well, and how goes the world with you now?*

Katy. Very well, only Mr. *Roger* come not so often to see me, as I could wish.

Frank. *Why, you are well acquainted with him then?*

Katy. Sure enough, for we understand one another perfectly.

Frank. *But did not, what he did unto you at first, seem a little strange?*

Katy. I'll tell you the truth, you remember you told me much of the pleasure and Tickling of Fucking, I am now able to add a great deal more of my own experience, and can discourse as well of it as any one. I am sure of my standing.

Frank. *Tell me then, I believe you have had brave sport, I am confident Mr.* Roger *cannot but be a good Fuckster.*

Katy. The first time he Fucked me, I was upon the Bed in the same posture you left me, making as if I had been at work, when he came into the Chamber he saluted and asked me, what I did, I made him a civil answer, and desired him to sit down, which he soon did close by me, staring me full in the face, and all quivering and shaking, asked me if my Mother were at home, and told me he had met you at the bottom of the stairs, and that you had spoken to him about me, desiring to know if it were with my consent. I returning no answer, but Smiling, he grew bolder, and immediately Kissed me, which I permitted him without strugling, though it made me Blush as Red as Fire, for the Resolution I had taken to let him do what he would unto me, he took notice of it, and said, what do you Blush for Child, come Kiss me again, in doing of which, he was longer than usual, for that time he took advantage of thrusting his Tongue into my Mouth. 'Tis a folly to lye, that way of Kissing so pleased me, that if I had not before received your Instructions to do it, I should have granted him whatever he demanded.

Frank. *Very well.*

Katy. I received his Tongue under mine, which he rigled about, then he stroked my Neck, sliding his Hand under my Handkerchief, he handled my Breasts one after another, thrusting his Hand as low as he could.

Frank. *A very fair Beginning.*

Katy. The End will be as good, seeing he could not reach low enough, he pulled out his Hand again, laying it upon my Knees, and whilst he was Kissing and Embracing me, by little and little he pulled up my Coats, till he felt my bare Thighs.

Frank. We call this getting of Ground.

Katy. Look here, I believe few Wenches have handsomer Thighs than I, for they are White, Smooth and Plump.

Frank. I know it, for I have often seen and handled them before now, when we lay together.

Katy. Feeling them he was overjoy'd, protesting he had never felt the like before, in doing this, his Hat which he had laid on his knees fell off, and I casting my Eyes downwards perceived something swelling in his Breeches, as if it had a mind to get out.

Frank. Say you so Madam.

Katy. That immediately put me in mind of that stiff thing, which you say men Piss with, and which pleaseth us Women so much, I am sure when he first came into the Chamber 'twas not so big.

Frank. No, his Prick did not stand then.

Katy. When I saw it, I began to think there was something to be done in good earnest, so I got up, and went and shut the Door lest the Maid should surprize us, who was below Stairs, I had much ado to get away, for he would not let me stir till I told him 'twas only to make fast the Door; I went down and set the Maid to work in the Out-house, fearing she might come up and disturb us, if she heard any noise. Having made all sure I returned, and he taking me about the Neck and Kissing me, would not let me set as before upon the Bed, but pulled me between his Legs, and thrusting his Hand into the slit of my Coat behind, handled my Buttocks which he found plump, Round and hard, with his other hand which was free, he takes my right Hand, and looking me in the Face, put it into his Breeches.

Frank. You are very tedious in telling your Story.

Katy. I tell you every particular. He put his Prick into my Hand, and desired me to hold it, I did as he bid me, which I perceived pleased him so well, that every touch made him almost expire, he guiding my Hand as he pleased, sometimes on his Prick, then on his Cods and Hair that grew about it, and then bid me grasp his Prick again.

Frank. This Relation makes me mad for Fucking.

Katy. This done, says he, I would have you see what you have in your Hand, and so made me take it out of his Breeches, I wondred to see such a Damn'd great Tarse, for it is quite another thing when it stands, than when it lyes down, he perceiving me a little amazed, said, do not be frighted, Girl, for you have about you a very convenient place to receive it, and upon a sudden pulls my Smock round about my Arse, feeling my Belly and Thighs, then he rubbed his Prick against my Thighs, Belly and Buttocks, and lastly against the Red Lips of my Cunt.

Frank. *This is what I expected all this while.*

Katy. Then he took me by it, rubbing both the Lips of it together, and now and then plucked me gently by the hairs which grow about, then opening the Lips of my Cunt, he thrust me backwards, lifting my Arse a little higher, put down his Breeches, put by his Shirt, and draws me nearer to him.

Frank. *Now begins the Game.*

Katy. I soon perceived he had a mind to stick it in; first with his Two Fingers he opened the Lips of my Cunt, and thrust at me Two or Three times pretty smartly, yet he could not get it far in, though he stroaked my Cunt soundly. I desired him to hold a little, for it pained me, having Breathed, he made me open my Legs wider, and with another hard thrust his Prick went a little further in, this I told him pained me extreamly, he told me he would not hurt me much more, and that when his Prick was in my Cunt, I should have nothing but pleasure for the pain I should endure, and that he endured a share of the pain for my sake, which made me patiently suffer Two or Three thrusts more, by which means he got in his Prick an Inch or two farther, endeavoring still to get more Ground, he so tortured me, as I cryed out, this made him try another posture, he takes and throws me backwards on the Bed, but being too heavy, he took my Two Thighs and put them upon his Shoulders, he standing on his Feet by the Bed side. This way gave me some ease, yet was the pain so great to have my Cunt stretched so by his great Tarse, then once more I desired him to get off, which he did, for my part the pain was so great, that I thought my Guts were dropping out of the bottom of my Belly.

Frank. *What a deal of pleasure did you enjoy, for my part had I had such a Prick, I should not complain.*

Katy. Stay a little, I do not complain for all this. Presently he came and kissed me, and handled my Cunt a fresh, thrust in his finger to see what progress he had made, being still troubled with a standing Prick, and not knowing what to do with himself, he walked up and down the Chamber, till I was fit for another bout.

Frank. *Poor Fellow, I pity him, he suffered a great deal of pain.*

Katy. Mournfully pulling out his Prick before me, he takes down a little Pot of Pomatum,[17] which stood on the Mantle-tree of the Chimney, oh says he this is for our turn, and taking some of it he rubbed his Prick all over with it, to make it go in the more Glib.[18]

Frank. *He had better have spit upon his hand and rubbed his Prick therewith.*

Figure 1.9   The seventh illustration of *The School of Venus*.

Katy. At last he thought of that, and did nothing else, then he placed me on a Chair, and by the help of the Pomatum got in a little further, but seeing he could do no great good that way, he make me rise, and laid me with all four on the Bed, and having rubbed his Tarse once more with Pomatum, he charged me briskly in the reer.

Frank. *What a bustle is here to get one poor Maiden-head, my Friend and I made not half of this stir, we had soon done, and I near flinched for it.*

Katy. I tell you the truth verbatim, my coats being over my Shoulders, holding out my Arse I gave him fair mark enough, this new posture so quickened his fancy, that he no longer regarded my crying, kept thrusting on with might and main, till at last he perfected the Breach, and took intire possession of all.

Frank. *Very well, I am glad you have escaped a Thousand little accidents which attend young lovers. But let us come to the sequel.*

Katy. It now began not to be so painful, my Cunt fitted his Prick so well, that no Glove could come straighter on a mans hand; to conclude, he was overjoyed at his victory, calling me his Love, his Dear, and his Soul, all this while I found his Tarse Rub up and down in my Body, so that it tickled all the faculties of my Cunt,

Frank. *Very good.*

Katy. He asked me if I were pleased, I answered, yes, so am I said he, hugging me close unto him, and thrusting his hands under my Buttocks, he lifted my Cunt towards him, sometimes handling the Lips thereof, sometimes my Breasts.

Frank. *This was to encourage or excite him.*

Katy. The more he rubbed the more it tickled me, that at last, my hands on which I leaned failed me, and I fell flat on my face.

Frank. *I suppose you caught no harm by the fall.*

Katy. None, but he and I dying with pleasure, fell in a Trance, he only having time to say, there have you lost your Maiden-head, my Fool.

Frank. *How was it with you? I hope you spent as well as he.*

Katy. What a question you ask me, the Devil can't hold it when it is a coming, I was so ravished with the pleasure, that I was half besides my self, there is not that sweetmeat or rariety whatsoever, that is so pleasant to the Palate as spending is to a Cunt, it tickleth us all over, and leave us half dead.

Frank. *Truly, I believe you did not believe it half the pleasure you have found it.*

Katy. Truly no, 'tis impossible till one has tryed it. So soon as he withdrew, I found my self a little wet about my Cunt, which I wiped dry with my Smock; and then I perceived his Prick was not so stiffe as before, but held down it's head lower and lower.

Frank. *There is no question to be made of it.*

Katy. This bout refreshed me infinitely, and I was very well satisfyed, then he caressing and kissing me, told me what a [great] deal of pleasure I had given him; I answered, he had pleased me in like manner, that he said more rejoyced him of any thing, we then strove to convince one another who had the most pleasure, at last, we concluded that we had each of us our shares, but he still said he was the better pleased of the two, because I was so well satisfied, which compliment I returned him.

Frank. *There is a great deal of truth in what you say, for when one loves another truly, they are better satisfied with the pleasure they give each other, then with that they themselves enjoy, which appears by a Woman, who if she really love a man, she will permit him to fuck her though she herself have no inclination thereunto, and of her own accord will take up her Smock, and say, get up dear Soul, and take thy fill of me, put me in what posture you please, and do what you will with me, and on the contrary, when the Woman hath a mind to be fucked, though the Man be not in humor, yet his complaisance will be as great towards her.*

Katy. I am glad I know this, I will mind Mr. *Roger* of it as I see occasion.

Frank. *Therein you will do very well.*

Katy. After a little pause, he got up his Breeches and sat down by me, told me he should be bound unto you so long as he lived, how he met you at the Stairs foot, where with your good news you rejoyced the very Soul of him, for without such tidings the Agony he was in for the love of me, would certainly have killed him, that the love which he had long time

Figure 1.10 The eighth illustration of *The School of Venus.*

had for me, encouraged him to be doing, but he wanted boldness and Rhetoricks to tell me his mind; that he wanted words to express my deserts, which he found since he enjoyed me to be beyond his imagination, and therefore he resolved to make a friendship with me, as lasting as his life, with a Hundred protestations of services he would do me, intreating me still to love him and be true unto him, promising the like on his part, and that he would have no friendship for any Woman else, and that he would every day come and Fuck me twice, for these compliments I made him a low Curtesy, and gave him thanks with all my heart. He then plucked out of his Pockets some Pistachios which he gave me to eat, telling me 'twas the best restorative in the World after Fucking; whilst he lay on the Bed, I went down to look after the Maid, and began to sing to take off all suspicion, I staid a while devising how to imploy her again, I told her I was mightily plagued with Mr. *Roger,* and knew not how to be rid of him, yet found her out such work as assured me I should not be molested in our sport by her.

Frank. *In truth you are grown a forward Wench.*

Katy. When I was got up Stairs again, I shut the door, and went to him, whom I found lying on the Bed, holding his standing Prick in his hand, so soon as I came, he embraced and kissed me, making me lay my powerful hand on his Prick, which did not yet perfectly stand, but in the twinkling of an eye it grew as stiffe as a Stake, by vertue of my stroaking.

Frank. *This we call rallying, or preparing to Fuck again.*

Katy. I now began to be more familiar with it then before, and took a great deal of satisfaction with holding it in my hand, measuring the length and breadth of it, wondering at the vertue it had to please us so strangely; immediately he shuffles me backwards on the Bed, throwing up my coats above my Navil, I suffering him to do what he pleased, he seizing me by the Cunt, holding me by the hairs thereof, then turned me on my Belly to make a prospect of my Buttocks, turning me from side to side, slapping my Arse, playing with me, biting, tickling and reading love lectures to me all this while, to which I gave good attention, being very desirous to be instructed in these misterys; at last, he unbuttoned his Breeches putting his Prick between my Buttocks and Thighs, which he rubbed up and down, and all to shew me how to act my part when we Fucked in earnest.

Frank. *I am certain your Person and Beauty pleased him extreamly.*

Katy. That is not my discourse now. But he put me in a Hundred postures incunting at every one, shewing me how I must manage my self to get in the Prick farthest, in this I was an apt Schollar, and think I shall not in hast forget my lesson. At last we had both of us a mind to ease our selves; therefore he lay flat on the Bed with his Tarse upright, pulled me upon him, and I my self stuck it into my Cunt, wagging my Arse, and saying I Fuck thee, my dear, he bid me mind my business, and follow my Fucking, holding his Tongue all this while in my Mouth, and calling me my life, my Soul, my dear Fucking Rogue, and holding his hands on my Buttocks, at last, the sweet pleasure approaching made us ply one another with might and main, till at last it came to the incredible satisfaction of each party.

Figure 1.11   The ninth illustration of *The School of Venus.*

Frank. *This was the second bout.*

Katy. Then I plainly perceived all that you told me of that precious liquor was true and knew there was nothing better than Fucking to pass away the time. I asked him who was the inventor of this sport, which he was not learned enough to resolve me, but told me the practique part was better than the Theorique; so kissing me again, he once more thrust his Prick into my Cunt, and Fucked me Dog fashion, backward.

Frank. *Oh brave, this was the third time he Fucked you.*

Katy. He told me that way pleased him best, because in that posture he got my Maiden-head, and besides his Prick this way went further into my Body then any other, after a little repose he swived me again Wheelbarrow fashion, with my Legs on his Shoulders.

Frank. *This was four times, a sufficient number for one day.*

Katy. That was the parting Fuck at that time, in swiving me he told me, he demonstrated the greatest of his affection unto me.

Frank. *I should desire no better evidence, but how long did this pastime last?*

Katy. 'Twas near Night before we parted.

Frank. *If you were at it less then three hours sure his Arse was on fire.*

Katy. I know not exactly how long it was, this I am sure the time seemed not long to me, and if his Arse was on fire, I found an extinguisher which did his business. And this Cousin, is the plain truth of what hath befallen me since last I saw you, now tell me what is your opinion of it all.

Frank. *Truly you are arrived to such a perfection in the Art of Fucking, that you need no farther instructions.*

Katy. What say you Cousin?

Frank. *Why I say you have all the Terms of Art as well as my self, and can now without Blushing call Prick, Stones, Bollocks, Cunt, Tarse, and the like names.*

Katy. Why, I learned all this with more ease than you can Imagine, for when Mr. *Roger* and I am alone together, he makes me often name these words, which amongst Lovers is very pleasing.

Frank. *Incunting is when one sheaths his Prick in a Cunt, and only thrust it in without Fucking.*

Katy. But he tells me in Company modesty must be used, and these words forborne.

Frank. *In Truth, when my Friend and I meet, we use not half such Ceremonies as does Mr.* Roger *and you, tell me therefore, what is the difference between Occupying or Fucking, and Sheathing or Incunting?*

Katy. Occupying, is to stick a Prick into a Cunt, and Riggle your Arse till you Spend, and truly that word expresses it fuller than any other. Fucking, is when a Prick is thrust into a Cunt, and you spend without Riggling your Arse. Swiveing, is both putting a Prick into a Cunt, and stirring the Arse, but not Spending; to Incunt, or Insheath is the same thing, and downright sticking ones Prick into a Cunt, beareth no other denomination, but Prick in Cunt.

Frank. There are other words which sound better, and are often used before Company, instead of Swiving and Fucking, which is too gross and downright Bawdy, fit only to be used among dissolute Persons; to avoid scandal, men modestly say, I kissed her, made much of her, received a favor from her, or the like; now let us proceed to the first Explication which you mentioned, and 'tis as good as ever I heard in my life. I could not have thought of the like my self.

Katy. You Compliment me Cousin, but I do not know well what you mean, they express Fucking by so many different words.

Frank. That is not unknown unto me, for example, the word Occupying is proper when a man takes all the pains and labor, Incunting is called Insheathing, from a similitude of thrusting a Knife into a Sheath. But men amongst themselves never use half these Ceremonies, but talk as Bawdy as we Women do in our Gossipings or private Meetings, if on one side we tell our Gossips or those that we trust in our amours, I Fucked with him and pleased him well, or he Fucked me and pleased me well, on the other side when they are among their Companions, they say of us, such a one has a Plagy wide Cunt, another tells of a straight Cunt, and the pleasure he received. 'Tis ordinary for two or three Young Fellows, when they get together, to give in their verdicts upon all the Wenches that pass by, saying among one another, I warrant you that Jade will Fuck well, she looks as though she lacked it, she hath a Whoreish countenance, and also, if her Mouth be wide or narrow they make their discants thereon, looking on their Eye-brows, for 'tis very certain, they are of the same colour with the hair of their Cunts.

Katy. Oh, but will men reveal what they know of us?

Frank. Yes, marry, of Common Whores they'll say any thing, but of their private Misses, the Gallants will be Damn'd before they will speak a word.

Katy. I am very glad of it, for I can scarce believe it of my self, that Mr. *Roger* should make me suffer so much Lewdness lately, and that I should suffer him to put me into so many Bawdy postures, truly I blush when I do but think of it.

Frank. Yet for all your Blushes, you were well enough pleased with what he did unto you.

Katy. I cannot deny it.

Frank. Well then, so long as you received no harm, there is no hurt done, if they did not love us, they would be Damn'd [if] they would take the pains to put us into so many different postures.

Katy. You say true Cousin, and I am absolutely perswaded Mr. *Roger* Loves me very well.

Figure 1.12   The tenth illustration of *The School of Venus*.

Frank. That you need not doubt of, since at first dash he tryed so many several ways of Fucking thee.

Katy. I shall never forget a posture he put me [in] the other day, which was very pleasant and Gamesome.

Frank. I hope you will not conceal it.

Katy. No indeed, but when once you know it, I am confident you and your Gallant will practice it.

Frank. Well, what is it?

Katy. Last Sunday in the Afternoon, my Mother being gone to Church, he having not seen me in Three days before, gave me a visit. So soon as he came in, being impatient of delay, he flung me on a Trunk and Fucked me; having a little cooled his courage, we Kissed and dallied so long, that his Prick which he showed me stood again as stiff as a Stake, then he flung me backwards on the Bed, flung up my Coats, opened my Legs, and put a Cushion under my Arse, then Leveling me right, he took out of his Pocket Three little pieces of Red, White, and Blew Cloaths, the Red he put under my Right Buttock, the White under my Left, and the Blew under my Rump, then looking me in the Face, he thrust his Prick into my Cunt, and bid me observe Orders.

Frank. This was a good beginning.

Katy. Yes, but it had a better Ending.

Frank. Let me know how.

Katy. As he thrust, if he would have me lift up my Right Buttock, he called Red, if the Left Buttock, he called White, if he meant my Rump, he called for Blew.

Frank. Oh brave, what perfection art thou arrived at.

Katy. Till he was well setled in the Saddle, he was not over Brisk, but soon as he was well seated, he cryed out like a Mad man, Red, Blew, White, White, Blew, Red, so that I moved Three several ways to his One, if I committed any mistake, he gentled reproved me, and told me that then I mistook White for Blew, or Blew for White. I told him that the Reason was, because the Blew pleased me more than any of the other.

Frank. The Reason was, because that the Blew being in the Middle, that motion made him thrust his Prick farthest.

Katy. I perceive you know too much Cousin, than to be instructed by me.

Frank. However go on, perchance I may learn something.

Katy. What would you have more? At last he holding his Tongue in my Mouth let fly, but he was so long at his Sport, that I spent twice to his once; at last he taught me a Trick to hold my Seed till he was ready to spend,[19] when he was, we spoke both with frequent Sighs and short breaths, so that when the Liquor of Life came, we scarce knew where we were.

Frank. Indeed they that at Spending make the least noise give the more pleasure, though some cannot abstain from it, and to excuse it say, that it is pleasure.

Katy. What do they mean, is it pleasure to make a noise, or doth the pleasure they receive by Fucking cause it?

Frank. My opinion is, that Fucking maketh them do it, for why may not great pleasure have the same effect upon us, as great pain hath, and you know Tickling often makes us cry.

Katy. How comes this to pass?

Frank. They get upon Wenches sitting boult up right with their Pricks in their Cunts, with a grim countenance, like St. George on Horse back, and so soon as they find the sperme come Tickling, they cry out, oh, there, there, heave up, my Love, my Dear, thrust your Tongue in my Mouth. To see them in that condition would make one who knoweth not the Reason, come with Spirits to help fetch them to life again, believing they were ready to dye.

Katy. Sure the Wench is very well satisfied, to see the man make so many Faces, provided the parties can fare well and not cry Roast Meat, that is, be very secret, I think the pleasure very lawful.

Frank. We were saying that the height of pleasure makes men cry out, I tell you so do Women too very often, for when they find it coming, they often Roar to the purpose, crying out, my Dear Rogue, thrust it up to the Head, what shall I do, for I dye with pleasure. Such Blades and Lasses Fuck in some private place, where they cannot be heard. Now some are such Drowsy Jades as nothing will move.

Katy. Say you so, pray what sort of Animals be they?

Frank. Why such as must be prompted by Frigging, and other ways to Raise their Leachery, but when once their Venery is up, their Cunt is like the Bridge of a Fiddle, which makes them mad for Horsing.

Katy. But do not they Spend?

Frank. Yes, they can't hold it, but Spend more than others.

Katy. That Wench, whose Gallant is so dull as he must want her Assistance to make his Prick stand, is very unhappy.

Frank. Now let us speak of them that do not spend with Fucking. First Eunuchs, whose Stones are cut out, their Pricks stand now and then, but they cannot emit any Seed, and yet their Pricks will so tickle, as they can make a Woman Spend, and Women in Turkey formerly made use of them, till of late a Turkish Emperor seeing a Gelding cover a Mare, Eunucks now have all Pricks and Stones cut off.

Katy. I abominate all these sort of People, pray don't let us so much as mention them, but let us talk of those Lads, who have swinging Tarses to please Women.

Frank. By and by, but I have not yet mentioned some People who say nothing in their Fuckings, but Sigh and Groan, for my part I am for those that are mute, those that make a noise being like Cats a Catterwauling.

Katy. But what part doth Woman act whilst she is Fucking with the man?

Frank. Don't run too fast, and thou shalt know all at last. Let us consider what progress we have made, we are now no forwarder than the manner of thrusting a Prick into a Cunt, and the pleasure there is in Spending, with the satisfaction of Kissing, handling, and other Love Tricks, of which we have not fully spoken, nor of its due time and place when to be practiced. This therefore shall be your this days Lesson, it being a very material thing, and of great consequence, for 'tis the chief end of Love, and the way how to please men.

Katy. Without doubt Cousin all this must be most excellent, and 'tis even that wherein I desire to be informed.

Frank. Let us put the case then. Thou wer't at handy Gripes with thy Lover, and didst not know how to make good the skirmish, whilst he is a laboring on thee, you must speak low with little affected Phrases, calling him your Heart, your Soul, your Life, telling him he pleaseth you extreamly, still minding what you are about, for every stroak of your Arse affords a new pleasure, for we do not Fuck brutally like Beasts, who are only prompted thereto for Generations sake by nature, but with knowledg and for Loves sake. If you have then any Request to make to the man,

Figure 1.13   The eleventh illustration of *The School of Venus.*

do it when he is at the height of his Leachery, for then he can deny the Woman nothing, and nothing mollifies the Heart more than those Fucking Actions; Some Jades have been so fortunate as to Marry Persons of Great Quality, meerly for the knack they had in Fucking; These Love Toyes extreamly heighten a mans Venery, who therefore will try all ways to please you, calling you his Soul, his Goddess, his little Angel, nay he will wish himself all Tarse for thy sake, so soon as he finds it coming, he will not fail to give thee notice of it by his half words and short Breathings; Remember these things I have told you, and look to your bits.

Katy. I warrant you, let me alone, but what posture do you usually put your self in?

Frank. *For the most part you must thrust your Buttocks towards him, taking him about the Neck and Kissing him, endeavoring to Dart your Tongue into his Mouth, and Rowling under his, at last clinge close unto him, with your Armes and Legs, holding your Hands on his Buttocks, and Gently Frigging his Cods, putting his Arse to you to get in his Prick as far as you can, thou knowest what follows as well as I can tell thee, only mind to prepare thee as I have informed you, and he will make mighty much of you, and though he give himself and all he is worth unto you, yet will he not think he hath done enough for you.*

Katy. Cousin, though your obligations are great, yet I poor Wench have nothing but thanks to return you, but the postures you have informed me of, I shall make use of as opportunities present, that my Gallant may perceive I love him.

Frank. *'Tis a common fault among young People only to think of the pres-*

39

ent *Time, but they never consider how to make their pleasures durable, and to continue it a long time.*

Katy. Let me have your instructions, who are so great a Mistress in the art of Love.

Frank. *But ha'nt you had Mr.* Rogers *company lately?*

Katy. Now and then I used to let him in, and he lay with me a whole night, which happiness I have been deprived of above this Fortnight, for my Mothers Bed being removed out of her Chamber, (which is Repairing) into mine, so that our designs tending that way have been frustrated ever since.

Frank. *But you see him daily, do you not?*

Katy. Yes he visits me daily, and Fucks me once or twice if there be time, now one time was very favorable unto us, for the Maid being gone abroad, my Mother bid me open the Door for him, which I did, and because we would not loose that opportunity, but take fortune by the forelock he thrust me again[st] the Wall, took up my Coats, made me open my Thighs, and presented his stiffe standing Tarse to my Cunt, shoving it in as far as he could, plying his Business with might and main, which pleased me very well, and though I was very desirous of the sport, yet he made a shift to spend before me, I therefore held him close to me, and prayed him to stay in me till I had done too, when we both had done, we went up Stairs, not in the least mistrusting any thing. But when my Mother was from home, we took our Bellies full of Fuck, if my Mother or any Company was in the House we watched all opportunities that he might encunt me, we were both of us so full of Fuck, that we did not let slip the least minute that was favorable unto us; nay more; we sometimes did it in fear and had the ill luck to be disturbed and forced to give over our sport without spending, if it proved a false alarm we went at it again, and made an end of our Swiving; sometimes we had the ill fortune, that in two or three days time he could only kiss and feel me, and we thought it happiness enough if we could but make Prick and Cunt meet, which if we did they seldom parted with dry Lips. At other times if we sat near one another, he would pull out his Prick throwing his Cloak over it, and with languishing eyes shewing it me standing, in truth I could but pity him, and therefore drew near him, and having tucked up my Smock, he thrust his hand into my Placket and felt me at his will, tickling my Cunt soundly with his finger, when he was once at it, he held like a Mastiffe Dog and never left till he made me spend. This is called Digiting and if rightly managed give[s] a Woman the next content to Fucking, this way he did to me, but the better is thus ordered. After a Wench is soundly swived, and that her Arse is wet with seed, the Man must keep her lying on her Back, then taking up the Lip of her Cunt, thrust in his finger into the hole through which she pisseth, (which is above the Cunt hole, and is made like the Mouth of a Frog) and then the Woman must be soundly frigged, which will make her start, and give her so much pleasure that some esteem it beyond Fucking. We grew every day [more] learnedly then [the] other, so that at last we found out a way of Fucking before Company, without being perceived by any of them.

Frank. *Pray tell me how that is?*

Katy. As I was once Ironing, my Mother being gone out of the Room, he came behind me, pulls up my Cloaths and puts his Prick between my Thighs, striving to get it into my Cunt; I feeling him laboring at my Arse, ne're minded what I was doing, so that I burnt a good Handkerchief by the means, when he saw he could not this way get his Prick in, he bid me bow down and take no farther care, for he would give me warning if any body came, but I going to stoop, he found the slit of my Coat behind, so small that it displaced his Prick, which made him curse and swear, because he was forced that time to spend between my Thighs.

Frank. *What pity was that.*

Katy. When the job was over and he had put up his tool again, I began to murmur at the ill fortune I had in burning my Hankerchief, which my Mother hearing, comes up and calls me Idle Huswife, protesting she would never bestow any more upon me, but Mr. *Roger* made my peace again, for he told my Mother, that it was done whilst I ran to the Window to see what was doing in the streets, not dreaming the Iron had been so hot.

Frank. *But all this while, you have forget to tell me the new way you have found out to Fuck before Company.*

Katy. The manner we found it out was thus, Mr. *Roger* gave me a Visit one Night, as we were dancing with some few of our Neighbors, he being a little flustrated with Wine set himself on a Chair, and whilst others danced, feigned himself a sleep; at last he pulled me to him, and sat me down on his knees, discoursing with him about ordinary matters, keeping my eyes fixed on the Company all the time, all this while having thrust his Hand in at my Placket behind, he handled my Cunt, whilst I felt his stiff standing Tarse thrusting against me, which he would fain have thrust through the slit of my Coat behind, but that was not long enough for him to reach my Cunt, and he durst not pull up my Coats, the Room was so full of Company. At last with a little Pen-knife he pulled out of his Twesers, he made a hole in the exact place, and thrust his Prick into my Cunt, which I was very glad of; we went leasurely to work, for we durst not be too busie for fear of being caught, though I received a great deal of pleasure, yet I held my Countenance pretty well, till we were ready to spend, when truly I was fain to bite my Lip, it tickled me so plaguily. An hour after, he Fucked my Arse again in the same manner, this way we often since before Company experimented, and I have often thanked him for his new invention.

Frank. Ah but this way is hazardous, and for all your biting of your Lip the Company might take notice of you, 'twere better therefore for you to hold down your head, and keep your hand before your Face, for then they could not perceive any thing, and would only have thought your head had Ached.

Katy. You say very true Cousin, and I shall observe that way for the future, indeed I must confess I have learned more of you then any one else, in this mistery of Fucking, and shall always acknowledg it.

Frank. Nay since you are my Schollar 'tis my duty to make you perfect, if therefore you want any more instructions pray be free with me and ask what you will.

Katy. After all these pleasures we have talked of, I perceive 'tis that part of a man which we call Prick contents us Women best; now I would fain learn of you, what sorts of Pricks are best and aptest to satisfie us.

Frank. You propound a very good and pertinent question, and I will now resolve it unto you. You must know then though there are Pricks of all sorts and sizes, yet are they briefly reduced to these three sorts, great ones, midling ones, and little ones.

Katy. Let us begin with the little ones, how are they made?

Frank. They are from four to six Inches long, and proportionably big; these are good for little, for they do not fill a Cunt as it should be, and if a Woman should have a great Belly, or have a flabby Cunt with a great pair of Lips to it, (which is a great perfection) or if the Cunt hole be low, which is a fault on the other side, it is impossible for such a Prick for enter above two or three inches, which truly can give a Woman but little satisfaction.

Katy. Well but what say you to the great ones?

Frank. Great horse Tarses hurt and open a Cunt too wide, nay they often pain tryed Women as well as Virgins, such is their strange bigness and length, that some men are obliged to wear a Napkin or cloath about them, to hinder then from going in too far.

Katy. Well what say you to the midling Pricks?

Frank. They are from Six to Nine Inches, they fit Women to a hair, and tickle them sweetly. As in Men so in Women too, there are great, small, and midling Cunts, but when all is done be they little or great, there is nothing so precious as a friends Prick that we love well, and though it be no longer then ones little finger, we find more satisfaction in it then in a longer of another mans. A well sized Prick must be reasonable big, but bigger at the Belly then at the Top, there is a sort of Prick

I have not yet mentioned, called the Belly Prick, which is generally esteemed above the rest; It appears like a snail out of it's shell, and stands oftner then those large Tarses which are like unweldy ladders, which take a great more time to Rear then little ones.

Katy. I have another question to ask you.

Frank. *What is it pray?*

Katy. Why do Men when they fuck us, call us such beastly names? Methinks they should court and complement us, I cannot conceive how love should make them so extravagant.

Frank. *'Tis love only that makes them use those expressions, for the greatest and chiefest cause of love, is the pleasure our Bodies receive, without that there would be no such thing as love.*

Katy. Pray excuse me, there I know you will tell me of Brutal love, and that may be, but there is other besides which you may know by it's lasting, whereas Brutality endures no longer then any other extravagant Passion, and is over so soon as the seed is squirted out of the Prick.

Frank. *Why then all love is Brutal, which I will plainly demonstrate unto you.*

Katy. Pray take the pains to do it, and I will not interrupt you.

Frank. *Though the pleasure passes away, yet it returneth again, and it is that which cherisheth love, let us come to the point, would you love Mr. Roger if he were gelt, and would you esteem him and think him a handsome Man, and fit for your turn, if he were impotent? What say you?*

Katy. Truly no.

Frank. *Therefore don't I speak truth, and if you had not a Cunt too for him to thrust his Prick into, and Beauty to make it stand, do not deceive yourself and think he would love you for any other good quality. Men love to please themselves, and though they deny it, believe them not, and the chief mark they aim at is our Cunts; also when we embrace and kiss them, we long for their Pricks, though we are ashamed to ask it, for notwithstanding all the Protestations of honor, the tears they shed, the faces and cringes they make, it all ends in throwing us backwards on a Bed, insolently pulling up our Coats, and catching us by the Cunts, getting between our legs and Fucking us. In short, this is the end of all;[20] most commonly those that love most, swive least, and they that Fuck oftnest have seldom a constant Mistriss, if they have, the love doth not last long, especially if the Mistriss were easily gained. 'Tis strange to see Women pretend to love with constancy, making it such a vertue, protesting that it is not Fucking they delight in, when we daily see them use it. To be short, all ingenious persons confess, that copulation is the only means of generation, and consequently the chief procurement of love.*

Katy. How learned are you Cousin in these misteries of love, pray how came you by all this knowledg?

Frank. *My Fucking friend takes a great deal of delight to instruct me, and love hath this excellency in it, that though at first we do not think of Swiving, yet is it the chief thing we aim at, and the only remedy to cure love.*

Katy. You have said as much on this Subject, as possibly can be expected.

Frank. *Now the reason why Men call us Women such beastly names, when they Fuck us, is because they delight in naming such things as relate unto that pleasure, for when they are in the Act of Fucking, they think of nothing but our Cunts, which makes them express themselves accordingly, saying my Dear Cunny, my little Fucking fool, my pretty little Tarse taker, and such like words which they use in the Act of Venery. This also proceeds from the attentiveness of our Spirits, when we are in copulation, and gives a lively Representation of the mind on the beloved object; for our very Souls rejoyce at these amorous embraces, which appears by the sweet union of two Tongues, which tickle one another in soft murmurs, pronouncing my Dear Dove, my Heart, my very good Child, my Chicken; all these are Emblems of affection, as my Dove, when they consider the Love of Pigeons, good Child, and Chicken, relate to the dearness of a Child, and harmlessness of a Chicken; my Heart, that is, they so passionately love the Woman that they wish they could reach her Heart with their Prick. In fine, all the words they use are like so many Hieroglyphicks, signifying every one of them a distinct sentence, as when they say my Cunny, it signifies they receive a great pleasure by that part, and you might add innumerable similitudes more. There are also very sufficient reasons, why they call every thing by it's right name, when they are Fucking us.*

Katy. How say you Cousin?

Frank. *First the more to celebrate their Victory over us, as when they once enjoy us, they take pleasure to make us blush with those nasty words. Secondly their thoughts and imaginations being so intent on the pleasure they take, they can scarce speak plain, and as they breath short, they are glad to use all the Monysyllabic words they can think of, and metaphorise as briefly as they can upon the obscane parts, what they usually called Loves Paradise and the center of delight, they now in plain English call a Cunt, which word Cunt is very short and fit for the time it is named in, and though it make Women sometimes Blush to hear it named, methinks indeed they do ill, that make such a pather, to describe a Monysyllable by new words and longer ways then is necessary, as to call a Man's Instrument according to it's name, a Prick, is it not better than Tarsander, a Mans-yard, Man Thomas, and such like tedious demonstrations, neither proper nor concise enough in such short sports. For the heat of love will neither give us leave or time to run divisions, so that all we can pronounce is, come my dear Soul, take me by the Prick, and put it into thy Cunt, which sure is much better then to say, take me by the Gristle, which grows at the bottom of my Belly, and put it into thy loves Paradise.*

Katy. Your very bare narration is able to make one's Cunt stand a tip toe, but after all this, would you perswade me that Mr. *Roger*, only loves me for Fucking sake?

Frank. *I don't say it positively, there is reason in all things, sometimes the Womans wit and breeding is as delightful as her Body. They help one another, some love for their Parts, some for meer Beauty. I have heard my friend say sometimes, when he hath heard me maintain an argument smartly, he was mad to be Fucking me on the spot, the cleverness of my wit so tickled him, that he could not rule his stiff standing Tarse, but desired to thrust it into my Body to reach the soul of me, whose ingenuity pleased him so much.*

Katy. I now find my self pretty well instructed in love tricks, and in all the intrigues Men use tending thereunto, but now let us speak of Maids, who are equally concerned with men in love, what is the Reason that they are so coy and scrupulous to be kissed, nay though we make them believe 'tis no sin to kiss?

Frank. *Oh, but they are fearful of being got with Child.*

Katy. What if I should be with Child? The abundance of sperm Mr. *Roger* hath spurted into my Cunt makes me mistrust it.

Frank. *Pho, fear no colors, if ever that happens I'll help thee out, for I have infallible remedies by me, which will prevent that in time of need.*

Katy. Pray Cousin let me have them.

Frank. *And so you shall if there be occasion, but to ease you of that fear and trouble, first know that these misfortunes are not very frequent, that we need [not] fear them before they happen. How many pregnant Wenches are there, that daily walk up and down, and by the help of Busques[21] and loose garbs hide their great Bellies till within a Month or two of their times, when by the help of a faithful Friend they slip into the Country, and rid themselves of their Burthen, and shortly after return into the City as pure Virgins as ever? Make the worst of it, 'tis but a little trouble, and who would loose so much fine sport for a little hazard, sometimes we may Fuck two or three years and that never happen[s], and if we would be so base 'tis easie to have Medicines to make us miscarry, but 'tis pity such things should be practiced in this time of Dearth, and want his Majesty hath of able Subjects, in which there are none more likely to do him Service then those which are illegitimate, which are begot in the heat of Leachery.*

Katy. I shan't so much for the future fear a great Belly, this I am sure of, it cannot but be a great satisfaction to a Woman, that she hath brought a Rational and living creature into the World, and that one whom she dearly loves had his share in getting it.

Frank. *You say very true, against the time of your lying in, 'tis but preparing a close and discreet Midwife, and after the Child is born have it nursed by some Peasants Wife in the Country till the Child be grown up and provided for, either by Father or Mother.*

Figure 1.14 The twelfth illustration of *The School of Venus.*

Katy. But, what do those poor creatures do, who are so fearful to be got with Child, that though their Cunt tickleth never so much, yet dare they not get a lusty Tarse to rub it, for methinks fingering is unnatural.

Frank. Why may be they have another way to please themselves.

Katy. What way pray can that possibly be?

Frank. I have somewhere read of a Kings Daughter who for want of a Prick in specie, made use of a pleasant device, she had a brazen statue of a Man painted flesh color, and hung with a swinging Tarse composed of a soft substance, hollow, yet stiff enough to do the business. It had a red head and a little hole at the Top, spupplyed with a thwacking pair of Stones, all so neatly done, it appeared natural, now when her desire prompted her, she went and eased nature, thrusting that Mascarade Prick into her Cunt, taking hold on the Buttocks, when she found it coming, she pulled out a spring, and so squirted out of the Prick into her Cunt a luke warm liquor, which pleased her almost as well as Swiving.

Katy. Lord, what can't leachery invent?

Frank. And no doubt but Men in their Closets have statues of handsome women after the same manner, which they make use of in the same way and rub their standing Pricks in a slit, at the bottom of their bellies proportionable deep, and in imitation of a Cunt.

Katy. This is as likely as what you said before, but pray go on.

Frank. Wenches that are not rich enough to buy statues must content themselves with dildoes made of Velvet, or blown in glass, Prick fashion, which they fill with luke warm milk, and tickle themselves therewith, as with a true Prick, squirt-

ing the milk up their bodies when they ready to spend, some mechanick Jades frig themselves with candles of about four in the pound; Others as most Nuns do make use of their fingers. To be short, Fucking is so natural, that one way or another Leachery will have it's vent in all sorts and conditions of People.[22]

Katy. This is pleasant enough, go on with your story.

Frank. Some Women that fear Child-bearing will not Fuck, and yet they will permit their Gallants not only to kiss them, but also to feel their skin, Thighs, Breasts, Buttocks and Cunts frigging the Men with their hands, rubbing their Cunts and bottom of their Bellies with the sperm, yet they will not permit the Man downright swiving.

Katy. What is next?

Frank. There are a sort of bolder Jades, who will suffer themselves to be Fucked till they feel the sperm coming, when immediately they will fling their rider out of the Saddle, and not suffer him to spend in them; some will tye a Pigs Bladder to the Top of their Pricks, which receives all without hazard. Some are so confident of their cunning, that they will let Men spend in them, but they will be sure it shall be before or after they have done it themselves, for all Physicians agree they must both spend together to get a Child, yet after all, most Women put it to hazard, and rather venture a great Belly than receive the pleasures but by halves, and stop in their full carier, who certainly are in the Right, for of a hundred Women that Fuck, scarce Two of them prove with Child, for my part, those that will follow my advice, should neither trouble themselves with care either before or after Fucking, for such fears must certainly diminish the pleasure, which we ought rather to add unto, for there is not the like content in this World as entirely to abandon ones self to a party Beloved, and to take such freedom and liberty one with another, as our Lust shall prompt us unto.

Katy. Though I believe Cousin you are weary with Discoursing, yet I must needs ask you another question or two before we part.

Frank. You hold me in a twined Thread. Ask what you please.

Katy. By the Symptoms you tell me of I am afraid I am with Child, for when ever Mr. *Roger* Fucks me we spend together, to give our selves the greater pleasure, now can you tell me any sign, or do you know any Reason why I should not be with Child?[23]

Frank. Yes marry can I, for besides spending together, the Woman if she have a mind to take, must shrink up her Buttocks close together, and lye very still till the Man have done, did you do so?

Katy. For matter of holding my Buttocks together, that I always do, but 'tis impossible for any so Airy a Wench as I am, to hold my Arse still in the midst of so great pleasure, no, I always shake it as fast as I can for the Heart of me.

Frank. That alone is enough to prevent it, for stirring so much disperseth the

Mans Seed, and hindereth it from taking place, that it cannot possibly joyn with the Womans, as for holding our Buttocks close, that none of us can help, for it is consistent with the pleasures we receive, to keep them as close as we can. Now Nature which maketh nothing in vain offereth us a better mark at the Cunt, thrusting it towards the Man, so that the Lips of the Cunt intirely Bury the Mans Tarse, that makes your Experienced Fucksters cry, Close, Close, which is to say, close behind and open before.

Katy. I improve more and more by your Discourse, as to my being with Child you have satisfied me, being not at all afraid of it, but pray tell me why men had rather we should handle their Pricks more than any other part of their Bodies, and why they take so much pleasure to have us stroak their Cods, when they are Fucking of us?

Frank. That's easily answered, for 'tis the greatest Satisfaction they receive, nor can we better make them sensible of the satisfaction they give us. Is it not reason to make much of a thing which gives us so much pleasure? 'Tis also very obligeing and grateful to the man; A Woman's hand hath great vertue in it, and is an Emblem of Love, for Friends when they first meet shake hands, now the Love of Man and Woman is more natural, for thence the body and mind partake; in short, though a Woman suffer a Man to Fuck her, spend in her, and have his will of her in every thing, yet if she don't take him by the Prick, 'tis a sign she cares not so much for him, nay, she ought when her Gallant is Fucking of her, and thrust up his Tarse as far as he can into her, to feel the Root of his Prick and make much of his Bollocks, and Nature hath ordered it so, that a Man at once receiveth Two pleasures, one from the Cunt, the other from the Hand, there being a great part of the Prick behind the Stones, which never entereth into the Cunt, but reacheth to a Mans Arsehole. This was so placed purposely for the Woman to handle it when she is in the very act of Venery. There is nothing belonging to the Privy parts, but if we consider good reason may be given why it is so, and to what use it serves, Nature having made all things in it's perfection to please us, if we know the true use of them. I have enlarged a little more on this Subject, because it hath some Relation to my concerns, I and my Fucking Friend having often experimented those feeling pleasures. Is it not Child a fine sight to see a little piece of limber Flesh, which hangs down at the bottom of our Friends Belly to grow stiffer and stiffer, till it be as hard as a Stone, and all this by vertue of Hand stroking?

Katy. This Question being now resolved, pray tell me, who hath the most pleasure in Fucking, the man or the Woman?[24]

Frank. That's hard to resolve, but if we look upon the running out of the Seed to be the material cause, then certainly the Woman hath most, for she feels not only her own, but the Mans too, but the Man feels only what comes from himself, but this Question cannot easily be resolved, because the man cannot be Judge of the Womans pleasure, nor she of the Mans.

Katy. But how comes it to pass, that both Sexes Naturally love and de-sire Copulation, before they have any experience or tryal of its pleasure?

Frank. *Man and Woman were ever joyned together from the beginning, and Copulation was ordered for the propagation and continuance of Mankind, to which Nature hath added so much delight, because the thing in it self is certainly so nasty, that were it not for the pleasure, certainly none would commit so filthy an act.*

Katy. What is it you call Love?

Frank. *'Tis a desire one half hath to unite it to the other half.*[25]

Katy. Pray take the pains to make this more plain unto me.

Frank. *'Tis a Corporal desire or the first motion of nature, which by degrees ascends up to Reason, where it is perfected into a Spiritual Idea; so that this Rea-son finds an absolute necessity of uniting one half to the other half, when nature hath what she Requires, that Idea or spiritual vapor by little and little dissolves it self into a white liquid substance, like Milk which tickling softly down through our Backbones into other Vessels, at last becomes the pleasure of which before 'twas the only Idea.*

Katy. What causeth that Idea to tickle so in it's passage?

Frank. *Because it pleaseth her, that she is nere communicating her self to the beloved object.*

Katy. Truly this is admirable, but why can't People (in the height of leachery) laugh since they are both so well pleased?

Frank. *Because the head partakes not of their pleasures, for all the Joy is di-vided between Cunt and Prick.*

Katy. This makes me smile.

Frank. *But you may think otherwise of it?*

Katy. How mean you?

Frank. *The Soul by the violence of this great pleasure descends and thinks no more of it self, but leaves the functions of reason empty and unprovided, now laugh-ter being a propriety of reason is with it anticipated, which is thus proved, when the Idea begins to pass through our Vessels, we find a kind of drowsiness and stu-pefaction of our senses, which demonstrates the privation of the soul from those parts, and the pleasure being so great in our secret members, it is not in the souls power to exercise any other faculty.*

Katy. Though these Lectures are very Learned for a young Schollar, yet will I reflect on them, but why do Men thrust their Pricks between our Breasts, Thighs and Buttocks, when we won't suffer them to put them into our Cunts, certainly this is a kind of blind love, for which I cannot imag-ine a true reason?

Frank. *You have given it an excellent Epithite (you remember what I said be-fore of the Idea) for the Members of the Woman is the part of the Man, Love being blind and not knowing where the conjunction is, provided, that the Man partake in it's pleasure in the conjunction of each Member, so that the Man finding the pleasure coming, friggs and rubs himself against the Woman, cheating his Reason, by the Idea to which that conjunction hath some resemblance, with what is true and natural to it, he is transported if in the beloved object, he feels any thing that makes the least resistance to his Prick, which makes him shuffe on harder and harder.*

Katy. You have cleared this point Cousin, but we have not yet spoke of Tongue kissing, which I reckon nothing but a meer fancy.

Frank. *Tongue kissing is another cheat, which desireth conjunction in any manner whatsoever, 'tis a true resemblance and representation of the Prick entering into the Cunt, the Tongue slides under another Tongue, but in so doing finds a little resistance by the lips of the recipient, and the resemblance of this object cheats the mind the better to imitate the Pricks entrance into the Cunt. When these kind of caresses are made, 'tis then we breath out our very hearts and Souls out of our Mouths, for it makes the lover think that his Prick should go after the same manner into the Cunt of her whom he kisseth, and I believe the Womans thoughts are not much unlike the Mans; in short, they do what they can to imitate Swiving after the liveliest manner, they can with their Tongues, which they thrust and rowl about in one anothers Mouths, as if they were a Fucking.*

Katy. Enough, enough of this Cousin, or else you'll make me spend, but why is the pleasure greater when the Woman gets upon the Man and Fucks him, then when she is passive and lyes under?

Frank. *I have already given you one Reason, and now I will give you another; 'tis a Correspondence of love, for Man and Woman you know are perfect and distinct Creatures, now the great love they bear one to another makes them desire to transform themselves one into the other.*

Katy. But still you do not tell me why they Fuck Topsie Turvy, and the Woman is a top who ought to be under.

Frank. *Yes but I have, but if there were no other reason this is sufficient, she ought not perpetually to work him at the labor Oar.*

Katy. I grant all this.

Frank. *Besides, it is a kind of Metamorphosis, for when the Woman is a top, the Man is possessed with feminine thoughts, and the Woman with Masculine passions, each having assumed the contrary Sex by the postures they are in.*

Katy. This is according to a former lesson you taught me, which I think I shall not forget.

Frank. *Pray, what was that?*

Katy. That one half desireth to be united to the other half.

Frank. *'Tis an assurance of a good principle, when the reasons and effects of the causes we infer are well deduced.*

Katy. I think we have spoken enough of all things relating to love, and therefore I think we may rest here.

Frank. *I agree with you in that particular, but pray be careful then not to forget any of your lessons.*

Katy. To help my memory pray then make me a short Repetition.

Frank. *First, we have spoken of the Effects which are stroaking, handling and kissing, then of the thing it self, and several ways of Conjunction, the several humors of Men and Women, their dispositions and sundry desires, we have unfolded love with its nature, properties and effects, it's uses how and in what manner it acts it's part, and the reasons of it, and I am sure if we have omitted any thing it cannot be of much consequence. Indeed there may be a Hundred other little particular love practices, which now we have not time to enumerate, first as to the uniting of one half to the other, the desires and ways of doing it, the tickling, Arse-shakings, cringes, sighings, sobbs, groans, faintings away, hand clappings, and sundry other caresses, of some of which we have already spoken; so that we will now make an end, and if there be any thing remaining, discourse it at another meeting.*

Katy. Well Cousin, give me your hand upon it.

Frank. *Why, I promise you I will. What needs all this pother between you and I?*

Katy. Well, I can but give you thanks, for the great favors you have done me, in thus instructing me.

Frank. *What needs all these compliments, do you know what you have thanked me for?*

Katy. For the patience you have had all this while to instruct my thick soul in all these love lessons, and of those most excellent reasons you give for every thing, making me perceive what an inexhaustible Fountain love is, this I am sure of, I never could have had a better informer to instruct me from it's first Rudiments, to it's highest notions imaginable.

Frank. *Pray no more of your compliments, love hath this excellency in it, that it intirely satisfyeth every body, according to their apprehensions, the most ignorant receiving pleasure though they know not what to call it; hence it comes, that the more expert and refined wits have a double share of it's delights, in the soft and sweet imaginations of the mind. What pleasant thoughts and sweet imaginations occur, when we are at the sport, and now it comes in my mind, I like this way of the Womans riding the Man beyond any other Posture, because she takes all the pains the Man ought to do, and maketh a Thousand grimaces, as the pleasure doth tickle her, and the Man is extreamly happy, for he seeth every part of the beloved upon him, as her Belly, Cunt and Thighs, he seeth and feeleth the natural motion she hath upon him, and the stedfast looking in her Face adds fewel to his fire, so that every motion of her Arse, puts him in a new extasie, he is Drunk with pleasure, and when love comes to pay the tribute which is due to their pleasures, they are both so ravished with Joy, they almost expire with delight. This is a Subject one might amply enlarge on if there were time.*

51

Katy. 'Tis impossible to represent every bodies imagination upon this subject, for methinks I could invent more postures then you have told me of, and as pleasing unto me, but pray whilst you are putting on your Scarfe to be gone tell me one more thing.

Frank. *Well, what is it?*

Katy. What is it [that] will make two lovers perfectly enjoy one another?

Frank. *Truly, that will require more of me then the putting on of my Scarfe, first we must talk of Beauty, which they must both have, then we must come to other particulars, which are too long to treat of now.*

Katy. However grant me my request, for the longer you are with me the greater is my pleasure, it is not so late, but you may stay a little longer, the truth is, you have put me so agog this day, that I can endure to talk of nothing but what relates to love.

Frank. *Well, I will do this, provided when I have done you will keep me no longer, you have almost sucked my well dry, turn up the glass, for upon my word I will stay no longer then this half hour.*

Katy. Then I will make the better use of my time, Cousin, I know not how it comes to pass, but when I am absent from my friend I always think of the pleasant pastime I have in his company, and not considering his other perfections, I am so strangely besotted with his Stones and Prick, that ever and anon I am fancying he is thrusting it into my Cunt, with all the force he hath, stretching my Cunt as a Shoemaker doth a straight Boot, sometimes, I think it tumbleth the very coggles of my heart, these imaginations make me so damnable Prick proud, that I spend with the very conceit of them.[26]

Frank. *This Ordinarily happens to all Lovers, and is a product of your desire, which Represents things of this Nature, so lively unto you, as if they were Really such, and your thinking of your Friends Prick more than any other part, plainly sheweth, that whatever Idea we have of the Person whom we Love, which Love brings into our minds, thoughts of the Privy Members, as being the cause of the immediate pleasure we take, the other Members though never so Beautiful, being but circumstances: As for example, a fair Black Eye, a fine White plump Hand, and a delicate Taper Thigh, makes a man consider the Cunts admirable structure, strangely exciting sensual Appetites, and make the Prick stand, which cannot any other wayes be eased but by spending.*

Katy. I understand this very well, but Cousin, since Beauty was the Subject we were upon, pray describe it unto me, and Represent a perfect enjoyment accompanyed with all the pleasures that go along with it.

Frank. *Beauty consists in Two things, first in the perfect and well proportioned lineaments of the Body, and secondly of the Actions thereunto belonging.*

Katy. I am much taken with these clear Divisions.

Frank. *There are some Women, which though they cannot properly be called handsom, yet have they such a* Jointy mien *as the* French *term it, as renders them extreamly taking.*

Katy. To talk of each feature is too tedious, my desire is only to have Beauty described.

Frank. Then will I begin with the Woman, and then speak of the Man. She must be a Young Lass of Seventeen or Eighteen years Old, pretty plump, and a little inclined to fat, straight, and of a good Statue and Majestical looks, having a well proportioned and noble Face, her Head well set on her Shoulders, sparkling Eyes, with a sweet and pleasant Aspect, her mouth rather of the bigger size than too little, her Teeth even and very White, her forehead indifferent, and without frowns, her Cheeks well filled up, Black Hair and a Round Face, her Shoulders Large and of a good breadth, a fine plump and smooth Neck, hard Breasts, that hang not down, but support themselves like Ivory Apples, an Arm proportionable to the rest, a skin neither too White nor too Tawny, but between both, and so filled with flesh that it hang not loose, a Hand White as Snow, and well set on at the Wrists; as to her Manners, first let her be neatly Drest, Modest, yet with lively Actions, let her words be Good and Witty, she must appear Innocent and a little ignorant before Company, and let her manage all her Discourse so, that it may tend to ingratiate her self with the hearers, and make her Person the more taking, still to keep her self within the bounds of modesty, and not to give the least encouragement to any to violate it, and if by chance any should offer an uncivil action or discourse to her, she must protest she knows not what they would be at, or what they mean, at Publick Meetings and Feasts let her be very demure, let her Eat and Drink but moderately, for you may know the humor of the Lass, as she is more or less affected with pleasures, and inclined to Diversions, which her words and Actions will easily detect, therefore excess is dangerous to Young Women, but if it be the General Frolick of the Company, she may indulge her self a little more liberty, especially if she be amongst those who have a good Repute in the World; to make her more compleat, she must Dance well, Sing well, and often Read Love Stories and Romances, under pretence to learn to speak well her Mother Tongue, she ought to have a tender Heart, even when she Reads of cruelty, though in one of these Romances.

Katy. You have made an admirable Description of a fine Woman.

Frank. I have not yet done with all the Perfections of the Body, but come to describe her naked, she must have a fine hard Belly well thrust out, for 'tis upon this delightful Rock where all Lovers are Ship-wrackt, her Stomach must be soft and Fleshy, fine small feet turning out at the Toes, which shews that her Cunt is well situated, her Calf of her Leg Plump and large about the middle, small and short Knees, substantial and Tapered Thighs, on which must hang a pair of Round hard Buttocks, a short Rump, and a slender Waste, the Reins of her Back very plyable for her Cunt sake, the heel of her Cunt must be full and hard, round beset and Trimed with dark coloured hair, the slit of her Cunt ought to be Six Fingers below her Navil, the skin whereof must be well stuffed out and slippery, so that when a Mans Hand is upon it, he cannot be able to hold it still in one place, but it will slide and come down to the two Lips of her Cunt, which ought to be red and strutt out, the Cunt hole ought to be of an exact bore to do Execution, and so contrived, that the Prick having forced the first Breast work, may come to the Neck of the Cunt, and so farther forceing before it the small skins, and getting half in, then having taken breath, they both strive again till the Noble Gentleman has got Field Room enough, and at last arrives at the enterance of the Matrix, where my fair Deflowred Virgin will find abundance of Tickling pleasure, but I speak of so perfect a Beauty, that her Gallant will be besotted with her, till he comes to have a fling at her Plumb Tree.

Katy. Having thus described a Lass in her full and Blooming Beauty, what must be the perfections of the Man, which when you have informed me according to your Doctrine, we will put the Two halves together?

Frank. To be short, he must be of a fair Stature and a strong able body, not of a Barbary shape like a Shotten Herring, which is proper to Women only, let him have a Majestick Gate, and walk decently, a quick pleasing Eye, his Nose a little Rising, without any deformity in his Face, his Age about Five and twenty, let him rather incline to Lean than Fat, his Hair of a dark Brown and long enough to Curl upon his Shoulders, a strong Back and double Chested, let him be indifferently strong, so that he may take his Mistriss in his Armes and throw her upon a Bed, taking up her Two Legs and flinging them over his Shoulders, nay he ought to Dance and handle her like a Baby, for it often happens, a Young Spark may have to deal with a Refractory Girl, who will pretend so much modesty, as she will not open her Legs, so that if he have not strength to force her, he will Spend in the Porch, and not Rub her Cunt with his stiff standing Tarse, he must have a well fashioned Foot, and a well proportioned Leg with full Calves, and not like Catsticks, and a pair of lusty Brawny Thighs to bear him up, and make him perform well. What, you seem to wonder at this? Oh, did you but know how enticing strong and vigorous Masculine Beauties are, especially when united to a Neat and perfect Feminine one, you would wish to enjoy no other pleasure, what a brave sight it is to see the Workman of Nature sprout out at the bottom of a Mans Belly, standing stiffly, and shewing his fine Scarlet Head, with a Thawcking pair of Stones to attend it's motion, expecting every minute the word of Command to fall on. I warrant it would alarm thy Cunt, which I would have thee always keep in readiness, that it may be able and ready to withstand the briskest onset the stoutest Tarse of them all can make: Be not afraid of having thy Quarters beaten up, though the Prick be never so big, indeed it may scare a tender Young Virgin, for it Thunders such a ones Cunt hole, and carries all before it.

Katy. What pretty sweet cruelty is this.

Frank. I tell you 'tis a Perfection in a man to have a Tarse so big that it will scare a Virgin, and this in short is the Description of a Complete Man.

Katy. Now demonstrate unto me a perfect enjoyment of persons qualified according to your Description.

Frank. In the Act of Copulation, let them both mind all manner of conveniencies, the Wench must in some things appear a little shame-faced, the Man cannot be too bould, yet I would not have her so bashful as to deny him when he demands Reason, and what belongs to Love: I would only have her modestly infer by her Eyes, that she hath a mind to do that which she is ashamed to Name, let her keep at a little distance, to egge on her Gallant, and make him the more eager, 'tis not becoming the Wench to prostitute her self, though she is glad to hear her Gallant often beg that of her, which she within her self wisheth he would desire; therefore the Man must have a quick Eye and regard all her Actions, Sighs and words, that so nothing she wants may escape his knowledg, but so soon as ever he hath Incunted, 'tis then past time to consider, but let him mind his Knitting, and wag his Arse as fast as he can, whilst she will shame-facedly hold down her Head and wonder at the Sweet Rape he commits on her Body. Let him make full and home thrusts at her Cunt, and let her lye ready to receive them, with her Legs as far a sunder as possible, if she is not much used to the sport, probably her Cunt at first may smart a little, or else it's possible she may complain out of pretended modesty, but let him not fear, for the hurt she receiveth will not be so great as the pleasure. If his Prick be never so big, if it do but stand stiff enough to make way 'twill enter at last, and the pleasure will be the greater; therefore the Wench ought to be very Tractable, and not refuse to put her self in any posture he shall demand of her; she should also encourage, Kiss him, and speak kindly unto him, chearing him up till he have finished the work he hath in Hand. I would have the Wench let the Man have a full Authority over her, and let her Body be totally at his disposal, let what will happen [happen]. She will at length find a great deal of sweet in it, for he will instruct her in what is fitting, and force her to nothing incongruous to Love and it's pleasures, if she be a seasoned Whore, she is to blame if she play the Hypocrite, and pretend modesty after her so long continuance in Fornication, and thereby loose a great deal of pastime. To conclude, I would have no Woman Tantalize a Man with her Hand, since she hath a more proper place to receive and bestow his Instrument, and 'tis a thousand pities so much good stuff should be lost, if she does indeed think the Mans Prick too big, she must for Love of him take the longer time, and try often anointing his Prick with Pomatum, and make use of all the other means she can imagine, and no doubt, in the Conclusion, be it never so big, she will get it in to both their contents.

Katy. These lectures Cousin, which you read unto me are far different from those my Mother Preaches, they treat of nothing but vertue and honesty.

Frank. Yes, yes, Cousin, so goes the World now adays; lyes overcome truth, reason and experience, and some foolish empty sayings are better approved of then real pleasures. Virginity is a fine word in the Mouth, but a foolish one in the Arse, neither is there any thing amiss in Fornication but the name, and there is nothing sweeter then to commit it; neither do Married People refrain, but run at Mutton as well as others, and commit Adultry as often as others do Fornication: Prick and Cunt are the chief actors in the Mystery of Love, the Ceremony is still the same, but I have said enough for once, and must not now pretend to reform the World, some are wiser than some, and the fools serve like foiles to set off the wise, with more advantage. But always take notice, the greatest pleasure of Swiving is secrecy, for thereby we keep a good reputation, and yet enjoy our full swinge of pleasure.

Katy. Your Doctrine is admirable, what doth other Folks faults concern us, let every body live as they please. But let us go on, and finish what we have begun, for methinks there is nothing so pleasing as love, and the Minuts we spend therein are the sweetest and most pleasant of our life. Hay for a good lusty standing Tarse, and a fine little plump hair Cunt, which affords us all these delights. I have but one question more to ask you, who are the most proper for love Concerns, Married Women or Maids?

Frank. Married Women without question, for they are deeper learned, and have had longer experience in it, knowing all the intrigues of that passion perfectly well.

Katy. Why then do some Men love Maids better?

Frank. Because they take pleasure to instruct the ignorant, who are more obedient and tractable unto them, letting them do what they please, besides, their Cunts are not so wide but fit their Pricks better, and consequently tickleth them abundantly more.

Katy. What is the reason then that others differ in this opinion, and choose rather to Fuck with Women?

Frank. Because as I have told you already, they have more art in pleasing, and the hazard is not half so great as with young Wenches.

Katy. What hazard to you mean?

Frank. Of being got with Child, which is a Develish plague to keep it private when the child is born, and besides the Mans Pocket pays soundly for it's maintenance, and the Woman shall have it perpetually hit in her Teeth by her Parents and kinsfolk, who will endeavor many times also to revenge it of the Man, if they have an opportunity; now if a Man deal with a Married Woman, there is none of this clutter, the Husband is the Cloak for all, and the Galllants children sit at his fire side without any expences to him that got them, so that this security make them Fuck without fear, and enjoy one another the more freely.

Katy. So that now I have nothing more to do, but to get me a Husband that I may Swive without fear or wit.

Frank. *No marry ha'nt you, and when you are so provided, as often as your Husband is absent or opportunities presenteth, you may Fuck your Belly full with your Friend, and yet you will love your Husband never the worse, 'tis only cheating him of a little pastime, and it is good to have two strings to ones Bow, and there is no doubt but you will be able to do them both reason, for there are few Men that are able to do a Womans business, & besides change of Fucking as well as dyet is very grateful, for always the same thing cloyeth.*

Katy. Well then Cousin, since I have taken your instructions, and that by your means I have learned all that belongs to the misteries of love, what will you say if I have some prospect of a Sweet-heart, whom I intend to make a Husband of?

Frank. *Do you ask my opinion if you shall marry?*

Katy. Yes indeed, what else?

Frank. *Leave all that to my care, I am old [and] excellent at such a business, and 'tis Ten to one if the party care for thee never so little, but that I compass thy design and bring it about, I have e're now gone through greater difficulties of that nature. Heark, the clock strikes, God be with you, we will speak of this more at large when we meet next.*

Katy. God be with you then dear Cousin till I see you again.

Frank. *And with you too. Adieu, Adieu.*

The end of the second Dialogue.

Quo me fata trahunt Nescio.[27]

FINIS.

2

The Pleasures of a Single Life
(1701),

The Fifteen Comforts of Cuckoldom
(1706),

and

The Fifteen Plagues of a Maiden-Head
(1707)

THE

PLEASURES OF A SINGLE LIFE,

OR,

THE MISERIES OF MATRIMONY.

Occasionally writ upon the many DIVORCES
lately Granted by Parliament.

Wedlock, Oh! Curss'd uncomfortable State,
Cause of my Woes, and Object of my hate.
How blessed was I? Ah, once how happy me?
When I from thy uneasy Bonds was free,
How calm my Joys? How peaceful was my Breast,
Till with thy fatal Cares too soon opprest,
The World seem'd Paradice, so bless'd the Soil
Wherein I liv'd, that Bus'ness was no toil;
Life was a Comfort, which produc'd each day
New Joys, that still preserv'd me from decay.
Thus Heav'n first launch'd me into pacifick Seas,
Where free from Storms I mov'd with gentle breeze;
My Sails proportion'd, and my Vessel tite,
Coasting in Pleasure's Bay I steer'd aright,
Ballac'd with true Content, and fraighted with Delight.
Books my Companions were, wherein I found
Needful Advice, without a noisy Sound,
But was with friendly, pleasing Silence taught,
Wisdom's best Rules, to fructify my Thought,
Rais'd up our Sage Fore-fathers from the dead,
And when I pleas'd, invok'd 'em to my Aid,
Who at my Study-Bar without a Fee would plead:
Whilst I Chief Justice sat, heard all their Sutes,
And gave My Judgment on their learn'd Disputes;
Strove to determine ev'ry Cause aright,
And for my Pains found Profit and Delight.

Free from Partiality, I fear'd no Blame,
Desir'd no Brib'ry, and deserv'd no Shame.
But like an upright Judge, grutch'd no Expence[1]
Of time, to fathom Truth with diligence,
Reading by Day, Contemplating by Night,
Till Conscience told me I judg'd aright.
Then to my Paper World I'd have recourse,
And by my Maps run o'er the Universe;
Sail round the Globe and touch at every Port,
Survey those Shoars where Man untam'd resort,
View the old Regions where the *Persian* Lord
Taught Wooden Deities first to be Ador'd,
Ensnar'd at last to Sacrifice his Life
To the base Pride of an Adult'rous Wife,[2]
And where the *Grecian* Youth to Arms inur'd,
The hungry Soil with *Persian* Blood manur'd,
Where bold *Buceph'lus* brutal Conduct show'd,
The force of monstrous Elephants withstood,
And with his Rider waded through a purple Flood.[3]
        Then would I next the *Roman* Fields survey,
Where brave *Fabricius* with his Army lay;
Fam'd for his Valour, from Corruption free,
Made up of Courage and Humility.
That when Encamp'd the Goodman lowly bent,
Cook'd his own Cabbage in his homely Tent:
And when the *Samaites* sent a Golden Sume,
To tempt him to betray his Country *Rome*,
The Dross he scoffingly return'd untold,
And Answer'd with a Look serenely bold,
That *Roman* Sprouts would boil without their *Grecian* Gold.[4]
Then eat his Cale-worts for his Meal design'd,
and beat the *Grecian* Army when he'd din'd.
        Thus would I range the World from Pole to Pole,
To encrease my Knowledge, and delight my Soul;
Travel all Nations, and inform my Sense,
With ease and safety, at a small Expence:
No Storms to plough, no passage-Sums to pay,
No Horse to hire, or Guide to show the way,
No *Alps* to clime, no Deserts here to pass,
No Ambuscades, no Thieves to give me Chase;
No Bear to dread, or rav'nous Wolf to fight,

No Flies to sting, no Rattle Snaks to bite;
No Floods to ford, no Hurricans to fear;
No dreadful Thunder to surprize the Ear;
No Winds to freez, no Sun to scorch or fry,
No Thirst, or Hunger, and Relief not nigh.
All these Fatigues and Mischiefs could I shun;
Rest when I pleas'd, and when I pleas'd Jog on,
And Travel thro' both *Indies* in an Afternoon.
      When the Day thus far pleasingly was spent,
And every Hour administer'd Content,
Then would I range the Fields, and flowry Meads,
Where Nature her exub'rant Bounty spreads,
In whose delightful Products does appear,
Inimitable Beauty ev'ry where;
Contemplate on each Plant, and useful Weed,
And how its form first lay involv'd in Seed,
How they're preserv'd by Providential Care
For what design'd, and what their Vertues are.
Thus to my Mind by dint of Reason prove,
That all below is Ow'd to Heaven above,
And that no Earthly Temporals can be,
But what must Center in Eternitie.
Then gaiz aloft whence all things had their Birth
And play my prying Souls 'twixt Heaven and Earth,
Thus the sweet Harmony o'th' whole admire,
And by due search new Learning still acquire,
So nearer ev'ry day to Truths divine aspire.
      When tir'd with Thought, then from my Pocket pluck
Some friendly dear Companion of a Book,
Whose homely Calves-Skin fences shall contain
The Verbal Treasure of some Old Good Man:
Made by long study and Experience wise,
Whose piercing Thoughts to Heav'nly knowledge rise,
Amongst whose Pious Reliques I could find
Rules for my Life, Rich Banquets for my mind,
Such pleasing Nectar, such Eternal food,
That well digested makes a Man a God,
And for his use at the same time prepares
On Earth a Heav'n in spite of worldly Cares.
The day in these Enjoyments would I spend,
But chuse at Night my Bottle and my Friend,

Took prudent Care that neither were abus'd,
But with due moderation both I us'd.
And in one sober Pint found more delight,
Then the insatiate Sot that swills all Night;
Ne'er drown my Senses, or my Soul debase,
Or drink beyond the relish of my Glass,
For in Excess good Heav'ns design is Crost,
In all extreams the true enjoyment's lost:
Wine chears the Heart, and elevates the Soul,
But if we surfeit with too large a Bowl,
Wanting true Aim we th' happy Mark o'er shoot,
And change the heav'nly Image to a Brute.
So the great *Grecian* who the World subdu'd,
And drown'd the whole Nations in a Sea of Blood;
At last was Conquer'd by the Power of Wine,
And dy'd a Drunken Victim to the Vine.[5]
My Friend, and I, when o'er our Bottle sat,
Mix'd with each Glass some inoffensive Chat,
Talk'd of the World's Affairs, but still kept free
From Passion, Zeal, or Partialitie;
With honest freedom did our thoughts dispense,
And judg'd of all things with indifference;
Till time at last did our delights invade,
And in due season Seperation made,
Then without Envy, Discord or Deceit,
Part like true Friends as Loving as we meet,
The Tavern change to a Domestick Scene,
That sweet Retirement, tho' it's ne'er so mean.
Thus leave each other in a chearful Plight,
T' enjoy the silent Pleasures of the Night,
When home return'd, my thanks to Heaven pay,
For all the past kind Blessing of the Day;
No haughty Helpmate to my Peace molest,
No treacherous Snake to harbour in my Breast;
No Fawning Mistress of the Female Art,
With *Judas* Kisses to betray my heart;
No light-tail'd Hyppocrite to raise my Fears;
No vile Impert'nence to torment my Ears;
No molted Off-spring to disturb my Thought,
In Wedlock born but G-d knows where begot;
No lustful *Massalina* to require

Whole Troops of Men to feed her Brutal Fire;[6]
No Family Cares my quiet to disturb;
No head-strong Humours to asswage, or Curb;
No Jaring Servants, no Domestick Strife,
No Jilt, no Termagent, no faithless Wife,
With Vinegar, or Gall, to sour or bitter Life.
      Thus freed from all that cou'd my mind annoy,
Alone my self, I did my self enjoy:
When Nature call'd, I laid me down to rest,
With a Sound Body, and a Peaceful Breast;
Hours of repose with constancy I kept,
And Guardian Angels watch'd me as I slept,
In lively Dreams reviving as I lay,
The Pleasures of the last precedent day:
Thus whilst I single liv'd, did I possess,
By day and night incessant happiness,
Content enjoy'd awak'd, and Sleeping found no less.
      But the curs'd Fiend from Hell's dire Regions sent,
Ranging the World to Man's destruction bent,
Who with an Envious Pride beholding me,
Advanc'd by Vertue to felicitie,
Resolv'd his own Eternal wretched State
Should be in part reveng'd by my sad Fate;
And to at once my happy Life betray,
Flung Woman, faithless Woman, in my Way:
Beauty she had, a seeming modest Mein,[7]
All Charms without, but Devil all within,
Which did not yet appear, but lurk'd, alas, unseen.
A fair Complexion far exceeding Paint,
Black sleeping Eyes that would have Charm'd a Saint;
Her Lips so soft and sweet, that ev'ry kiss,
Seem'd a short Tast of the Eternal Bliss;
Her set of Teeth so Regular and white,
They'd show their Lustre in the darkest night;
Round her Seraphick Face so fair and young,
Her Sable Hair in careless Tresses hung,
Which added to her Beauteous features, show'd,
Like some fair Angel peeping through a Cloud.
Her Breasts, her Hands, and every Charm so bright,
She seem'd a Sun by Day, a Moon by Night;
Her Shape so ravishing, that ev'ry part,

Proportion'd was to th'nicest Rules of Art;
So awful was her Carriage when she mov'd,
None could behold her but he fear'd and lov'd,
She Danc'd, well Sung, well finely play'd the Lute,
Was always Witty in her Words, or Mute;
Obliging not reserv'd, nor yet too free,
But as a Maid divinely bless'd should be;
Not vainly gay, but decent in Attire,
She seem'd so Good, she could no more acquire
Of Heaven, no more then what she had, and Man no more
    desire:
Fortune, like God and Nature too, was kind,
And to these Gifts a copious Sum had joyn'd.
Who could the Power of such Temptations shun,
What frozen *Linick* from her Charms could run;[8]
What Cloister'd Monk could see a Face so bright,
But quit his Beads, and follow Beauty's light,
And by its Lustre hope to shun Eternal Night.
I so bewitch'd, and poyson'd with her Charms,
Believ'd the utmost Heaven in her Arms,
Methoughts the goodness in her Eyes I see,
It Spoke her the Off spring of some Deitie.
Now Books or Walks would no content afford,
She was the only Good to be ador'd,
In her fair Looks alone delight I found,
Loves raging Storms all other Joys had drown'd.
By Beauty's *Ignis Fatuus* led astray,[9]
Bound for content I lost my happy way
Of Reason's faithful Pilot now bereft,
Was amongst Rocks and Sholes in danger left,
There must have perish'd, as I fondly thought,
Lest her kind Usage my Salvation wrought;
Her happy aid I labour'd to obtain,
Hop'd for success, yet fear'd her sad disdain,
Tortur'd like dying Convicts whilst they live
'Twixt fear of Death, and hopes of a Reprieve.
First for her smallest Favours did I sue,
Crept, Fawn'd and Cring'd as Lovers us'd to do.
Sigh'd e'er I spoke, and when I Spoke, look'd pale,
In words confus'd disclos'd my mournful Tale.
Unpractised in Amour's fine Speeches coin'd,

But could not utter what I well design'd.
And by her Charms 'gainst bashfulness I Strove,
And trembling sat, and stammer'd out my Love;
Told her how greatly I admir'd and fear'd,
Which she 'twixt Coyness and compassion heard,
Grutch'd no expence of Money, or of Time,
And thought that not t'adore her was a Crime;
The more each Visit I acquainted grew,
Yet every time found something in her new,
Who was above her Sex so fortunate
She had a Charm for Man in every state;
Beauty for th' Youthful, Prudence for the Old,
Scripture for the Godly, for the Miser Gold;
Wit for th' Ingenious, silence for the Grave,
Flatt'ry for the Fool, and Cunning for the Knave:
Compounded thus of such Varieties,
She had a Knack to every Temper please,
And as her self thought fit was every one of these.
I lov'd, I sigh'd and vow'd, talk'd, whin'd and pray'd,
And at her Feet my panting heart I lay'd;
She smil'd, then frown'd, was now reserv'd, then free,
And as she played her part oft changed her Key;
Not thro' fantastick Humour but design,
To try me throughly e'er she would be mine,
Because she wanted in one Man to have,
A Husband, Lover, Cuckold and a Slave.
So Travellers before a Horse they buy,
His Speed, his Paces, and his Temper try,
Whether he'll answer Whip and Spur, thence Judge,
If the poor Beast will prove a patient Drudge,
When she by Wiles had heightened my desire,
And fann'd Loves sparkles to a raging Fire;
Made now for Wedlock, or for *Bedlam* fit,[10]
Passion hav'n got the upper-hand of Wit,
The Dame by pitty, or by Interest mov'd,
Or else by Lust, pretended how she lov'd;
After longer sufferings, her Consent I got,
To make me happy, as I hop'd and thought,
But oh, the Wretched hour I ty'd the *Gordian* Knot.[11]
      Thus thro' mistake I rashly plung'd my life,
Into that Bag of Miseries a Wife.

With joyful Arms I thus embrac'd my fate,
Believ'd too soon, was undeceiv'd too late;
So hair-brain'd fools to *Indian* Climates rove,
With a vain hope their Fortunes to improve;
There spend their slender Cargoes, then become
Worse Slaves abroad than e'er they were at home.
When a few Weeks were wasted I compar'd,
With all due moderation and regard,
My former freedom, with my new restraint,
Judging which State afforded most content,
But found a Single Life as calm and gay,
As the delightful Month of Blooming *May*,
Not chill'd with cold, nor Scorch'd with too much heat,
Not Plung'd with too much dust, nor drown'd with Wet,
But pleasing to the Eyes, and to the Nostrils sweet.
　　　　But Wedlock's like the Blustring Month of *March*,
That does the Body's Maims and Bruises search,
Brings by Cold niping Storms unwelcome pains,
And finds, or Breeds, Distempers in our Veins;
Renew old Sores, and hastens on decay,
And seldom does afford one pleasing day,
But Clouds dissolve or raging Tempest blow,
And untile Houses like a marry'd Shrow;[12]
Thus *March* and *Marriage* justly may be said,
To be alike, then sure the Man is mad,
That loves such Changling Weather where the best is bad.
　　　　Tho' I once happy in a single Life,
Yet Shipwrack'd all upon that Rock a Wife,
By Gold and Beauties Pow'rful Charms betray'd,
To the dull drudgery of a Marriage-Bed;
That Paradice for Fools, a Sport for Boys,
Tiresome its Chains, and brutal are its Joys,
Then Nauseous Priest craft that too soon appear'd,
Not as I hop'd but worse than what I fear'd,
All her soft Charms which I believ'd devine,
Marriage I thought had made them only mine;
Vain hope, alas, for I too early found,
My Brows were with the Thorns of *Wedlock* crown'd.
Jealousies first from Reason rais'd a doubt,
And fatal Chance th'unhappy Truth brought out;
Made it so plain from all Pretences free'd,

That wicked Woman no Excuse could plead;
And if she wants device to hide her shame,
Hell can no Umbrage for Adult'ry frame.
      I thought it prudence the Disgrace to hide,
Tho' rav'd and Storm'd, she Pardon beg'd and Cry'd,
Yet with false Protestations strove to Charm,
The Cuckold to believe she'd done no harm,
Tho' taken by surprize (O curse the day)
Where all the Marks of past Enjoyments lay,
And she disorder'd by her lustful freeks,[13]
Had shame and horrour Struggling in her Cheeks:
Yet made Essays to clear her Innocence,
And hide her Guilt with Lyes and Impudence;
For lustful Women like a vicious State,
Oft stifle Ills by others full as great,
But I convinc'd too plainly of her Guilt,
All her false Oaths and quick Inventions spoilt,
Which when she'd used in vain she blush'd and Cry'd,
And own'd her fault she found she could not hide.
      This I forgave, she promis'd to reclaim,
Vow'd future truth if I'd conceal the shame;
But what Strange Adamantine Chain can bind,
Woman Corrupted to be just or kind:
Or how can Man to an Adultress shew
That Love, which to a faithful Wife is due.
I struggled hard, and all my Passions checkt,
And chang'd Revenge into a Mild Respect,
That Good for Ill return'd might touch her near,
And Gratitude might bind her more than fear;
My former Love I ev'ry day renew'd,
And all the Signals of Oblivion shew'd:
Wink'd at small faults, would no such Trifles mind,
As accidental Failings not designed.
I all things to her Temper easie made,
Scorn'd to reflect, and hated to upbraid;
She chose (and rich it was) her own Attire,
Nay, had what a proud Woman could desire.
      Thus the new Covenant I strictly kept,
And oft in private for her Failings Wept,
Yet both with seeming Cheerfulness these Cares,
That bring a Man too soon to drisled hairs.[14]

But all the kindness I dispens'd in vain,
Where Lust and base Ingratitude remain.
Lust, which if once in Female fancy fix'd,
Burns like Salt-petre with dry Touchwood mix'd:
And tho' cold fear for time may stop its force,
'Twill soon like Fire confin'd, break out the worse,
Or like a Tide obstructed, reassume its course.
    No Art could e'er perfume the stinking *Stote*,[15]
Or change the lecherous Nature of the *Goate*.
No skillful Whistler ever found the flight,
To wash or bleach an *Ethiopian* white.
No gentle Usage truly will Asswage
A Tyger's fierceness, or a Lyon's rage,
Stripes and severe Correction is the way,
Whence once they're thro'ly Conquer'd, they'll obey.
This Whip and Spur, Commanding Rein and Bit,
That makes the unruly head-strong Horse submit,
So stubborn faithless Woman must be us'd,
Or Man by Woman basely be abus'd.
    For after all the endearments I could show,
As last she turned both Libertine and Shrow,
From my Submission grew perverse and proud,
Crabbed as Varges, and as Thunder loud;[16]
Did what she pleas'd, would no Obedience own,
And redicul'd the patience I had shown.
Fear'd no sharp threatnings, valued no disgrace,
But flung the Wrongs she'd done me in my face;
Grew still more head-strong, turbulent and Lewd,
Filling my Mansion with a spurious Brood.
Thus Brutal Lust her humane Reason drown'd,
And her loose Tail oblig'd the Country round;
Advice, Reprooff, Pray'rs, Tears, were flung away,
For still she grew more wicked ev'ry day;
Till by her equals scorn'd, my Servants fed
The Brutal Rage of her adultrous Bed.
Nay, in my absence truckled to my Groom,[17]
And hug'd the servile Traytor in my Room;
When these strange Tydings Thunder-struck my Ear,
And such Inhumane Wrongs were made appear,
On these just Grounds for a Divorce I sued,
At last that head-strong Tyrant Wife subdued,

Cancel'd the marriage-bonds, & Bastardiz'd her Brood.
   Woman, thou worst of all Church-Plagues, farewel;
Bad at the Best, but at the worst a Hell;
Thou truss of Worm wood, bitter Teaz of Life,
Thou Nursery of humane cares a *Wife*.
Thou Apple-Eating Traytor, who began
The Wrath of Heav'n, and miseries of Man;
And ha'st with never-failing diligence,
Improv'd the Curse to humane Race e'er since.
Farewell Church-Juggle that enslav'd my Life,[18]
But bless that Pow'r that rid me of my Wife.
And now the Laws once more have set me free,
If Woman can again prevail with me,
My Flesh and Bones shall make my Wedding-Feast,
And none shall be Invited as my Guest,
But my good *Bride*, the *Devil*, and a *Priest*.

FINIS.

The

Fifteen Comforts

of

Cuckoldom.

Written by a noted Cuckold in
the New-Exchange *in the* Strand.

To the Reader.

The Town being diverted of late with a great many Comforts, several of the Gentlemen and others of the cornuted Society belonging to Horn-Fair *not thinking those Comforts compleat without those of Cuckoldom, they requested me to undertake the Performance thereof, as having had some experience for many Years in Wives cokesing their Husbands in the very Moment they designed to put a pair of Antlers on their Heads for fear of being gor'd by their Neighbours;[1] whilst other good Wives are as often Picking their Husbands Pockets to pay now and then for a By-Blow: I have experienced those kind Wives too who are commonly upon the religious Point of going to Lectures, when alas they had no other Business at Church than to meet their Gallants, who presently coaches 'em, because they den'y love Jolting. But for Brevity passing the several Dispositions of Men's Wives, as such as are Melancholly many Times for Delay or Defeat, whilst others are preparing to make the Markets at the Play-house or Spring-Garden; or else to the Bath, when Bathing is the least part of their Errand, I shall draw too the Comforts which we enjoy by our Wives good Nature to others, which to their Fancies is as sweet as Muskadine[2] and Eggs.*

The First Comfort of Cuckoldom.

As I last Night in Bed lay Snoring,
I sweetly dreamt of Drinking and of Whoring,
Which waking me from a most pleasant Sleep,
To my dear Wife I very close did creep,
And offering to give her what I shou'd,

Quoth she, you Fumbler you can do no good,
Give me the Man that never claps his Wings,
But always Life and Courage with him brings,
'Tis such a one wou'd please; but as for you
If Night and Morning some small matter do;
You think you've done your due Benevolence,
When I with thrice your Labour can dispence.
This Reprimand my Courage soon did cool,
And fearing Combing with a Three-Legg'd-Stool;
I very fairly went to Sleep again,
And left her of my Manhood to complain.

The Second Comfort of Cuckoldom.
No sooner had I chang'd my single Life,
And had confin'd my Carcass to a Wife;
But she was always Gadding up and down,
To take the various Pleasures of the Town;
How e're I only reckon'd this to be,
The airy Frisks of her Minority,
Till shortly finding an Old Hag wou'd pay
Her Visits oft, and take her Day by Day
Abroad, indeed this gave me some Mistrust,
That this old weather beaten Devil must
Be some Procurer, and resolv'd to watch
Their Waters, where shou'd I the Bitches catch,
But in a Bowdy-house in *Milford-lane?*
So going in a Passion home again,
At twelve at Night my Doxie likewise came,[3]
Whom I in mod'rate Terms began to blame;
Telling her that old Witch with whom she went,
Abroad a Days by Rogues was only sent
About to Wheedle young and tender Maids
To Ruine, till they turned common Jades.
You Lie, (reply'd my hopeful graceless Dear)
I'll have you know, I'll never sin in fear,
Besides for she of whom you think Amiss,
That sweet obliging Gentlewoman is
A tender-hearted Bawd that ne'er made Whore,
But ever us'd such as were broke before.
Now finding her so bad at Seventeen,

73

Thinks I by that time she has Thirty seen,
She'll be a Whore in Grain; but by good hap,[4]
She dy'd within a Year of Pox and Clap.

The Third Comfort of Cuckoldom.

It was my Fortune to be joyn'd to one,
As pretty as was shin'd on by the Sun;
For on my Word her Eyes were full and gray,
With ruddy Lips, round Cheeks, her Forehead lay
Archt like a snowie Bank, which did uphold
Her native Tresses, that did shine like Gold;
Her azure Veins, which with a well shap'd Nose,
Her whiter Neck, broad Shoulders to compose:
A slender Waste, a Body strait and Tall,
With Swan-like Breasts, long Hands, and Fingers small,
Her Ivory Knees, her Legs were neat and clean,
A swelling Calf, with Ancles round and lean,
Her Insteps thin, short Heels, with even Toes,
A Sole most strait, proportion'd Feet, she goes
With modest Grace; but yet her Company,
Did not a Month enjoy, before that I
Was Prest for Sea, and being on the Main,[5]
For thirty Months I then return'd again,
Where finding in my absence that my Wife
Three Brats had got, a most uneasie Life;
Both Day and Night I led the lech'rous Whore;
Who seeing how I Curst, and Bann'd, and Swore,[6]
A Bag or two she shew'd me cramn'd with Gold,
Which Treasure I no sooner did behold,
But then I Kist my loving Wife and leapt,
For very Gladness that my Horns were Tipt.

The Fourth Comfort of Cuckoldom.

Above a Year or two I always thought
My Wife so good that she cou'd not be naught,
Till one Night coming home I caught a Spark
Sat in my Parlor by her in the Dark,
In mighty Pet I call'd for Candles strait,[7]
Doubting that I poor Fool was come too late:
T'avert the Burthen which is made to grow

On such who enters into Cuckold-Row.
How er'e as I was thinking of the best,
And as I nothing saw content'd rest,
My am'rous Wife's Gallant, before he went,
Did shew enough t' encrease my Discontent
For he wou'd slily pull her Petticoat,
Nod, Wink, and put into her Hand a Note,
Whisper her in the Ear, or touch her Foot
With many other private Signs to boot,
All which confirm'd my Jealousie the more,
And made me think 'em to be Rogue and Whore,
But as I knew my Wife a bawling Slut,
My Horns into my Pocket did I put
For Quietness, which yet I seldom had,
So I thro' Cuckoldom run really Mad.

The Fifth Comfort of Cuckoldom.
When I poor I unto a Wife was bound,
I wish I had been Bury'd under Ground,
For to my Grief I found her both before
And after Marriage too to be a Whore.
But when I found the Beast of such a Breed,
Soldier turn'd, and with a Baw'd agreed
To let her out at half a Crown a Week
Who undertook she shou'd not be too seek;
For Custom, but said, she must for her pains,
From th' insatiate Whore have double gains.

The Sixth Comfort of Cuckoldom.
Finding my Wife by Whoring nothing get,
But to maintain her Sparks ran me in Debt;
Her Whoring gratis made me really vext,
So Shop I shut, and fled to *Holland* next.

The Seventh Comfort of Cuckoldom.
While I was but into the Country gone,
To give some Chapmen there the gentle Dun,[8]
Mean time a Rubber she with some had play'd[9]
And in the Powd'ring Tub was quickly laid,
Unknown to me, and had been secret still,

But that the Surgeon bringing in his Bill
When I came Home, the Murder so came out,
And still my Wife is Whore enough [no] doubt.

The Eighth Comfort of Cuckoldom.
A sordid Lech coming very old
To tempt my Spouse with Silver and with Gold,
She told me of't, and said, she cou'd not fawn,
On him, or's Gold, to lay her Soul in pawn.
By this I thought her Honest, till my maid
Inform'd me shortly what Lewd Tricks she play'd.
I Twitted then my Wife's Hypocrisie,
Who Imprudently did Reply to me;
Old Flesh she Loath'd, as having in it left
No Gravy, and of all it's Juice bereft,
But if the Flesh was Young and to her mind,
She to one Dish would never be confin'd.

The Ninth Comfort of Cuckoldom.
By my Dear Wife, in turning up her Tail
To bear the Threshing of her Gallant's Frail,[10]
A Groat (which always is a Cuckold's Fee)
Under the Candlestick I've laid for me;
Besides good Peck and Booze, so till she's Dead,[11]
She may and will Whore on to get me Bread.

The Tenth Comfort of Cuckoldom.
As Strangers flatter'd with deceitful Snow,
Fall in a Deadly Pit they do not know,
So was I hamper'd in a Marriage Noose,
In Marrying one that did frequent the Stews,[12]
As well as Cuckold me at Home; but she
Transacting Whoredom with great Secresie,
Like other Neighbours, to avoid the Name
Of Cuckold, I as private hid her shame.

The Eleventh Comfort of Cuckoldom.
When I found Cuckolds to Encrease apace,
I Marry'd one with such and Ugly Face
That one wou'd thought the Devil wou'd but grutch
So foul a Figure as my Wife to touch;

Yet being at a Friendly Club one Night,
A Raskal came and Cuckol'd me for spight.

The Twelfth Comfort of Cuckoldom.

What signifies a Man to fret and fume,
Till Grief and Sorrow makes his Flesh consume
Because his Wife in Actions may be light
And to his Face will horn him Day and Night;
This Comfort may alleviate his Woe,
That Cuckold's without doubt to Heaven go.

The Thirteenth Comfort of Cuckoldom.

If it's my Fate (I oftentimes would cry)
To have a Wife that will play wantonly,
I soon wou'd tame her, or at least I shou'd
Be Hang'd for her but I wou'd make her good.
But faith it is my Luck to light upon
Such Ware, that will a *Caterwoulling* run,
And cannot help it, for to have her full
Of Sport, she run away a Soldiers Trull.[13]

The Fourteenth Comfort of Cuckoldom.

When at *Horn-Fair* I see how ev'ry Year
Whole droves of Cuckold's thither do appear
The very sight thereof wou'd make one swear
That none but Cuckolds in the Nation were;
Especially if those who are not known
For Cuckolds too the Title wou'd but own,
And such as are not summon'd would appear,
In those Accoutrements we ought to wear,
Which are our Horns, a Pick-Axe and a Spade,
That Paths may for our Wives be even laid.

The Fifteenth Comfort of Cuckoldom.

If that our wives will tick their Souls on Sin,[14]
'Tis vain to make about their Ears a din,
For that exasperates their will the more,
And where in private may in publick whore;
So then the Scandal coming to all Ears,
Each Neighbour will not only fling his Jeers
Upon us, but the Boys will hoot us too,

And point their Fingers at us where we go,
As if we were not come of human Blood,
Because they do perceive we've Horns to bud;
But to avoid so base and curst a Life,
The only way's to Live without a Wife.

FINIS.

The

Fifteen PLAGUES

of a

MAIDEN-HEAD.

The First Plague.
The Woman Marry'd is Divinely Blest,
But I a Virgin cannot take my Rest;
I'm discontented up, as bad a Bed,
Because I'm plagued with my Maiden-head;
A thing that do's my blooming Years no good,
But only serves to freeze my youthful Blood,
Which slowly Circulates, do what I can,
For want of Bleeding by some skilful Man;
Whose tender hand his *Launcet* so will guide,[1]
That I the Name of *Maid* may lay aside.

The Second Plague.
When I've beheld an am'rous Youth make Love,
And swearing Truth by all the Gods above,
How has it strait inflam'd my sprightly Blood?
Creating Flames, I scarcely should withstood,
But bid him boldly march, not grant me leisure
Of Parley, for 'tis Speed augments the Pleasure.
But ah! tis my Misfortune not to meet
With any Man that would my Passion greet,
Till he with balmy Kisses stop'd my Breath,
Than which one cannot die a better Death.
O! stroke my Breasts, those Mountains of Delight,
Your very Touch would fire an Anchorite;[2]
Next let your wanton Palm a little stray,
And dip thy Fingers in the milky way:
Then having raiz'd me, let me gently fall,
Love's Trumpets sound, so Mortal have at all.
But why wish I this Bliss? I wish in vain,
And of my plaguy Burthen do complain;
For sooner may I see whole Nations dead,
E'er I find one to get my Maiden-head.

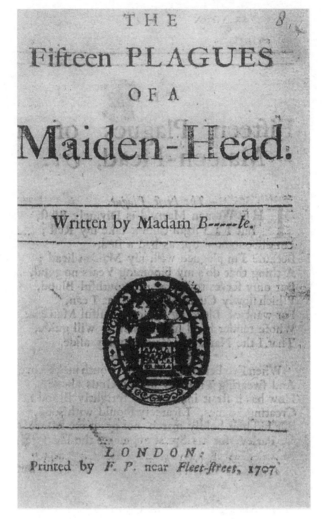

Figure 2.1 The title page of *The Fifteen Plagues of a Maiden-Head*.

The Third Plague.
She that her Maiden-head does keep, runs through
More Plagues than all the Land of *Egypt* knew;
A teazing Whore, or a more tedious Wife,
Plagues not a Marry'd Man's unhappy Life,
So much as it do's me to be a Maid,
Of which same Name I am so much afraid,

Because I've often heard some People tell,
They that die Maids, must all lead Apes in Hell;
If so, 'twere better I had never been,
Than thus to be perplex'd: *God save the Queen.*

The Fourth Plague.
When trembling Pris'ners all stand round the Bar,
In strange suspence about the fatal Verdict,
And when the Jury crys they Guilty are;
How they astonish'd are when they have heard it.
When in mighty Storm a Ship is toss'd,
And all do ask, What do's the Captain say?
How they (poor Souls) bemoan themselves as lost,
When his Advice at last is only, Pray!
So as it was one Day my pleasing Chance,
To meet a handsome young Man in a Grove,
Both time and place conspir'd to advance
The innocent Designs of charming Love.
I thought my Happiness was then compleat,
Because 'twas in his Pow'r to make it so;
I ask'd the Spark if he would do the Feat,
But the unperforming Blockhead answer'd, *No.*
Poor Pris'ners may, I see, have Mercy shewn,
And Shipwreck'd Men may sometimes have the Luck
To see their dismal Tempests overblown,
But I poor Virgin never shall be F——.

The Fifth Plague.
All Day poor I do sit Disconsolate,
Cursing the grievous Rigor of my Fate,
To think how I have seven Years betray'd,
To that dull empty Title of a Maid.
If that I could my self but Woman write,
With what transcendent Pleasure and Delight,
Should I for ever, thrice for ever Bless,
The Man that led me to such Happiness.

The Sixth Plague.
Pox take the thing Folks call a Maiden-head,
For soon as e'er I'm sleeping in my Bed,
I dream I'm mingling with some Man my Thighs,

Till something more than ord'nary does rise;
But when I wake and find my Dream's in vain,
I turn to Sleep only to Dream again,
For Dreams as yet are only kind to me,
And at the present quench my Lechery.

The Seventh Plague.
Of late I wonder what's with me the Matter,
For I look like Death, and am as weak as Water,
For several Days I loath the sight of Meat,
And every Night I chew the upper Sheet;
I've such Obstructions, that I'm almost moap'd,[3]
And breath as if my Vitals all were stop'd.
I told a Friend how strange with me it was,
She, an experienc'd Bawd, soon grop'd the Cause,
Saying, *for this Disease, take what you can,*
You'll ne'er be well, till you have taken Man.
Therefore, before with Maiden heads I'll be
Thus plagu'd, and live in daily Misery,
Some Spark shall rummage all my Wem about,[4]
To find this wonderful Distemper out.

The Eighth Plague.
Now I am young, blind *Cupid* me bewitches,
I scratch my Belly, for it always itches,
And what it itches for, I've told before,
'Tis either to be Wife, or be a Whore;
Nay any thing indeed, would be poor I,
E'er Maiden-heads upon my Hands should lie,
Which till I lose, I'm sure my watry Eyes
Will pay to Love so great a Sacrifice,
That my Carcass soon will weep out all its Juice,
Till grown so dry, as fit for no Man's use.

The Ninth Plague.
By all the pleasant Postures of Delight,
By all the Twines and Circles of the Night,[5]
By the first Minute of those Nuptial Joys,
When Men put fairly for a Brace of Boys,
Dying a Virgin once I more do dread,
Than ten times losing of a *Maiden-head*;

For tho' it can't be seen, nor understood,
Yet is it troublesome to Flesh and Blood.

The Tenth Plague.
You heedless Maids, whose young and tender Hearts
Unwounded yet, have scop'd the fatal Darts;
Let the sad Fate of a poor Virgin move,
And learn by me to pay Respect to Love.
If one can find a Man fit for Love's Game,
To lose one's Maiden-head it is no Shame:
'Tis no Offence, if from his tender Lip
I snatch a tonguing Kiss; if my fond Clip[6]
With loose Embraces oft his Neck surround,
For Love in Debts of Nature's ever bound.

The Eleventh Plague.
A *Maiden-head!* Pish, in it's no Delight,
Nor have I Ease, but when returning Night,
With Sleep's soft gentle Spell my Senses charm,
Then Fancy some Gallant brings to my Arms:
In them I oft the lov'd Shadow seem
To grasp, and Joys, yet blush I too in Dream.
I wake, and long my Heart in Wonder lies,
To think on my late pleasing Extasies:
But when I'm waking, and don't yet possess,
In Sleep again I wish to enjoy the Bliss:
For Sleep do's no malicious Spies admit,
Yet yields a lively Semblance of Delight.
Gods! what a Scene of Joy was that! how fast
I clasp'd the Vision to my panting Breast?
With what fierce Bounds I sprung to meet the Bliss,
While my wrapt Soul flew out in ev'ry Kiss!
Till breathless, faint, and softly sunk away,
I all dissolv'd in reaking Pleasures lay.

The Twelfth Plague.
Happen what will, I'll make some Lovers know
What Pains, what raging Pains I undergo,
Till I am really Heart-sick, almost Dead,
By keeping that damn'd thing a Maiden-head.
Which makes me with Green-sickness almost lost,[7]

So pale, so wan, and looking like a Ghost,
Eating Chalk, Cindars, or Tobacco-Pipes,
Which with a Looseness scowers all my Tripes;[8]
But e'er I'll longer this great Pain endure,
The Stews I'll search, but that I'll find a Cure.[9]

The Thirteenth Plague.
Let doating Age debate of *Law* and *Right*,
And gravely state the Bounds of Just and Fit;
Whose Wisdom's but their Envy, to destroy
And bar those Pleasures which they can't enjoy.
My blooming Years, more sprightly and more gay,
By Nature were design'd for Love and Play:
Youth knows no Check, but leaps weak Virtue's Fence,
And briskly hunts the noble Chace of Sense!
Without dull thinking I'll Enjoyment trace,
And call that lawful whatsoe'er do's please.
Nor will my Crime want Instances alone,
'Tis what the Glorious Gods above have done:
For *Saturn*, and his greater Off-spring *Jove*,
Both stock'd their Heaven with Incestuous Love.

The Fourteenth Plague.
If any Man do's with my Bubbies play,
Squeeze my small Hand, as soft as Wax or Clay,
Or lays his Hands upon my tender Knees,
What strange tumultuous Joys upon me seize!
My Breasts do heave, and languish do my Eyes,
Panting's my Heart, and trembling are my Thighs;
I sigh, I wish, I pray, and seem to die,
In one continu'd Fit of Ecstasy;
Thus by my Looks may Man know what I mean,
And how he easily may get between
Those Quarters, where he may surprize a Fort,
In which an Emperor may find such Sport,
That with a mighty Gust of Love's Alarms,
He'd lie dissolving in my circling Arms;
But 'tis my Fate to have to do with Fools,
Who're very loth and shy to use their Tools,
To ease a poor, and fond distressed Maid,
Of that same Load, of which I'm not afraid

To lose with any Man, tho' I should die,
For any Tooth (good Barber) is my Cry.

The Fifteenth Plague.
Alas! I care not, Sir, what Force you'd use,
So I my Maiden-head could quickly lose:
Oft do I wish one skill'd in *Cupid's* Arts,
Would quickly dive into my secret Parts;
For as I am, at Home [in] all sorts of Weather,
I kit, ———as Heaven and Earth would come together,[10]
Twirling a Wheel, I sit at home, hum drum,
And spit away my Nature on my Thumb;
Whilst those that Marry'd are, invited be
To Labours, Christnings, where the Jollitry
Of Women lies in telling, as some say,
When 'twas they did at Hoity-Toity play;
Whose Husband's Yard is longest, whilst another
Can't in the least her great Misfortune smother,
So tells, her Husband's Bauble is so short,[11]
That when he Hunts, he never shews her Sport.
Now I, because I have my Maiden-head,
Mayn't know the Pastimes of the Nuptial Bed;
But mayn't I quickly do as Marry'd People may,
I'll either kill my self, or shortly run away.

FINIS.

3

Gonosologium Novum

(1709)

Gonosologium Novum:

or, a

NEW SYSTEM

Of all the Secret Infirmities and Diseases,

Natural, Accidental, and Venereal in

MEN AND WOMEN,

That Defile and Ruin the Healths of themselves and
their Posterity, obstruct Conjugal Delectancy and
Pregnancy, with their various Methods of Cure.

THE
PREFACE

Sixteen Years ago, or more, I had wrote something upon the Heads of the en-suing Treatise, which I then had thoughts of Printing; but by one means or other of Business, I was put by, so that it lay dormant among my Papers, almost quite for-gotten, till upon Printing the last (viz. Sixth) Edition of my Book of the Venereal Disease, lately Publish'd, it came occasionally into my Mind, and which upon a fresh perusal, I resolved to Print with that; but the Fifth Edition of that Book sell-ing off faster than expected, and the Sixth in hast call'd for, I had not time to model it, and digest it into that Order and Method as the many observations I have made since in my Practice, did require, and therefore left it out, with an intention how-ever to Print it by way of Appendix to that Edition the first opportunity I had, with such necessary Alterations and Additions as should recommend it, beyond its being thought any Imposition upon the Buyers of that Book. Accordingly, it is now done, and Printed with the same Letter, on the same Paper, for the better conveniency of those that please to bind it up with that; and tho' it contains full twelve Sheets, which by rate makes a half Crown Book or more, it is charg'd but at eighteen Pence, which is the same or less than it would have swell'd the other Book to, had it been Printed with it, so that both for Matter and Price, 'tis presum'd 'twill not be found unacceptable.

The motive of my Printing a Treatise of this Nature, was from the numbers of People coming daily to me with the Complaints of Secret Infirmities *and* Diseases *of divers kinds,*[1] *many of which neither they, nor the Physicians or Surgeons they had consulted, could account for; and their Cases most commonly resisting the usual Methods in Practice, and their meeting afterwards with my Book, gave them other sort of Thoughts concerning themselves, which upon enquiring into, comparing, and coming to me about, I can safely declare, I found, that not one in ten of the* Secret Maladies *complain'd of, but had its rise Originally from the* Venereal Taint, *and I was daily more and more convinc'd of the Truth thereof, because no Methods whatever would effect a Cure, but the powerfully* Antivenereal; *I mean as to those Maladies that were* Venereal, natural Infirmities and Diseases were *otherways to be accounted for. I say, the many Indispositions both Men and Women, labour'd under, from unknown (as to Original, and Unthought of, as well as Perplexing and Troublesome) Causes, and the thousands in this Nation that do still labour under the like Inconveniences to their grief, put me upon the Thought of writing this Appendix, that such as know not (having already fruitlessly try'd, that is the Womankind, all the old Midwives, Nurses and good Women in the Town; and even many of them Physicians and Surgeons also) may be directed where to have Cure for their imagin'd uncurable Distempers, which some through Modesty or Bashfulness, or believing there can be no Cure, are quite discourag'd from seeking after.*

How many married Men and Women have complain'd to me of Seminal *and other* Weaknesses, Gleets, &c. *to their depriving them of having Children?*[2] *How many totally defective or incapable of performing the Conjugal Duty, being wholly abridg'd of that pleasing Sensation, and that from* Venereal *as well as Natural and Accidental occasions, is almost incredible to consider? and which many times upon a very little necessary Direction and Medicine have been restor'd, tho' of divers Years standing, and to their apprehensions for ever irrecoverable; and doubtless there are many more, which by labouring under (as they think irrepairably) the same Inconveniencies, live unhappy Lives, Women that can have no Children thinking it their Faults, when the defect is on the Man's side, and Men knowing themselves defective, charge it on the Woman's, and Women with known Infirmities charge it on their Husbands, to the occasioning Discontents, Animosities and worse Breaches, which by a little prudent management and proper administrations, may probably be remedied to the satisfaction of one and t'other as the ensuing Appendix 'tis hop'd will evince.*

And as there are Numbers that labour under and are afflicted in their Secret Parts, *with* Infirmities *and* Diseases *hindering Conjugal Conversation and Procreation, and which more than any thing, (especially the modest Class of People,) give them great Concern and Trouble, this will inform them as to the Nature, Cause and Cure of those* Maladies; *and not only that, but also how to prevent the like*

*Injuries in those that may fear them, or by any inconsiderate rashness or inadver-
tency, may before they are aware, be brought into them: For here Young People are
shewn what Constitutions they are of, and at what Age it is best, and whether and
when it is convenient for them to Marry, for the preservation of their Healths; for
many by too early Marriages, enervate their Strength, or bring themselves into Diseases, &c. And as young People in Marrying, aim at Pleasure more than any thing
else, they will herein find the inconveniences that follow by the excessive devoting
themselves, to those Pleasures. Old People or Impotent Ones, are directed, the Cause
and Cure of their Imbecilities, and the many Inconveniences and Injuries that attend late Marriages in both Sexes.* Barrenness *in* Women *and* Conception *is
treated of to advantage, and many things for the Publick Good, is observ'd, as*
Weaknesses, Whites, *&c. in Woman-kind, which if not abused by the Vicious, will
turn to excellent purposes of those whose Cases require Information and Help,
which as it was a Treatise wanted, so by it wise People will be improv'd upon reading it, and all People better'd by rightly considering it. Women will see by it all the*
Secret Infirmities *and* Diseases *they themselves are subject to, and the Causes
and Cure thereof; and Men can have no Disease in their private Parts, or Infirmity
from any Cause; but it is here taken notice of, with the Dangers that attend it, and
way of Cure, which will prove greatly advantageous to each Sex, and set them to
rights in their Opinions, concerning divers Matters, which they before were strangers
to, and at a loss to account for, or be inform'd about: For when this is read and consider'd by them, they will be capable of judging whether the Disease or Infirmity,
be from themselves or from others, and be no longer wrongly charg'd, some Men
bearing the blame when the Fault is their Wives, and Women when its their Husbands, to the Cause of frequent Differences, as aforesaid, which this will be a means
of reconciling, tho' many times at last it appears to proceed from neither of them, that
is, by any Act of theirs, but from Natural, &c. Causes, which however were it not for
this Book, they would have been at a loss to understand.*

*But if any should complain the Discourse is too plain, or that it may sully the
Minds of them that read it, my advice is, that such would lay it aside, for if those
that read it, cannot manage or subdue their Passions, they are not fit to be acquainted with such Matters; for as it was intended for the use of several Persons
Diseas'd and Infirm, it was such of them only as were suppos'd to be peculiarly distinguish'd for their Virtue, at least so much as not to let their unruly Passions sway
them, and the Virtuous will never make an ill but good Use of it. If we are blam'd
for directing People that are in Extremity, or labour under* Infirmities *and* Diseases *of the* Private Parts, *how to get a Cure, we may have reason to accuse him,
says Venette,[3] that form'd those Parts, and even blame him also for giving us the
Vine, because People are inebriated with its Juice; and by the same rule likewise that
it is blam'd, should all our ancient and modern Writers be censur'd, who have done
the same, but in a much more open manner, for there is nothing herein but what is*

discours'd in a Physical way, and in the modestest Terms Anatomy would allow. Why were not the Works of Aristotle, Plato, Plutarch, Catullus, Juvenal, Horace, Virgil, *who have all wrote of Generation, and Natural Pleasures; as also* Petrarcha, Bocacio, Marsilius Ficinus, Platina, Equicola, Hieronymus Mengus, *Dedicated to Cardinal* Paleolus, Delrio, Sprenger, Flaminius Nobilis *who wrote of Love, in an Amorous Way, tho' he was one of the greatest Divines of his time, and who, after having been employ'd by order of Pope* Sixtus V. *in the Edition of the Latin Bible, thought it neither Dishonest or Unworthy of himself to compose that Book, as the Masterpiece of his Life; I say, Why were not they blameworthy and silenc'd?*[4] *By the same rule, says* Venette, *all the Casuists ought to be burnt for teaching so many things upon this Subject; and the Jesuit* Sanchez *should not be exempted from blame, who has made a great Volume of the most Secret Matters that pass between Married Persons.*[5]

Venette *tells us, if modestly speaking of affairs of the* Secret Parts *be blamable, neither St.* Austin, *St.* Gregory of Nice, *nor* Tertullian *should be perus'd, who all speak of Conjugal Affairs in such terms, as he durst not Translate. And by the same rule, one would suppress the Book of* Secrets of Women, *by* Albertus Magnus, *wherein he sets forth a great many things to provoke to Love.*[6] *And in fine, the Books of Physicians and Anatomists ought not to be seen, if the Complaints above recited were just and reasonable, for the Books of Physick and Anatomy, as* Cowper, Gibson, *&c. and of Midwifry, which have Figures, priviledg'd;*[7] *also St.* Jonbert's *Book of* Vulgar Errors, *wherein he treats the Action of the Parts of both Sexes, and which he Dedicated to* Margaret *of* Navarre, Henry the Great's *Grand-mother: Also that of* Ambrose Parry, Laurentius *of Generation,* Maricean, *which speaks of* Child-birth, *with Figures that seem Lewd and Immodest, and was Translated into English by Dr.* Chamberlain:[8] *Monsieur* Dionis *of Generation, and many others, are daily sold, and found very useful for the good of the Publick, so far as to direct for the Cure of some difficult Maladies, whose* Causes *and* Cures, *we could not so well account for, did we not peruse them, as we are oblig'd to do, from a Life-saving Principle, upon such urgent Occasions; and therefore in a modest Way, I say, to shew how and by what means, in this Appendix, People may have their* Infirmities *and* Diseases *known and redress'd, surely cannot be a Crime, since the true and real Intent in Publishing it, was for their Benefit and Preservation, as no doubt but the use of it in time will make appear.*

But before I end this Preface, I cannot but observe that there are a great many People, who under such Misfortunes as the ensuing Appendix treats of, out of a modest reservedness, instead of applying to the Physicians, they in other Cases make use of, because they would not that any who know them, shoul'd know their Secret Infirmities, *do choose to run to This and That* QUACK *for Cure, and the more obscure he lives, the better as they think it suits their Purpose, and who, upon their*

Figure 3.1   Portrait of John Marten from the Frontispiece
of *A Treatise of all the Degrees and Symptoms of the Venereal
Disease in both Sexes* (1708).

assuring them of Cure, they presently trust, till at length they find their Mistake,
by their Ignorance and Unsuccessfulness, there being so many Quacks, Mountebanks, Fortune-tellers, *&c. in the Town, and all pretend to great Matters, that it*
is a great Chance but they fall into the Hands of one or the other; 'tis necessary
therefore to point out who are Quacks, *at least those that profess by their Bills dis-*
tributed about the Town, and pasted up at every pissing Place, the Cure of Venereal *and other* Diseases, *which as they know nothing of, so the People by know-*
ing them, may avoid and shun them.[9]

Those sort of Quacks *of our own Nation, make the concealing their Names a principal part of their Business; for in their Bills you never see who they are, or from whence they came, and so know not who you go to; only that in this or that Ally, or Court, next to the* Frying-Pan *says one, at the* Golden-Ball *says another, at the* Hand *and* Urinal *says a third, in* Magpy-Ally *says a fourth, lives a Doctor that Cures all Incurable Diseases, whether* Venereal *or otherwise; one of them but the other day a* Taylor, *another a* Journey-man *Baker, another a* Gun-Smith, *another a* Country-Barber, *another a* Merry-Andrew *to a* Mountebank, *another a* Foot-man, *and so of the rest: And if they be* Forreigners, *to be sure are some* High-German *Doctors of great extraction and Learning, that can do great Feats, at least they'll tell you so, for still you must take their Word for it, as well as for their Skill; for God knows who they are, what or whence they came, for if were regular Practicers, they would soon tell you so. It is by them that many poor Wretches are deluded and bubled out of their Mony and Lives; and if they escape Death, are frequently brought into some languishing condition, it may be one or the other of those mention'd in the ensuing Appendix, which by their Villainous management are too often render'd past the Power of Art to rectify.*

But t'other Day there comes a young Fellow to me with a Clap, *for Cure of which he said he had apply'd to the Foreign* Quack *at the* Hand *and* Urinal *in* Holborn, *who, after managing him according to his Skill; and before the Malignity was expel'd, gave him a pint Bottle of Turpentine-drink and a Powder, for which he took ten Shillings, and by which he told him his Running would be stopped, which indeed was so to a tittle, for it was immediately dislodg'd and thrown down upon one of his* Testicles, *to the creating a very big inflam'd and painful humoral Tumour, which if had not been forthwith remedied, or had been under his Outlandish Direction, would have prov'd sufficiently mischievous and dangerous. Also a Gentlewoman, some time since, came to me, by direction of a Friend of hers that I formerly Cur'd, who had a* Venereal Running, *which she got from her Husband, and had been for Cure in the Hands of one of the* Quacks *aforemention'd, who telling her 'twas only the* Whites, *gave her Restringents which stopt it, and told her she was well, she believ'd the same, and paid him three Pounds for doing it; but a while after she fell into Pains, and Breakings out almost all over her Body, and at length complain'd of a Soreness in her Throat and Palate, which, upon inspection, I found to be Ulcerated, both Tonsils and Palate; I put her into a proper method and Cur'd her, which otherwise would have been her Ruin.*

But a day or two ago, the following Letter was brought, of a Case and Management, which, the better to shew the fallacy of such that pretend to what they do not understand, I shall so far trespass upon the Reader's Patience as to incert it, and is this:

Dear Sir,

I Crave your Patience and leisure to read the following Relation, and then your skilful and sagacious Judgment.

About seven Weeks ago I unhappily got a *Clap*, for Cure of which I apply'd my self having met with one of his Bills, to the *German* or *Dutch Quack*, at the *Hand* and *Urinal* in *High-Holborn*, who told me, between stammering and speaking, oh! he would Cure me presently, and gave me Purges for five or six times, and then some Medicines he call'd Strengtheners; insomuch, that in about three Weeks, I heard no more of my *Running Nag*, and paid him, and as he assur'd me, thought my self well, and away I went well satisfy'd; but in about three Weeks time after, I began to be in Pain all over me, and grew upon me more and more, that I could scarce walk; every one call'd it a Rheumatism. I had a Physician who came to me, and enquiring into my condition, whisper'd me in the Ear that it was the *Pox*; but I forgot to tell you that when the Pains encreas'd, I was advis'd to Sweat, which I did with *Venice Treacle*, &c. whereupon I had Blotches all over me that turn'd to white mealy Scabs, which my Physician said were *Pocky* ones, and order'd me something for the present, which set me upon my Legs a little, that I made a shift to go in a Coach to that d——d *Quack* that *Poxt* me, to shew him how I was, who, a P—gue take him, told me I had got it a-fresh, and that I must drink his *Royal Decoction*, as he call'd it, which would Cure me, but I d——d his Ignorance and Knavery, and with a few hearty C—ses, God forgive me, I left him, wishing him to have my Distemper. The next day I saw my Physician again, to whom I told the whole Story, as I have now done to you, who laugh'd at my Folly, as well he might, that I should be drawn in, and bubled by one of the most notorious *Quacks* of the Town, which, he says, he and every one knows him to be, he knowing him to be such many Years: But upon enquiring of my Physician what I must do to be well, he told me I must be Salivated out of hand,[10] and advis'd me to you; telling me that you lately Cur'd a very good Friend of his, a Knight, that he recommended to you, who no body else could Cure, and that you was a Man of Judgement and Honour, and would do me Justice. I therefore having told you the whole Story, desire you, good Sir, to consider of my Case against this Night, when, about seven a Clock, I will wait of you at your House, and

beg of you by all that is Sacred, you would put me in a proper
Method, and finish my Cure with all the expedition you can, for
which you shall be honourably and gratefully rewarded; but you
must excuse me, dear Sir, that I am oblig'd to desire you never to
enquire, who or what I am, or the Physician's Name that advis'd
me to you, because by that means I shall come to be known, for
whatever you must have, I will pay you down before-hand, to
avoid your suspecting me. I hope, Sir, for all what my Doctor says,
it may be done without Salivation, but when I wait of you, you
will know better. Why do you and others of the Profession, suffer such a Dog to live under your Noses? send him packing with
a P-x to him to his own Country, to kill the People there with
his d—'d *Turpentine* and *devilish Decoction*, for I have been told
since that he has spoil'd several. Good Sir, don't fail being in the
way at seven at Night; in the interim favour me with a line by this
Porter whether you receiv'd my Letter, fairly Seal'd in three
Places; and one thing more I have to request of you, that you
would not let this be seen by any, but burn it as soon as you have
read it, my Hand being remarkable, and thousands of this Town
know it. I beg your Pardon for this tedious Scroll, and am, Dear
Sir,

Your most humble and most obedient
(tho' unknown) Servant.

Friday Morning.

*This letter sufficiently shews the Ignorance of the Man in those Cases, and how
it can be thought or imagin'd by any, he should be otherways than Ignorant, who,
for all his Life-time, as far as I know, at least for many Years, has got his Living by*
casting of Piss, *and* Telling of Fortunes, *as we are told by an Advertisement
lately Publish'd in the News-Papers; and which, it seems, will be demonstrated in
a Book preparing for the Press by one Dr.* Fitcherton, *a regular Physician;*[11] *as
also that a Book of that Disease set forth by that* Quack, *is all other Mens Works.
So far I know my self of it, having run it over, that great part of it is my Book of
the* Venereal Disease *abridg'd, he having transcrib'd in many places, the very
Words and Sentences, and dispos'd many of the Paragraphs in the same Order as
mine are, which is such Plagiary, that I have directed some hints to that worthy
Gentleman that is answering his Book, which I hope he will so far favour me as to
incert. Such is the ill Nature of Foreign Audacious* QUACKS, *who care not what
they do, who they Steal from, or who they Ruin, so they get but the Mony, which
is all their Aim and Design; but 'tis hop'd by the Methods now a taking to suppress
all Foreign and Domestick* Quacks, Mountebanks, Fortune-Tellers, &c. *which
are the very Pest of the Nation, he, who is one of the Tribe, will be Silenc'd, and*

shewn better Manners than has been taught him in his own Country and made to know, that tho' the Mob may for a while, yet the Wise part of the People of England *are not to be so abus'd by Strangers.*

From this very Quack, *sometime since, came a Gentleman to me, who by taking his Drink, which he calls the* Royal Decoction, *has brought into an involuntary emission of Urine, had such a Propensity as that he could not hold it a minute, but would come away in his Breeches, insomuch that he was difficultly sav'd from a* Diabetes: *He was from a plump fleshy Man, brought by drinking that Decoction, into a thin, wasting, declining Condition, and tho' he went thro' his Method for thirty Days, was so far from being Cur'd of his Indisposition (which that* Quack *told him was the* Pox, *which I aver, and can make it appear, was nothing of that Disease) that he was rendered much worse, even to the endangering a* Consumption *as well as a* Diabetes, *which might have cost him his Life. I undertook him and Cur'd him, and he had twenty Guineas for my Pains. These Relations afore spoken of, I aver and can prove to be Fact; as also others under the same* Quack's *hands, taken notice of in my Book of the* Venereal Disease, *Sixth Edition, to which I refer the Reader for further Satisfaction; and have besides, divers other well attested Relations and Accounts of his managing* Venereal People, *which as opportunity offers, may be made Publick by*

From my House in *Hatton-Garden*, the
further end of the Street on the left
Hand beyond the *Chappel*, as you turn   *John Marten.*
in from Holborn,
John Marten, *Surgeon*,
writ over the Door, *London*,
Decemb. 20th, 1708.

CHAP. II

Of the Imperfections, Defects, Imbecilities and Diseases of the Secret Parts of Women, *which Defile and Ruin the Healths of themselves and Posterity, obstruct conjugal Delectancy and Pregnancy, with their various methods of Cure; as also of* Generation *and* Conception, *and the Causes and Cure of their Miscarriages.*

As Man therefore (as I at first obsrev'd) was by the great Creator most curiously made, and the Structure of his Parts in the most exquisite Order contriv'd; so Woman, and her Parts ministring to Generation, are no less admirable in every respect, as we shall by and by shew, in giving a Description thereof; and unless we enquire as particularly into the Parts of

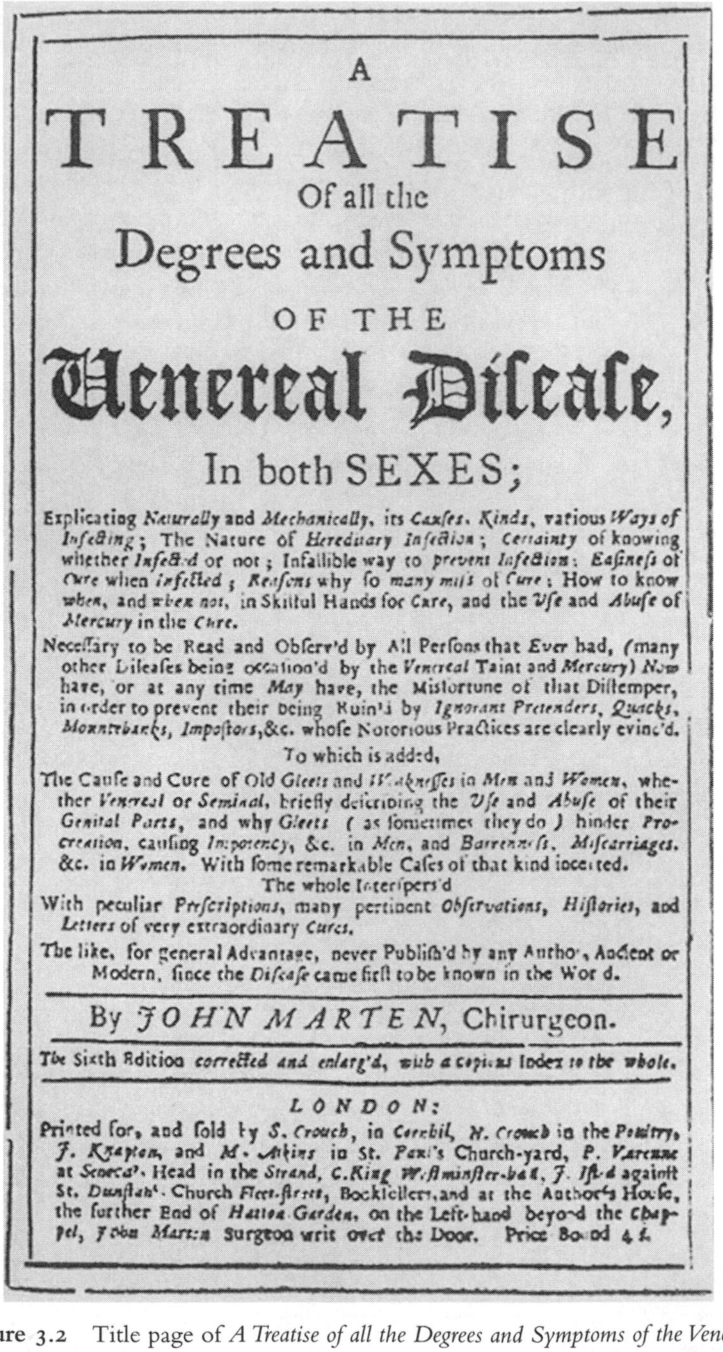

A

TREATISE

Of all the

Degrees and Symptoms

OF THE

Uenereal Diſeaſe,

In both SEXES;

Explicating *Naturally* and *Mechanically*, its *Cauſes*, *Kinds*, various *Ways of Infecting*; The Nature of *Hereditary Infection*; *Certainty* of knowing whether *Infected* or not; Infallible way to *prevent Infection*; Eaſineſs of *Cure* when *infected*; *Reaſons* why ſo *many miſs* of *Cure*; How to know *when*, and *when not*, in Skilful Hands for *Care*, and the *Uſe* and *Abuſe* of *Mercury* in the *Cure*.

Neceſſary to be Read and Obſerv'd by All Perſons that *Ever* had, (many other Diſeaſes being occaſion'd by the *Venereal* Taint and *Mercury*) *Now* have, or at any time *May* have, the Misfortune of that Diſtemper, in order to prevent their being Ruin'd by *Ignorant Pretenders*, *Quacks*, *Mountebanks*, *Impoſtors*, &c. whoſe Notorious Practices are clearly evinc'd.

To which is added,

The Cauſe and Cure of Old *Gleets* and *Weakneſſes* in *Men* and *Women*, whether *Venereal* or *Seminal*, briefly deſcribing the *Uſe* and *Abuſe* of their *Genital Parts*, and why *Gleets* (as ſometimes they do) hinder *Procreation*, cauſing *Impotency*, &c. in *Men*, and *Barrenneſs*, *Miſcarriages*, &c. in *Women*. With ſome remarkable Cases of that kind inceſted.

The whole Interſperſ'd

With peculiar *Preſcriptions*, many pertinent *Obſervations*, *Hiſtories*, and *Letters* of very extraordinary *Cures*.

The like, for general Advantage, never Publiſh'd by any Author, Ancient or Modern, ſince the *Diſeaſe* came firſt to be known in the World.

By *JOHN MARTEN*, Chirurgeon.

The Sixth Edition *corrected and enlarg'd*, *with a copious Index to the whole*.

LONDON:

Printed for, and ſold by S. *Crouch*, in *Cornhil*, *N. Crouch* in the *Poultry*, *J. Knapton*, and *M. Atkins* in St. *Paul's* Church-yard, *P. Varenne* at *Seneca's* Head in the *Strand*, C. *King Weſtminſter-hall*, *J. Iſted* againſt St. *Dunſtan's* Church *Fleet-ſtreet*, Bookſellers, and at the Author's Houſe, the further End of *Hatton-Garden*, on the Left-hand beyond the Chappel, *John Marten* Surgeon writ over the Door. Price Bound 4 ſ.

Figure 3.2 Title page of *A Treatise of all the Degrees and Symptoms of the Venereal Disease, in both Sexes* (1708). *Gonosologium Novum* was published as an appendix to the 1709 sixth edition.

Woman, as we have of Man, we cannot come to the distinct Knowledge of the business of Generation.

The Parts of a Woman that are calculated for that Office, are very curious and very useful, and as every Man's Passion is inflamed at the sight of them, so every curious Man is desirous of their being treated upon, being willing to know where and how he was form'd. When a Man at any time is Dissected, the place of Dissection is not so crowded, but when it happens to be a Woman, the Spectators would willingly be more numerous, did not Modesty in those concern'd forbid it, in turning away the Crowd, as not worthy of the Sight, which is called, and that justly enough, pretty and fine. But I go on.

It has been the method of divers [authors] that have given an Anatomical account of the *Genital Parts* of Woman, to begin first with the external or outer Parts of the Privity; which I should also here have done, but that willing to pursue the same Order in Women, as I have already done in Men, shall first begin with the internal Parts of the Privity, which may properly enough be divided into four Parts, *viz*. The Privities, which is that part as appears at first sight without Dissection, the *Womb*, the *Testicles*, and the *Vessels* that prepare and carry, called the *Spermatick Vessels*, which I shall, for reasons already mentioned, now speak to, (tho' the last in order) and are of two sorts, *viz. Arteries* and *Veins*, and are also in number two as in Men, springing from the great Artery, a little below the Emulgents,[12] passing down toward the *Testes*, differing from those in Men, which are by a direct course, when in Women they are with much twirling and winding among the Veins, which yet notwithstanding they are when stretcht out to their utmost length, shorter than those in Men, by reason Mens descend out of the *Abdomen* or *Belly* into the *Scrotum* or *Cod*, when in Women they have a far shorter passage, reaching only to the *Testes* or *Stones* and *Womb* within the *Abdomen* or Belly.

Those *Veins* in Women are also two, the right Vein springeth from the Trunk of the *Vena Cava* under of a little below the Emulgent, and the left springeth from the Emulgent of the same side, both which in this descent, have no more windings than in Men, and therefore are considerably shorter than theirs are, and not united before they come to the *Stones*, as they are in Men, but are divided into two Branches, the greater passing to the *Stones*, the lesser to the *Womb*, for the nourishment both of it self, that is, the *Womb*, and the Infant that is therein; by which means 'tis that the *Menstrua* or *Terms* in Women with Child, flow for the first Months, and not out of the Coats of the *Uterus* or *Womb*, as some imagine; for when a Woman is not with Child, the same Blood slips away through several small passages that open into the circumference of the bottom of the *Womb*, and

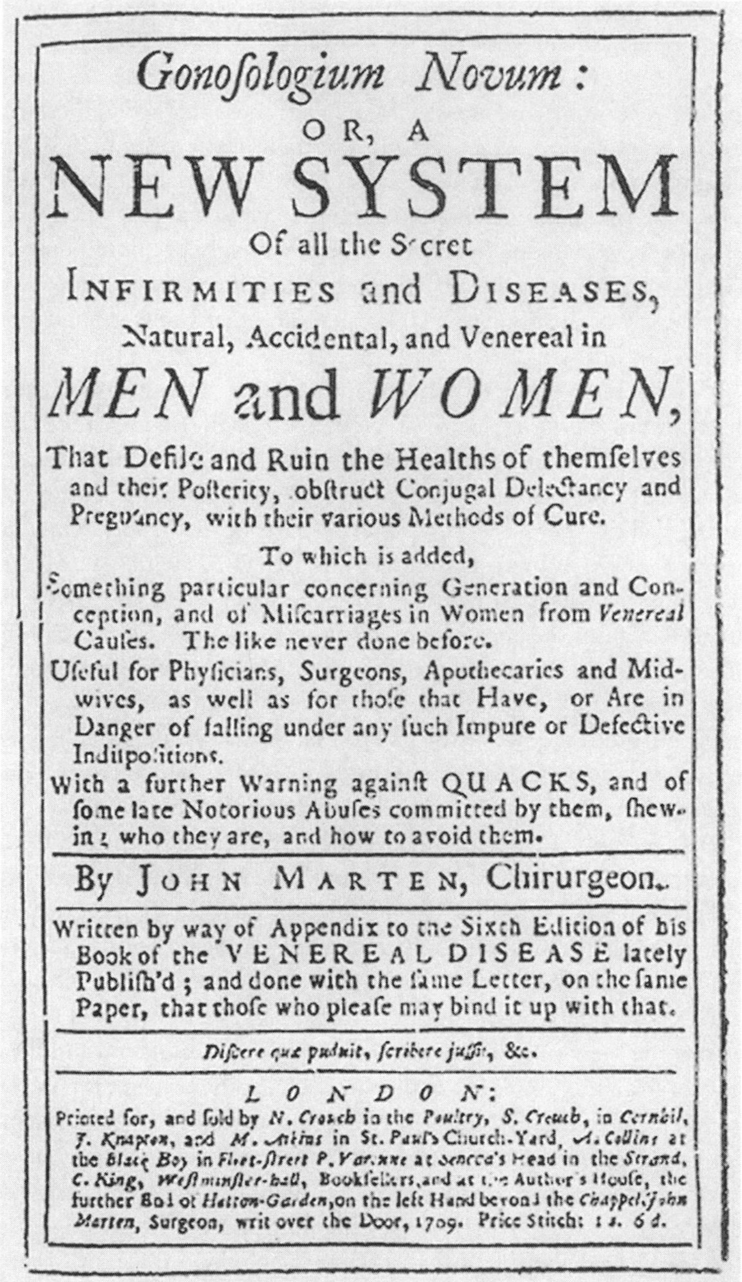

Gonosologium Novum:

OR, A

NEW SYSTEM

Of all the Secret

INFIRMITIES and DISEASES,

Natural, Accidental, and Venereal in

MEN and *WOMEN,*

That Defile and Ruin the Healths of themselves and their Posterity, obstruct Conjugal Delectancy and Pregnancy, with their various Methods of Cure.

To which is added,

Something particular concerning Generation and Conception, and of Miscarriages in Women from *Venereal* Causes. The like never done before.

Useful for Physicians, Surgeons, Apothecaries and Midwives, as well as for those that Have, or Are in Danger of falling under any such Impure or Defective Indispositions.

With a further Warning against QUACKS, and of some late Notorious Abuses committed by them, shewing who they are, and how to avoid them.

By JOHN MARTEN, Chirurgeon.

Written by way of Appendix to the Sixth Edition of his Book of the VENEREAL DISEASE lately Publish'd; and done with the same Letter, on the same Paper, that those who please may bind it up with that.

Discere quæ pudnit, scribere jussi, &c.

Printed for, and sold by *N. Crouch* in the *Poultry, S. Crouch,* in *Cornhil, J. Knapton,* and *M. Atkins* in St. Paul's Church-Yard, *A. Collins* at the *Black Boy* in *Fleet-street* P. *Varenne* at *Seneca's Head* in the *Strand, C. King, Westminster-hall,* Booksellers, and at the Author's House, the further End of *Hatton-Garden,* on the left Hand beyond the *Chappel, John Marten,* Surgeon, writ over the Door, 1709. Price Stitch: 1 s. 6 d.

Figure 3.3   Title page of *Gonosologium Novum* (1709).

falls into its Cavity, from whence it makes its *exit* through the *Vagina* or neck of the *Womb* every Month; and this is what is call'd the *Menstrual Blood*. These little passages are plainly visible in those that are Dissected soon after Child-birth, or in the time of the *Menstrual Flux*. Both Arteries and Veins are covered with one common Coat from the *Peritonaeum*, some branches of which sometimes in big-belly'd Women, let out their Blood, as aforesaid, and that longer than the first Months only, especially when there is more than is necessary for the nourishment of the Child in the Womb; therefore 'tis not to be wondered at, neither should it cause such fears as the Women and Midwives also are frequently in, so as to run them upon Bleeding and giving Medicines to stop it, to the injuring of the Woman, because in those Cases they nevertheless go out their full time, without any manner of danger of Miscarrying, because, as hinted before, the Blood comes from the Vessels in the neck of the *Womb*, and not from those of the bottom; which were it so, would by giving the Blood such vent as to occasion Miscarriage: So that it appears the use of these *Spermatick Vessels* is not only to minister to the nourishment of the *Fœtus*, and of the Womb as beforesaid, but also for the expurgation of the *Monthly Courses* in Womankind.

The *Testicles* or *Stones*, or rather *Ovaria* in Women (for says *Culpeper* they have such kind of Toys as well as Men)[13] differ from the *Stones* in Men both in their situation, formation, magnitude, coverings, substance and use; first in situation, they being within the Body in Women, situated on each side, about two Fingers breadth from the bottom of the *Womb*, to the sides whereof they are connected or knit by a strong Ligament; the design of which situation being suppos'd by Nature to make Women more passionate than they would otherwise be for Generation; but to be sure are more conveniently there plac'd than elsewhere, for that their commerce and alliance with the *Womb*, requires an immediate communication.

As for the form of the *Stones* in Women, they are flat on the sides, and in their lower part oval; their Superfices are more rugged and unequal than in those of Men, differing in magnitude according to the Womans Age, for in those that are newly come to maturity they are about half as big as those of Men, or about the bigness of a small Pigeons Egg, but in such as are in Years they grow less and are harder, tho' in some Women they have been observ'd to grow preternaturally to a vast bigness, even to contain several quarts of Liquor, as we have observ'd in such as have had Dropsie of the *Womb*.[14]

The Stones in Women have but one Membrane that encompasses them round, unless on their upper side, where the *Vasa Preparantia* enter them, where another Membrane encompassing those Vessels and springing from the *Peritonæum*, involve them about half way. Upon the removing this cover, the Substance of the *Stones* appears whitish, altogether different from the Substance of Mens *Testicles*: For theirs, as have been observ'd, are compos'd of Seminary Vessels, which put together so as to be extended without breaking, are twenty or thirty Ells long; But the *Stones* of Women principally consist of a great many Membranes and small Fibres, loosely united one to another, among which there are several little Vessels or Bladders full of a clear Liquor, and which are commonly took for Eggs, and from thence it comes that the Female *Testicles* are called *Ovaria*, tho' are what *Hippocrates* and *Galen*,[15] with their Followers, have suppos'd to be *Seed* stor'd up in them, as if they supply'd the place of the *Vesiculæ Seminales* in Men; but Dr. *Harvey*[16] (according to *Aristotle*) and also many other learned Physicians and Anatomists in their and our time, deny all *Seed* to Women, tho' they emit this Liquor upon Copulation, and sometimes much of it, which is taken for their Seed, "For," says Dr. *Harvey*, "some Women emit no such Humour as this which they call *Seed*, and yet do Conceive"; "yea," says he, "some that after they begun to emit such Humour upon Copulation, tho' indeed they took great Pleasure in the Act, yet grew less Fruitful than before." There are also infinite Instances of Women, who, tho' they have great Pleasure in the Act of Coition, yet send forth nothing of that which they call *Seed*, and yet at the same time Conceive: So that both from the place of its emission, and from its consistence, it is apparent that the Humour which Women send forth in Copulation cannot be *Seed*, but a clear Liquor shed thro' the Pleasure taken in the Act, to render the passage more slippery and the delight in the Act more pleasing and easy both to the Man and Woman, and that which occasions the Woman to Conceive is the Man's Impregnating one or more of the Womans *Ovaria*, or little Eggs in the *Testicles*, each having about twenty of several sizes, which when so Fœcundated by the Man's *Seed*, are separated and conveyed into the *Womb* by the *Tubae Fallopianae*, which are sufficiently enlarged upon the Act of Copulation as well as all other of the *Genital Parts*, and are truly Eggs, analogous to those of Fowl and other Creatures, as appears upon their being boil'd, they having the same Colour, Tast, and Consistency with the white of Bird Eggs, which want not Shells as theirs do, because they always remain in the Body, and when fœcundated in the *Womb*, are thereby sufficiently defended by it.

The *Womb* of Woman or *Matrix* (from its being as a Mother to conserve and nourish the Fœtus) is seated in the *Hypogastrium* or lowest part of the *Abdomen* or *Belly*, in the middle of that large hollow that is call'd the *Pelvis* or Basin, and is formed by the *Ossa Illii*, the Hip, the *Ossa Pubis* and the *Os Sacrum*. In this Cavity it is placed between the passage of Urine or

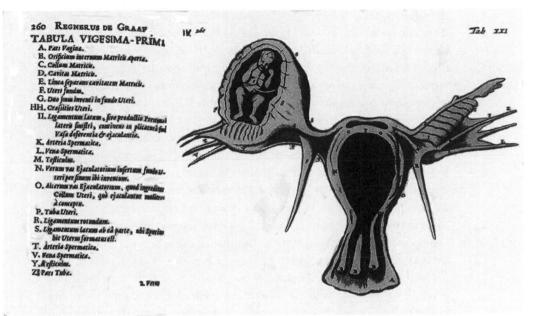

Figure 3.4 Illustration from Regnier de Graff, *De mulierum organis generationi inservientibus* (1672)

the Bladder, and the strait or right Gut, to shew Fond Man that he has little reason to be Proud, when he considers that he was Conceiv'd and Bred
betwixt the places Ordain'd by Nature to discharge the Excrements, being
the very Sink of the Body, which if he did but consider aright, and from
whence his Original sprang, might from it sufficiently draw an Argument
of Humility; the hindmost part of the Womb is loose, that it may be extended as the Child increases, but its sides are ty'd fast by two pair of Ligaments; the first Pair of which are so contriv'd as to keep the *Womb* from
falling upon its Neck, which is called among Women and Midwives a
bearing down, occasioned by relaxation of those Ligaments, but if they at
any time are broken or immoderately relaxed, as sometimes they are,
by Falls, Bruises, &c. then the *Womb* descends, and sometimes falls out,
turning inside outwards, and is both very troublesome and dangerous to
Women: The second Pair of these Ligaments, call'd the round or Worm-
like Ligaments, do, according to *Vestingius, Diemerbroeck*, &c. receive a small
Seminal Vessel from the Womans *Testes* or *Stones*, and *Tubae*, which they
conduct or lead down to the *Clitoris*, into which they are incerted, and
ought rather to be accounted *Vasa Deferentia* than Ligaments; for which
reason, what Women emit from about the *Clitoris* in the Act of Copulation, they think to be true *Seed* conducted thither by those *Seminal Ducts*
or Passages: But *Regner de Graef* says,[17] there are no such Ducts, and affirms
that these Ligaments reach not the Clitoris, but are terminated above the
Os Pubis, towards the Fat of *Mons Veneris*, near the *Clitoris*, being divided
into many parts or jags, and that Humour or Liquor which Women emit,
doth issue out of the *Lacunae* or little Pores or Passages in the *Vagina* of the
Womb, and lower part of the *Urinary* Passage, and also form the *Meatus* in
the Neck of the *Womb*, and is a ferous Petuitous Matter flowing out (the
same as the *Prostatal Liquor* is by Man upon Erections, &c.) in some in a
great quantity in the Act of Coition, to lubricate the *Vagina* of the *Womb*,
and causes, as said before, the greater pleasure both to the Woman and
the Man; which tho' some Authors deny, and say it is the Womans Seed,
Anatomy shews to the contrary; for that they have no *Seed*, but *Ovaria*, or
little Eggs in their *Testicles*, which are impregnated and fæcundated by the
Man's *Seed*, so as that thereby they conceive.

The Substance of the Womb is whitish, nervous and compact in Virgins, but a little spongy and soft in Women with Child. In Virgins it is
about two Fingers breadth broad, and three long, and while they retain
their Virginity, its cavity or hollowness is so small, as that it will hardly hold
a large Hazel Nut; but in those that have had Children, it will hold a small
Walnut. Its *Cervix*, or lesser Neck of Passage of the Womb, is an Inch or
more in length; its Cavity as it opens to the *Vagina*, is compar'd to the

Mouth of a Tench; *Galen* likens its passage to that in the Glans of a Man's *Penis* or *Yard*,[18] and is so strait and narrow in Virgins, as scarce wide enough to admit a Crow's Quill, unless just before and after the flowing of their *Menses*, when it widens a little, especially in lustful Maids. When a Woman has conceiv'd with Child, its inner Orifice does either shut up, quite closing its sides together, or is daubed up with a slimy yellowish Humour,[19] so that nothing then can enter into the Womb; whence it is that Women with Child have not so great a propensity, nor take nothing near the pleasure (nay, sometimes 'tis painful) in the act of Copulation. The Womb in shape is like a Pear, only a little flattish above and below, but in Women with Child it becomes more round, and is divided by a Line that goes lengthways, much like the Seam that is in a Man's Cod. It hath two Membranes, the outer, which is common, is strong and double, arising from the Peritonæum; the inner, being proper, is fibrous and more porous: Betwixt those two Membranes there is a certain carnous and fibrous Contexture, which in Women with Child, together with the said two Membranes, do imbibe so much of the nutritious Humours that then flow thither, that the more the *Fœtus* increaseth, the more fleshy, fibrous, and thick, doth the Womb grow; so that in the last months of a Womans being with Child, it becomes an Inch thick, and sometimes two Fingers breadth, tho' it be extended to so much greater compass, than it has when a Woman is not with Child; and yet, which is very strange, and to be observ'd, the Womb becomes as thin as before, within the compass of sixteen or seventeen days after a Woman is brought to Bed, not being then above half a Fingers breadth, and contracts it self into so small a compass as to be held in ones hand.

    The Arteries of the Womb spring partly from the Spermatick and Hypogastrick, and run along the Womb, bending and winding, that they may be extended without danger of breaking, when the Womb is stretched with the Child. By these Arteries it is that the *Catamenia* or *Monthly Courses* of Women flow in greatest quantity into the Womb it self, and by the branches opening into the Neck of the Womb, less quantity of the menstrual Blood flows, and out of the Sheath of the Womb the Courses flow in small quantity, and begin to appear in Virgins about the twelfth, fourteenth, or fifteenth year of their Age, at which time also the Hair of their Privities begins to put forth, their Voices and Judgment strengthen, and they begin to distinguish Virtue from Vice; Nature then putting a Veil upon their Privy-parts, to signify that Honesty and Modesty ought there to be Establish'd. In Women with Child, the Courses very rarely flow, and the wanting of them, is the first *Item* in marry'd Women that are Pregnant (unless any Distemperature) of their having Conceiv'd. The Reason or

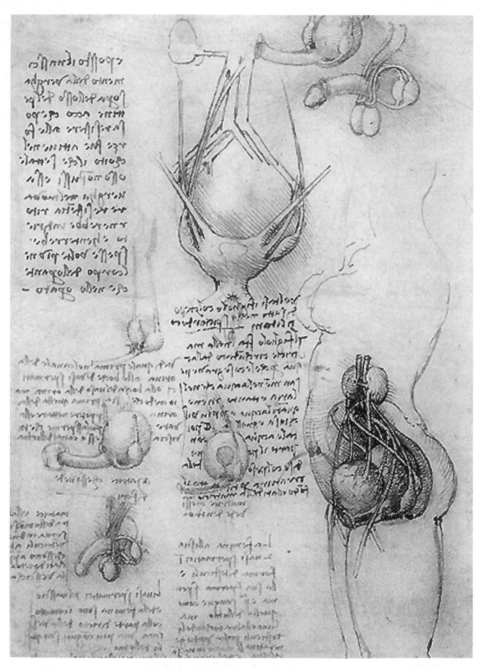

Figure 3.5 Leonardo da Vinci, *Study of the Female Reproductive System* (c. 1509), showing the homology between male and female organs.

Cause why Blood should so periodically every Month flow from Woman-kind, has been much in Dispute, tho' not difficult to be assign'd; some say, and those the Ancients, that they flow by the influence of the Moon, as supposing the Element had the Dominion over Womens Bodies, which if so, than all Women of all Ages and Temperaments would have their Courses at the same periods and revolutions of it, at the same time; which they have not, as daily experience sufficiently shews: But the Time has not been so much contended about, but the ill and offensive Quality of that Menstruous Blood, has been as much or more asserted by divers Authors; as first from the Pain it gives many Women in the Evacuation, which they say is because it is acrimonious, nay venomous. They say likewise, that the malignity of that Blood is so great that they excoriate by meer Contact, the *Glans* and *Perputium* of a Man, upon his having to do with a Woman at that time; nay, some affirm, that by a Man's Copulating with his Wife when she has her Courses upon her, he will get the *Venereal Disease*, for that the *Menstrual Blood* is infectious: They say further, that the breath of a Menstruous Woman, or one that has her *Courses* upon her, will give a lasting Stain to Ivory, or a Looking-glass; and that a little of the Blood drop'd upon a Vine, or Corn, or any other Vegetable, will blast or cause the same to die: That if a Woman with Child be defiled with the *Menses* of an-other Woman, it will cause her to miscarry: That if a Dog tastes the *Courses* of a Woman, he will run mad: That if a man tastes them, 'twill render him Epileptick; which, with almost innumerable other ridiculous and foolish Fancies, tho, related by grave and great Authors, are yet justly to be re-jected, as having no foundation of Truth or Reason to support them.

The *Vagina* or Sheath of the *Womb*, contiguous to the *Cervix*, is so call'd because it receives the Man's *Yard* in time of Copulation, like a Sheath; it is likewise call'd the Portal or Door of the Womb, and its greater Neck, to distinguish it from the other, a little before spoke to. This Sheath is a soft and loose Pipe, rugous or uneven on its inside, with orbicular Wrinkles, of a nervous but somewhat spongy Substance, which Lust causes to puff up in the Act of Copulation, the better to embrace and clasp the Man's *Yard* more closely, and is about six or seven, some say eight Inches deep, and as wide as the strait Gut, the better to contract it; but yet in the respect of Age, *&c.* it differs in length, width and looseness; and according as a Woman is more or less inflam'd with Lust. Therefore Man and Women that have no natural or accidental Impediments in those Parts, need not be sollicitous but that their *Genitals* will be proportionable, and fit each the other; and in Women, Nature has so admirably contriv'd the Sheath of the *Womb* so, as that it will suit with every Man's *Yard*. The aforesaid wrinkles on the inside of the Sheath or greater Neck of the *Womb*, are much more numerous and close set in Virgins, and those Women that seldom accompany with Man, or that have never borne Children, than in those that have had many Children, and in Whores that use frequent Copulation, or those that have been long and much troubled with the Whites.[20] This Sheath has very many Arteries and Veins, some of which open into it, and through which sometimes the *Menses* flow in Women with Child that are *Plethorick*, for they cannot come from the Womb it self, unless Abortion follow, as we before shew'd, which has put many Women and Midwives under a fear, thinking when a show of their *Menses* has appear'd, that they shall presently Miscarry; which is because they have not judgment to discern whether it flows from the Arteries or Veins in the Sheath, or from the Womb; but these things have been sufficiently spoken to already.

These Vessels we speak of, bring plenty of Blood to those parts, in the *Venereal* Encounter, which heating and puffing up the *Vagina*, much encreaseth the pleasure, and prevents the Man's *Seed* from cooling before it reaches the *Uterus* or Womb of the Woman. All along the Sheath there are abundance of Pores from whence a thin Humour always flows, especially in Copulation, and increases the Womans pleasure, and is suppos'd to be her *Seed*; the contrary of which, with the Reasons, we have already sufficiently explicated, and need say no more about. Near its outer end under the Nymphs, in its upper part, it receives the Neck of the Bladder. This Passage or Sheath is so narrow in Virgins, that at their first conversation with a Man, it is more pain than pleasure, as those that have lost their Maidenheads well know; for it is not to be entered by the Man's erected *Yard* without pain, by reason of the extension the Man's *Member* necessarily makes, even so as to break (say many Authors) from small Vessels, from whence Blood issues, and is the certain sign (however the pleasing one) of Virginity: And not only is the pain to the Woman, but sometimes to the Man also, if her Body be very strait, as we have already observ'd; yet when once the Womans Chastity is forfeited, it is wide enough to admit the largest *Yard*, and is so much from being a pain then, or being troublesome, because of its largeness, that it really adds much to the pleasure and satisfaction of the Woman.

The *Hymen*, otherwise call'd the *Virgin Zone*, or *Girdle of Chastity*, is a thin nervous Membrane, interwoven with fleshy Fibres, and endow'd with many little Arteries and Veins, behind the insertion of the Neck of the Bladder, with a hole in the midst that will admit the top of one's little Finger, whereby the Courses flow. When this Hymen is broken, as it is, or at leastwise distended at the first Bout, or time of Copulating, it never closes again; and the Blood that the Woman sheds at that time, is the sign or token of her Virginity; and which, as said before, when the Man perceives,

PRÆSENS *figura uterum à corpore exectum ea magnitudine refert, qua postremò Patauij dissectæ mulieris uterus nobis occurrit, atq; ut uteri circunscriptionem hic expressimus, ita etiam ipsius fundum per medium dissecuimus, ut illius sinus in conspectum ueniret, una cum ambarum uteri tunicarū in non prægnantibus substantiæ crassitie.*

A, A.B,B Vteri fundi sinus.

C,D Linea quodāmodo instar suturæ, qua scortum donatur, in uteri fundi sinum leuiter protuberans.

E,E Interioris ac propriæ fundi uteri tunicæ crassities.

F,F Interioris fundi uteri portio, ex elatiori uteri sede deorsum in fundi sinū protuberans.

G,G Fundi uteri orificium.

H,H Secundum exteriusq; fundi uteri inuolucrum, à peritonæo pronatum.

I,I et c. Membranarum à peritonæo pronatarum, & uterum continentium portionem utrinq; hic asseruauimus.

K Vteri ceruicis substantia hic quoque conspicitur, quod sectio qua uteri fundum diuisimus, inibi incipiebatur.

L Vesicæ ceruicis pars, uteri ceruici inserta, ac urinam in illam proijciens. Vteri colles, & si quid hic spectādum sit reliqui, etiam nullis appositis characteribus, nulli non patent.

s VIGE·

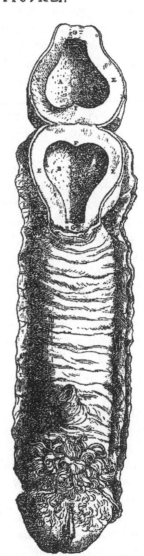

Figure 3.6   Vesalinus, *Fabrica* (1543), showing the homology between the uterus and the penis.

concludes and is satisfied in himself that he has married a Maid, tho' many a Man has been mistaken in that point, the Womans bleeding at the first Assault being not always the certain sign of a Maiden-head, no more than when that Blood is wanting, it is to be concluded, a Woman for that reason had before forfeited her Virginity, because it does not always necessarily follow that the Bride must bleed upon the first Embrace; for the Hymen may be corroded by sharp Humours flowing through with a long continuance of the *Courses*; or from the dripping of the *Whites* which many Maids as well as Women are infested with; also from other Causes, as one that I knew, who from a wanton Inclination, broke it with her Finger, and others that I have heard of, by using some convenient Instrument for the satisfying of their Lust; or if a Maid be so indiscreet as to be married in the time her *Courses* are upon her, or within a Day after they have left her, or a day or two before they flow, at which time the *Hymen* and wrinkled Membrane of the Sheath are so relaxed (as before observ'd) that the Bridegroom's *Virile Member* may enter without any manner of Obstruction, whereby he may suspect tho' without Cause, that he had not married a Maid. These things have in some been the cause of very unhappy Lives. In old Maids the *Hymen* is so strong sometimes as that it cannot be penetrated by the Bridegroom without very great difficulty, and not without extraordinary Pain both to the Bridegroom and Bride. In some it is naturally quite clos'd up, by which means their Courses are stopt to the injuring their Healths, and endangering their Lives, and cannot be remedied, but by Chirurgical Operation; but that I shall speak to particularly, when I come by and by to treat of the Infirmities and Diseases of those Parts.

It is in the integrity of this *Membrane*, together with the straitness of the *Vagina*, that Virgin Innocence consists; and Virginity is said to be lost, when by the admission of the Man's *Yard*, the former is forcibly or violently broken, or loosned and distended, and the latter widened; tho' yet, as said before, it may be violated by other means; and tho' Virginity once lost, or as said before, the *Membrane* broken or distended, can never be restor'd or clos'd again, yet an artificial Maiden-head, mimicking the true, may be obtain'd, and is what numbers of Harlots have acquir'd, and thereby impos'd upon the Men, by only constringing the *Genitals*, and bringing them to their almost former straitness, and this they do by Baths and Fomentations prepar'd of Astringent Ingredients, by using which to the Privy Parts, as also to the Breasts (which latter upon lying with Men, and Conceiving, grow, especially in some, great, soft and flagging) contracts both the Parts and them so effectually, as scarcely to be discover'd, even by the most understanding Midwife; and when they come to be Brides, the better to deceive their Husbands, have either a little blooded their Shifts before-hand, or placed a little Fish-bladder of Blood so, as to be broke in the Encounter; or have appointed the Day of Marriage to be at the declension of their Courses, complaining at the time of Embrace a little of Pain to colour the matter, and make the Bridegroom believe it was the very first Bout; but this being so commonly done, as doubtless may be affirm'd, no more need to be said, or the Prescriptions of the Medicines to straiten, here set down, lest those that are yet Chaste should take the hint, as some giddy Girls may, upon the Presumption, and so the easier forfeit that Virtue which should be their peculiar Care to preserve, and the more, because many Men now-a-days in this degenerate Age, (tho' it cannot but be allow'd the Men are generally as bad or worse than the Women) are so very inquisitive, or shall I say suspicious, judging them by their own false Steps, that on the Nuptial Night, if they find no emission of Blood from the Womans Body upon the Encounter, tho' there be all the other Signs and Tokens of her Virginity and Chastity, yet are presently apt to believe themselves impos'd upon, and for that reason will hardly be reconcil'd to their Bride; when they, poor Women, are sufficiently impos'd upon by the Men, who probably have lain with several Women before that time, yet, hard is their Case, there is no rule by which they can come with certainty to the knowledge thereof.

In ancient times great notice was taken of those Things on the Womans side, and even now in many parts of the World, as in *Morocco, Poland*, &c. they have Virginity in such reverence, that after the married Couple go to Bed, the Company invited, waits in the next room, till they have Copulated, when the Bride Shifts her self, which Shift is brought out by some grave Matron appointed, and if they find the Tokens of Virginity thereon, they make joyful Acclamations, in which all the Kindred joyn, and the next Day carry her Shift in Publick Triumph about the Town, like a Banner, that all the People may be Witness of the Brides Virginity, and the People follow with Musick, Singing, and Dancing: But if they do not find those marks of Virginity on her Shift, every one of the Guests, according to the custom of the *Polanders*, throws down his Glass, and all the Jollity is at an end, and the Brides Kindred are quite out of Countenance: Then the Guests commit a thousand Extravagancies in the House, they break the Pots and the earthen Cups, put a Horse's Collar about the Brides Mothers Neck, make her drink out of one of those broken Cups, and upbraided her for not having been more watchful of her Daughters Chastity; and after they have treated her with all the vile Language imaginable, the Company breaks up, the Friends of the Bride keep within Doors for some time, being asham'd to go abroad, till the Wonder and Ignominy is somewhat over, upon which, the Bridegroom may put away his Bride if he pleases, or if he keeps her, he must resolve at the same time to put up with abundance of Reproaches and Affronts that he will meet with. Thus we see how Maiden-heads are valued abroad, when at the same time the Bride may not be in Fault for Reasons we gave before.

And indeed here also most Husbands are such Fools as to covet the difficult task of getting a Maiden-head the first Night, and glory in the imaginary Conquest, measuring their Wives Virtue, by the labour of that first Attack, when it does not always happen, and the Wife not the less Chast, as aforesaid; neither, as said before, is it a hard matter to impose upon such Husbands, when their dependance is only upon that feeble Testimony, for the wisest of Men, King *Solomon*, in his *Proverbs* tells us, There are three things hard to be known, yea four, but the fourth he could by no means account for, namely *the way of a Man with a Maid*, or to explain his Meaning, *the Track of a Man in a Virgin, that is to know whether she had lain with a Man or no.*[21]

But all this while, in speaking about the preservation of this *Hymen* or *Virgin Zone*, I must not here forget to observe, that there are some that not only differ and contend about the Figure, Substance, Place, and Perforations of the *Hymen*, but even are doubtful whether such a thing be or not, which as some positively affirm, so others as flatly deny: And even that famous Man *Regner de Graef* himself, the most Industrious and Accurate Inquirer into those Parts, confesses that he always sought it in vain, tho' he endeavour'd it, and had opportunities in divers People of various unsuspected Ages: all that he could find, he says, was a different straitness and different corrugations, which were greater or lesser as were their respective Ages. Whether therefore it is to be found in all People, is not to be asserted; *Realdus Columbus* also says, it is seen very seldom, these are his Words, viz. "Under the *Nymphae* in many but not in all Virgins, there is another Membrane, which when it is present, (which is but seldom) it stoppeth, so that the Man's *Yard* cannot be put into the Orifice of the Womans *Womb*, for it is very thick above towards the Bladder, and hath a hole by which the Courses flow out."[22] And adds, that he had observ'd it in two young Virgins, and in one elder Maid. *Ambrose Parry* the Surgeon,[23] says, "That *Tunicle* or *Membrane* call'd the *Hymen*, is suppos'd by many, and those learned Physicians, to be, as it were the enclosure of the Maidenhead or Virginity of the Maid," but declares he could never find it in any, seeking it in Virgins of all Ages, from three to twelve, of all that he had under his Hands in the Hospital of Paris, where he was one of the Surgeons; yet confesses at last he once saw it in a Virgin of seventeen Years old, in whom it was so strong, that at her Marriage it hindered her Copulating:

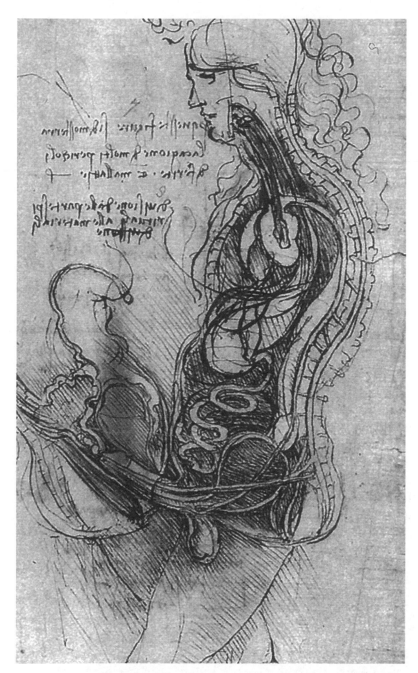

Figure 3.7   Leonardo da Vinci, *Study of Human Intercourse* (c. 1509).

The Mother to whom the Virgin made her complaint, desir'd *Parry* to examine her, who did, and found the Tunicle so thick, that he was forc'd to cut it asunder with his Scissars, after which she could suffer her Husband, and bore him Children.

Sometimes this Virgin *Tunicle* is so strong and so thick, as that by the endeavors and strength of an ordinary Man, it is not to be broke, and the fault not the Man's neither; and I don't doubt but there are many married Maids now in our time, who are apt enough to blame their Husband's inability, and the Husband at the same time content to bear the imputation, when all the while the fault is on the Womans side, by the over-thickness of the *Hymen*, so that the Man cannot, as desir'd, penetrate her.

John Wierus in *Lib. de prof. daemon. cap.* 38. writes of a Maid at *Camburge*,[24] whose *Hymen* was so strong, as not to permit her *Monthly Terms* to flow out, which caus'd a great Tumour and distention of the Belly, with as great Torment, as if she had born the Pains of Child-birth, and so much resembled it, that Midwives were call'd to her, who upon examining her, did all agree and affirm that she was in Labour, tho' the Maid at the same time did aver she had never known Man: At length, upon her Pains continuing long, the aforesaid *Wierus* the Physician was called, who being informed of her Condition, and that she had made no Urine for three Weeks, and what was almost spent with great Watchings, loss of Appetite, and Loathing, examined the grieved Place, and found the Neck of the Womb stopped with a very thick Membrane, which hinder'd the passage from sending out the *Menstrual Blood*, the lodging of which was the cause of all the Torment; he presently therefore sent for a Surgeon, and order'd him to divide that Membrane, which being done, there issued forth as much black congealed and putrefied Blood as weighed eight Pounds, as the discharging of which in three days time, she recovered, and was free afterwards of all Disease and Pain.

But tho' some are of the Opinion there is no such *Hymen* in Virgins, yet others and the greater number assert there is.

Avicen writes, That in Virgins, there are *Tunicles* in the Neck of the Womb, composed of Veins and Ligaments very little, rising from each part of the Neck, which at the first time of Copulation are wont to be broken, and the Blood to run out.[25]

Almansor also says, That in Virgins, the passage of the Neck of the Womb is very wrinkled, or narrow and strait, which is broken at the first time of Copulating with a Man.[26] And the late ingenious Dr. *Drake* says, that in those few which he had an opportunity to examine, he did not remember he ever missed the *Hymen* in any, where he had just reason to depend upon finding it, if it were constant; and that the fairest view he ever had of it, was in a Maid who died at about thirty Years of Age.[27]

The *Carunculae Myrtiformes*, or *Myrtle-berry Caruncles*, so called from their resembling *Myrtle-berries*, lie close to the *Hymen*, there are four of them, the largest standing uppermost, just at the mouth of the passage of the Urine, which it shuts, after making Water; just against this at the bottom of the Sheath of the Womb there is another, and in each side one; but of these there is only one in Maids, and that is the first, the other three are not properly *Caruncles*, but little Knobs made of the angular Parts of the broken *Hymen*, roll'd into a heap by the wrinkling of the *Vagina*, and appears never but after having Copulated with a Man.

Thus having as much as is necessary describ'd the Parts of the Vagina; its Use from what has been said, may without difficulty be easily understood, all knowing, that know any thing, that it is to receive the Man's *Yard*, being Erected; to direct and convey the Man's *Seed* into the Womans *Womb*; to serve for a Pipe or Conduit for the *Menses* to flow through, not mentioning its being a Passage through which the Birth is protruded.

The *Pudendum Muliebre* or Privates of Women, are next to be consider'd, and that which offer themselves to view without any deduction are the *Fissura Magna* or great Chink, with its *Labia* or Lips, the *Mons Veneris*, and Hairs, which are called by the General Name of *Pudenda*, because when they are bared they bring *Pudor* or Shame upon a Woman. St. *Au[gu]stin* says the same, and that we can command all our other Parts, yet cannot oblige the *Privy Parts* to Obedience.[28]

The *Fissura Magna* or great Chink, is called by *Galen Cunnus*, which signified to Conceive; *Hippocrates* calls it *Natura*; it is also by others call'd *Vulva, Poreus, Concha*, and many other Names, according as Fancy has led People, and to please a lascivious Humour; some valuing themselves for their notable Faculties of imposing this and that Name on it, which are yet not worthy to be observed here.

The *Chink* reaches from the lower part of the *Os Pubis* to within an Inch of the *Fundament*, and is in ordinary siz'd Woman about six Inches in length, being by Nature made so large, the better to be extended in Childbearing. It is less and closer in Maids than in those that have had Children, but the length in all makes the *Perinæum* or distance between the lower end of the Chink and the Fundament not above an Inch long. The Chink has two Lips cover'd with Hair a little curled, and begins to grow there about the age fourteen, which Lips towards the *Pubes* grows thicker and more full or protuberant, and meeting upon the middle of the *Os Pubis* makes that bunching up or rising at the bottom of the Belly that is covered also with Hair, and is called *Mons Veneris* or the *Hill of Venus*, chiefly consisting of Fat, which is the reason of its bunching so up, and which is so convenient, by the appointment of Nature, as that it secures the Bones of the Pubes of the Man and Woman, which are placed underneath it, from hitting one against another, and the Hair of each part from grating one another in the Act of Copulation, which were it not for this Fat, would cause Pain instead of Pleasure.

There was a Lady who had the Lips of her *Matrix* so closely join'd, that her Husband could never have entrance; she had only a small Orifice in the middle, that afforded a passage to her Urine and the *Menstrual Blood*: but having recourse to Surgery, and the two Lips being artfully separated both above and below, she had several Children afterwards: And it was observ'd afterwards that her Husband in a Jocose Way, said, the Surgeon had cut too far, but at the same time owned his Wife was obliged to the Surgeon, because it very much facilitated her Delivery in Child-Birth. There was another young Woman that laboured under the same misfortune, but she chose rather to have her Marriage disannul'd, than to endure the Operation, besides the Shame that would attend it, and the Discourse that might be rais'd upon it deter'd her, for that a Lady's being viewed by the Judges Order at *Paris* by the most noted Physicians and Surgeons there, upon the Question and Contest about her Virginity, gave occasion for their Fans and Snuff-Boxes being Painted afterwards with undecent Postures.

When the Chink is opened by drawing aside the *Labia* or Lips, that which offer themselves next to our View are the *Nymphae* or *Clitoris*. The *Nymphae* or Nymphs, or as others *Alae* or Wings, are so called because they stand next to the passage of the Urine on each side it, and keep the Lips of the Privities and Hair from being wet as the Urine spouts out of the Bladder, being two fleshy soft productions beginning at the upper part of the Privities, where they make that wrinkled membranous Production which cloaths the Clitoris like a Fore-skin, and answers very like to the *Preputium* or Fore-skin of a Man's *Yard*, and are almost triangular, and which for their Shape and Colour, being soft and red, are compared to the Thrils that hang under a Cock's Throat, and are larger in grown Maids than in young, and grow larger upon the use of *Venery* and after the bearing of Children, for in the Act of Copulation they swell and extend themselves by the influx of the Animal Spirits and Arterial Blood, necessarily flowing thither upon the transport of that Pleasure.

I have read that in some Women the *Nymphae*, and also the *Labia*, are naturally so long, that they are not only troublesome, but hinder their Copulating, and that according to the report of *Leo Affricanus*,[29] it is what often happens to the *African* Maids; and are infirmities so common in the Southern Parts of the World, that there are Fellows who make it their business to walk up and down the Streets of Towns, bawling *Who wants to be cut?* and such indeed ought to be cut rather than suffered to hinder Procreation.

We have already spoken of the use of the *Nymphae* to defend the Urine from wetting the Lips, which they do, by peculiarly guiding and turning strait the Stream of the Womans Urine as it comes out of the Bladder, causing it to make that hissing Noise as is observ'd when evacuated, and which the shortness and width of the passage of Urine in Women, (which is much shorter and wider than that in Men, as the extraction of large Stones out of their Bladder, without cutting, testify) and their squatting and forcing posture when they make Urine, very much contributes to.

Betwixt the Nymphs, in the upper part of the *Pudendum* of Privities, is plac'd the *Clitoris*, which singifies lasciviously to grope the Privities, and is a fleshy Substance which jets out a little, called by some *Virga* or *Yard*, because in Shape, Situation, Erection, and Substance it is very like a Man's *Yard*, differing only in length and bigness, tho' in some Women it is as big as some Mens *Yards*, but generally is as big as one's Finger, of a long and round Body, lying under the Fat of the *Mons Veneris*, and puffs up in Venery, swelling and straiting the Orifice in the act, so as to embrace the Man's *Yard* more eagerly and closely, and with more notable Delight and Pleasure in the Act; but unless in the Act, it is seldom to be seen in most Women, unless when the Lips are drawn aside, tho' it is easily to be felt in all. In those called *Hermaphrodites* it is so long and big, as to be able to converse with Women in the manner of Men.[30] Dr. *Drake* tells us, that sometimes by extraordinary means it will be extended almost to the bigness of a Man's Yard, which at all times it resembles very exactly in shape, excepting that it is not perforated as that is, having no hole in it (tho' it really by the natural impression at the end, looks and feels as if there was a passage). The extraordinary size and propendance, says the aforesaid Doctor *Drake*, sometimes out of the Body in Infants, makes the Women mistake such Children for that sort of Monsters they call *Hermaphrodites*. Of this sort, says he, I had one brought to me upon another occasion, the *Clitoris* of which hung out of the Body so far at about three Years old, that it resembled very much a *Penis* or *Yard*, but it wanted the Perforation, and instead of that, just behind it, the Urine issued at a hole, which was nothing else but a corner of the *Rima*, the *Clitoris* filling all the rest of the Orifice; so that the Parents mistook it for a Boy, and as such Christned it, and as such esteemed it when it was brought to me; but the Neighbors who had notice of this appearance, called it an *Hermaphrodite*.

Platerus tells us he saw a *Clitoris* once in a Woman, as big and as long as the neck of a Goose.[31] Indeed the *Clitoris* in a Woman is very like a Man's *Yard*, its end is like the *Glans* or *Nut* of a Man's, and erects and falls as a Man's does, and as in Men the seat of the greatest Pleasure is in the *Glans* or *Nut*, so is this in Women, for therein is the rage and fury of Love, and there has Nature plac'd the peculiar seat of Pleasure and Lust, from whence 'tis call'd *Amoris Dulcedo* and *Aestrum Veneris*; for the Man's *Yard* rubbing in Copulation against the Womans *Clitoris*, causes those excessive Ticklings, delightful Itchings, and transporting Pleasures to both Sexes; and the more of that Serous Matter (before spoken of) the Woman sheds in the Act, the greater still is the Pleasure in both, for as the Man's *Yard*, and principally the *Nut* of it, fills with Spirits in the Actions of Love, so also does the Womans *Clitoris* at the same time, which conjunctly together, gives that charming Delight to those Parts, and the whole Animal Functions, which, as to relate is inexpressible, so in the Act sometimes it is almost unbearable, especially where both Parties meet with equal Desire and Freedom; for if we love Persons whose Inclinations are answerable to ours, and whole Parts are proportionable, our Flame is happy, and nothing but Pleasure, Delight, and Tenderness, is the consequence of our lawful Love; for the Enjoyments which attend the Actions for the continuance of our kind, are the highest gratifications of our Senses that can be.

But it has been often disputed which takes most Pleasure in the Act of Copulation, the Man or the Woman; some say one, and others the other, and that as the Man's *Seed* is the chief efficient and beginning of Action, Motion and Generation, yet that the Woman affords *Seed*, and effectually contributes in that point to the Procreation of the Child, as is evinced, say they, by strong Reasons; as first, were it not so, her *Seminal Vessels* and *Genital Testicles* had been given her to no purpose, which cannot but be allow'd to be of use, their Nature being as receptacles to treasure up, operate and afford Virtue to the *Seed*; and to back this, they urge, that if Women do not eject *Seed* when they Copulate, it is observed that they frequently fall into strange Diseases, such as Hysterick Indispositions, Womb Furies, and the like, as oftentimes young Widows and Virgins are known to do; and the Cure of those Diseases consists chiefly in frequent Copulations, by which is apparently by the effect, that they are never better pleas'd, or appear more brisk and jocund than when they are often satisfy'd that way, whence it is an inducement to believe they have more Pleasure and Titillation in the Act than the Men, (at leastwise for the sake of Health have frequently more occasion) for Nature is more delighted when Ejection is on both sides, and both Parties are better pleased; for the Enjoyment by ejection and reception is doubled, and the Act of Coition more desirable. Others will not have it that either the Man or the Woman enjoy most Pleasure in mutual Caresses, but that to both of them 'tis so excessive as to be diffi-cult to determine which exceeds, not but that it is allow'd, the Man's *Privy Parts* are more sensible than the Womans, because they are all Nervous, when the Womans are but partly Nervous and partly Fleshy, and so by consequence not altogether so sensible; besides, other reasons in *Anatomy* which conform the same, and which are too tedious here to have been taken notice of, not accounting for their way of Living, their firmer Minds and stronger Fancies, and also hotter Nature, sharper Blood, &c. which makes me believe that Women are not so sensibly, or altogether touched to the quick in the Act, as the Men are, unless in some *Virago's* or Women that have hot *Wombs*, of sanguine florrid Complexions, red Hair'd, merry Dispositions, &c. who are generally more Lustful that Weakly or some other sort of Women, and their Desires so restless and excessive, by giv-ing themselves up to the Pleasure, as not to be satisfy'd with many Men, even as if they had a Furor of Madness of the Womb, of which I shall speak particularly by and by, when I come to treat of the Diseases of the *Womb*; such Women, I say, there are, and some that I have heard of to confess they could scarcely ever be satisfy'd by all that their Husbands could do, which is the reason, I believe that those Physicians, who have probably heard the same, have asserted that Women take more Pleasure in the mutual Embrace than Men, even to a third part of the Enjoyment (therein condemning all for some, which is the wrong way of reckoning), but I cannot tell how to determine it any otherwise than that the Pleasure the Man takes is short and soon at an end, and sometimes the intermission long, but with the Woman it is almost endless, by reason that she can hold out beyond what one Man can afford her; nay, as soon as she has done with one, she read-ily, and with as great or greater Pleasure receives another, and so a third, and onwards, being almost always ready for the Embrace, and ever pleas'd with it, else why do many of them, even marry'd Women, that are wanton, not being satisfy'd with what their Husbands can do, procure to them-selves with their Fingers, or other more proper Instrument, a Pleasure that supplies the room of a Man's Embraces, for which reason the *Clitoris* in Women is call'd the *Contempt of Men*; and not only do marry'd Women that are Buxom use such means, but, as I have heard, is a practice very common among other Women of all Ages, viz. Widows, or such whose Husbands are absent, Maids, and even by Girls at Boarding-Schools, to their irrepairable Disgrace, that practice being almost as rife among them, as *Friction* among School-Boys, and of which, as I am credibly inform'd, several young Girls were not long since detected, in at a certain Boarding School in this Town.

In short, to both Sexes the pleasures of Love are quick and excessive, the thoughts of which, with an agreeable Object, strikes us perfectly Chill, which afterwards by the Spirits recoiling, makes us glow. 'Tis the same in both Sexes, and the Thoughts inexpressible; and if the Thoughts and Act were not extremely pleasing, a Man of Sence, or Woman of Wit, would never submit to the practice: But, as I said before, it is excessive; for we see the strictest Hermit, and the most precisely Grave and Religious, look pleasantly upon an agreeable Woman, smile at the talking of the Pleasures of Love, and are charm'd at the thoughts thereof, so that it favours not of Smut or Bawdry.

The *Clitoris* has two pair of Muscles, which serve to erect it, and straiten and narrow the Orifice of the Sheath, and has also Veins and Arteries, which are somewhat large. In some Eastern Countries the Clitoris in Women is so large, that for its deformity and filling up the passage, the better to facilitate, as they think, Copulation, they cut it quite out, or else hinder its growth by searing it, and is what they call Circumcising of Women: But of these things, and of *Hermaphrodites*, as also of the odd and ridiculous Customs and Manners of many Countries, concerning the ordering, using, and abusing of the *Genital Parts* of both Sexes, I have particularly, not with a little pains explicated in my sixth Edition of the *Venereal Disease*, from Page 352 to 384; to which I refer the Reader, that is willing to be satisfied in those matters, I thinking it unnecessary to make repetition of them here.[32]

I shall therefore, having given what description of the Woman's *Genitals* is necessary to serve the present purpose, begin and proceed in the discovery of the Infirmities and Diseases incident to their *Privy Parts*, with their Causes and Cure, and shall, by the way, give a Hint concerning *Generation* and *Conception*, and shew the Causes and Cure of Miscarriage in Women, which few that I know of, and none, in the like method, have undertaken so particularly and intelligibly to set forth.

At the Age of fourteen years, as hinted before, the Menstrual Blood in Virgins begins to break forth, at which time also, it being the years of *Puberty*, they begin, from a natural Instinct, to entertain Lust, and are capable of Conceiving, and feel something of a titillation to, or desire after the *Venereal* Pleasure, which in some is so vehement as not to be satisfied, till, by means of Provocation, and the opportunity of wanton Dalliance with Man, they forfeit their title to the Angelical Character; whereby young Girls who have too much liberty given them of being in Men's company, and especially about that age, are, for want of a discreet Conduct, by the design'd Wills and Temptations of Men, sooner overcome than at other times. Which is a caution worth the observation of such Parents who have young amorous Daughters, that they would not suffer them to be at Balls, Plays, or Interludes, without some faithful Attendant; and that they keep them not long from marrying, lest they should marry themselves; for as all young People, from a natural Instinct, desire marriage Embraces, it is a Duty incumbent on Parents, that have Children of a hot Temperaments, and sanguine Complexions, to provide in time such suitable Matches for them, as may make their lives comfortable, rather than to cross their Inclinations, by afterwards putting a restraint on their Affections; which has been found by experience, to hasten them to commit such follies as have brought as indelible Stain upon themselves and Families, by throwing themselves into the unchaste Arms of the next alluring Tempter that comes in their way; for when Virgins arrive to the years of *Puberty*, their Minds are naturally stirr'd up to *Venery*, and their Imaginations are fired with unusual Fancies, tho' in some much more than in others, and especially those who give up themselves to Pleasures, Pastimes, frequenting Mens Company, wanton Discourses, high Feeding, and the like, whereby the Humors are heated, and the Desire augmented, which even in some, sometimes is so insuperable, that if Enjoyment is deny'd, or they use not those means so customary among many Women, to pleasure themselves, it brings them into *Cachexia's*, ill habits of Body, Hysterick Fits, Greensickness, or other inconveniences, which by all the *posse* of the most fortuitous Medicines that Art can invent, will scarcely be remedied. To know the amorous Inclinations of young Virgins, mind their eager and earnest gazing at Men, affecting their Company and Conversation, &c. which sufficiently prompts them to desire Coition: As also the same may be observ'd in young brisk Widows, or those whose Husbands are gone abroad, who not being satisfied without the usual Conversation, oftentimes break the Bond of Modesty, and give themselves up to unlawful Embraces, or take other methods to allay the fury of their desire, as I before hinted; not that I at the same time encourage early Marriages, for they are inconvenient to most; and is marrying unseasonably, which often times exhaust the Vital Moisture of young People, and cause them to become so enfeebled, as that with the best of Medicines they will not be restored.

Inequality of Years in the Parties marry'd, is another great error; when a young Man to advance his Fortune in the World, marries a Woman old enough to be his Grandmother; between whom, instead of that love and delight which ought to be in marry'd People, nothing but bitter Quarrels, Strifes, Jealousies, and Discontents, are observ'd in their Conversations. The like may be said, tho' with something more excuse, when an old doting Fellow marries a young Virgin, in the prime of her Youth and Vigour, who whilst he vainly strives to please her, is hastening himself to the Grave; for that the more he endeavors, the more he is exhausted. For as in green raw Youth it is unfit and unseasonable to Marry, so to marry in old Age is altogether as preposterous; for as they that enter upon it too soon are presently exhausted, grow Consumptive, &c. so those that defer it till they are old, are alike liable to the same inconveniencies, besides forfeiting their gravity and conduct, losing that honour due to their years, and instead of being said to be fine old Men, they undergo the Title of *Old Fools*, and too often become young *Cuckolds*, especially if they meet with Wives that are Bucksom as well as Young, who have much Beauty, and little Chastity.

But when we speak of Ages most fit for to undertake a marry'd State, we must shut out, as uncapable, *Eunuchs*, and others of both Sexes, render'd unfit by accident, or that are born defective; neither is every Age, tho' never so well equipt, fit to tast the pleasures of a Matrimonial State. Young People are too feeble, and the Old too languishing; Infancy and Puerility are too ignorant as to the productive part, and old Age, tho' well acquainted with the manner, yet are destitute of the Matter which Nature requires for procreation.

But to come to the point; when the Man arrives to *Puberty*, that is, when the Voice changes, and grows more loud and rough, or harsh, which proceeds from the encrease of the natural Heat in the *Thorax:* When Hair grows on the *Privy Parts*, and Titillations, or amorous Motions are felt to stir there, which in some young Men is, as said in another place, about the sixteenth, in others about the seventeenth, and in some not till the eighteenth year of their Age; then, I say, a Man may be capable of caressing a Woman so as to get Children; he at that time being fired with the heat of Love's Passion. Then, I say, a Man is capable, if in a disposition, to get Children; but it is better that Loves Flames be suppressed till riper years; for it is better then for himself, and he is better capable of getting stronger and more firm and healthy Children, which time is about the twenty fifth year of his Age. We have read indeed of Boys that have got Children at seven or eight years of Age, and of Girls of ten or twelve that have had Children, from their robust and vigorous Nature; but I cannot believe it; for the weakness of Parts, and dryness of Temperament, besides other occurrences in those parts, cannot possibly afford Matter for Generation: And in Women-kind the indubitable Sign of their being ripe for a Man, and in a capacity for bearing Children, is when the *Menstrua* flow, and not before, and which seldom or never appear to that purpose, till the thirteenth, fourteenth, and, in some, sixteenth Year of their Age, as said before; and the best time for Women to marry, in order to have strong healthy vigorous Children, is about the eighteenth or nineteenth Year, not but some have born

Figure 3.8   Plate from John Browne, *Myographia Nova, Or a Graphical Description of all the Muscles in the Humane Body* (1698).

Children at the fifteenth year of their Age, and young Men got them at the same, but then the Off-spring has been either weakly or infirm, or the Birth never brought to perfection, especially when the Male has polluted himself by *Friction*, and thereby weakened his *Seminal Vessels*, and the Woman used artifice to titillate, either with her Fingers or other Instrument in use among them; but when the Man is in his twentyfifth Year, and the Woman in her twentieth, and both retain their Virginity till they Copulate, and those People born of healthy sound Parents, not tainted with any ill Stamen, and each of them well in Health, of good Constitutions, and full of Love and Vigour, there will proceed the best, most vegete, lovely, healthy and strong Posterity.[33] Concerning which I could greatly enlarge, but time and designed Brevity will not allow.

Marriage that is, with suitable Matches, is commendable, establish'd so by the Laws of God and Man, no station more happy or more honourable, where there is Love and Agreeableness; it was held in great esteem from the beginning of the World, and that among all sorts of People and Sects; the *Romans* held Marriage in great esteem, and so did and do the *Jews*; the *Lacedemonians* when they instituted Festivals, as they usually did, would not admit of any single Men among them; and as the fault in those days were wholly on their side, if they were not marry'd, and any of them came to their Festivals, they were, as soon as discover'd, order'd to be whipt by Women, as unworthy Members of the Republick, and none but marry'd Men suffer'd to bear any Office. So that marry'd Men throughout the World (as an encouragement to Matrimony) had highly the preference and advantages of those that lived single.

As Marriage therefore is honorable, so it should by every Couple be made pleasant to each, that is, the Man should please his Wife, and the Woman her Husband; in the conjugal Affair there should be a reciprocal Harmony and Friendship, which they each to other are bound in Duty to observe: The Husband is to render to his Wife what she expects, that is, due Benevolence, and the Wife to her Husband what he desires; not that a Man should caress oftner than he is capable; for the Woman to desire that, is an injury to his Body; but when he is in capacity, and nothing on the Womans side to hinder, there it is his Duty to perform, if for no other reason than to please his Wife, and ought not to deny her: On the other side, a Man is not to desire his Wife but when she is in condition, 'tis his Duty at some times, tho' never so much inclined, to forbear her, as when the *Terms* flow, as shall be by and by further observ'd, and when she is near her Time, for then the Woman has no manner of inclination; when the *Terms* flow it cannot be done but imprudently, and, as it may happen, injuriously; and when near Delivery, or at some times when they are big, endangers their coming before their time, or causes an ill Disposition of the Child in the Womb, by the necessary posture and shaking a Woman undergoes in the Act.

As the *Menses* in Virgins begin commonly to flow at fourteen, so in most Women they generally continue to flow to forty four, at which time, for the most part, they cease Child-bearing, unless they be such that are very healthful, strong of Body, and have always liv'd temperately, and some such have been known to bear Children at fifty five Years, but this very rarely happens, tho' the *Courses* in some flow till then, which however is more from an Indisposition of Body, than any natural Cause, and commonly indicates a dangerous State of Health. But if Men are inclin'd to Marry, and desirous to have Children, they must mind to wed with such as are within the aforesaid Age, or else blame themselves if they meet with a disappointment, tho it has been known, that old Men that have liv'd their time with temperance, and been free from Diseases, have, by marrying with young brisk Women, had Children, even tho' they have been seventy years of Age, and some that have been extraordinary lusty, have, as we have read, had Children at fourscore; but we may say of such, as in another Case, *Rara avis in Terris.*[34]

Men and Women cease to engender differently, according to their Strength and Constitutions, those that are naturally very Amorous and Lascivious, soonest leave off, their natural heat being wasted when they come to years sooner, by the too profuse use of the Sports of Love when young. Some Men, as said before, are capable of procreating at seventy, others not at fifty five, and few after sixty, tho' some Sparks of Lust haunts the old Man's Head, and his Inclination is often good, tho' the Power be too weak to put that Will in act; yet we have heard of some that have got Children at seventy, eighty, nay a hundred, but it is looked upon as Prodigy.

Women cease Teeming, tho' they cease not to engender at forty five or fifty, tho' some that I know have conceived at fifty two; but when the *Menstrua* cease flowing, 'tis a certain sign they will Teem no more, there being wanting what is necessary to form and nourish the Birth in the *Womb*. But when the man is very vigorous, tho' old, and the Woman has her *Courses*, tho' in years too, there it is possible Conception may ensue, because so long as the *Menstral Flux* remains, the prolifical Faculty is preserv'd; yet *Pliny* says, "That *Cornelius* (who was of the House of the *Scipio's*) being in the sixty second Year of her Age, and her *Courses* long before left her, bore *Volusius Saturnius*, who was Consul."[35] And *Valescus de Tarenta* also affirmeth, "That the same Woman that bore a Child in the 62d year of her Age, having had one also before, in the sixtieth and sixty first Year,"[36] therefore it is to be suppos'd, that by reason of the variety of the Air, Region,

Diet and Temperament, the *Menstural Flux* and Procreative Faculty in Women ceaseth, in some sooner, in others later, which variety also taketh place in Men; for in them, altho' the *Seed* be *Genitable* for the most part in the fourteenth Year, yet it is not Prolifick or Fruitful till about the eighteenth, some say the twentieth: And whereas most Men beget Children until they are sixty Years Old, and many to the Age of seventy, yet there are some known to have begot Children in the 80th Year of their Age. *Pliny* recites, that King *Masinissa* begot a Son when he was eighty six Years Old; and also that *Cato* the Censor begot a Child after he was Fourscore. Indeed it is no great wonder to hear of Old Men having Children, when they have a Young Wife to work upon, but to hear of Women of sixty, or upwards to bear Children, is something strange, and is almost as incredulous as the Story of *Averoes* of a Womans Conceiving in a *Bath*,[37] by attracting the Sperm or Seminal Effluxion of a Man admitted to Bath in the same Water; which is a new and unseconded way to Fornicate at a distance, when the Rules of Physick assure us there is no Generation without a joint Immission or Corporal and carnal Contaction, and joint Emission also, nor that virtually unless the Parties be pregnant; for the want of that is an effectual Impediment, and utterly prevents the Success of a Conception, and therefore how a Woman of threescore or more, whose Courses have long before left her, her Intellects decay'd, and Parts dry'd almost up, should Conceive, is a Mystery: I know there are some who believe its possibility, and with the same Parity of Reason may believe what Sir *Thomas Brown* in his *Vulgar Errors* explodes,[38] *viz.* That Generations by the Devil are probable, (which indeed a certain Wench with Child, would have had it believ'd, and reported it as Fact, for that, as she said, she had never lain with Man) or else, as they argue, how came the Daughters of *Lot* with Child? who were only as they alledge, impregnated by their sleeping Father, or Conceived by Seminal Pollution received at a distance from him; and that 'tis possible for the Devil by contriv'd delusions of Spirits, to steal the Seminal Emissions of Men, and transmit them into their Votaries in Coition, whence ensues Conceptions; which is all Imposter, and such Jargon that none but deluded Souls will Believe or give Credit to, tho' is what many Wantons abroad would be glad the World was so credulous as to hearken to, for the easier and better saving their Credit. 'Tis said that our magnify'd *Merlin* was thus begotten by the Devil, which is no other than a groundless Report; but from thence it is, they say, his Prophetick Spirit had its rise, and that as he was begot by the Devil, he had the Faculties of his Father the Devil, to foresee and foretel Events and strange Matters of Persons and Things to come.

There are others that say 'tis not impossible for Women to Conceive

A Secundarum pars interior membranofa.
B Secundarum pars exterior carnofa, &
   infinitis venarum ofculis referta.
D Meatus ab vmbilico fœtus ad collum &
   axillas deuolutus.

Figure 3.9   Plate from Charles Estienne, *De dissectione partium corporis humani* (1545).

without gross Immissions, for that the Seminal Spirits and Vaporous Irradiations, containing the active Principle of the *Seed* will do it, and for Instance, they tell us, that imperforate Persons, and such under Puberty or fourteen Years of Age, have Conceiv'd, without any immission at all. As also, say they, may be conjectured in the Coition of some Insects, wherein the Female makes intrusion into the Male; and from the continued Ovation in Hens, from one single Tread of a Cock, and little stock laid up near the vent sufficient for durable Prolification: And altho' also in human Generation, the gross and Corpulent Seminal Body may return again, and which we most times know does, yet nevertheless Conception is had by what is carried (*viz.* the Spirit of the *Seed*) with it: Yet that little Portion that remains, we find is not always sufficient, nor will it but here and there hold good, that Conception is had without Bodily Immission. But I shall enlarge no further on these matters now.

Women are sooner Barren than Men, because their natural Heat, which is the cause of Generation, is more predominant in them than in Men, and the more because they are moister, as their *Monthly Purgations* and the softness of their Bodies demonstrate, which native Heat concocts their Humours into proper Aliment, which if they wanted, they would grow Fat.

Women seldom have Children after forty five, but Men Procreate longer, as aforesaid, for we read that in *Campania*, where the Air is clear and temperate, Men of 80 Years of Age, marry young Virgins and have had Children by them, which shews that Age in Men hinders not Procreation, unless they exhaust their Strength in their Youth by too much Masturbation or Friction with the Hand, which custom too frequently practis'd, so debilitates the Spermatick Vessels and Parts adjacent, that Inclinations to *Venery* are lost, and the *Yard* shrivel'd up, of which I have already spoken sufficiently in my Sixth Edition of the *Venereal Disease* aforementioned, and need not stand here to repeat.

It was the Opinion of that profound Philosopher *Hippocrates*,[39] that Youths at the Age of 16 or 17, having much Vital Strength, are capable of getting Children, and also that the force and heat of Procreating Matter constantly increases till 45, 50, and 55, and then begins to flag, the *Seed* by degrees becoming Unfruitful, because the natural Spirits being extinguish'd, the Humours are dry'd up; but this, as observ'd before, falls otherwise to some, for that we read of a Man in *Sweedland* who was married at an hundred Years old, to a Bride of thirty, and had many Children by her, but he was such a hale, lusty constitution'd Man, and of so fresh a Countenance, that those who knew him not, took him to be no more than about fifty Years of Age.

As for the time for Man and Wife to Copulate, in order to Generate, Physicians speak differently, for that Custom is a second Nature, and all People may safely Caress when their Inclinations are strongest, only that they observe to be not too furious, or use it too frequently, especially in hot weather; Men embrace most that have been most accustomed to it, and so does Women, that is, they enjoy the Pleasures of Matrimony most, because the passages of Generation are more open, more large and big, than those who never Copulated at all, or that never had any other Idea of the thing than Reading or Dreaming of the Pleasures of Love; Men and Women that are very Lustful, and yet retain their *Seed*, are subject to many Disorders, which we see particularly in some vigorous strong Green-sickness Girls, who have not an opportunity of expressing their Desires otherwise than by their rouling Eyes, Looks and Gestures; but those that have often tasted of the Pleasures of Love, and for many Reasons *perforce* retain their *Seed*, there it does them much less Injury, the Parts being open and capacious to receive it, that the retention is not so hurtful.

Some Men and Women embrace with more eagerness at one time, others at other times; some Men cannot Caress till a Glass of Wine is in their Heads, and some Women with no great Pleasure, till the time just before and just after the flowing of their *Courses*, and then dalliance to heighten the Thoughts and quicken and enliven the Spirits, renders both so very Amorous, that the Act is done with greater Pleasure; and this either Day or Night is to purpose, tho' Men generally at Nights, and Women generally in the Mornings seem most inclinable. Upon a full Stomach 'tis absolutely an Injury for Men and Women to Caress, for nothing spoils our Stomachs and weakens Digestion more than ardent Love; some Physicians say, that to Caress in the Day-time, is worse than in the Night, but, as said before, when both are well inclin'd, whether Day or Night, then is the best Season for both Sexes to Caress. As to the frequency of Caressing, that is according to Constitution, some are capable of lying with several Women several times in the space of a Night, others cannot embrace above one, and her but one time. I have been told by some that they have Caress'd several Women for several nights successively, and given them entire Satisfaction; but such *Virago's*, if such there be, (for it is not enough to be wanton with Women, but to be able to shew one's Manhood to please them) must, in the end, find it to enervate and wast their Strength and Spirits, so as to render their *Seed* Infertile. I know Fancy carries a Man far, and that's the reason that a Beautiful Woman, or one that he likes, strikes a Man to the quick, and if a Man can exceed in the Amorous Embrace, 'tis certainly most with a handsome Woman, the Idea let in by the Eyes being fixt in the Head with which the Fancy is touch'd, that immediately runs to the *Privy*

Nolim exiſtimes ma
tricem hoc loco ſuum ſi-
tum ſeruare: ſed aliquā-
tulum in latus conuer-
ſam fuiſſe, ad vaſorum
quæ ad ipſam pertinent
commodiorem explica-
ionem.

Figure 3.10 Plate from Charles Estienne, *De dissectione partium corporis humani*
(1545).

Parts, and puts them into motion, for 'tis Beauty we admire in Women; that is the powerful Sting that Tickles, Excites and Charms us to the Desires and Delights of Love. What Priviledges over Men, have handsome Women? Beauty strikes an awe into the most barbarous Breast, Charms the Surliest and most Morose Tempers, there is no resisting a Beautiful Woman in a lawful way; she has our Inclinations, Assistances, and Performances at all times, manages us as she pleases, draws Men of all Ranks to admire her, and even takes us Captive against our Wills.

A Man that has a Beautiful Wife and can resist her Charms, where every Faculty is agreeable, cannot properly be said any more to be a Man, yet how frequently do we see such Men leave their so agreeable Wives, and take up with any nasty Drab, the thoughts only of which is a sufficient Surfeit. Every thing about us is immediately put into motion at the sight of a pretty Woman, and if her Conversation and Humour be agreeable to her Appearance, that motion, if not prudently resisted, will be put into Action, for Love is nothing else but a desire of Beauty; Ugliness to the contrary is the reverse of that, which at its appearance, becalms our Tempers, checks our Raptures, flattens our Desires, and at once proves to us an Antidote against Lechery, as was a great Masculine Woman I once saw at *Woodstock*-Fair in *Oxfordshire*, who had a beard like a Man, Ugly and Ungainly, so as to draw the Eyes of all People of both Sexes to look upon her with Detestation and Abhorrance: But presently again at the sight of a fine beautiful Woman, just after the sight of so deform'd a Piece, we are made to feel Fire that inflames us to a desire of Copulation, when at the appearance of an Unhandsome, Ugly, or Deform'd One, as said before, we as soon feel Ice in our Breasts, which freezes our Passions and locks up our Desires; therefore as a pretty or beautiful Woman is far more Desireable, so the Caressing such a One must needs be more delightful; and doubtless, if a Man at any time can exceed the bounds of Nature, 'tis with such a One, which is able to attract Love, when no force besides will do it; Love, that is, Beauty, being as strong as Death, and by which we are drawn as with Chains of Iron. But I shall proceed now to the Infirmities and Diseases of Women, hindering Copulation and Procreation, and shall, first, lay down those attending Virgins, which Marriage without the help of Surgery, will not Cure.

And such Infirmities are preternatural, as when the *Pudenda Virginum* or Vulva is quite clos'd with a Membrane, or else but a very little Perforation left, and is incident either from the Birth, or afterwards joined together upon an ill affected Ulcer in those Parts. Sometimes a preternatural *Caruncle* shuts the *Os Vulvae*, and in others a Membranous Coalition of the four *Carneous Monticuli*, whereby the fore-parts of the *Vulva* are shut up, sometimes very close, as may easily be perceived by the Eye, or by the Finger. In those Cases Incision with a Knife must be made, to divide the Membrane, using afterwards a *Speculum Matricus*, with a small Pipe perforated through its whole length to help the Cicatrizing, which must be done the common way, with drying Unguents or Lotions, or both; in order for Operation, the Patient must be laid on her Back, and her Knees rais'd and opened as wide as she can, and then Incision must be made with a crooked Incision-knife, beginning at the top, and then a leaden Pipe is to be put into the Orifice. Sometimes the passage is open, but the *Vagina* or Neck of the *Womb* is clos'd, and that wholly or in part only, and that either Naturally, or through an Ulcer, or by an Excrescence, and may happen both to Maids and Women, in which latter, hard Labour may occasion, by tearing and inflaming the Parts, so as to become raw and adhere together: The *French Pox* sometimes causes the like Disasters to Women, as I have observ'd fully in my Sixth Edition of the *Venereal Disease*; those Cases, I say, are known by the Sight and Feeling of a skilful Surgeon, but best known and regretted by the Husband, who upon Trial, finds he is not capable of entring his Wife's Body, for that upon endeavouring, she complains of prodigious Pain, and is not able to suffer him, but upon forcing, causes her to cry out, as bad as if stuck with a Sword. In some again the inward Orifice of the *Womb* is so clos'd, as not to admit of a small Probe, caused through cold Humours gathered there, or the Man's *Seed*, or her *Menses* long retained, whereby when they are heap'd upon it, causes such a Swelling as to close the Mouth thereof; and in some, has such an effect, as to harden the Mouth of the *Womb*, and cause great Pain both in the sides of the *Womb* and *Belly*, hardly able to be endured, and at length throws out a thin stinking black Matter, which if not timely remedied, both by proper Medicaments and Surgery, after the manner before directed, proves to be Incurable.

If it be an Excrescense that stops the passage, Medicines must be apply'd that are drying and discuffing, to hinder the increase of the Flesh, and after that, Medicines must be us'd to lessen it, or eat it away, which are *Escarotick*. The Following one is good.

> *Take Myrrh, Aloes, and Frakincense, of each a Dram Birthwort Root, Pomgranate Flowers, and Catechu, of each two Scruples, Burnt Allom two Drams, make all into a Powder, and with as much Egyptian Oyntment as is sufficient; make it into a Liniment, with which smear the superfluous Flesh twice or thrice a day with the Fingers, or put up a Pessary smear'd with it, fastning it with Strings to the Waste or Thighs.*

But if this does not eat it away in some time, or it should grow much painful, it must be extirpated, or cut off with such an Instrument as we extirpate a *Polypus* out of the Nose.

When any of these accidents happen to Virgins, they seldom perceive them till they come to be married, and the pain, instead of pleasure, puts both the Wife and the Husband upon considering the Cause, which if they do not presently find out, and get remedied, proves vexatious, and stirs up Feuds, Discontents and Animosities between them; for the Female Sex like not to be call'd Marry'd Maids, any more than the Men love to be accounted Incapable, which many think themselves to be, when all the while it is their Wives fault.

It is known, or should be known to all Physicians, that the *Venereal* Appetite, or Lust in Women, is nothing more than a tender sense and tickling of the extended *Clitoris*, as before observ'd, caus'd, by the influence of Seminal Matter abounding in the two glandulous Prominencies, and other glandules of the *Vagina*, and is what, according to nature, should be moderate; however it sometimes happens that it exceeds what it naturally ought, and again sometimes falls out to prove very deficient.

The languishing of the *Venereal* Appetite in Women, is frequently occasion'd by the smallness or want of *Genital Liquor*, and its want of Spirits; proceeding sometimes from other Diseases, as the *Whites, Scurvy*, or the like; which how to discover, is the art or main thing, and is what ought to be understood, because it may happen from a default in the Structure or confirmation of the *Privy Parts*, and if so it admits of no Cure; but if not from a natural Cause, but from some Disease, it probably may be cured, or at leastwise to be of no danger, save the rendring the Woman Barren, which however may be remedied, if proper Medicines be timely apply'd; and that which most supplies *Genital Liquor*, is juicy nourishing Food, and volatile Aromatick Medicines, such as Musk, Civet, Ambergrise, or the use of those Medicines prescrib'd already for Deficiencies in Men; or the Woman may foment her *Privy Parts* with the Infusion of Ants with the Nest, and imbrocate the *Groins* and *Privities* with Oil of Ants, Pismires, or *Cantharides*, or with Aromatick Oils, or Apoplestick Balsam, prepar'd with Civet, Musk, &c.

Sometimes the *Venereal Appetite* in Women is deprav'd, and Copulation and Conception hindred, when the *Seminal Humour* contain'd in the glandulous Substance of the *Vagina*, is either too long retain'd, or otherwise kept in and not emitted by some fault in the *Vagina*, where it becomes sharp, saltish, or somewhat acid, exciting sometimes in the places through which it passes, such an itching, as that they can scarcely forbear scratching before People, and even oftentimes to that degree as to make the

Blood come. This violent Itching frequently disturbs Sleep, and is some-times accompany'd with a desire of Copulation. To remedy this, is with mild Laxatives and Sudorisicks inwardly, and to use outward Applications to the part, to allay the acrimony of the Humours. Inwardly the follow-ing is good.

> Take Mercurius Dulcis fifteen Grains, Trouches Alhandal half a Scruple, Syrup of Buckthorn as much as is sufficient to make into a mass, which form into four Pills, to take in a Morning, every other or third day; and at other times to drink a Decoction of Elder, Fumitory, Sorrel, Succory, Scabious, Roots of Bryony, Polypody, black Hellebore, and the like.

And to use either of the following outwardly.

> Take Ointment call'd Nutritum an Ounce, Oyntment of Tutty and To-bacco of each two Drams, mix and anoint the Lips of the Privities; but if the acid Humours retain'd there should corrode the Lips of the Privities, and occasion Wheals, Pushes, Scabs, Warts, &c. whether with itching or not, call'd Epinictides, procur'd from foul Em-braces, then a Preparation of Mercury ought to be added, or else use the following Lotion.

> Take Lime-water a Pound, Mercurius dulces a Dram, mix and inject into the Vagina, and also wash the Lips and other parts affected, twice, thrice, or four times in a day; which will cure, or else the Woman will be as unfit for Copulation, as Procreation or Conception.

But if the Venereal Appetite is superabundant, and exhalted to the pitch of a Delirium, it is then call'd Furor Uterinus, or Fury or Rage of the Womb, so as that the Party is not to be satisfied without Venery, and is a disorder incident as well to Virgins as marry'd Women and Widows, they discover-ing their malady by their talking obscenely, and being peevish and fretful, if thwarted in it, and do ramble through the Streets from place to place, and sollicit to Venery whomever they meet with, and if they receive a de-nial, it is with the highest Indignation: Sometimes they wantonly uncover themselves before Men, and let all their discourse favor of Bawdry and Smut; such are the dismal Effects of that Disease, which if not cured, ter-minate into Madness: In time 'tis cured without any great difficulty, espe-cially if strong Emeticks be exhibited, and a spare Diet enjoyn'd, when also Specificks that extinguish the Genital Liquor, such as Agnus Castus Seeds, Roots of Water Lillies, Lettice, Rue, Purslain, Seeds of Hemlock, Hemp, and Pop-pies, made either into an Emulsion or Decoction, either of which, or this that follows, will abate the Effervescence of the Blood, and by consequence the Turgescence of the *Seminal Liquor*, especially if Bleeding be frequently us'd.

> *Take the four greater Cold Seeds of each a Dram, Hemp Seeds two*
> *Ounces, Water-Lilly Seeds, and Agnus Castus Seeds, of each two Drams,*
> *Seeds of Hemlock a Dram, with a Quart of Purstane Water, make an*
> *Emulsion according to art, adding when strain'd, juice of Lemons and*
> *Pomgranats, of each two Ounces, Sugar of Lead ten Grains, liquid Lau-*
> *danum sixty Drops, Syrup of Citrons and Poppies, of each an Ounce,*
> *mix all together, to drink four or five Spoonfuls twice or thrice in a day.*

And when the Case is inveterate, we use also outwardly to the *Womb*, Cataplasms, Baths, and Formentations of Man-drake, Night-shade, Hemlock, Poppy, Rue, Purslane, and the like, but the quickest, certainest, and most pleasant Remedy, says *Parry*, is by tickling the Neck of the *Womb* with the Fingers, after fomenting the parts to warm them, anointing the Fingers at the same time with Ambergriese, Civet, and Musk, whence the Womans Matter and sharp Vapours will flow out, by the force the Woman makes upon the pleasure of Tickling, which is also almost as delightful as her Copulating with a Man.[40]

The *Green-sicknesss*, or *White Fever* in Virgins, frequently, if of long duration, so as to disorder the whole Body, causes Barrenness, and takes off the edge of the *Venereal* Desire, for several notable alterations in Women happen at the first arrival of their *Seminal Liquor*, and in case it be too long retain'd, and consequently corrupted and alter'd, it puts the whole mass of Blood, Juices and Spirits into a ferment, and disorder; whereupon an evil Disposition of the whole Body, with paleness of Skin, which looks somewhat livid and ugly, attended with a bluish Circle under the Eyes, anxiety, and sadness, &c. without any manifest cause, are introduc'd; whereby all *Venereal Inclinations* are at once quasht, there being in such no desire, and when they marry in this condition, which is vulgarly said to cure all, it oftentimes renders such Persons worse, and far from conceiving or bearing Children; for in such Cases I have known incurable Barrennesses to happen. But in some again Copulation cures, such as are sanguine, full of Juice, having a burning and itching in their *Gentials*, with the imagination of *Venery*, the *Seminal Matter*, which is in great abundance, distending the *Testicles*, and stirs up a natural Titillation in their *Genital Parts*, so as scarcely to forbear imposing upon their wonted modesty.

It has been observ'd, that the Green-sickness happens as soon to brisk forward Maids, as to those that are naturally dull and spiritless, whereby they have all of a sudden, become pensive, sad, and anxious, and it not only invades Virgins, but Widows and Women retired from Men, who while their Husbands were with them, were free from the Disease, and upon the disuse of *Venery*, have fallen into this condition.

The cure of this Indisposition depends upon the correcting the fault of the *Genital Liquor*, and removing the vitious *Crasis* of the Blood, which will remedy and remove the incident Symptoms, whereby Inclinations to *Venery* will be promoted, and Procreation effected; and this must be done by volatile altering Medicines, that have a peculiar virtue of fortifying the Blood and Spirits, and making active the unactive Humours, such as volatile Salt of Amber, *Armoniack*, Myrrh, Castor, and the like; or this that follows is good.

> *Take Steel prepar'd with Sulphur two Drams, Salt of Amber and Armo-niack, of each a Dram, Essence of Myrrh half an Ounce, Powder of Cas-tor a Dram, Mace, Nutmegs, Pepper, Zedoary Roots, of each a Scruple, Camphir half a Scruple (which, by the way, tho' some say is cold, and so extinguishes Seed, is a great mistake; for it is naturally hot, volatile and penetrating, and increases Seed). Conserve of Baum and Citron, of each six Drams, with Syrup of Coral as much as is sufficient to make it into an Electuary, of which to take the quantity of a Nutmeg, three times a day, drinking after it a Glass of rich Wine.*

All disorders of the *Menstrual Flux*, which are Diseases peculiarly in-cident to Womankind, frequently obstruct Procreation, if not Copulation; for it being a monthly Evacuation of Blood by their secret Parts, caus'd by an extraordinary Fermentation and Rarefaction of the mass of Blood, and a peculiar fermentative Power of the *Glands* of the *Womb*, which being in-capable to be contain'd within its ordinary Bounds, breaks forth at the Ar-teries of the *Vagina*, as we have particularly observ'd, and flows for three or four days, at which time the Fermentation ceasing, the quantity grows less and less, and so goes off till the next period, which is duly once a month, in some a few days sooner, and in others so much later, excepting when Women are with Child, or when they give Suck. Now this monthly Evac-uation of the *Courses*, is said to be disorder'd when the *Flux* is either defi-cient, or too plentiful, or deprav'd.

The deficiency of the monthly *Terms*, is call'd, tho' improperly, a *Sup-pression of the Terms*, and is occasion'd either by a default of the *Blood*, or of the *Womb* and Vessels thro' which it flows; if it be by the former, that is de-fault of the Blood, it is from its acidity, being gross, tough, and fix'd, pro-ceeding from the disorder of the Stomach, whereby it becomes unfit for a due fermentative Expansion. Sometimes the Vessels of the *Vagina* or Neck of the *Womb*, are obstructed by a viscid Phlegm; and sometimes the side of the *Vagina* are exulcerated, or otherwise hurt, so as to grow together, and cause a deficiency of the wonted Flux. Cold sometimes is the cause whereby the Blood is coagulated, and Food difficultly digested, also the too frequent use of Acids and other things, thicken the Blood, and cramp its Fermentation. If the deficiency of the *Terms* is from the *Womb*, and its obstructed Vessels, the Symptoms will shew it, but the greatest difficulty is to distinguish this preternatural State from the natural Suppression of the *Terms* by Impregnation, they being accompanied with almost the same Symptoms; yet the Patients growing still worse and worse, with an universal Paleness, decay of Appetite, continu'd Pains in the Head, difficulty of Breathing, unusual Beatings of the Arteries, and the like, and this continuing beyond the third Month, we may conclude that the Suppression is preternatural.

This Distemper is cur'd the more easily, or the more difficultly, as it is of later or longer standing, and, if too long neglected, brings on divers other Diseases, such as Jaundice, Dropsies, Asthma's, various Ulcers of the Parts (as we shall observe by and by) disorders of the Stomach, Melancholy, &c. and at length Death it self. Therefore the Cure ought to be set upon in time, and is to be done by rectifying the *Chylification* of the *Ventricle*, amending the Crudity of the Blood, and removing that viscidity of the Humours which obstruct the Vessels of the *Womb*.

To accomplish this, universal Remedies which evacuate upwards and downwards, must be given, after which Bleeding in the *Saphena* will come in, and after that Digestives must be premis'd; for the first, *Antimony* or *Asarabacca*, is very proper, being indeed of excellent virtue, and therefore needful to be repeated; or she may purge with *Coloquintida* and black *Hellebor*, or with this that follows.

> *Take of Pil. Hiera with Agarick, fifteen Grains, Calomelanos the same weight, Extract of black Hellebor half a Scruple, Droches of Alhandal four Grains, with syrup of Mugwort, make into six Pills, take three at Night and three the following Morning, repeating them every fourth or fifth day; and in the intermitting days let this that follows be given.*

> *Take of Arcanum Duplicatum of Mynsicht three Drams, opening Crocus of Steel half an Ounce, Salt of Wormwood a Dram; mix them together, and divide them into twelve Papers, one of which to be taken Night and Morning in a Glass of good White-Wine.*

But if the Case be very stubborn, *Volaile Aromaticks*, with *Gum. Ammoniacum* must be added, not forgetting the use of *Baths, Fumigations, Fomentations, Pessaries*, and the like, nay even some Cases have been so inveterate, as that for the better of forcing and opening those obstructed Passages, we have been forc'd to have recourse to *Cantharides*, both inwardly and outwardly apply'd; for such a Distemper, unless in time remov'd, utterly spoils Procreation, and much impedes Copulation.

★　★　★　★　★　★　★　★　★　★　★　★　★　★

For Man and Wife to use Coition, in order to get Children, when either of them are not in Health, but have some Sickness or Disorder on them, be what it will, is an Error, and a very great one; for by that means if the Woman happens to Conceive, it turns to the disadvantage of the Child, who is born, either with abundance of ill Humours inherent, or proves but indifferently well stockt with Wit, or is afflicted with some languishing Disease, which being rivetted into the Stamen or natural Habit of the Child, is not to be Cur'd by all the the Art that can be us'd; so that if it lives, it becomes a sickly infirm Child, and perhaps miserable to it self for ever, as well as troublesome to its Parents and all about it; tho' that fam'd Surgeon in his time, *Ambrose Parry*,[41] and others also say, that Sickly or Diseased Parents do sometimes get sound and healthy Children, and gives the reason thereof.

All sorts of Sadness, Trouble and Sorrow, are direct Enemies to the Delights of *Venus*, and ought especially to be avoided; and therefore when a married Couple are to use Coition, in order for Conception, all that should be first banish'd and forgot, for if a Woman Conceives when her Spirits are afflicted, it will have a very ill effect upon the Child that shall then be begot, even such as many times is never after to be remedied: Therefore it is advis'd that they lay aside all Passion, Vexation, anxious Thoughts and Trouble, before they begin to make use of those means, that from an inherent Instinct, Nature has ordain'd to that purpose; and it would be necessary also that they cherish their Bodies with some generous Restoratives, and get their Imaginations Charm'd with sweet and melodious Airs, that their Spirits might be rais'd to the highest pitch of Inamour, that so by their being rendred Brisk, Airy, and Vigorous, Conception may ensue, not but at the same time all excess is to be avoided, for that instead of raising, will allay and flatten the briskness of the Spirits, and render them dull and languid, whereupon Conception will be rather hindred, than furthered.

Hesiod advises all married People not to use Copulation when they return from Burials,[42] but when they come from Feasts and Plays, lest that their sad, heavy, and pensive Cogitations, should be so transfus'd, and engrafted into the Issue or Child that may be begotten; for the natural Habit or Temper of the Parents, like Diseases, are transfer'd to the Child, in every respect, as they were in at the begetting thereof, and proves an Hereditary

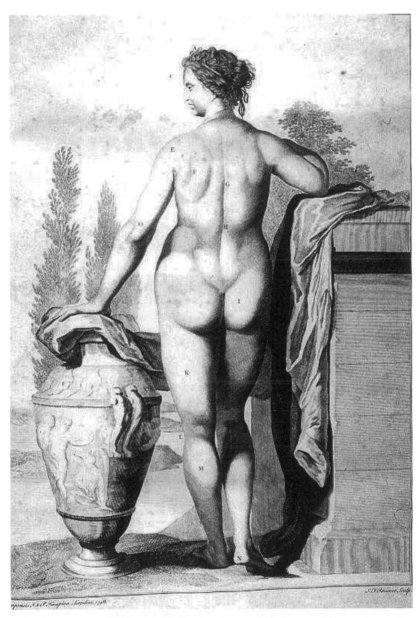

Figure 3.11 Copperplate illustration from Bernhard Albinus, *Tables of the Skeleton and Muscles of the Human Body* (1749).

Title of Good or Ill, as they themselves were in at the time of that Conception. And we sometimes see this much more remarkable, when Parents that are Crook'd-back'd, get Crook'd-back'd Children; those that are Lame, Lame Children; those that are Leprous, Leprous; those that have the Stone, the Stone; those that have the Phtisick, the Phtisick; and those that have the Gout, the Gout; and so of other Distempers; the *Seed* following the Power, Nature, Temperature and Complexion of him that engendreth it. So likewise, *e contrario*, those that are in Health and of sound Habits, get healthy and sound Children, born with a good Stamen, which nothing but excess, irregularity or accident, will to any measure injure. It is likewise absolutely necessary that Married People in their mutual Embraces in order for Children, do come together and meet each other with all the imaginable Ardour and Love, so as that neither of them want motives to the performance of the Act; for if either of their Inclinations flag, or Spirits are not fired, they will certainly fall short in what Nature requires, and the Woman will either miss of Conception, or else the Child prove weakly in its Body, or defective in its Understanding; therefore 'tis advisable that before they begin their Conjugal Embraces, to invigorate their mutual Desires, and make their Flames burn with a fiercer Ardour, by those toying and endearing ways that Love is a better Artist to teach, than I am to write; tho' *Ambrose Parry*, when the Fault is on the Womans side, in behalf of them (who he says, are generally more slow and slack to the Act than the Men) speaks plain in his Book of Surgery, *pag.* 593. in telling us, "That when the Husband comes into his Wifes Bed-Chamber to Caress her in order to Conception, and finds her cold to the Act, he must entertain her with all kind of Dalliance, wanton Behaviour, and Allurements to *Venery*, by Cherishing, Embracing and Tickling her, and that not abruptly to break into the Field of Nature, but rather to creep in by little and little, intermixing more wanton Kisses, with wanton Words and Speeches, handling her Secret Parts, and Breasts, that she may take Fire and be inflam'd to *Venery*; for so at length the *Womb* will wax fervent with a Desire of Copulation, which then is the more likely opportunity for Conception. "But," adds he, "if all these things will not suffice to inflame the Woman, or raise her Desire of Copulating with her Husband, it well be necessary first to foment her Secret Parts with a Dedoction of hot Herbs made with Muscadine, or other rich Wine; and put a little Musk or Civet into the Neck or Mouth of her *Womb*; and when she perceives a tickling sensation of Pleasure there, she is to advertise her Husband thereof, that at the very instant and Moment of that desire, he may embrace her, by which means a Child may be formed and born."

It is affirmed by divers good Authors that have wrote concerning

Conception, that if a Woman on the fourth Day after her *Courses* break down, drinks but six ounces of the juice of Garden Sage, with a little Salt dissolv'd in it, and her Husband presently after has conversation with her, she will infallibly Conceive. And *Aetius* also affirms, that the *Aegyptian* women, by the use of this only Remedy, became fruitful after a raging Plague that had been amongst them. And some say that Garlick has such an effect by way of *Pessary*, as that many who have despair'd of ever having Children, have Conceiv'd by thrusting up high in the Privities a head of it heated with Oil of Spike, and wrapt in a fine Rag, as aforesaid; for that it powerfully forces the *Courses*, and cleanses and delights the *Womb*, which before was foul and injur'd, so that Conception soon follows. And when all is done that Nature can require, the Man must take care he does not part too soon from the Embraces of his Wife, lest some sudden interposing Air should strike cold into the *Womb*, which, as I observ'd before, may occasion a Miscarriage, and thereby deprive them of the Fruit of all the Labour and Pains, which they had before taken to procure a Child. And when after some small convenient time, the Man has withdrawn himself from his Wife, let her, as said before, betake herself to Rest, with all serenity and composure of Mind, and keep her self clear of all anxious, perplexing and disturbing Thoughts, or any kind of perturbation or uneasiness whatsoever; and to remember as much as she can, for a while at least, to keep the same order of lying on her Back, and not turn her self out of the posture on which she first reposes her self; and as much as may be to avoid Coughing and Sneezing, which by the violent shaking or concussion of the Body, is a great Enemy to Conception, especially if it happens soon after the act of Coition. And also from time forward she should endeavour that her body be neither costive or loose; getting of Cold should as much as possible be prevented, for Coughs by that means causes a forcing: Likewise all sweet Scents, especially to those that are *Hysterical* or subject to Vapours, should be abandon'd, as should be the eating of sharp Salt and windy Foods and Medicines; by which observance and regularity Conception will be furthered and preserved, and the Woman go the end of her time, safely and cheerfully, where I shall leave her to be manag'd by her Midwife, whose business it is then, more properly than mine, both to Deliver her safe, and preserve her thro' her Month to her going abroad, and being in a condition again to Bed with her Husband, in order for the making more work for Mrs. Midwife.

FINIS.

4

Venus in the Cloister

(1725)

VENUS

IN THE

CLOISTER:

OR, THE

NUN in her SMOCK.

Vows of Virginity *should well be weigh'd*:
Too oft they're cancell'd, tho' in Convents made.
GARTH.[1]

DEDICATION.

TO

The Duchess of

★ ★ ★ ★ ★ ★ ★ ★.

Madam,

As I have the utmost Pleasure, upon all occasions, in obeying Your Grace's
COMMANDS, I hope in the Performance of the last Task enjoined me, that I
have made these celebrated DIALOGUES speak English in a smooth, natural,
and agreeable Manner. I could not render the Title otherwise than I have done, it
being a Literal Version of the Original.* As to the Design of their Composition,
whatever any Pretender to Sanctity may object, the same just Apology ought to be
made for them with which Quevedo concludes his VISIONS: He that rightly
comprehends the Morality of this Discourse, shall never repent the reading of it.[2] I have this Plea to urge in my own behalf, for the Liberty I have taken
of inscribing them to Your GRACE, that I have only followed the Example of the
Abbé du Prat, who has himself dedicated them to that Polite Lady the Abbess of
Beaulieu whom he addresses in the following manner. ————

---

* Venus dans le Cloître: ou, la Religieuse en Chemise.

TO
Madam D.L.R.
The most worthy Lady Abbess
of Beaulieu.

Madam,

As it would be very difficult for me not to perform what your Lady-ship seemed so earnestly to desire of me, so I have no Ways deliberated on that Request of reducing, as soon as possible, into writing, the agree-able Entertainments in which your community bears so great a part.

I am too solemnly engaged in the gallant Undertaking to look back or excuse myself from this Work, on Account of the difficulty which may occur to me in giving to Voice *and* Action *That beautiful Fire with which they were animated and enlivened. I know not if I shall have well performed my Duty, and satisfied your expectations: The Exercises of two or three Mornings will discover to you the Truth, and make you sensible, that if I have not a great deal of Eloquence, I have at least a very good Memory, to relate faithfully the greatest Part of Things that are passed. I have proposed so much your Satisfaction in this Work, that I have passed by indifferently all the Reasons which might hinder me from it, the Fear only lest it should fall into other Hands was the Cause that made me de-lay the Sending it to you for some small Time: I would myself have been the Bearer, if the present Posture of my Affairs would have permitted me, rather than trust a Packet of this Consequence, either to the Hazard of the Post or even a Special Messenger.*

For, to speak plainly, what Confusion would it be both for me and for you, Madam, if such Secret Conferences *should be made publick?*[3] *If Actions which are not blamed because they are not known, should be-come a new Subject of Criticism, and furnish with Arms those who would attack Us? What Posture would our poor* NUN *be in, if an unlucky ac-cident exposed her* Naked *to the eyes of the curious? What Embar-rassment! What Shame! What Confusion! All these Considerations are strong, but you would be obeyed, and have treated as light and timid Re-flexions, Reasons the most cogent and solid.*

But whatever be the Event, it will not affect me; for, to talk less Gravely, I shall only say, that there is nothing to be apprehended from the Conduct of Sister AGNES, *whose Destiny introduced her into these Scenes; since, as I have drawn her Picture, she is represented in the strictest observation of her Vows.*

For in Reality, to begin with Poverty,* *Can any One shew herself*

---

* The Nuns at their Profession take three vows, *viz*, of Poverty, Chastity, Obedience.

more detached from Worldly Goods, *than to strip herself voluntarily into her* Smock? *Could she in her Words and Actions display the Beauty of* Chastity *in a greater Lustre than by taking for her Rule* Pure Nature? *In short, if we would make Proof of her implicit* Obedience *in all Things, without Exception, we shall find that she has shewn herself as docile as any One of our* Novices.

Inform your greatest Intimates what you shall judge Proper for them to know, and believe me without reserve,

MADAM,
Your most obedient
And most affectionate Servant,
L'ABBÉ DU PRAT.

Thus for Monsieur du Prat.

May it please your GRACE,

As I began with QUEVEDO's *own Apology, I shall conclude with Sir* Roger L'Estrange,[4] *and apply to our* French Abbé, *what he does to his* Spanish Knight.

These DIALOGUES *are full of* Sharpness *and* Morality, *and have found so good Entertainment in the World, that they wanted only* English *of being Baptized into all* Christian Languages. I am,

(With the profoundest Respect)

Your Grace's
Most devoted Servant,
★ ★ ★ ★ ★

Dialogue I.

★Sister AGNES, Sister ANGELICA.

AGNES. Ah Lard! Sister *Angelica*, for heaven's Sake do not come into our† Cell¶; I am not visible at present. Ought you to surprize People in the Condition I am in? I thought I had shut the door.

ANGEL. Be quiet, my dear, what is it gives thee this Alarm? The mighty Crime of seeing thee shift thy self, or doing [something] somewhat

---

★ The Nuns call each other *Sister.*

† In Convents no one says *my*, it is always *our*; because in Monasteries they make Profession of having no Propriety of any Thing; all Things are supposed to be in common: So that it is *our* Cell, *our* House, *our* Garden, *our* Shoes, &c.

¶ Chambers in Convents are called Cells.

more refreshing? Good Friends ought to conceal nothing from one another. Sit down again upon the Mattress;* I'll go and shut† the Door.

AGNES. I'll assure you, Sister, I should have died with Confusion had
any one but yourself thus surprized me; but I know you love me, and
therefore I have no cause to fear any thing from you, whatever you might
have taken Notice of.

ANGEL. Thou hast reason, my Child, to talk after this Manner; and
though I had not all the Affection for thee, a tender Heart is sensible of,
yet shouldst thou apprehend nothing on that Account. Seven Years are
now passed since I was professed a Nun: I came into the Convent at thirteen, and I can say I have made no Creature in the House my Enemy by
my ill Conduct, having ever an utter aversion of speaking ill of People, and
taking the most inward Pleasure and Satisfaction in the World to serve any
one of the Community. This manner of acting has gained me the Affection of the greatest Number, and above all, entirely engaged me that of our
Superiour, the Abbess, which stands me in no small stead upon Occasion.

AGNES. I know it and have often wondered how you could even manage those of a different Party;¶ undoubtedly you must have a great deal of
Wit and Address to win such People. For my Part, I could never torture
my self in my Affections, or labour to make Friends of those who were indifferent to me. This is my *Foible*, who am an Enemy to Restraint, and
would always act with Liberty.

ANGEL. It is certainly very agreeable to let ones self be guided by that
pure and innocent Nature, by following intirely the Inclinations which she
gives us, but Honour and Ambition, which have long since troubled the
Repose of Cloisters, oblige those who come into them to divide themselves, and do often that with Prudence, which they cannot do by Inclination.

AGNES. Which is as much as to say that a great many who believe
themselves Mistresses of your Heart, possess only the Picture of it, and that
all your Protestations assure them very often of a Good which in Reality
they do not enjoy. I should be afraid, I assure you, to be of that Number
and fall a Victim to your Politicks.

ANGEL. Ah! my dear, thou dost me wrong. Dissimulation has nothing to do with Friendships so strong as ours. I am intirely thine; and had
Nature made me of the same Blood and Spirits with thee, she could not
have given me more tender Sentiments than those I now perceive with

---

* The Nuns have seldom Beds, but lie on stuffed Quilts or Mattresses.
† The Nuns have no Locks to their Doors.
¶ In these Houses there are always Parties.

such excess of Pleasure. Let me embrace thee, that our Hearts may talk to each other in the Tumult of our Kisses.

AGNES. Ah Lud! how you squeeze me in your Arms; Don't you see I am naked to my Smock? Ah! you have set me all on Fire.

ANGEL. Ah! how does that Vermillion, which at this instant animates thee, augment the brilliancy of thy Beauty? That Fire which sparkles in thy Eyes, how amiable does it make thee? How lovely! must a young Creature so accomplished be thus reserved? No, no, my Child, I'll make thee acquainted with my most secret Actions, and give thee the Conduct of a sage and prudent Religious;* I do not mean that austere and scrupulous sageness which is the Child of Fasting, and discovers its self in Hair and Sackcloth: There is another less wild and savage, which all People of better informed Judgment make profession to follow, and which does no less suit thy amorous Inclination.

AGNES. My amorous Inclination! Certainly my Physiognomy must be very deceitful, or you do not perfectly understand the Rules of that Art. There is nothing touches me less than that Passion; and since the three Years that I have been in Religion† it has not given me the least Inquietude.

ANGEL. That I doubt very much, and if thou wouldst speak with greater Sincerity¶ thou wouldst own that I have spoke nothing but the Truth. What, can a young Girl of sixteen, of so lively a Wit, and a Body so well formed as thine, be cold and insensible? No, I cannot persuade my self to think so: Every thing thou dost, however so negligent it is, convinces me of the contrary, and that *Je ne scay quoy* that I saw through the Crevice‡ of the Door before I came in, convinces me that thou art a Dissembler.

AGNES. Ah dear! I am undone!

ANGEL. Indeed thou hast no reason to say so. Tell me a little whether thou couldst apprehend any thing from me, or hadst any Cause to be afraid of a Friend? I spoke this to thee with Design to make thee my Confidant in a great many other Things relating to my self. Really these are pretty *Bagatelles;*5 the most scrupulous make use of them, and they are called in conventual Terms, *The Amusement of the Young, and the Pastime of the Old.*

---

* Those of both Sexes who make Profession of a Conventual-Life are called *Religious.*

† In Religion, means after they have taken their Vows of Profession; a cant Word in Monasteries, especially in Nunneries.

¶ Recommending Sincerity, we see, is much older than some of our modern Malevolents would have it.

‡ Some Readings have it Key-hole, but not so properly, the Nuns having no locks to their Doors. I therefore in this Case make use of Crevice.

AGNES. But pray what did you perceive thro' the Crevice?

ANGEL. Thou perfectly tirest me with this Conduct. Know for certain, that Love banishes all Fear; and that if we would both of us live with that Harmony and perfect Understanding, as I desire we should, thou must keep nothing from me nor I hide any Thing from thee. Kiss me, my little Heart; in the Condition thou are at present, a Discipline* would be of good use to chastise thee for the small return thou makest me for the Friendship I shew thee. Ah Lard! in what good Plight thou art! what delicate proportion of Shape! Let me —

AGNES. For heaven's Sake let me alone, I am not able to recover from my Surprize. But in good earnest what did you see tho'?

ANGEL. Dost thou not know, my little Fool, what it was I could see? Why I saw thee in an Action, in which I will serve thee my self, if thou wilt, and in which my Hand shall now perform that Office which thine did just now so charitably to another part of thy Body. This is that grand Crime which I discovered, and which my Lady Abbess† of **** practises, as she says, in her most innocent Diversions, which the Prioress¶ does not reject, and which the Mistress of the *Novices*‡ called *The Ecstatic Intromission*. Thou wouldst not believe that such holy Souls were capable of employing themselves in such profane Exercises. Their Carriage and outside have deceived thee; and this exteriour of Sanctity, with which they so well know how to deck themselves on Occasion, has made thee believe that they live in their Bodies, as if they were only made up of nothing but the Spirit. Ah! my Child, how shall I instruct thee in a great many Things of which thou art ignorant, if thou wilt but place a little Confidence in me, and discover to me the present Disposition of thy Mind and Conscience? After this I will make thee my Confessor, I'll be thy Penitent, and I protest thou shalt see my Heart as open, as if thou thy self wert sensible of it's genuine Movements.

AGNES. After all this, I think I ought not to doubt of your Sincerity, for which Reason I shall not only inform you what you desire to know of me, but I would also do my self that sensible Pleasure to communicate to you even my most secret Thoughts and Actions. This will be a general

---

* A Discipline is a sort of Cat of Nine Tails with which they whip themselves in Monasteries.

† The Head or Superiour of some Orders of Nuns is so called.

¶ Prioress is next in Dignity to the Abbess.

‡ Mistress of the *Novices* is she who hath the Care of the Probationers, who are to try for a Twelve-Month whether they like the State of a Nun, and during that Time are called *Novices*.

Confession* of which I know you have no design to make any Advantage, but of which the Confidence I shall repose in you, will only serve to unite us both in the strictest and most indissoluble Chains of Friendship.

ANGEL. Without doubt, my dearest Soul, and thou wilt observe as we proceed, that there is nothing more sweet and agreeable in the World, than a true Friend, who might be the depositary of our secret Thoughts, and even our very Actions. Ah how comfortable are the Openings of Hearts in the like Occasions! Speak then, my Minion, I am coming to sit down by thee on the Mattress. There is no Necessity to dress thee, the Weather gives thee Leave to continue as thou art; I think thou art the more lovely for being so, and the more thou approach to the State in which Nature produced thee, thou hast more Charms and Beauty. Embrace me, my dear *Agnes*, before we begin, and confirm by thy Kisses the mutual Protestations we have given to love each other for ever. Ah! how pure and innocent are thy Kisses! how full of tenderness and sweetness! what Excess of Pleasure do they afford me! Truce a Moment, my little Heart, I am all on Fire, thou makest me mad with thy Caresses. Ah Lard how powerful is Love! and what will become of me if simple Kisses thus lively animate and transport me!

AGNES. Ah! how difficult it is to contain our selves within the Bounds of our Duty, when we give ever so little the Reins to this Passion! Would you believe *Angelica*, how wonderfully these Toyings, which in the main are nothing, have wrought upon me? Ah, ah, ah, let me breathe a little; methinks my Heart is too much locked up at present! Ah how do these Sighs comfort me! I begin to feel within me a new Affection for you, more strong and tender than before! I know not whence it proceeds, for can simple Kisses cause such disorder in the Soul? It is true you are very artful in your Caresses, and all you do is extraordinary engaging; for you have gained me so much, that I am now yours more than my own. I am even afraid that in the excess of that Satisfaction which I have tasted, there may be somewhat intermixed, that may give me Cause to reflect upon my Conscience; this would give me a great deal of trouble: For when I am obliged to speak to my Confessor of these Matters, I die with shame, and know not how to support my self. Lord how weak we are, and how vain are our Efforts to surmount the smallest Sallies and lightest Attacks of corrupted Nature?

ANGEL. Thou art now arrived where I expected thee. I know thou wert always a little scrupulous on many Things, and that a certain tenderness of Conscience hath not given thee a little Pain. Thus it is to fall into

---

*A general Confession is that of ones whole Life.

the Hands of an ill-instructed and ignorant Director.* For my Part, I tell thee, that I was instructed by a very learned Man with what Air I ought to comport my self to live happily all my Life, without doing any Thing that might shock the Observation of a regular Community, or which might be directly opposite to the Commandments.

AGNES. Do me the Favour, Sister *Angelica*, to give me a perfect Idea of this good Conduct; believe me entirely disposed to hear you, and suffer my self to be persuaded by your Reasonings, when I cannot refute them by stronger. The Promise that I made you to open my self fully to you shall be no less observed; since you will insensibly in my Answers to you, re-mark on what foot I stand, and you will judge by that sincere Discovery in all Things I shall make you, of the good or bad Ways I am to follow.

ANGEL. My Child, thou wilt perhaps be surprized at the Lessons I am going to give thee, and thou wilt be astonished to hear a Girl between nineteen and twenty, so intelligent, and to have penetrated into the deep-est Secrets of religions Policy. Do not believe, my Dear, that a Spirit of vain Glory inspires my Words: No, I am satisfied I was less enlightened than thou wert at thy Age, and that all I have learnt, hath succeeded an extreme Ignorance; but I must also tell thee, that I should accuse my self of Stu-pidity, if the Care which several great Men had taken to form me, had not produced some Fruit; and if the Understanding of several Languages which they have taught me, had not caused me to make some Progress by the reading of good Books.

AGNES. My dear *Angelica*, begin your Instructions, I desire you, I die with Impatience to hear you; you never had a Scholar more attentive than I shall be to your Discourse.

ANGEL. As we are not born of a Sex to make Laws, we ought to obey those we find, and follow as known Truths, a great many Things, which pass with a Number of People only for Opinions; we know we are indispensably to do Good, and avoid Evil. But as all do not agree, what to call Good or Evil, and that there is an infinity of Actions for which we have the utmost horrour, that are notwithstanding received and approved of by our Neighbours; I shall teach thee in a few Words, what a Reverend Father Jesuit, who had a partic-ular Affection for me, told me at the Time when he endeavoured to open my Understanding, and make me capable of the present Speculations.

As all your Happiness, my dear *Angelica*, (for so he called me) depends upon a certain Knowledge of the religious State you have now embraced, I shall draw you a naked Picture and pre-scribe you the Means to live in your Solitude without any Un-

---

* The same as Confessor.

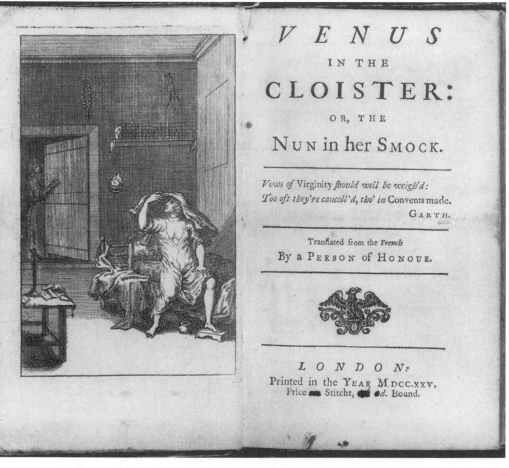

VENUS

IN THE

CLOISTER:

OR, THE

NUN in her SMOCK.

Vows of Virginity *should well be weigh'd:*
Too oft they're cancell'd, tho' in Convents made.
GARTH.

Tranſlated from the *French*
By a PERSON of HONOUR.

LONDON:
Printed in the YEAR M.DCC.XXV.
Price ▬ Stitcht, ◆ ◆*d.* Bound.

Figure 4.1   The frontispiece and title page of *Venus in the Cloister* (1725).

easiness or chagrin proceeding from your engagement. To proceed then with Method in the Instruction I am about to give
you, you must take Notice that *Religion,* (by this Word I mean all
monastick Orders) is composed of two Bodies, one of which is
purely celestial and supernatural, the other terrestrial and cor-
ruptible, which is only the invention of Men. One is political, the
other mystical with Reference to Christ, who is the Head of the
true Church. One is permanent, because it consists in the Word
of God, which is unalterable and eternal; and the other subject
to an infinity of Changes, in as much as it depends on the Word
of Man, which is finite and fallible.

This being supposed, we must separate these two Bodies, and
make a just Distinction between them, in order to know to what
we are obliged; and to do this well is no small Difficulty. Policy, as
the more feeble Part, is so closely united to the other, which is the
stronger, that both are almost blended together, and the Voice of
Man confounded with that of God. From this disorder, Illusions,
Scruples, and those Racks and Tortures of Conscience which often cast a poor Soul into Despair, take their Origin: And that
Yoke which ought to be light and easy to wear, is become, by the
Impositions of Men, excessively heavy and insupportable to the
Generality of Mankind.

Amidst this thick Darkness, and so visible an Alteration of all
Things, One must only hold fast by the Trunk of the Tree, without
putting ourselves in Pain to embrace the Boughs and Branches; we
must content our selves to obey the Commands of the Soveraign
Legislator, and hold for certain, that all those Works of Supererogation to which the Voice of Men would engage us, ought not to
cause in us one Moment of Inquietude: In obeying the Commands
of God, we must consider whether his Will be written with his own
Finger, or proceeds from the Mouth of his Son; or whether only
from the Voice of the People: So that Sister *Angelica* may without
Scruple, lengthen her Chains, embellish her Solitude, and giving her
self a gay Air in all Things, make her self familiar with the World.
She may, as much as Prudence will permit her, dispense her self with
putting in Execution that *Fratras** of Vows and Promises which she
indiscreetly made between the Hands of Men,† and resume the

---

* This word in *French* means *Trifles.*

† Nuns take their Vows of Profession after a year's Noviceship or Probation, holding
their Hands up between the Hands of a Bishop.

same Liberty she was in before her Engagement, by following only her original Obligations.

This is what, continued he, regards interiour Peace: As for the exteriour, you cannot without sinning against Prudence, dispense with the Laws, Customs, and Manners to which you submitted your self at your Entrance into the Monastery. You ought also to appear zealous and fervent in Exercises the most painful; if any Interest of Glory or Honour* depend on those Employments, you may furnish your Cell with Hair and Sackcloth, Thorns and Briars, and merit by that devout Equipage, as much as they who indiscreetly wound and lacerate their Bodies.

AGNES. Ah! how I am ravished to hear you! the extreme Pleasure which I take makes me interrupt you, and that Liberty of Conscience which you begin to give me by your Discourse, hath rid me of almost an infinite Number of Troubles which tormented me. But continue, I beseech you, and teach me what was the design of Policy, in establishing so many Orders, the Rules and Constitutions of which, are so rigourous.

ANGEL. One must consider in the Foundation of all Monasteries, two Master Workmen, that is to say, the Founder and Policy. The Intention of the former was very often pure, holy, and far distant from the Designs of the other; and without having any other View than the Salvation of Souls, it proposed Rules and Manners of Life, which he believed necessary, or at least useful for advancing in the spiritual Warfare, and the Good of our Neighbour; it was for this End that Desarts were peopled, and Cloisters erected. The Zeal of one alone inflamed a great many, and their principal Employment being to sing continually the Praises of the true God, they drew by these pious Exercises, to them, whole Companies, which united themselves to them, and became one Body. I speak of what passed in the Fervour of the first Ages; for as to others one must reason differently, and not think that this primitive Innocence, and this fine Character of Devotion preserved it self very long, which gradually mixed it self with what we see at present.

Policy, which cannot suffer any Thing defective in the State, seeing the Increase of these Recluses, their Disorder and Irregularity, was obliged to make use of it's Power; it banished a great many, and retrenched the Constitutions of others, as to what it did not think necessary for the common Interest: It had a Mind to rid it self entirely of those *Leaches*, who through laziness and horrible sloath, would live on the Labour of poor

---

* Was not this good Father an admirable Casuist now?

People; but this Buckler of Religion with which they cover themselves, and the Judgment of the Vulgar, of which they had already made themselves Masters, gave Things another Turn; so that these Communities were not entirely unuseful to the Common-Weal.

Policy, then looked upon these Houses as so many Common-Sewers, into which it might discharge it self of it's Superfluities; it makes use of them to ease Families, whom a great Number of Children would make poor and indigent, if there were not Places for them to retire to; and that their Retreat may be secure, without any Hopes of Return, it invented Vows, by which it pretends to bind us, and tye us indissolubly, to that State which, we have embraced: It makes us even renounce the Rights which Nature has given us, and separates us from the World in such Manner, that we make no part of it. You comprehend me so far?

AGNES. Yes, but whence comes it that this cursed Policy, which of free People hath made us Slaves, approves more of those Rules which are rude and austere than those which are less rigorous?

ANGEL. The Reason is this: Policy considers Monasticks of both Sexes as so many Members cut off from its Body and as Parts divided, the Life of which it does not esteem in particular to be useful to any Thing, but rather prejudicial to the Publick. And, as it would appear to be an Action very inhuman to rid itself of them openly, it had Recourse to Stratagems; and under pretense of Devotion, it engaged these poor Victims to be their own Murderers, to macerate themselves with so many Fastings, Penances and Mortifications, that at last the poor Innocents sink under the Burden and make Room by their Death for others, who must be as miserable as themselves, if they are not more enlightened. Thus, a Father is often the Executioner of his Children, and without thinking of it, sacrifices them to Policy, when he believes he offers them to God.

AGNES. Ah wretched Effect of a detestable Government! you give me Life, my dear *Angelica*, in drawing me by your Reasons out of the broad Road I was in; very few People put in Practice more than my self all Kinds of Mortifications, even the most rude and violent. I am torn to Pieces with Stripes of the Discipline, in Order to combat often the innocent Movements of Nature, which my Director passed upon me for horrible Disorders. Ah! why should I have been thus abused! without Doubt it is from this cruel Maxim, that moderate Orders are despised, and those which have every Thing in them frightful and horrid, praised and elevated to the Skies. Oh God! dost thou suffer thy holy Name to be thus abused in such unjust Executions! dost thou permit Men thus to personate and mock thee!

ANGEL. Ah! my Child, these Exclamations, plainly convince me that thou wantest yet some Ray to enlighten thee universally in all Things: But let us rest here; thy Mind is not capable at present of a more delicate Speculation. *Love God and thy Neighbour*, and be satisfied, that the whole Law is included in these two Commandments.

AGNES. What *Angelica*, would you leave me in any Error?

ANGEL. No, my dear Heart, thou shalt be fully instructed, and I will put into thy Hands a Book which shall completely make thee intelligent, and, by which thou shalt learn with Ease, what I cannot explain to thee but very confusedly. Here it is, take it.

AGNES. Enough. Ha! what is it I see, I have dipt into that pleasant Passage you were just now mentioning: *That Cloisters are the Common-Sewers, whereinto Policy discharges it self of it's Ordures!* and I think no one could speak after a lower and more abject Manner.

ANGEL. It is true, the Expression smells a little strong; but it is no more shocking than that of another Author, who says, that *Friers and Nuns were in the Church, what Cats and Mice were in* Noah's *Ark*.

AGNES. You are in the right, and I admire the easiness with which you discourse of these Things, and would not for all that is most dear to me, that the Crevice in the Door had not given Birth to this Entertainment: Yes, dear *Angelica*, I have penetrated into the Sense of every Word you spoke.

ANGEL. Very well; will you make a good Use of what hath been said? And shall this beautiful Body which hath been guilty of no manner of Crime, be again treated like the most infamous and most consummate Villain in the World?

AGNES. No, I design to make it amends for the bad Weather I caused it to suffer. I beg it's Pardon, and particularly for a very rude Discipline which I made it very sensible of by the Advice of my Confessor.

ANGEL. Kiss me, my poor Child, I am more touched at what thou tellest me, than if I had experienced it my self; this Correction must be the last thou shalt inflict upon thy self: But does it still pain thee?

AGNES. Alas! my Zeal was indiscreet, I thought the more I laid on, the more I merited; my good plight of Health, and my Youth made me sensible of the least Stroke; so that at the conclusion of this fine Exercise, I found my back Apartment all on Fire: I don't know whether I have not some Wound in those Parts, for I was altogether transported when I committed this so sensible an Outrage upon it.

ANGEL. You must let me make it a Visit, My Mignonne,[6] that I may see how far an ill-managed Zeal may carry one.

AGNES. Oh Lud! must I suffer this! you speak then in earnest. I cannot bear it without Confusion. Oh! Oh!

ANGEL. To what Purpose is all what I have been saying, if you are still enslaved by a foolish shame-facedness? What Harm is there in granting what I ask of you?

AGNES. 'Tis true, I am in the wrong, and your Curiosity is no wise blameable; take then that Satisfaction you desire.

ANGEL. Oh! let us see then unveiled that beautiful Countenance that has hitherto been always covered! kneel down upon the Mattress, and hold down thy Head a little, that I may observe the Violence of thy Stripes! Ah! Goodness of Heaven, what Patch-Work is here? what Variety of Colours? Methinks I see a piece of China Taffeta: Sure one must have a great deal of Devotion for *the Mystery of Flagellation*,* thus to illuminate† ones Thighs.

AGNES. Well, and hast thou sufficiently contemplated that innocent Outrage? Oh God! how you handle it, let alone, that it may recover its former Complection and divest it self of this strange Colour. What, dost thou kiss it?

ANGEL. Do not be against it, my Child, I am a Soul the most compassionate in the World; and as it is a Work of Mercy to comfort the afflicted, I think I could not caress them too much to acquit my self willingly of that *Devoir*.[7] Ah! how well formed is that Part! And what *Eclat* and Beauty does that whiteness and good plight that there appears, bestow upon it! I perceive also another Place which is no less participant of the Kindness of Nature, it is *Nature it self.*

AGNES. Take away your Hand, I beseech you, from that Place, if you would not blow up a Fire not easily to be extinguished. I must own my Weakness, I am a Girl the most sensible you ever knew; and that which would not cause in any other the least Emotion, very often puts me entirely into the utmost Disorder.

ANGEL. So! then thou are not so cold as thou wouldst have persuaded me at the beginning of our Discourse! and I believe thou wilt act thy Part as well as any one I know when I shall have put thee into the Hands of five or six good Friers. I could wish on that Account that the Time of the Retreat,¶ into which, according to Custom, I am going to enter, might be de-

---

* Some Readings have it *Flogging*, but the Term being too vulgar, I am of their Sentiment who read it *Flagellation*.

† This Term is taken from Painters in Miniature and Water-Colours, as when they colour Prints or Maps with Water-Colours, they call it *illuminating*, such a Map or Print.

¶ The Nuns are obliged, every one, singly to retire for eight Days once every Year at least, into their respective Cells, and have no Conversation with the rest of the Community there. Eight Days are supposed to be past in Devotion, and such Retirement is called, *The Spiritual Retreat,* or *Retreat.*

ferred, that I might go along with thee into the Parlour:* But no Matter, I shall comfort my self with the Recital thou wilt make me of every Thing that shall have passed; that is, whether the *Abbé*† shall have acquitted himself better than the *Monk* or the *Feuillant*,¶ than the Jesuit; and in short, if the whole *Fratraille*‡ shall have given thee plenary Satisfaction.

AGNES. Ah! I fancy I shall be much embarrassed in these Kinds of Entertainments, and that they will find me a meer Novice in Feats of Love.

ANGEL. Do not put thy self in Pain about that, they know what Methods to make use of with every Body, and one Quarter of an Hour with them will make thee more knowing, than all the Precepts thou couldst have from me in a whole Week. There, cover thy Back-side for fear it should catch Cold: But stay, it shall first have this Kiss from me, and this, and this.

AGNES. How toying thou art? Dost believe I would suffer these Fooleries, unless I knew there was nothing criminal in them.

ANGEL. If there was, I should commit a Sin every Moment, for the Charge I have over the Scholars§ and Pensioners, obliges me to visit their Back-houses very often. It was but yesterday, I whipped one, more for my own Satisfaction, than for any Fault she had committed. I took a singu-

---

* Parlours in Nunneries, are those Rooms where the Nuns see Company, of which they have several in every House, separated from each other by Walls; so that one Company cannot hear another Company in a different Parlour. These Rooms are divided in the middle with an Iron Grate, so as to make two Apartments, the Inward and the Outward; and into the Inward the Nuns come, without coming out of their Inclosure, and the Visitors come into the Outward by a Key, given through a Grate by the Portress at the Entrance of the Monastery.

† *Abbé* here does not signify an Abbot, or superiour of a Monastery of Men, but one who holds some Sine-Cure, of which there are a great many in *France*, and abundance of them not in Priests-Orders, and as great Libertines and Debauchees as one could wish. They go in the short Habit, that is, in a short black Suit and Cloak; they wear fine Bands, and most of them very sparkish in their Dress: Take Snuff, go to Plays and Operas, play at Cards, and talk Love to the Ladies.

¶ The Order of *Feuillants* was established in the Year 1565 by *John de la Barriere*. They follow the Rule of St. *Benedict,* and St. *Bernard;* formerly they went unshod with Sandals. They wear fine white Stuff, they are called *Feuillants*, from *Feuille* a Leaf, because they carry in their Arms a Branch with Leaves.

‡ We have no one word in *English* to signify what this Word *Fratraille* does in *French*, which means a *Friarly-Crew.*

§ In some Nunneries they teach young Ladies all Sorts of fine works, who are allowed also to learn to dance, sing, and play on the Musick. When their Masters come to teach them they come out of the Enclosure into a large Room, the School-Mistress sitting in a little Parlour with an Iron Grate. Those who go home are called Scholars, those who board and lie within the Enclosure are called Pensioners.

lar Pleasure in looking on her; she was very pretty, and only thirteen Years old.

AGNES. I long for that Employment of School-Mistress, that I might take the like Diversion; I was struck with that Fancy, and I should be even ravished to behold in thee, what thou hast so attentively considered in my Person.

ANGEL. Alas! my Child, what thou askest does not at all surprize me; we are all formed of the same Paste. Hold, I'll put my self into thy Posture. So! Take up my Petticoat and Smock as high as thou canst.

AGNES. I've a strong Temptation to take my Discipline, and so order it that these twin Sisters may have nothing to reproach me withal.

ANGEL. Ouf! Ouf! Ouf! what Havock thou makest. This Kind of Diversion does by no means please me, but when it is not too violent. Truce, truce, if thy Devotion should tempt thee to renew this Exercise, I should be ruined. Lud what an inflexible Arm thou hast! I have a Design to make thee Partner in my Office.* but that requires a little more Moderation.

AGNES. You have a great deal of Reason to complain indeed, this is not the tenth Part of what I received: I'll defer the rest to another Opportunity, something must be allowed to your want of Courage. You must know this Place looks now more beautiful; a certain Fire, which enlivens it, gives it a Vermillion, more pure and brilliant than *Spanish* Wool. Come a little nearer to the Window that the Light may discover all it's Beauties. So, that's well. I could never be weary of looking at it: I see all I could wish even to it's Neighbourhood. Why do you cover that Place with your Hand?

ANGEL. Alas! thou mayest look upon it as well as the rest: If there be any ill in this Operation, it cannot Prejudice any body, and does not in the least trouble the Tranquility of the Publick.

AGNES. How can it, since we make no more a Part of it? Besides, hidden Faults are half pardoned.†

ANGEL. You have Reason, my Dear, for if one practised in the World¶ as many Crimes, to speak comformably to our Rules, as are committed in Cloisters, the Government would be obliged to correct the House, and cut off the Current of these Disorders.

AGNES. And I believe that Parents would never suffer their Children

---

* Of School Mistress.

† This alludes to this Italian Proverb. *Un Peccato celato e Mezzo perdonato.*

¶ This is a Cant Word amongst the Nuns, who call themselves People out of the World; among whom nothing is more common than to say, when I was in the World I did this, when I was in the World I was so unhappy as to do that, &c. So that by being in the World, they mean before they became Nuns.

to come into our Houses, and be professed amongst us, if they knew our Disorders.

ANGEL. You need not doubt it; but as the greatest Part of these Faults are secret, and Dissimulation reigns more in Cloisters than elsewhere. All who live in these Retirements do not see them; but serve themselves to decoy others. Besides, very often the particular Interest of Families prevails above all other Considerations.

AGNES. Confessors and Directors of Convents* have a particular Talent to make those poor Innocents fall into their Snares, who snap at their Bait, vainly imagining they have found an invaluable Treasure.

ANGEL. 'Tis true, and I have proved it by Experience in my self, I had no manner of Inclination for Religion. I fought couragiously against the Arguments of those who would persuade me to it, and I should never have been a Nun, if a Jesuit, who then governed this Monastery, had not intermeddled: An Interest of the Family obliged my Mother, who loved me tenderly, and was very averse to give her Consent. I stood out a long while, because I did not foresee that the Count *de la Roche*, my eldest Brother, in Right of his Nobility, and the Custom of the Country, possessed himself of all the Estate of the Family, and left six of us without any other Support than what he promised us, which, according to his Humour, was to have been but very little. In short he allotted me ten Thousand Florins†️ out of his Pretensions, to which he added four Thousand more; so that at my Profession in this Convent, I brought in, for my Portion, fourteen Thousand.¶ But, to return to the Address and Cunning of him who inveigled me, you must know it was so ordered, that I should come into his Company one Day after Dinner, when I went to pay a Visit to one of my Cousins, who was a Nun; and who died with extreme Desire to see me cloathed in the same Habit with her self.

AGNES. Was not this Sister *Victoria*?

ANGEL. It was, being then all three of us in the same Parlour, the Jesuit, Sister *Victoria* and my self: We began with those Complements and Civilities People generally use in their first Interviews, which were succeeded by a Discourse of this Loyalist,‡ touching the Vanities of this Life, and the Difficulty of working out ones Salvation in the World, who in-

---

* Convent is the same as Cloister, and is applicable to those of Men and Women, except to the Jesuits Houses, which are called Colleges, forsooth.

† Ten Thousand Florins, reckoning every Florin at *1s. 6 d. English* is *750 £.* Sterling.

¶ *1400* Florins, is *1050 £.* Sterling.

‡ The Founder of the Jesuits was *Ignatius Loyola*, a *Spaniard*, Loyalist then means the same as a Jesuit.

sensibly very much disposed my Mind to be seduced by him: This, how-ever, was nothing but light Preparations: He was Master of a great many other Subtilties to insinuate himself into my Interiour, and make me en-ter into his Sentiments. He sometimes told me, that he observed in my Physiognomy the true Character of a religious Soul;* that he had a par-ticular Gift in making a just Discernment, and that I could not, without doing an Injury to God, (for these were his Words) consecrate to the World a Beauty so perfect as mine was.†

AGNES. He was not out in his Judgment as to the last: But what An-swer did you make to all this?

ANGEL. I immediately opposed these first, Arguments to others I made use of, which he soon destroyed by a wonderful Artifice. *Victoria* too gave a helping Hand to delude and cheat me, and shewed me Religion¶ on that side, which might make it appear amiable and lovely, and, with great Dex-terity and Address, concealed from me every thing, that might give me the least Shock or Disgust. In that, the Jesuit, who, as I have been since in-formed, had made a great many Conquests, even the most difficult, made use of his utmost Efforts to compleat mine, which he accomplished by the Picture he drew me of the World, and of Religion; and constrained me, by the Force of his Eloquence, strictly to embrace his Party.

AGNES. But yet tell me what was it that he said, which could be ca-pable of exercising such an absolute Power over your Soul?

ANGEL. I must relate it to thee in it's full Extent, for he kept me three Hours at the Grate; thou shalt know only that he proved to me by these Arguments, which I imagined very strong, that this was my Vocation, in which only I could work out my Salvation; that out of it he had no Surety for me nor my Way; that the World was full of nothing but Rocks and Precipices; that the Excesses of religious Persons‡ were of more Value than the Moderation of Worldlings; that the Quiet and Contemplation of the one was, in the same time, more sweet and meritorious, than the Action and all the Troubles of the other: That it was only in Cloisters, where one could treat familiarly with God, and consequently, that, to make ones self worthy of a Communication so elevated and holy, one must fly the Com-pany of Men. That it was in these Places, that the Remains of the ancient

---

* True religious Cant; tho' these spiritual Physiognomists are frequently out. I know a young Gentleman, who was told for certain by one of them, that he knew he had a Vocation to be a Priest by his Eye: But he proved a false Prophet, the Gentleman being now a Physician.

† O rare Casuist!

¶ By Religion here is meant, entring into a Convent or Monastery.

‡ Nuns and Friars

Fervour of Christians was preserved, and where one might see the true Image of the primitive Church.

AGNES. No one could speak with greater Eloquence, and at the same time with more Artifice; for I observe he did not mention a Syllable of Rigours and Austerities to fright you.

ANGEL. Thou art mistaken, he forgot nothing: But the Pains and Mortifications which he spoke of, were seasoned with so much Sweetness that I did not think them ill-tasted. I will conceal nothing from you, said he; these devout Societies, of which I hope you will increase the Number, labour Night and Day, by their Austerities and Penances, to overcome Pride and the Insolence of Nature; they exercise over their Senses a Violence which always lasts, without dying their Soul is separated from their Body, and, despising equally Pain and Pleasure, they live as if they were only made up of the Spirit. This is not all, (continued he with a persuasive Tone) they all make a rigorous Sacrifice of their Liberty, they despoil themselves of all their Riches, and impose on themselves by solemn Vows the Necessity of a perpetual Virtue.

AGNES. This Disciple of *Loyola* was a Master Orator, I should be glad to know him.

ANGEL. You know him very well, and I shall inform you of some little Particulars of his Life, which will convince you that he knows more than One Person. But I must finish his Harangue. See here, young Lady, said he, a great many Chains, Rigours, and Mortifications that I present you; but, believe me, these holy Souls, whom I speak of, glory in this Yoke; they are proud of this Servitude, and there is no Pain so rude, that offers it self to them, but they willingly undergo it, and esteem it a great Reward; all their Love and Passion is for Jesus Christ: It is he alone that sets them on fire at the least Touch, it is he who is the only Master of their Heart, and who knows how to make all their Pains and Sufferings to be succeeded with incredible Sweetness, and Excess of Joy.*

AGNES. Without Doubt you were charmed with this fine Discourse.

ANGEL. Yes, my Child, this Mountebank persuaded me; his Words changed me in a Moment. They tore me from myself, and made me seek with Ardour, that which I had ever fled from with Constancy. I became the most scrupulous Creature in the World, and, because he had told me, that out of a Convent I could not work out my Salvation, I imagined, before I came into one, that I had all the Devils in Hell at my heels: Since that time he himself undertook to put me into a good State, he gave me that Knowledge, which was capable of drawing me out of that Darkness

---

* This is going through Stitch.

he had plunged me into; and it is to his Morality that I owe all the Peace and Quiet I now enjoy.

AGNES. Tell me then, quickly, who is this wonderful Person?

ANGEL. It is *Pere de Raucourt.*

AGNES. O the Enchantor! I went once to Confession to him, and I took him for the most devout Man in the World. It is true he knows the Address of gaining Hearts to perfection, and persuades every Thing he desires. But I take it very ill of him to leave me in the Error he found me and, whence he might have disengaged me.

ANGEL. Ah! he was too prudent thus to put himself in any Danger. He saw thee in an extraordinary Bigotry, and horrible Scruples; and knew that it would not be so easy a Matter to bring a young Girl from one extreme to another. Besides, if one Saint could give sight to all that were blind, he would have no Miracles to work in others; you understand me: That is to say, if thou hadst had Faith, thou wouldst have been healed; and if this sage Director had found in thee any Dispositions to have followed his Prescriptions, he would have served thee as thy Physician.

AGNES. I believe it, but I had much rather lie under that Obligation to you: Paint me then, I beseech you, some little Picture of the Life of this same Saint.

ANGEL. I will, my little Heart, kiss me then, and embrace me as lovingly as thou didst just now. Hah! hah! that's well. Ah! how am I charmed with thy lovely Mouth and Eyes! one only Kiss of thine transports me more than I am able to express.

AGNES. Begin then. Ah! you are a great Kisser!

ANGEL. I am never weary of caressing that which I find so lovely. Since then, my Dear, thou knowest *Pere de Raucourt,* I need not tell thee, that he is the most intriguing Person in the World, the most *Adroit* and witty. I shall only tell thee, that, in the point of Friendship, he is the most delicate Creature living; and, as he thinks he is somewhat deserving, one must have a great many good Qualities to please him. Amongst all his Conquests he reckons none more glorious, than that which he made on a young Nun, of a Monastery in this City, whose Name is Sister *Virginia.*

AGNES. I have heard her mentioned as an accomplished Beauty, but I am ignorant as to other Particulars.

ANGEL. She is one of the most beautiful Creatures living, if the Picture, our Lover has drawn of her, does not flatter. She hath as great a share of Wit as she can desire; she is gay and lively, touches several Instruments of Musick to admiration, and sings with Charms capable to enchant Hearts the most insensible. It is but some Months since that our Jesuit has entirely gained her, and they both enjoy that sweet Tranquility which compleats the Happiness of Lovers, when Jealousy gave birth to that Disorder I am going to relate.

There was, in the same Monastery, a certain Nun, to whom that Father had made a Profession of Friendship, and whom he had visited a great many times on that account: He had also received some Favours, capable firmly to engage a Man that had but a little Fidelity: However, the Brightness of *Virginia's* Beauty captivated his Soul. He disengaged himself entirely from his first Attach, and shewed nothing to that poor Creature, than the exterior and Appearances only of a true Love. She soon perceived the Change, and clearly saw another partook of his Affection: She dissembled, however, her Chagrin, and finding that she had to do with a Rival, who surpassed her in every thing: she had no Design to attack her, but swore the Ruin of him that despised her.

The more easily to bring about what she had resolved upon, she studied the Hours and Moments which *Virginia* bestowed in entertaining this religious Lover; and, as she had learnt by Experience that he was not to be satisfied with Words only, or slight Favours, she had Reason to believe she might surprize them in certain Exercises, the Knowledge of which might make her Mistress of the Fate of her faithless Lover. It was a long Time before she could discover any Thing to convince her of his Falshood. She plainly saw three or four Times this good Father warm his Hands in her Bosom, and kiss one another with an incredible Ardour; but this passed with her as no more than so many little *Bagatelles* or Amusements, and as she knew that People in Cloisters looked upon these Actions as *Peccadillos,** which might be easily washed off with a little *Holy Water*, she said nothing, in Expectation of a better Opportunity.

AGNES. Ah! how am I afraid for poor *Virginia!*

ANGEL. Our Lovers, who never dreamt of the Ambushes laid for them, took no Measures to defend themselves against them. They saw one another two or three Times a Week, and corresponded by Billets, when Prudence obliged them to separate themselves for any Time from each other, for fear of giving any Room for ill Tongues. The Father's Letters were expressed in very strong yet tender Terms, insomuch that they entirely gained *Virginia's* Soul. He came to see her after eight Days Absence and observed by her Eyes and Countenance, that he should obtain that which she had hitherto ever refused him. In the mean while her Rival was not idle, for having a good Intelligence with the Mother Portress,† she was

---

*Venial Sins.

† A *Nun* so called on Account of keeping the Keys of the Doors of the *Nunnery*, and its *Parlour*.

informed of the Jesuit's Arrival, and not doubting but after so long an Interval that they would proceed to those Privacies which she herself had so long wished for, she flew, all transported with Jealousy, to a Place near the Parlour,* where by the Means of a little Hole she had purposely made, she could discover the least Motion of those that talked together, and hear their most secret Conversation.

AGNES. Here my Fears increase. Ah! how could I curse that curious Devil, thus maliciously to trouble the Repose of two unhappy Lovers.

ANGEL. To the End that the Depositions she designed to make, of what she should see, might be received without Difficulty; she took another Nun with her, who might give the same Testimony. Being therefore both posted at the Place I mentioned, they perceived our two Lovers entertaining each other more by their Looks and Sighs than Words. They pressed each other's Hand, and beholding one another with a languishing Air, they spoke some tender Things which proceeded rather from their Heart, than Lips. This amorous Contemplation was followed by opening a little square Window, about the middle of the Grate, and which was made use of to put in Packets of the larger Size, that should be at any Time directed to the Nuns. Now, it was that *Virginia* by this Means gave and received a Thousand Kisses, but with Transports so great, and such surprizing Sallies, that Love it self could not increase the Fire. Ah! my dear *Virginia*, began our passionate Lover, will you then that we rest here? Alas! what little return do you shew to those who love you! and how well do you understand how to practise the Art to torment them! In what, replied our Vestal, is it possible for me to present you with any Thing, after having given you my Heart? Ah! how tyrannical is your Love! I know what it is you desire: I know too at the same time that I have had the Weakness to make you hope for it; but I am not ignorant that this is my Riches, my whole Treasure, my All, and that I cannot grant it you without reducing my self to the last Extremity. Cannot we remain as we are, enjoy together agreeable Moments, and taste those Pleasures so much the more perfect as they are pure and innocent? If your Happiness, as you tell me, depends entirely on the Loss of that which I hold most dear, you cannot be happy, but only once, and I always miserable, since it is a Thing which never can be recovered when once suffered to be lost. Believe me, let us love like Sister and Brother, and give this Love all the Liberties we can imagine, except that *one Thing* only.

---

* *Parlour*, is a Room (of which there are several in every *Nunnery*) into which the *Nuns* come to talk with Strangers: It is divided in the Middle by an Iron Grate, and contrived so that those in one *Parlour* cannot hear what is said in another. Strangers come into it through a Gallery, having first received a Key from the Mother Portress.

AGNES. And did he answer nothing to all this?

ANGEL. No; he spoke not one Word; but leaning his Head upon his Hand, in a melancholy Posture, he looked upon her with Eyes full of Languishing, which spoke for him. After which, taking her by the Hand through the Grate, he said unto her with a very moving Air; we must then change our Method, and love otherwise than we did before. Can you do this *Virginia?* For my Part I can retrench nothing of my Love: The Rules which you prescribe me, cannot be received by a true Lover. At last he exaggerated with so much Fire the Excess of his Passion, that he entirely disconcerted her, and drew from her a Promise, to grant him in a few Days that one *only Thing* that could make him perfectly happy. He then made her come nearer to the Grate, and having made her get upon a Stool of a convenient Height, he conjured her to let him satisfy at least his Sight, since all other Liberties were forbidden. She obeyed him after some Resistance, and gave him Time to handle those Places consecrated to Chastity and Continence. She on her Side would also satisfy her Eyes with the like Curiosity: And the Father who was not insensible, found easily the Means to gratify her, and she obtained of him what she desired, with less Difficulty than what he obtained of her. This was the fatal Moment to them both, and what our Spies desired, who contemplated with an extraordinary Satisfaction the most beautiful Parts of the naked Body of their Companion, which the Father discovered to their View, and handled with the Transports of a furious Lover. One while they admired one Part, then another, according as the officious Father turned and changed the Situation of his Paramour; so that while he considered her before, he exposed her Posteriors to their View, for her Petticoats on both Sides were taken up as high as her Girdle.

AGNES. Methinks I see her, so naturally have you described this Adventure.

ANGEL. In short, they finished these little Toyings, and our two Sisters retired with a design to break the Chain of these ill-managed Amours, and hinder the Effect of *Virginia's* Promise. By a particular good Luck for this poor Innocent, the Nun whom her Rival had taken with her to observe this Interview, had a very tender Friendship for her, and endeavoured to find out a Way how to ruin the Father, without hurting her for whom she had so great an Affection. She gave her to understand what she knew of her Conduct; assured her, she would do nothing to her Prejudice, provided she would promise to break entirely with that Father, and never for the future to have any Communication with him. *Virginia* all ashamed at what she heard, engaged to do every Thing that was desired of her, only earnestly begging that the Father's Reputation might be preserved, because it was impossible to hurt one, without injuring the other. She protested she would never see him more, and that Letter which she was going to write to him, to give him Advice never to come to her again, should be the last he ever should receive from her. These Conditions were accepted of by both the Nuns, tho' with some Difficulty. They embraced *Virginia* with whom they fell in Love, and said, in leaving her, that they would supply the Place of the good Father, and contract a strict Friendship with her.

AGNES. She was very well off. I believe she owed this Indulgence to her Beauty, and her other Qualities which rendered her, without Doubt, even lovely to her very Enemy.

ANGEL. Her History does not yet end here. *Virginia* wrote immediately to *Pere de Raucourt*, and in her Letter informed him of all what had passed, and the Conditions to which she had engaged her self to save both their Reputations. She represented to him the Danger to which he would expose himself in coming to see her, and gave him to understand that it would be impossible for her to receive his Letters, if he did not make use of a particular Intrigue to avoid their Interception. She concluded with Protestations of a constant Love, being Proof to all the most rude Attacks of Jealousy; and made him hope that Time would disperse this Storm that threatned them, and make them more happy than ever. I do not say with what Surprize the good Father received, and read this Letter; he was thunderstruck, and saw that it was not convenient for him to return an Answer, and that he must give Way to his ill Fortune that opposed his Happiness in the very Instant, as he was going to participate of it.

Three Weeks had passed of this Widowhood, when *Virginia* grown sick of her Solitude, found by a wonderful Address, the means how to learn News from her Lover, and to make him also partake of what related to her. She feigned she had forgot to send to *Pere de Raucourt* a square Cap, which he had given her to make up for him in the Time of their past Familiarities. Her Rival told her she had nothing else to do but give it her, and that she would send it him by a *Touriere.** This was accordingly done: The Messenger was instructed what Words she should use in delivering it. She punctually acquitted her self of her Commission; and the Father, after having received the Cap, desired her to wait a Moment in the Church, in order to gain Time to think on what he saw. After a little Reflection, he doubted of the Stratagem, opened one Part of the Cap, and found there a Letter from *Virginia*; without much examining of it, he immediately wrote an Answer, and put it into the same Place, which he stitched up as well as he could with a Needle and Thread. He returned to the *Touriere*, whom

---

* A *Lay-Sister* so called, who goes abroad and carries Messages to, and from the Nuns.

he desired to carry back the Cap that it might be made more fitting, since it was much too little for him, that he had tried it on a great many of the College, that he might spare the Party the Trouble she must necessarily have in altering it, but that he could not find one Father that it could fit; and as to her Part, he was very much obliged to her for the Patience which she underwent in waiting for him so long. The good Sister answered by her several Bowings* the Civilities of the Father, and carried back the square Cap to the Monastery; which by Order of her that gave it her she put into the Hands of *Virginia*, who was even ravished to hear News from him whom she loved, and that her Artifice had so well succeeded.

AGNES. It must be owned that Love is very fertile in Invention.

ANGEL. This Commerce lasted more than a Month, there was always something to be mended in this venerable Cap: Once in three Days it must be carried to the College, and carried back to the Monastery. No one, however, imagined that there was any Thing mysterious in all this, no one took Notice of it, and they might have still made use of this Postillion, had not an unlucky Accident thrown him out of his Employment.

AGNES. Ah dear; I fancy the *Touriere* smelt out the Nose-gay, was it not so?

ANGEL. No, thou art deceived. It happened from the ill Humour of the Jesuit's Porter one Fast Day, who perhaps was out of Temper because he had not emptied his Dram-Bottle as usual. The *Touriere*, who had a great many Messages to deliver, and amongst the rest, that of the square Cap; rung two or three Times at the College Gate to deliver her Errand with all Expedition. This good Brother† came out of the Garden where he was, in great haste and out of Breath, as thinking it to be some Bishop, or Archbishop, or other Person of Quality, that had rung thus magisterially, but was surprized to find it to be only the good Sister, who had nothing else to say but desire him to give the *square Cap* into the Hands of *Pere de Raucourt*.

This same Brother being wearied with so many Visits, grew very angry, and said that this *Cap* walked backward and forwards very often, and that he would put it into the Hands of a Man that should make it undergo the Mortification of a Retirement. The *Touriere* excusing herself as well as she could, withdrew; and the *Rector*,¶ who waited in the Porter's Room

---

* The Nuns never make Court'seys, but bow their Bodies.

† The *Jesuits* as all other Orders, have their *Lay-Brothers* for their Servants, who wear the same Habit with themselves but are the Servants to the House, and never enter into Orders, as the *Nuns* have their *Lay-Sisters* in the same Manner who never sing in the Choir.

¶ The *Superiour* of a *Jesuit's* College is always called *Rector*.

for a Companion, to go out with him,* having heard the Dialogue, called the Brother, who would know the Reason of the Squabble and why he treated after so rude a Manner, People that had to do with those of the House. The Porter, seeing himself thus *chaptered*† by his Superiour, told him what he thought of the *Cap*, assuring him that it had made at least twenty Journeys from the College to the Monastery; and that without doubt there was some Design covered in this Management, and that if it pleased his Reverence he would visit this Piece of Goods, which he said was Contrebande,¶ which he instantly did, and with one Cut of his Scissars, delivered the *square Cap* of it's fifteenth Child, which descended in a right Line from *Virginia*.

AGNES. Ah Lard! what Difficulty one has to save ones self when pursued by an unhappy Destiny that has sworn ones Ruin. But what's the Event of all this?

ANGEL. The Father was confined in another Province, and poor *Virginia* was mortified with some Penances: And hence comes the Proverb; *Qui'ly a bien de la malice sous le Bonnet quareé d'un Jesuite.* There is a great deal of *Malice* under the *square Cap* of a *Jesuit*.

AGNES. It was for her alone I was in Pain, but tell me how this came to the Knowledge of the Prioress?

ANGEL. It would be too long to tell you at present. In the first Conversation after my Retreat I shall Discourse more on this Subject. I shall shew you two Children of the *square Cap*, and inform you of the Fate of their Father and Mother. Think only at present, my dearest Soul, that I am going to pass eight or ten Days in a very mellancholy Manner, since it debars me from having Conversation with thee. I am going to write to three or four of my good Friends, that they may come and see thee in the mean while. They are an *Abbé*, a *Feuillant*, and a *Capucin*.

AGNES. Lord what a Piece of Patch-Work is here! Ah Dear! what would you have me do with all these People whom I have no Knowledge of?

ANGEL. Thou hast nothing else to do but to be obedient, they will teach thee enough for thy understanding the Duty, in order to satisfy them, and content thyself. Here, take this *Book* which I lend thee, make a good use of it; it will instruct thee in a great many Things, and give thy

---

* No Jesuit, or other religious Person goes abroad without a Companion of the same House and Order.

† *Chaptering* means reprimanding, a Term used in religious Houses, because generally those Reprimands are made by the Superiour in the Chapter-House.

¶ *Contrebande* Goods in *French*, is the same as *prohibited*.

Mind all the Quiet thou can'st desire. Kiss me, my dear Child; for all that long Time I shall be absent from thee. Ah! how I could pass my Retreat with a great deal of Pleasure, if the Director I shall have were as amiable and docile as thou art! Adieu, my Heart: Put on thy Cloaths; keep secret all our Friendships, and prepare thy self to give an account of all thy Diversions when I come out of my Exercise.

Dialogue II.

Sister ANGELICA, Sister AGNES.

ANGEL. The Lord be praised, I begin to breathe: never in my whole Life was I more loaded with Devotions, Mysteries and Indulgences, than since I left thee. Lord, how I am tired with so much Supererogation. How dost do? What, nothing to say? What is it thou laughest at?

AGNES. I am quite ashamed to appear before you. I fancy to my self that you know already the most minute Particular that hath happened to me in your Absence.

ANGEL. And from whom should I have learnt it? Thou ralliest me very handsomely. Come into our Cell, and think where thou wilt begin to make me a faithful Recital of thy Adventures. For my part I come out of the Hands of a meer Savage, that would make a mind differently disposed than mine fall into Despair: I mean my *Director*,* who is a Man the most tormenting, and most ignorant of his Profession. O' my Conscience, I believe he has made me gain all the Indulgences and Pardons that ever were granted from GREGORY the *Great*, to BENEDICT the *Fourteenth*.† Had I given entire Credit to him, I must have made my Body all over Blood with the Disciplines he enjoined me; not because in my Confessions, I discovered to him many Sins of Malice, but because he fancied that the Way to Paradise must be as dry, meagre and Skeleton-like as himself, and that to be a little agreeable, and in good Plight, was sufficient to merit all kinds of Pennances. Judge by this how I passed my Time, and whether I have not Reason to be very chagrin and uneasy on that Account.

AGNES. For my part I must tell you, that you have given me Directors that have no less tired me, than yours have you. I cannot tell whether I have gained any Indulgences with them, but I am certain that to gain them a great many People do not do so much as we have done.

---

* The *Nuns* call their *Confessors*, Directors.

† This is the present Pope, Cardinal *Orsini*, to whose Time from *Gregory* the Great is about 1100 Years.

ANGEL. I am of thy Mind. But tell me some little News of our Abbé, and inform me whether he is capable of any thing.

AGNES. I saw him the first, and found in him most Fire; there is nothing more lively and fuller of Spirit, and it is a Pleasure to hear him talk. I was at the Recreation* after Dinner, when I was told he wanted to speak with me. As I knew my Lady† was indisposed, I bid the Porteress tell him to go into the great Parlour,¶ and that he should not be out of patience. I made him wait for me above a good Quarter of an Hour, for I went to put on another Veil and Guimpe,‡ that I might appear before him a little proper, and that I might answer the Expectation, he had of seeing one of whom he had been presented such an agreeable Picture. In respect to him I made semblance of being somewhat shy and ignorant, giving very serious Answers to the Civilities he shewed me: But this did no ways discourage him; on the contrary, he took occasion to tell me very boldly, that he very well knew that Beauties were permitted to talk with an Air of Indifference, which would but ill become any other; but that he had room to hope, that visiting me on the Recommendation of my best Friend, such Interview would not but be a thing very agreeable to me.

ANGEL. He passes for a Man of Wit, and one may say, that his great Travels, attended with much Experience, have added to those Advantages Nature has given, all the Perfection he stood in need of.

AGNES. I don't know what you told him of me, but I found he made very considerable Advances for a first Visit. He turned the Discourse on the Rigours and Austerities of religious Houses, and endeavoured to persuade me, by an Infinity of Arguments not to follow the indiscreet Zeal of the Generality, treating as ridiculous, all those who foolishly made use of all sorts of Mortifications. He made me laugh by the Relation he gave me of what happened to him in *Italy* with a certain Nun, on account of the Address he made use of, in order to see her as often as he desired; and how at last he received from her those Favours which were the Fruit of his continued Attendances. He assured me, that before that Intrigue, he always be-

---

* The Nuns after Dinner and Supper have about an Hour and half to divert themselves in Chit Chat, or other Diversions, which Time they call Recreation.

† By my Lady, is meant the Abbess, or Superiour of a Nunnery.

¶ The *Great Parlour* is what is appropriated to the Use of the *Abbess*, into which no *Nun* can go without express leave of the *Lady Abbess*, or when she is sick or indisposed, which was the present Case.

‡ *Guimpe*, is the Nuns Head-Dress, made of Cambrick, or fine Linnen, through which they put their Faces; it comes close under the Chin, and, falling on their Breast, makes a large kind of Band, reaching over their Shoulders.

lieved that Nunneries were the Places only where Chastity fled for it's Preservation, and that he was ever persuaded that these recluse Souls lived in a Continency as perfect as that of Angels, but that he was well satisfied of the contrary; and as nothing that is perfect suffers a moderate Corruption, and that every Thing retains in it's Corruption the same Degree that it had in it's Goodness, he had observed that nothing was more dissolute than the Recluses and Bigots, when they have an Opportunity to divert themselves. He shewed me a certain *Instrument* of *Glass*, which he had of her I have been telling you of; and he assured me, that she told him there were above fifty of them in their House, and that every one, from the *Abbess* down to the last *Profest* handled *them* oftner than their *Beads*.

ANGEL. Very well. But thou tellest me nothing relating to thy self.

AGNES. What would you have me tell you? He is the most playful and toying Man in the World. At the second Visit he made me, I could not help bestowing on him some small Favours. He combated all my Reasons with such strong Morality, and so artful withal, that he rendered all my Efforts entirely useless. He shewed me *three Letters* from our *Abbess*, which convinced me that whatever I did was no more than treading in her Steps. She passed whole Nights with him, and in her *Letters* called him nothing else but the *Abbé de Beaulieu*. I represented to him, that the Grate was an insurmountable Obstacle, and that of Necessity he ought to content himself with some Toyings, for that it was impossible for him to advance any farther. But he soon convinced me, that he was more knowing than I, and shewed me two Boards, which he removed, one on his side, and the other on mine, which opened a Passage sufficient for any one Person. He told me, that it was by his Advice that my Lady had disposed them after this manner, and that she called them, The Streights of Gibralter; and told him, that he ought by no Means to venture the Passage, without being furnished with all the Things necessary, especially if he designed to stop at *Hercules's Pillars*. In short, after several Disputes and Contests on both sides, the *Abbé* passed the *Streights*, and arrived at the Port, where he was well received. But this was not without some Pain and Difficulty, and that too after his assuring me, that his Entrance should not be attended with any bad Consequences. I permitted him to sojourn there so long as might make him happy, this was the seventh Day of *August*, A Day that my *Lady* used to employ in extraordinary Ceremonies, but which her Indisposition obliged her to put off till the next Month. He told me, that the second Year of her being Abbess, she had created an Order of *Knighthood*, which was composed only of *Priests*, *Abbés*, *Monks*, and other religious Persons and Ecclesiasticks. That those who were admitted, took an Oath to keep secret the *Mysteries* of the *Order*, and called themselves *Knights* of the *Grille*,* or *Knights* of St. *Laurence*.† That the Collar, which was given them on the Day of their Creation, was composed of my Lady's *Cyphers* and *True-Love's Knots* alternately; and on the bottom hung a golden Medal, representing the Patron of the Order lying all naked on a *Grille*, or *Gridiron*, in the middle of the Flames, with these Words. ARDOREM CRATICULA FOVET; that is, *The Grille augments my Fires*. He shewed me the Collar that was given him, and after some Presents he made me of several curious Books, we took leave of each other till another Opportunity.

ANGEL. What you tell me, in relation to this Order instituted by my *Lady*, is no new Thing to me. My Lord Bishop of ★★★★ is the first Knight, the *Abbé Beaumont* the second, the *Abbé du Prat* the third, the *Prior* of *Pompiere* the fourth. These are the principal, and the first created; they are followed with *Jesuites*, *Jacobines*,¶ *Augustines*, *Carmelites*, *Fathers* of the *Oratory*, and the *Provincial* of the *Cordeliers*. So that at the last Promotion, which she made a Year ago, the Number was two and twenty. But you must observe, that there is a great deal of Difference amongst them, and that they cannot enjoy all of them the same Privileges. There are some of them who call themselves *Blue Ribands*, and these are they which are the most puissant, and know the *Secrets* of the *Order*, and who manage my Lady's Affairs, as my Lady has the Conduct of theirs; as for the rest, their Power is limited. They have their settled Boundaries which they cannot pass and have no other Advantages than of Aspirers to the supreme Class or Dignity, till, by their Zeal, Prudence, and Discretion, they shall have rendered themselves worthy to be permitted to make their grand and last Profession. Of all religious Persons, only the *Capucins*‡ are excluded, because that Beard of theirs which disguises them so much hath rendered them odious to our Abbess, who says that she cannot imagine that any one of the Sex can wish well to those Satires. But, now I think of it, tell me some News of *Pere Vitalis* of *Charenton*.

AGNES. I should never have believed, any more than my Lady, that a *Capucin* could be capable of any Gallantry, if this good Father had not by his Conduct convinced me to the contrary. He came to see me three Days

---

* Here is a material *Double Entendre*, *Grille*, in *French*, signifying a *Nun's Grate*, and a *Gridiron*.

† Saint *Laurence* was broiled to Death on a *Gridiron*.

¶ *Jacobines* are the same as *Dominican-Friars*, so called in *France*, because their principal Convent is at *Paris*, in the *Rue St. Jaques*.

‡ The *Capucins* after they have taken their *Vows* of *Profession* never shave or cut their Beards, which makes some of them have terrible long ones.

after the *Abbé*, we went into the *Parlour* of St. *Augustine*,* and there it was that he bestowed on me more Flourishes than I could have expected from a Courtier by Profession, and spoke besides so much *en Debauché* as I was ashamed to hear from the Mouth of a Man, whose Habit and Beard preached nothing but Pennance, proceed[ing] Words indeed in the beginning favouring only of a little Libertinism, but in the end, as dissolute as the greatest *Debauché* could make use of. I could not help discovering to him my Astonishment, and give him to understand, that he was too excessive in his Transports, which made him behave himself with a little more Moderation. He gave me three Visits during your Retreat; but in the last he obtained very little of me, because the Parlour where we were had not those Conveniencies of the other. I shall only tell you that he afforded me sufficient Cause of Laughter, having by meer Strength displaced one of the Bars of the Grate, and, thinking he had made a Way large enough for him to pass through, he ventured on it much against my Inclination; but he could by no means bring it about, for, having got through his Head and one of his Shoulders with a great deal of difficulty, his Hood caught hold of one of the Spikes on the outside, in such a manner, that he had much ado to stir, and could not disengage himself from this Trap. I could not see him in this Condition without bursting out into a loud Laugh. I immediately assisted him to retreat, and made him put the Bar into it's former Position. He gave me three or four Books, which he mentioned to me in his first Visit, and went away highly dissatisfied with his Adventure.

ANGEL. I am sorry for this Disorder, for, without doubt, he was very much daunted.

AGNES. Daunted! Oh Lord! he is a Man indeed to be daunted! there is not a more impudent Thing in the World: Oh, I shall have him here again before the end of the Week. He promised me, *The Collection of the secret Amours of* Robert d'Abrissel. He began to relate the whole History, but I believe it to be false, and counterfeited at pleasure.

ANGEL. Thou art mistaken, there is nothing truer; and several grave Authors say that he used to lie with his Nuns in order to prove their Chastity; and to observe at the same time in himself, how far the Force of that Virtue, which fights against the Temptation of the Flesh, might extend. He believed he merited a great deal by his Conduct; which gave occasion to *Godfrey* of *Vendome,* to treat this Devotion as pleasant and ridiculous in a Letter which he writes to St. *Bernard*, where he calls this Fervour a new Kind of Martyrdom.

---

* The *Nuns* give always some Saint's Name to their *Parlours* to distinguish them one from the other.

AGNES. It must be own'd, there are a great many Abuses practised in Convents; and I am no longer surprized that so many People have an Aversion for them. The *Feuillant*, whom I saw during your Retreat, shew'd me plainly the defective Places of the present Government, in relation to religious Orders. He is a Man who, considering his Youth (for he is but six and twenty), is Master of all the Sciences that may make a Person accomplish'd, of what Character soever he be. He discours'd on all Subjects whatsoever, but with an Air entirely disengag'd and which has nothing in it of the Pedant.

ANGEL. I plainly see he pleased thee. He is well made, and a beautiful young Fellow. For my part, I call him nothing else but my *large white Thing*.* In what Parlour were you?

AGNES. I saw him twice: The first time was in the Parlour of St. *Joseph*, and the second in that of my Lady.

ANGEL. Very well; which is as much as to say, that he passed the *Streights*. He has a great deal of Merit, and one takes a pleasure in shewing him one's Person.

AGNES. He gave me two little Phials of Essence, which smelt wonderfully. He was perfum'd from Head to Foot, and had such a lively Colour that I fancied he made use of the Pencil; but I was satisfied to the contrary at last, and the Red proceeded only from that Ardour of his Passion, and his being newly shaved. His Entertainment and little Toyings, pleased me infinitely, and I had no Difficulty of granting him the Passage which I so much disputed with the Abbé. I only represented to him, that he had Cause to fear lest the Fooleries that passed between us two, be not attended with a third. I understand you, replied he, and drew at the same time out of his Pocket, a little Book, which he gave me, written in *French*, called, *Remedés† doux & faciles contre l'embon point dangereux*.[8] He told me, that he would teach me what I should do in the like Occasion. He put into my Mouth a Piece of Conserve, which I found had no disagreeable Taste, I know not whether it had any hidden Virtue, but he soon put himself into a Condition of arriving at *Hercules*'s Pillars.

ANGEL. Which is to say, that the great white Thing gained thy Heart?

AGNES. Most certainly he shared it with the Abbé. I cannot tell to whom I could give the Preference. One Thing indeed shocked me in the *Feuillant*. Having perceived about his Neck a Reliquary¶ of Silver gilt,

---

* Alluding to the white Habit those Fathers wear; a Description of which we have before given.

† The Title of this Book is one of those *double Entendres*, which cannot be translated.

¶ A Box, or Case for Relicks.

which he wore next his Heart, I had the Curiosity to open it, but I was very much surprized to find nothing else in it but Hair, and Hairs of different Colours, divided in several Compartments figured and very well designed.

He told me that these were the Favours of all his Mistresses, and begged of me in like manner to encourage his Devotion; and that he would acknowledge the Favour that I should bestow upon him, by putting it into the most beautiful Place of that Repository. What think you? In short, I satisfied him. I forgot to tell you, that it had, in Letters of Gold, this Inscription, in the Middle of a Chrystal, which covered all this fine Ware, *Relicks of St. Barbe.*★ On the Top of the Reliquary was engraved a *Cupid* on a Throne, and the loving Fool prostrate at his Feet, with these Words, which I well remember, though they were in *Latin*: AVE LEX, JUS, AMOR.[9] I blamed him for this Irreverence, which I treated as profane; but he did nothing but laugh at me, and said, he could not refuse giving this Worship to those who deserved all sorts of Adoration, and that if he knew but how to decipher seven other Letters which were on the other Side, I should exclaim much more; and indeed turning it about, I saw these seven following: A.C.D.E.D.L.G. He would never tell me the meaning of them, tho' I often desired him in the most pressing manner. I pretended to be out of Humour with him, but he saw very well that I would do him no great Injury, whereupon he embraced me again, and so we took our leaves of each other.

ANGEL. I am infinitely pleased, my dear Child, that every thing succeeded according to my Wishes. This is nothing but a Specimen, in regard to what I design to do for thee; and I'll take care to bring thee acquainted with a Jesuit, to whom, without doubt, thou wilt give the Prize; and thou wilt be obliged to own that Father more excellent than all others. But he is jealous to excess in his Intrigues, which is the only Fault thou wilt ever find in him: He is otherwise a handsome Man, full of Gallantry, and excellently well spoken, and is ignorant of nothing that may bring him to the Knowledge of a Person of our Sex.

AGNES. This Imperfection is very great, for which reason I cannot by any Means suit my self to him.

ANGEL. Why so? Thou wilt have a great deal of difficulty to find a Man who loves sincerely, and not jealous. I remember to have known a *Benedictine,* who believed that all the Nuns of St. *Benedict* could not receive Visits from one of any other Order, without doing an Act of Injustice, and

---

★ The double *Entendre* consists in this, that Barbe in French signifies both *Barbara* and *Beard*.

that in such Case they robbed him and his Brother Monks of all those Favours which they bestowed upon the *Capuchins*. Hear how he reasoned: One cannot doubt but Men, who are in Religion are subject to the same Passions and Movements of those who are in the World.* It is in this view, said he, that the Founders of Orders, who were very much enlightened, never erected Cloisters for their own Sex, but at the same time built those for Women, to the end, that, without having recourse to Strangers, they might comfort each other from time to time as to the Rigour of their Vows. In the Beginning this was practiced according to the Intention of their Institutors, which caused no Scandal; but at present these Places partake of the general Corruption. One has no Difficulty to find the *Benardin* Monk with the *Dominican* Nun, the *Cordelier* with the *Benedictine*, and from this horrible Confusion there can be produced nothing but Monsters.

AGNES. This Thought was pleasant enough.

ANGEL. Alas! cried he, what would all these holy Founders say, at the Sight of so many adulterated Conversations, were they to return upon the Earth! What Thunders, what Anathemas would they not fulminate against their own Children! Would not St. *Francis* send back the *Capuchins* to the *Capuchinesses*, the *Cordeliers* to the *Cordelieres*! Would not St. *Dominic*, St. *Bernard*, and the rest, make all these Wanderers to come back again into the ancient Road of their Rules and Constitutions? that is to say, the *Jacobins* to the *Jacobines*, and the *Feuillants* to the *Feuillantines*. But what would become, said I, of the *Jesuits* and the *Carthusians?* For neither St. *Ignatius*† nor St. *Bruno*¶ ever composed any Rules for our Sex. O that *Spaniard*, said he, has very well provided for that, he did it on purpose that his Followers might rove with Impunity amongst them all. Besides following his Fancy, which was a little upon the *Pedaraste*,‡ he put them into Employments, where amongst the Youth they find those Satisfactions which they prefer to all the Diversions they might have with others.

As for the *Carthusians*, continued he, as Retirement is strictly enjoined those Fathers, they seek in themselves the Pleasure which they cannot go

---

* The religious of both Sexes call all that do not live in Cloisters, *People that are in the World*, believing themselves to be out of it.

† St. *Ignatius*, sirnamed *Loyola*, was a *Spaniard*, and Founder of the Order of the *Jesuits*.

¶ St. *Bruno*, Founder of the *Carthusians*, a strict Order: they never eat Flesh, speak to each other but twice a Week, Thursdays and Sundays, when they dine in common; at other times eat a-part, each in his own Cell and wear always a Shirt made of Horse-Hair.

‡ *Pederaste*. This Word is derived from the *Greek*, and means a Lover of young People. Some malicious Folks would say, a Lover of Boys. The *double Entendre* consists in this, that the Jesuits Employment is chiefly to teach Youth.

and find amongst others; and by means of a strong and furious Battle, conquer the most rude Temptations of the Flesh. They repeat the Fight as long as their Enemy can make Resistance. In this Combat they employ all their Vigour, and call these sorts of Expeditions, *The Battle of Five to One.* Well, what do you think? Did not the Disciple of St. *Benedict* talk very learnedly?

AGNES. Undoubtedly, and I should have taken a singular Pleasure to have heard him.

ANGEL. There is nothing more certain than that these Things are practised, and that if even in this Disorder some Regulations were kept, Things would go much better than they do. It is but a Year ago that a young Nun would not have been so unfortunate as she afterwards was, had she had to do with the Provincial* of her own Order, instead of one of another. Thou hast heard talk, perhaps, of Sister *Cecilia.*

AGNES. No, tell me, I beseech you, what you know of her.

ANGEL. Sister *Cecilia* is a Nun of the Order of St. *Augustine*, and *Pere Raymond* was then Provincial of the Jacobins. I will not tell you what Method he took to insinuate himself into the Mind of this poor Innocent, who had been inaccessible to every one before; but thou shalt only understand that he acquitted himself so well, that never Friendship in the World was so strictly observed, and they could not rest a Moment without seeing one another, or receiving from each other some little News.

This was taken notice of by the Community, and the *Augustine* Provincial who governed this House, having been inform'd of it, was all in Despair, because he could never gain any Thing upon her, though he endeavoured by all sorts of Ways to corrupt her. She was the most beautiful Creature in the whole Monastery. Being shocked after so sensible a Manner, he wrote to the Superiour, and gave her strict orders to have a watchful Eye over *Cecilia*'s Conduct. It was very easy for that Prioress soon to discover some little Indiscretions, because no body stood upon their Guard; however, these were no more than petty Fooleries, which, not withstanding, were sufficient to give a Handle to a jealous Person who had it in his Power to ill-treat a poor Religious.† However, he formed no direct Design against her, but laid hold of this Opportunity to obtain from her that which he could not accomplish before. He wrote to her himself, that it might make no Noise, and forbad her coming to the Grate till he came himself to the Convent. He was then twenty Leagues off.

---

* *Provincial* is one chosen out of the Body of a religious Order, to preside over all the Convents of a whole Province or Country.

† Another Name for a Nun or Friar.

AGNES. But were there no Proofs produced against her of her having done any thing remarkable or worthy of a severe Reprehension?

ANGEL. Oh! that is easily done; People know how to find Means when they have a Mind to ruin any one. But however, all the Mischief had not befallen her, had she not been ill-advis'd. When the Provincial arrived, he told her that it was upon the Informations he had received of her ill Conduct that he came thither; that it was a shameful Thing for a young Nun, as she was, to abandon her self up to those Actions which could not be named but for their Infamy; and that it was a Thing the most disagreeable in the World to him, to find himself under a Necessity to inflict on her an exemplary Punishment. *Cecilia*, who was no ways culpable before but in some little Indiscretions, as leering Looks, and gentle Touches, said, that it was very true, that she had very often seen *Pere Raymond*, whom he talked of, but that she knew, at the same time, that she never had any Affair with him that deserved any particular Reprehension; that she turned him off immediately as soon as she received his Orders, and that she shewed by this that there was no very strict Engagement between them. The Provincial, to come at what he aimed at, changed his Discourse, and spoke in Terms more tender, and represented to her that if she underwent any Kind of Mortification, it must be entirely owing to her self; that she could remedy the Disorder she had been the Cause of, and that it would be very easy for her to avoid those rigorous Corrections which would inevitably be her Destiny to undergo, if she did not make use of those Advantages she was Mistress of. He took her at the same time by the Hand, which he pressed very amorously, looking on her with a Smile which might make her sensible of the Disposition of her Judge's Heart.

AGNES. And did not she make use of all that was most engaging in her, to avoid the Danger in which she saw her self involved?

ANGEL. No, she took a quite contrary Method to what she ought to have followed: She imagined that he only intended to try her; that he talked to her after this manner, and had no other Design but to judge by her Weakness of what she was capable of in relation to intriguing with the other good Father. Upon this ill Foundation she answered him, who was all on fire for her, with only Coldness, and Words scarce so much as indifferent; which changed the Heart of her Lover, who from a tender Suitor, became an implacable Judge. He proceeded then against her according to Form of Process: He received those Depositions which Jealousy and Flattery had put into the Mouth of several of the Community and condemned this poor Girl to be whipped till the Blood came, to fast Fridays with Bread and Water, and to be excluded the Parlour for six Months: So that one may say that she was punished for being too sage, and for not letting her self be corrupted by the Brutality of her Superiour.

AGNES. Lord, how this touches me! I look upon this poor Nun as an innocent Victim sacrificed to the Rage of a furious Letcher; and I make no difference between her and the eleven thousand Virgins.

ANGEL. Thou art much in the right on't; for they say that they were murdered for not satisfying the Passion of one Man, and she barbarously ill treated on the same Account. As there is no Animal in the World more luxurious than a Friar; so there is nothing more malicious and vindictive when one despises their Passion. I have read, upon this Subject, the History of a certain *Capuchin*, in a Book called *The Goat in a Heat*.* But now I think of it, tell me what were the Books they gave thee in my Retreat.

AGNES. With all my Heart: They are very pleasant ones I assure you. See here is the Catalogue.

> *Fruitful Chastity*. A Curious Novel.
> *The Passport of the Jesuits*. A Gallant Piece.
> *The Prison enlightened*: or, *The Opening of the Little
>   Wicket*, with Figures.
> *The Journal of the* Feuillantines.†
> *The Prowess of the Knights of S.* Laurence.
> *The Rules and Statutes of* C★★★★★★ Abbey.
> *A Collection of Remedies against* l'Embonpoint d'an
>   gereux.¶ *Composed for the Commodity of the
>   Nuns of St.* George.
> *The Extreme Unction of dying Virginity*.
> *The Apostolical* Orvietan, *Composed by the Four Orders
>   Mendicant*,‡ ex precepto sanctissimi.
> *The Cut—A———se of the Friers*.
> *The Pastime of the Abbés*.
> *The* Carthusian's *Battle*.
> *The Fruits of the Unitive Life*.[11]

I think I have not omitted one in this List. I have read five or six of them which please me wonderfully.

---

* The *Capuchins* wearing long Beards, are in Derision called Goats.

† Nuns so called, the Men of that Order are called *Feuillants*: See the earlier Notes.

¶ Those who understand *French* will know the Author's Meaning.

‡ The Four Mendicant Orders are those of St. *Augustine*, St. *Dominic*, St. *Francis*, and the *Carmelites* so called from Mount *Carmel* where they have a Convent, on which Mount lived the Prophet *Elias* they say as an *Eremite*, and from whom they also say they descended.

ANGEL. O' my Conscience! I think they have given thee a whole Library. If the Insides answers the Titles, as I doubt not but they do, these Books must be very diverting. Thou hast enough in them to improve thy Mind and make thee as thou shouldst be, that is, universally knowing in all Sciences. For there are those, who though they are in the midst of much Light, have, notwithstanding, certain Doubts which give them a great deal of Pain, the Consequences of which are often very dangerous. I shall tell thee a Story upon this very Subject which happened in the Abbey of *Chelles*.

AGNES. Certainly you must have had wonderful Intrigues to learn all, even the most secret Things, that have happened in Cloisters.

ANGEL. Thou must know that the Abbess of that House being of a very hot Constitution, used to bathe herself for some Weeks in Summertime. This Bath was made according to the Direction of the Physician, who to make it the better, prescribed a certain Rule and Method to be observed, without which it would be of no manner of Benefit. It was entirely to be prepared the Evening before the Day on which it was to be made Use of, and the Water to lie all Night long 'till the next Day, when it was to be made Use of at certain set Hours. Perfumes and Essences were not wanting, they were employed to Profusion, and every Thing also that might sooth the Sensuality of my Lady entered into that Composition.

AGNES. These are the Physicians, which be a false Complaisance, thus keep up the *Foibles* and weak Sides of their Patients.

ANGEL. No doubt. However, a certain Nun of that House, called Sister *Scholastica*, about eighteen, seeing all these great Preparations for my Lady and perceiving the Bath was ready that very Evening, formed in her Head a Design as well in order to refresh and comfort herself, (as to the Inconveniences of the Season) as to cool her inward Heat, which is no small one, to take hold of the Opportunity and make every Evening a Proof of that salutary *Lavabo*. In short, she continued to do so for eight Evenings successively, and found it gave a Brilliancy and Lustre to her Complexion and that she slept much better. She came out of her Cell about nine o'Clock and almost naked to her Smock, she went to the Place where every Thing had been prepared and got ready; when whipping off her Petticoat and Smock in a Moment, plunged herself naked into the Tub, where she washed and rubbed herself all over and came out afterwards as clean, pure and beautiful as *Eve* in Paradise during her State of Innocence.

AGNES. Was she not discovered?

ANGEL. Thou shalt hear presently. One Evening that *Scholastica* was refreshing herself as usual, an old Nun that was not then asleep, having heard somebody walking along the *Dormitory** at an Hour when according to their Rules all the Nuns ought to be a Bed went out of her Cell, and after having in vain sought for the Person whom she had heard came to the Place where the Bath was, and soon perceived by the Light of the Moon, a Nun all naked wiping herself with a Napkin and just going to put on her Smock. The good old Nun thinking it was the Abbess, retired immediately, asking Pardon for her advancing so far. *Scholastica*, who spoke not one Word, knew very well that this good Mother† was deceived, and had taken her for another. She went away after having given the other Time to retire, and was resolved to come there no more for fear of being discovered.

AGNES. And did it end here?

ANGEL. No, the Thighs of poor *Scholastica* paid for it very severely.

AGNES. How? What, did that pretty Creature undergo any Displeasure?

ANGEL. The Venerable Mother I just now mentioned, reflecting the next Morning on what she had seen the Night before, believed it very proper to find out my Lady and to make a particular Excuse for that Accident, which could be attributed to nothing but an evil Curiosity. This was very unhappy for poor *Scholastica*. The Abbess was entirely in a Surprize, it gave her Grounds to believe that she had participated only of the Remains and disgustful Relicks of some infirm Person of the Community. She spoke of it the next Day in her Chapter, and commanded under *holy Obedience*¶ that Nun who made Use of the Bath to own her Crime. *Scholastica* was none of the most scrupulous, and having a good Share of Wit, held her Tongue. This Silence put the Abbess into the utmost Despair. She cried, thundered, and threatned every Body but to no Purpose. At last, by the Advice of a Friar, she put in Practice a very pleasant Stratagem. She called all the Nuns together and told them that there was one amongst them excommunicated and in the State of Damnation for not revealing what she had commanded *in Virtue of holy Obedience*. That a very learned and holy Man had put her into a sure and infallible Way to discover her, but that she would permit her yet to speak that she might avoid by that Means those rude Penances which she would draw upon herself by her formal Disobedience.

---

* *Dormitory*, or *Dortoir*, is that Gallery in Cloisters on each Side of which are the Cells, or little Chambers, of the Religious of both Sexes.

† Nuns after seven Years of Profession, that is seven Years after they have taken their Vows, are called *Mothers*, and in some Orders *Dames*, 'till then they are only *Sisters*.

¶ The Nuns make three Vows after a whole Year's Noviceship or Probation, *viz.* of *Poverty*, *Chastity* and *Obedience*. So that to disobey any Command under *holy Obedience*, is looked upon as a manifest Breach of their Vow, and the greatest Crime that can be committed.

AGNES. Ah Lard! in this Perplexity I tremble for poor *Scholastica*, for the Advices of Friars are every one of them always pernicious.

ANGEL. My Lady seeing this last Effort proved ineffectual, followed the Advice that was given her. She caused a Table to be set up in a certain Room and to be covered with a Funeral Pall. In the middle of this Table was placed the Chalice* of the Sacristy.† Things being thus disposed, she commanded all the Nuns to go one after another into the Room, and touch with their Hand the Foot of the Sacred Vessel, (for so she called it) which was exposed upon the Table, that by this Means she could discover her who had 'till then concealed herself, because she should no sooner have put her Fingers upon that Sacred Cup, but the Table would presently tumble down to the Ground and discover by a secret Virtue from high, her that had been thus criminal. This was done about nine o'Clock at Night in the dark. The Nuns went accordingly into the Room, and touched the Foot of the Chalice as they were directed. *Scholastica* was the only one that did not dare to do so for fear of being discovered and touched only the Pall. After which she retired with all the rest into another Room, which was also without Light, where the Abbess made them come to her one after another, 'till the whole Ceremony should be finished. Now it must be observed that she had blackened the Foot of the Chalice with Oil and Lamp-black, so that it was impossible to touch it without carrying away some Signs of it. Having then lighted a Candle in the Room where she was, she examined the Hands of all the Nuns and found that every one of them had touched the Cup but *Scholastica*, who had nothing of Blackness upon her Hand as the others of the Community had. This made her conclude that she was the Criminal. This poor Innocent finding herself cheated by a false Artifice, had Recourse to Tears and Excuses and was acquitted for a couple of Disciplines, which she received before the whole Company. Well! this was only that Exterior of Religion impiously enough made Use of, which put her into such a Fright and which she never would have been sensible of had she but made some little Reflection upon the Impossibility that there was of making a Discovery by so ridiculous an Artifice.

AGNES. Very true, but the Abbess should have pardoned her Youth and Beauty.

ANGEL. She might indeed have done so, but she did not, and I have heard say, that the first Discipline she ordered her lasted near a Quarter of

---

* Chalice is the Communion Cup.

† Sacristy is a Kind of Vestry-Room, where they keep the Priest's Vestments, Plate, and other Church Ornaments.

an Hour. Judge then by that what a Condition must have the Thighs of this poor Soul been in.

AGNES. Without doubt much like mine when I shewed them to you. If it was in my Power I would send to the Gallies for his Life that cursed Counsellor of the Abbess, and if it happened to me, I would have laid so many Trains, by the Means of my Friends without* for that Friar, that he should have repented of his Stratagem.

ANGEL. Dost imagine that if he had thought it had been *Scholastica* that was to have been disciplined he would have advised as he did? No, no. He imagined as well as the Abbess that it was some old Nun or some in-firm Person that had been thus surprized; and this was what made the Abbess so uneasy in her Mind, to be as she believed, bathed in the Ordures of such People.

AGNES. For my Part I believe she was comforted when she knew it was *Scholastica*, for one is not disgusted at a young Girl handsome and well made as you have represented her. The Penance she underwent makes me think of *Virginia* and the Children of the Jesuit's Square Cap.

ANGEL. I must shew thee a couple of them, which I have here in my Casket. One is from *Pere de Raucourt* and the other from *Virginia*. Here take this first and read it to me.

AGNES. This is like a Woman's Hand, every Thing looks so negligent and careless.

Ah Lord! my dear Child, how does this Correspondence by Letters begin to give me the greatest Uneasiness in the World! it does nothing but add Fuel to my Fire and gives me no manner of Comfort; it tells me Virginia *wishes me well, but it informs me at the same Time that it is impossible for me to enjoy her. Ah! what strange Movements doth such a Mixture of sweet and bitter cause in a Heart so formed as mine is! I have often heard that Love bestows sometimes Wit on those who were unprovided of it, but I am sensible of a quite contrary Effect in me and I can speak it for a Truth, that it hath taken away from me what it hath given to oth-ers. A great many perceive this Change but they are ignorant of the Cause. I preached yesterday at the Nuns of the Visitation. I never was more animated; I should, conformably to my Subject, have entertained my Audience with Mortification and Penance, and I talked of nothing in my whole Discourse but of Affections, Tenderness, Sallies and Transports. It is you,* Virginia, *that cause this Disorder. Take then Pity of my Wan-*

---

* By *without*, they mean those who are in the World, as they call all those who do not live in Convents, and take the three Vows.

*derings, and study how to find the Way to bring me back to my Senses.
Adieu.*

ANGEL. Well, *Agnes*, what dost thou think of this Child got in Haste?

AGNES. I find it worthy its Father, and capable, all naked as it is of
Cloaths and Ornaments, to preserve not only one Heart it is in Possession
of, but even to excite in it new Movements.

ANGEL. Thou art much in the Right on't, for in Love the most negligent Style is the most persuasive, and very often all the Eloquence of an
Orator hath not been able to raise in a Soul those sweet Transports which
are not the Effect of a lofty, but expressive Term. It is a Truth which I can
witness, since I have frequently experienced it myself. But let us see a little if *Virginia* expresses herself as well as her Lover.

AGNES. Give me the Letter that I may read it.

ANGEL. Here, take it. It is rather a Billet than a Letter, for the whole
does not make above five or six Lines.

AGNES. Her Hand does not differ much from mine.

*Ah! how artful are you in your Expressions, and how well do you know
how to trouble the little Quiet that remains in a poor Innocent that loves
you! Can you with any Reason ask if I think of you? Alas! my Dear,
consult your own self, and believe that we cannot both of us be animated
with the same Passion, without being sensible of the same Resentments.
Adieu,* think of the breaking of our Chains! *Love makes me capable
of any Enterprize. Ah! in me what Weakness does it cause, my dearest
Soul, adieu.*

ANGEL. Is it not true, that thou findest this Billet more tender than the
Letter?

AGNES. Most certainly, one may say it is all Heart, and that two or
three Periods express as much the Disposition of a Lover as three Pages of
a Romance. But I do not see that it is an Answer to that which we read
from *Pere de Raucourt*.

ANGEL. No, it is an Answer to another which they have not sent me.

AGNES. The Unhappiness of these poor Lovers touches me, especially
I cannot but have an extreme Compassion on the Mortifications of *Vir-
ginia*, for without doubt she passes her Time at present in a great deal of
Chagrin and Uneasiness, and leads a very wretched and miserable Life.

ANGEL. If she had not kept the Letters and Billets that were directed
to her she had not been so unhappy, for they could not else have discovered the Design she had of running away from the Monastery.

AGNES. It is of that she speaks, undoubtedly, when she says in her Billet, *Think of the breaking of our Chains.* I should never have thought of the true Sense of those Words. Oh! the poor Child, how miserable would she have been had she endeavoured to have put that Design in Execution and had failed! Alas! what is not Love capable of when it sees itself encountered?

ANGEL. As soon as the Rector of the Jesuits was apprized of what had passed, by the Letter which he found in the Cap, he gave Notice of it to her Superiour, who went immediately with her Assistant to visit *Virginia's* Cell where they found in her Casket a vast Number of Billets, and other *Bagatelles*, which evidently convinced her of the Truth of what she would not have believed had she not seen it. As she loved *Virginia* very well, so she would not have taken those Measures she did in proceeding against her, could she any wise have concealed it, but she moderated the Correction which the Constitutions prescribed.

AGNES. The Jesuit was more happy, for he came off by only changing his Province.

ANGEL. Oh! these Affairs are not passed over so easily as thou imaginest. He is at present out of the Society. Thou must know that in the Society, as every Thing turns and is established upon Esteem and Reputation, it is impossible for a Man of Honour to stay in it after he hath lost by some Accident or other in the Minds of his *Colleagues*, those two Things which so agreeably sooth and flatter the Minds of Men. *Pere de Raucourt*, seeing himself fallen by the Misfortune I just now mentioned from that high Degree of Glory which he had acquired by his Merits, and which he had always retained by his Prudence, made little Account of the Indulgence which his Superiors offered him, and thought of nothing more than leaving them, which he did sometime afterwards and retired into *England*.

AGNES. But what must a Man, who has no other Estate than his Learning and Philosophy, do in a strange Country?

ANGEL. That which he can do. He can by his fine Genius make himself more useful to a Commonwealth, if they would employ him, than all the Artisans that compose it. He can by his fine Pen give Life and Vigour to the Laws, tho' never so opposite to the Inclinations of the People. He can carry the Glory of a Nation to Climates the most remote and distant. In short, there is no Employment whatsoever which he cannot worthily discharge, and whom the State may not greatly benefit by. As what I say is not without Reason, so is it not without Example. And I have heard from a *Dominican*, that a Male-content of their Order was at the Court of that Kingdom where *Raucourt* is retired to, and that he makes a considerable Figure in Quality of Resident, or Envoy, from a certain Prince of *Germany*.

AGNES. Undoubtedly he would have carried *Virginia* thither could they have brought about their Designs. Alas! there would be but a very few Recluses of either Sex if they had but Time given them to reflect upon the Advantages of an Hour's Liberty and the dreadful Consequences of a fatal Engagement.

ANGEL. Why dost thou talk after that Manner? Cannot we taste Pleasures as perfect within the Enclosure of our Walls as they which are without? The Obstacles which oppose themselves serve only to make us relish them the better, when after having dexterously surmounted them, we possess that which we desired. It would be malicious and ungrateful to censure the Diversions of Nuns and Friars. For I should say to such People, Is it not true that Continence is a Gift of God, which he bestows *Gratis* on whom he pleases, and of which he does not grant the Bounty to any but on those whom he will vouchsafe to honour. This being supposed, he will not make those give any Account of that Gift who have not received it.

AGNES. I conceive the Strength of that Argument, but it may be said that the Vows by which we have so solemnly engaged ourselves to him, make us responsible to him.

ANGEL. Ah! dost thou not see plainly that those Vows which thou madest between the Hands of Men are only mere Sing-Songs? Canst thou reasonably oblige thyself to give that which thou hast not? And which thou canst not have, if it does not please him to whom thou offers it to bestow it upon thee. Judge by this of the Nature of our Engagement, and if in Rigour we are bound to fulfill them according to Conscience and our Promises since they contain in them a moral Impossibility. Thou canst say nothing to destroy this Way of reasoning.

AGNES. It is very true; and this is what ought to make us easy in our Minds.

ANGEL. For my Part, I can tell thee that nothing gives me the least Chagrin. I pass the Time with an Equality of Mind which makes me insensible to the Pains which fatigue others. I see all Things, I hear all Things, but few Things are capable of moving me, and if my Repose was not troubled by some corporal Indisposition, no one in the World could live with greater Tranquility.

AGNES. But in a Conduct so opposite to that of other Cloisters, what think you of the Disposition of their Souls, and those Actions which are attended, as they preach, with so many Merits? Do they not tempt you by the Hope they propose? They may tell us that Libertinism is often capable to furnish us with Reasons to ruine us. For what is more holy than the Meditation upon heavenly Things in which they employ themselves?

What is more laudable than that high Piety which they put in Practice; and must the Tears and Austerities with which they mortify themselves pass for fruitless Works?

ANGEL. Ah! my Child! how weak are these Objections? Thou must know that there is a great deal of Difference between Licentiousness and Liberty. In my Actions I very often follow what is agreeable to the latter, but never suffer myself to fall into the Disorders of the former. If I prescribe no Bounds to my Pleasures it is because they are innocent and never hurt by their Excess those Things for which I ought to have a Veneration. But thou wouldst have me tell thee what I think of those melancholy Fools, whose Way of Living charms thee. Dost thou not know that what thou callest Contemplation of divine Things is nothing in the Bottom but a profound Laziness, incapable of all Action? That the Movements of this heroic Piety which thou makest such a Clutter about, proceeds from nothing but a distempered Reason; and to find out the general Cause which makes them tear and flay themselves, one must look for it in the Vapors of a black Humour or the Weakness of their Brain.

AGNES. I take so much Pleasure in hearing of you discourse, that I proposed all this on Purpose as a Difficulty of which I had no manner of Doubt. But I hear the Bell which calls us.

ANGEL. 'Tis to the Refectory,* after Dinner we may continue our Discourse.

Dialogue III.

Sister AGNES, Sister ANGELICA.

AGNES. Ah! how agreeable is the Beauty of the Day! it revives my Spirits. Let us both retire into this Walk, that we may be far from any Company.

ANGEL. It is impossible to find in the whole Garden a properer Place to walk in, for the Trees that are round us will afford as much Shade as is necessary to screen us from the Heat of the Sun.

AGNES. That is very true, but I am afraid, lest my Lady should come and turn us out, for in this very Place she chuses to recreate herself in after Meals.

ANGEL. Thou has no Cause to apprehend that, she is at present out of Order; and if thou didst but know the Cause of her Indisposition, thou wouldst laugh heartily.

---

* In Monasteries the Room or Hall where they dine or sup is called the Refectory.

AGNES. She was very well yesterday.

ANGEL. Very true, the Distemper seized her but last Night only, and thou must have been in a profound Sleep not to have perceiv'd it, for her squawling alarmed the whole Dormitory: I design'd to have diverted ourselves with this Adventure in the Morning, but our Discourse insensibly carried us to far different Subjects.

AGNES. Indeed I never hear any News 'till it is very publick.

ANGEL. Thou must know then that my Lady places one of her principal Diversions in feeding all Sorts of Animals, and that she does not content herself with having an Infinity of Birds of every Country, but has made familiar to her even Tortoises and Fishes: And as she does not hide this Folly, and that all her Friends know that she calls this Employment the Charms of her Solitude; they all strive to contribute to her Diversion by making of her a Present sometimes of one Beast, sometimes of another. The Abbot of St. *Valery* having heard that she made tame and familiar to her, even Carps and Pikes, sent to her four Days ago two live Barnacles, and two Lobsters also alive. After having cut the Wings of these two half Ducks, she ordered them to be put into the Fish Pond, and would bestow all her Application to bring up the Lobsters. For this Reason she made a little Tub be brought into her Chamber which she caused to be filled with Water, and the Lobsters to be put into it. It would give me a great deal of Trouble to tell thee what Care she took for their Preservation, even to throw them Sweet-Meats and Pistaches. In short, she was resolved to feed them with Victuals the most delicate.

AGNES. This Sort of Pastime is innocent and excusable in young People.

ANGEL. Last Night, by an unlucky Accident, Sister *Olinda,* who had Orders to change every Day the Water of the Tub to refresh the poor Things, had forgot to do so, which was the Occasion of all this Disorder. Thou must remember that last Night it being very hot, one of the Lobsters, which found himself incommoded with the Heat he felt, got out of the Tub and crawled a long while upon the Floor, 'till finding himself without any Comfort, he resolved to return back again to the Water, which he had left, as to his most natural Element. But as it was much more easy for him to descend than to mount up, he was obliged to have Recourse to the Water in my Lady's Chamber-pot, where without examining whether the Water was salt or fresh, he posted himself in that Vehicle. Sometime after our Abbess had a strong Propensity to piss, and being half asleep and without going out of Bed, took up the Urinal: But alas! she thought she should have died of the Fright! This wicked Lobster, which found himself bedewed with a Shower a little too hot, launched himself up towards that Place where he imagined it came, and took such strict hold of it with one of his Claws, that he left those Marks which will remain four or five Days at least.

AGNES. Ha! ha! ha! what a pleasant Adventure was this?

ANGEL. In the very Moment she gave such a Cry as waked all the Neighbourhood: She cast the Chamber-pot upon the Floor, and rising up in Haste, called every Body to her Assistance; in the meanwhile that Animal, which never tasted a Morsel so delicious, did not quit his Hold. The Mother-Assistant and Sister *Cornelia*, were the first that came to help her; they had much ado to forbear laughing at such a Spectacle. However, they refrained as much as possible, and were obliged to cut off the Claw of this Sacrilegious Beast, who would not 'till then leave his Prey. The Mother-Assistant retired, and Sister *Cornelia*, who is my Lady's Confidant, passed the rest of the Night with her in order to comfort her. And this is the Cause of the Indisposition of our Abbess, and what, in all Probability, will hinder her from interrupting our Discourse.

AGNES. Ah! I should not dare to appear, if an Accident like this had befallen me, and especially if it should have come to any other Peoples Knowledge.

ANGEL. Indeed there was a great deal of what she ought to be ashamed of; she shewed nothing, however, which she had not very often shewed to others, and the Knights of the Order have put their Hands in the Place where the Lobster had fixed his Claw.

AGNES. Which of them is her best Friend?

ANGEL. I do not know, but I know very well that a certain Jesuit visits her very often and partakes with her of those Privacies which makes him be known to be one of the blue Ribbons: I perceived her one Day with him in a very warm and brisk Discourse; and another Time, after she had parted from the same Person, I found in the Parlour a fine Napkin moisten'd in certain Places with a Liquor somewhat viscous, which she had dropped near the Window: I took no Notice of this Affair to any one, I only observed, that this Loss gave her some Uneasiness.

AGNES. What had she to apprehend? The Bishop on whom she entirely depends is at her Discretion, and at the Visitation that he made of this Monastery, he enjoined nothing but what she had prescribed him before.

ANGEL. It is very true, she is Mistress of all, and the Directors and Confessors are received and changed merely at her Pleasure.

AGNES. Ah! I could wish with all my Soul that the Confessor in Ordinary, which we have at present, did but displease her as much as she does me, what say you?

ANGEL. It is certain he is very austere, and that he is capable to give those who do not know how to behave themselves, a great deal of Uneasiness; but for we that do, it is very indifferent whether we make Use of him, or another less rigorous.

AGNES. For my Part I cannot tell him of the least *Peccatille*, but he is presently upon the high Ropes. For a Thought that I shall accuse myself of, he will enjoin me Mortifications and horrible Penances, and make me fast two Days for the least Movement of the Flesh that I shall confess myself of. Besides, I do not know how to spin out Time enough to keep him employed, for Fear of saying some[thing] that may shock him: And I cannot conceive what you do who hold him so long.

ANGEL. Ah! Dost think I am so great a Ninny as to declare to him all the Secrets of my Heart? Far from it: As I know he is extremely rigid, I only tell him such Things as he can by no Means take Hold of. He can never conclude by what he hears from me, but that I am a Child of Prayer and Contemplation, who is not acquainted with all the Movements of corrupted Nature, which makes him not dare to question me about those Matters. The rudest Penance he enjoins me, is only five *Pater Nosters, and the Litanies*.

AGNES. Well, but what is it you tell him then? For only for breaking Silence or rallying any of the Community, which is nothing, he will preach to me a Quarter of an Hour.

ANGEL. All these Faults being particularly mentioned with their Circumstances, the smallest of them become sometimes the most considerable, and this is what makes thee a Subject worthy [of] Reprehension. But stay, this is what I do, hearken to the Confession I made last. After having most humbly desired his Blessing, with my face held down, my Hands joined, and my Body half bent, I began after this Manner.

> Father, I am the greatest Sinner in the World, and the weakest of Creatures, I fall almost every Day into the same Faults.
>
> I accuse myself of having troubled the Tranquility of my Soul, by universal Divagations, which have put my Interiour into Disorder.
>
> Of having not sufficient Recollection of Spirit and of having been too much inclined to exteriour Occupations.
>
> Of having stopped too much at the Operations of the Understanding, bestowing therein the greatest Part of my Prayers to the Prejudice of my Will, which is become dry and barren.
>
> Of suffering myself once more to be bound by Affections, and exposed thereby to miserable Distractions, and a Laziness of Spirit, contrary to the Methodical Perfection of Contemplatists.

Of having too much conserved in me, all that was of me, without disengaging my Heart from Things created by a generous Act of Annihilation of Self-Love, Interests, Desires and Wills, and of my whole Self.

Of having made an Offering of my Heart, without having given it a previous Tranquilization, and divested it of the Trouble of Passions too moving, and of ill regulated Affections.

Of too much suffering myself to be carried away by the Inclinations of the old Man, and the Bent of unrepaired Nature, instead of divorcing myself from all, to gain all.

Of not having been solicitous of renewing myself, by a Review of myself, in myself, and to make in myself a Reparation of every Thing that was fallen in me, &c.

Well, *Agnes*, thou mayest judge of the Piece by the Sample. This is not the third Part of my Confession, but the Remainder made me no more criminal than the Beginning.

AGNES. Certainly I should be very much to blame to lay Penances on Sins so spiritualized. However, this is the only Way to deceive the Curiosity of young Directors, and avoid the Reprehension of the old.

ANGEL. The latter are generally the least tractable, for I never found any of the young ones, since I have been in the Community, but what were indulgent enough.

AGNES. It is true they are not equally rigorous; witness he who pushed Devotion so far into the Souls of two of our Sisters, that they found themselves very much incommoded for nine Months after.

ANGEL. Ah Lord! there must be a great deal of Address to conceal these Things and hinder their being known by those that are without. The Bishop himself knew nothing of the Matter, but when greater Proofs could not be given of it. This makes me think of an *Italian* Jesuit who confessing one Day, a young *French* Gentleman, who had learnt the Language of the Country, made an Exclamation without thinking of it, which sufficiently discovered his Weakness. The Penitent accused himself of having passed the Night with a young Creature of the principal Families of *Rome,* and that he enjoyed her according to his Desires. The good Father looking very attentively upon the Person who spoke to him, and who was very beautiful and well made, forgot the Place he sat in, and imagining himself to be in free Conversation, so much was he transported, asked him if the young Woman was handsome, what Age she might be of, and how often he had to do with her? The other having answered him, that he had found her an accomplished Beauty, that she was no more that eighteen, and that he had killed her three Times. *Ah! Qual Gusto, Signor*, cried he out aloud, which is to say, Ah! Lord! what Pleasure.

AGNES. This Sally was not unpleasant, and very capable of exciting the Heart of a Penitent, to repent of such like Faults undoubtedly.

ANGEL. What wouldst thou have? These are Men like others. And I have heard it said by one of my Friends who was occupied in those Employments, that very often a Confessor would not expose himself so much to Incontinency in a Brothel, as in hearing his *Devotes* whisper in his Ear.

AGNES. For my Part, I should find, I think, abundance of Diversion in this Employ, provided I might be suffered to chuse my Penitents: I should take a great deal of Pleasure to hear them, and my Imagination would be very lively touched by the Recital they would make of their Fooleries. All this could not prove but an extreme Satisfaction on my Side.

ANGEL. Alas! my Child! thou dost not know what thou desirest. If a *Devote* affords a Confessor some little Pleasure by a frank and open Recital of her *Foibles*, there are a Thousand who tire them with their Repetitions, load them with their Scruples, and whom they might sooner draw out of an Abyss than their Doubts. Sister *Dosithea* alone was more than three Years pestering the Ordinary Director of the House with her Questions; she took up almost all his Time, there was Scarce any Respite for any Body else. In vain did he represent to her that these curious Researches by which she tormented her Conscience, in fancying that she never had taken sufficient Care to examine it, were not only unprofitable, but even vicious and contrary to Perfection. He could gain nothing upon her, and was obliged to leave her to herself, and let her continue in her Error.

AGNES. However, methinks at present she is very reasonable, and I remember once when we were obliged to lie both together, which was while the Dormitory was building, she was not only very far from scrupulous, but I found her at that Time too free, besides a Thousand little Playings to which she excited me, by relating a Hundred Stories, the most slippery, and most lascivious in the World.

ANGEL. I plainly see that thou dost not know how she came out of the profound Darkness, into which Superstition had plunged her. Her Confessor bore no Part in her Deliverance. One may say that it was mere Devotion that produced this Change, and which out of a young Creature extremely scrupulous, formed a Nun entirely reasonable. I'll tell thee what I had from her own Mouth in Relation to this Affair.

AGNES. I do not conceive this: For to say that Devotion could rid any one of their Scruples, is the same Thing as to say, that a blind Man is capable of forcing another from a Precipice.

ANGEL. Only hear me out, and thou wilt find that I have advanced nothing but what is true. Sister *Dosithea,* as one may observe by her Eyes, was born of a Complexion the most tender, and most amorous in the World. This poor Creature at her Entrance into Religion, fell into the Hands of an old Director superlatively ignorant, and so much the more an Enemy to Nature, as his Age rendered him unable to taste all these Pleasures she proposeth to us. Finding therefore that the Inclination of his Penitent tended towards the Flesh, and that the Weaknesses which she accused her self of every Day were a certain Proof, he believed it to be his Duty to reform this Nature, which he called corrupted, and that it was permitted him to raise himself up as another Repairer of it. To bring his Design about, he immediately cast into her Mind all the Seeds of Doubts and Scruples, and Pains of Conscience, as he could think of or imagine: And in this he the more easily succeeded, as finding in her a great Disposition thereto, and that the ingenuous Confessions he had frequently heard from this Innocent convinced him of the extreme Tenderness she had in Relation to what regarded her Soul.

He drew her then the Picture of the Way to Heaven, in Colours so rude, that it was capable of discouraging a Person less zealous, and less fervent than *Dosithea.* He talked to her of nothing but the Destruction of this Body which opposed itself to the Enjoyment of the Spirit, and the horrible Penances which he loaded her with were, according to him, Means absolutely necessary, without which it was impossible for her to arrive at the Heavenly *Jerusalem.*

Dosithea being not capable of defending herself against these Arguments, suffered herself blindly to be led by an indiscreet Devotion, with which she became infatuated. The simple Practice of the Commandments passed with her as of little Value, unless attended with the Works of Supererogation; and even then with all this, she was ever in continual Fear of the Punishments of the other World, with which she was so frequently threatned. As it is impossible here below to destroy in us that which they call Concupiscence, she was never at Peace with herself. This was a War without any Intermission, which she imprudently waged against her poor Body, and the cruel Battles which she fought were rarely succeeded by any short lived Truce.

AGNES. Alas! how was she to be pitied! and what Compassion should not I have had for her, had I seen her in that straying wild Condition.

ANGEL. As her amorous Nature caused, as she told me, her greatest Faults, she neglected nothing that might extinguish her Fires the most innocent: Fastings, Hair and Sackcloth were made Use of, and the changing to a Director more reasonable than the former could not make any Diminution of her Folly. She was four whole Years entire in that Condition, and would have continued so till now, had not an Act of Devotion cured her. Amongst the many Advices she received from her ancient Director, this was one she practiced with an unparalleled Regularity, and it was to have Recourse to a Picture of *Saint Alexis,* the Mirror of Chastity,[12] which was in her Oratory, and to prostrate herself before it whenever she should find herself pressed with Temptation, or when she perceived in herself those Movements of which she so often made Confession. One Day then, when she found herself more moved than ordinary, she had Recourse to her Saint: She represented to him with Tears in her Eyes, her Face to the Ground, and her Heart elevated to Heaven, the extreme Danger she was in, recounting to him with a wonderful Simplicity and Candour, how fruitlessly she had defended her self and made Use of all her Efforts to repress those violent Transports, of which she had then such lively Sentiments.

She accompanied her Prayer with Penance, and the Discipline which she took in Presence of that blessed Pilgrim. But as it is reported of him, that he was no Ways touched with the Beauty of his Wife on the Wedding Night when he went away from her, the beautiful Body of this Innocent exposed naked before him made no Manner of Impression upon his Mind, and the Strokes which she laid upon her so plentifully, created in him no Spark of Compassion. After having thus flayed herself she began a new with this good *Roman,** and retired as victorious to practise with Tranquility those Exercises which were less fatiguing.

Agnes. Lord! what Ravage does Superstition make in a Soul it governs.

Angel. Scarce had *Dosithea* left her Cell when she felt all her Body in a Fire, and her Mind carried her to the Knowledge of a Pleasure she never knew before. An extraordinary Titillation animated all her Senses, and her Imagination filling itself with a Thousand lascivious Ideas, left this poor Nun half vanquished. In this piteous Condition she returned to her Intercessor, she redoubled her Prayers, and conjured him, by all that Devotion could most sensibly suggest, to bestow upon her the Gift of Continency: But her Fervour did not rest here. She resumed the Instruments of Penance, which she made Use of for a Quarter of an Hour, with an Ardour the most foolish and indiscreet in the World.

Agnes. Well, and did not all this give her some little Comfort?

Angel. Alas! very far from it! she retired to her Oratory† more trans-

---

* St. *Alexis* was born in *Rome.*

† In every Nun's Cell there is a little Partition like a Closet, but without any Door, where there are Shelves for their Books, and where they say their private Prayers.

ported with Love than before. It rung to Vespers;* she had much ado to stay out the whole Service: A Thousand Sparkles of Fire flew from her Eyes, and without knowing what she suffered, I wondered at her Restlessness and her not continuing in one Posture a Moment.

AGNES. But whence proceeded all this?

ANGEL. From the extreme Heat which she felt so sensibly in every Part of her Body which she had disciplined. For thou must know that these Sorts of Exercises, far from being capable of extinguishing those Flames that consumed her, had on the contrary increased them more and more, and reduced that poor Child into such a Condition, that she could, as it were, no longer resist them. This is easy to conceive, inasmuch as the Strokes of the Discipline she bestowed upon her Posteriours, having excited the Heat over all the Neighbourhood, had sent thither the purest and most subtle Spirits of the Blood, which to find an Issue conformable to their Nature were all on Fire, pricked in the most lively Manner, those Places where they were assembled, in order there to make some Overture or Passage.

AGNES. Did the Battle continue long?

ANGEL. It began and ended in one Day's Time. As soon as Vespers were over, *Dosithea*, though she had not been all this while addressing herself directly to Heaven, went immediately and prostrated herself in her Oratory: She prayed, wept, and sighed, but all to no Purpose. She found herself more oppressed than ever: And in order to insult anew, and with greater Violence, that opiniated Nature, takes her Discipline in Hand, and pulling up her Coats and Smock to her very Navel, and tying them about her with a Girdle, she had no Mercy on her poor Thighs, and that Part which had caused all her Sufferings, which then lay entirely bare and uncovered. This Rage having lasted some Time, her Strength failed her by this cruel Act; she had scarce so much left her as to set her Cloaths at Liberty, which exposed her more than half naked. She rested her Head upon her Mattress, and making Reflection upon the State of poor Mortals, which she called miserable and wretched, being born with such Movements which they condemned, though it was almost impossible to repress them. She fell into a very great Weakness, but it was a very amourous one, which the Fury of her Passion had caused, and made this young Thing taste such a Pleasure which ravished her to the very Skies. At this Moment Nature, inciting all its forces, broke through all the Obstacles which opposed its Sallies; and that Virginity, which till then had been in Prison, delivered it

---

* The Afternoon Service so called, beginning generally at Two o'Clock.

without any Aid or Succour with the utmost Impetuosity, leaving its Keeper extended on the Floor, as a certain Sign of her being discomfited.

AGNES. Ah! Lard! I wish I had been present!

ANGEL. Alas! my Dear, what Pleasure wouldst that have been to thee? Thou wouldst have seen that Innocent half naked, her Mouth smiling with those amorous gentle Contractions, of which she knew not the Cause! Thou wouldst have seen her in an Ecstacy, her Eyes half dying, and without any Strength or Vigour, fall beneath the Laws of undisguised Nature, and lose in Defiance to all her Care that Treasure, the keeping of which had cost her so much Pain and Trouble.

AGNES. Very well, and it is in this that I should have placed my Pleasure, to have considered her thus naked, and curiously to have observed all the Transports which Love would have caused in the Moment she was vanquished.

ANGEL. So soon as *Dosihea* recovered from this Syncope,[13] her Mind, which before had been buried in the thickest Darkness, found itself in an Instant developed of its Obscurity; her Eyes were opened, and reflecting on what she had done and on the little Virtue she had received from the Saint whom she had so much invoked, she knew that she had been in an Error; and thus by her own Force raised herself through surprising *Metamorphoses* above all those Things which before she dared not look upon, and entertained nothing more than an entire Contempt for those to which she had the greatest and most violent *Attach*.

AGNES. That is to say, that from being scrupulous, she became indevout, and that she made no more Offerings to all the minor Saints she adored before.

ANGEL. You take this wrong, but I do not wonder at it, it is natural for People that will not give themselves Time to reflect, to do so. She did nothing in this but what she ought to have done; she awaked from that profound Lethargy in which she had so long been lulled, through the Ignorance and ridiculous Impositions of Men, to practice a reasonable Devotion. But the best Things are too frequently misrepresented, the Reason is, Men look through the wrong End of the Perspective: And I make no doubt, but if our Discourse were to be published to the World, but some narrow-soul'd ignorant Bigot would speak as ill of it, as thou didst of *Dosithea's* Conduct; whereas I have said nothing to thee but what is no Ways contrary to the Doctrines of the Church. It is true, as my Aim is to instruct thee in the Truth, so have I made Use of a very free and open Manner, and called Things by their proper Names; if any should unreasonably be scandalized hereat, let them reflect that they themselves in

Confession are full as open; nor is in the spiritual Courts the Gravity of my Lords the venerable Bishops, ruffled by hearing, in Matters of Divorce Things mentioned in Terms the most plain and open: And Actions to which the unthinking Vulgar would think lewd and lascivious, have been ordered by their Reverend Paternities, as Inspections of Bodies in Cases of Impotency and Suspicion of *Judaism*; in which latter Case it is ever done in Court, where the *Inquisition* prevails, before my Lords the Inquisitors, where the suspected Person is turned up and handled very judiciously, to see whether by the Volubility of the Fore-Skin he be a true uncircumcised Christian. Now as it would be highly ridiculous to accuse these holy Fathers of the Church of Lasciviousness or Ribaldry, for what they piously do to find out the naked Truth of Things; so it is equally unreasonable and ridiculous to infer, that one cannot throw off Superstition, without falling into Impiety. This was Sister *Dosithea's* Case, she found by Experience, that these Whippings and Flagellations of her Posteriors, rather augmented than diminished her Fires; a very silly and ineffectual Remedy then against Concupiscence: And if I call it sinful, I should not be in the Wrong, especially since, as I have been credibly informed, it is made Use of by lewd Persons to excite their Letchery. She likewise experienced that it was the sovereign Physician that we must have Recourse to in all our Weaknesses; that Temptations were not in the Power of the Faithful, and that in a Soul the most humble and submissive, there rise sometimes involuntary Thoughts and Motions which are not in themselves any wise criminal, and without Consent never can be so. Thou seest by this Time that I have spoken nothing but the Truth, when I told thee it was mere Devotion that rid her of her Scruples. The same Thing almost happened to an *Italian* Nun, who having very often prostrated herself before an Image of an Infant newly born,* which she called her little Jesus, and had conjured him several Times to grant her the same Thing, by these tender Words, which she uttered with an extraordinary Affection, *Dolce mio Giesú, fatte mi la gratia,*&c.[14] Seeing that all her Prayers were ineffectual, she imagined that it was the Infancy of him she called upon was the Cause, and that she should find her Account much better in addressing herself to the Image† of the Eternal Father, which represented him in a more advanced Age. Upon which she returned to her little Lord, as she called him, whom she reproached for his little Virtue, protesting that she would never amuse her-

---

* Nudities are certainly very improper to excite chaste Desires.

   † In the Church of *Rome* they suffer such Images to be carved and painted, but as to the Lawfulness of it, let those whose Business it is, look to it.

self any more with Children such as he was, and so left him, telling him in the Words of this Proverb: *Chi s'impaccia con Fanciulli, con Fanciulli si ritova.*[15] Thou, my dear Soul, who understandest *Italian*, seest the horrid Effects of Superstition, and to what Extreminities of Folly, to speak no worse of it, Ignorance may sometimes carry us.*

AGNES. Indeed this Example is a sensible Proof of it, and that the Simplicity of this Nun was not to be paralleled. The *Italians* do not pass, however, for Fools; they say, on the contrary, they have a great deal of Wit, and that few Things can escape their Penetration.

ANGEL. That is very true generally speaking, but one ever finds some People that are not so enlightened as others. Besides, to have Doubts and Scruples is not always a Sign of Stupidity.

For thou must understand, my dear *Agnes*, (that excepting in Matters of Religion) there is nothing sure and certain in this World; there is no Party or Set of Men, but are furnished with Arguments to maintain their Tenets, and that we have nothing commonly but false and confused Ideas of Things which we fancy we know perfectly well. Truth, moreover, is unknown to us, and all the diligent Researches and Artifices of Men who have seriously applied themselves to find her out, have not yet made us sensible where she is, though they believe they have infallibly made the Discovery.

AGNES. How then must we guide our Minds in an Ignorance so universal?

ANGEL. We must, my Child, if we would not abuse ourselves, take all Things from their Origin, look upon them in their simple Nature, and at last judge of them conformably to what we see in them. We must above all Things avoid suffering our Reason to be prejudiced, or possessed by the

---

* I can easily believe the Probability of this Story: I was told abroad something like it, by a Monk of St. *Benedict*'s Order, who was a very learned good Man, and an utter Enemy to such Fooleries. He told me in their Parish Church there was an old rotten worm-eaten Image of the blessed Virgin, maimed in several Parts, which had been for many Years the Object of the Devotion of all the old Women in the Country. The Bishop, who after the Visitation of the Church, was scandalized at it, removed it privately, and had a fine Statue of Marble, which he sent for from *Rome*, set up in the same Place. A good old Woman who knew nothing of all this, for the old Image was removed with the utmost Secrecy, the Bishop otherwise, so great was the Peoples Folly, feared an Insurrection. The good old Woman, I say, came into the Church, mumbling her Beads, where after she had kneeled before this new Image some considerable Time without looking up, so intent was she on looking on her Chaplet, she rose up to curtsey to our Lady, but not seeing what she expected, in a violent Passion made in these Words a loud Exclamation, *Good Lord! what have they done? Lord have Mercy upon us, they have taken away my good old Lady, and put this young sinical Whore in the Room of her.*

Sentiments of other People, which commonly are nothing but mere Opinions. And we must, in short, have it stand on its Guard, that it let not itself be taken by the Eyes and Ears; that is to say, by a Thousand external Things, which are made Use of to seduce us, but always to keep our Minds free and disengaged from all the silly Thoughts and nizey Maxims, with which the Vulgar are infatuated, which like a Beast, runs indifferently after every Thing that is offered to it, provided it be covered with some Appearance of Good.

AGNES. I conceive all this very well, and even believe one might push your Reasonings yet much farther, and herein comprehend a great many Things you have omitted. I must own I take an extreme Pleasure to hear you, though you were not so young and beautiful as you are; your Mind alone makes you amiable and lovely. Give me a Kiss.

ANGEL. With all my Heart, my dearest Soul, I am ravished to think I can give thee Pleasure in any Thing, and to have found in thee a Disposition to receive the Lights thou stoodst in Need of. When we have our Mind developed of Darkness and disembarrassed from all Sorts of Inquietude, there is not a Moment of our Life in which we do not taste some Pleasure, and in which also we may not create a Subject Matter of Merriment and Recreation on the Pain and Scruples of which others participate. But let us leave off this Piece of Morality in which I am insensibly engaged. Kiss me, my Mignonne, I love thee better than my own Life.

AGNES. Well then, are you now satisfied? But you do not think that we may chance to be observed where we are?

ANGEL. Ah! what Reason have we to be afraid? Let us go into this Arbour; we can be seen by no one here. But I am not yet satisfied. O kiss me ever with the Kisses of that Mouth! O let me, dearest Angel, let me—

AGNES. Truce, *Angelica*, a little, and give me Leave to breathe. You are really too unreasonable. But tell me, my Dear, what dost thou think of these Caresses!

ANGEL. Think of? Why I'll tell thee the very same as some of the greatest and most learned Divines. No less a Man than Cardinal *Bembo*, a Man venerable for his Learning and exemplary Piety, as one may see related by *Castiglione* in the Fourth Book of his COURTIER,[16] made a most Excellent Oration of Love and Kissing to the Dutchess of *Urbino*, wherein he says, — O Lord, now I think of it, I have it here in my Pocket. This Book, thou must know, was wrote originally in *Italian*, and has for its Excellency been translated into all the Languages of *Europe*.* This was

---

* It is now translated into *English* and printed for Mr. *Curll* over against *Catherine-Street* in the Strand.

made *French* by The Abbé *Joyeuse.* — Stay, Let me see. — Oh! here is the Place. Read, my dearest Soul, and be informed.

AGNES. With all my Heart.

> *Because the Influx of a Beauty, when present, gives a wonderful De-light to the Lover, and sets his Heart on Fire, awakens and liquifies certain Virtues dormant and congealed in the Soul, which nourished with the genial amorous Heat, diffuse themselves, and flow bubbling about his Heart; sending through the Eyes those Spirits, which are Vapours the most subtile, composed of the purest and most lucid Particles of the Blood, which receive the Image of Beauty, and dress her with a rich Variety of a Thousand different Ornaments.*

> *Whereupon the Soul is delighted, and with a kind of Wonder grows astonished, and yet is full of Joy; and, as it were, stupefied with Excess of Pleasure, feels that Fear and Reverence which Men usually are affected with in sacred Things, and thinks herself in a Paradise of Bliss and Joy. The Lover then who considers only the Beauty of the Body, loses this Treasure and Happiness as soon as the beloved Object by her Departure leaves his Eyes without their Light, and consequently the Soul, like a Widow without her Joys. For Beauty thus removed at a Distance, that amorous Influx does not set the Heart on Fire, as it did when present.*

> *Hence the Passages grow dry and arid, and yet the Rememberance of that Beauty shines in such Sort in those Powers of the Soul, that they endeavour to diffuse the Spirits, which, finding the Passages closed up, cannot sally out, though they strive to do so; and being thus debarred, wound and torture the Soul, and give it those sharp Stings that tender Infants feel with pain when they breed their Teeth.*

> *Hence come the Tears, the Sighs and Tortures of Lovers; because the Soul always afflicts itself, and is in Pain, and grows almost mad, 'till the dear beloved Object returns, and then she is immediately at Ease and respires; and being entirely intent upon it, feeds her self with the most delicious Food in the World.*

But what is all this to Kissing?

ANGEL. It is, however, a true Description of Love. I own, my Dear, I mistook the Page. This Lecture notwithstanding is not *mal a propos*. But, here, give me the Book. I only mistook the Pages. It is in the Leaf before, there: *A Woman then,* &c.

AGNES. To continue.

> *A Woman then, to please her good Lover, besides blessing him with pleasant Looks, familiar and secret Discourse, jesting, little Liberties, and*

soft Touches of the Hand, may lawfully, and without Reproach, indulge
him in the Ecstacy of a Kiss. For since a Kiss is a Conjunction of the Soul
and Body, it is to be feared lest the sensual Lover, will be more inclined to
the Part of the Body than the Soul; but the rational Lover knows well, that
though the Mouth be a Part of the Body, yet it is a Passage for the Words
which are the Interpreters of the Soul, and for the inward Breath which is
also called the Soul, and therefore has such Delight in joining his Mouth
with that of his Beloved with a Kiss. Not to excite in him any dishonest
Desire, but because he feels that this Junction opens a Passage to the Soul,
which drawn by mutual Desire to each other, transfuse themselves alter-
nately into each other's Bodies; and thus mingling themselves so intimately
together, they have each two Souls, and one thus compounded, rules as it
were two Bodies; for which Reason a Kiss may be said rather to be the
Union of Souls than Bodies, because it has such Force and Energy as to
draw the Soul to it, and separates it, as it were, from the Body.

For this Reason did all chaste Lovers long eagerly for Kisses, as what
strictly united Souls. And for this Reason does PLATO, *the Divine*
Lover say, That in Kissing, his Soul came as far as his Lips, to de-
part out of the Body.

And because separating the Soul from sensual Objects, and uniting
it with intellectual, may be signified by a Kiss. Solomon *in his divine*
Book of the Canticles, *cried out in an Ecstacy and Rapture,* Oh! that
he would kiss me with the Kiss of his Mouth! *to express the ardent*
Desire he had that his Soul might be ravished by divine Love, to con-
template celestial Beauty, so that by intimately uniting herself to it, the
Soul may abandon the Body.[17]

ANGEL. There's enough, what follows you have read just now. But I
will lend thee the Book, it is well worth thy Perusal. What dost thou think
now, my lovely *Agnes*? Has not Love found an admirable Orator in our
Cardinal?

AGNES. But was he a Cardinal when he made this same Oration?

ANGEL. No, but he was made so soon after; he was then, however, in
Holy Orders, which some Cardinals never are.

AGNES. If a Lay-man had said half as much he would have been, perhaps, censured of Libertinism.

ANGEL. It may be so, but the Cardinal gained the Applause of the
whole Court of *Urbino* for that Harangue, in which had he thought he had
deservedly given any Scandal, he would have retracted it; neither would
Castiglione have dared to insert it in this Book, which he knew was liable
to the Censure of the Inquisition. Come then, my little Soul, and —

AGNES. What?

ANGEL. Give me another Kiss.

AGNES. And, what then?

ANGEL. Why then another. Lord, thy Kisses have nothing common in them. Give me one *a la Florentine*.

AGNES. I fancy you are out of your Senses. Does not all the World kiss after the same Manner? What do you mean by kissing *a la Florentine*?

ANGEL. Come a little nearer and I'll shew thee.

AGNES. Lord! you have set me all on a Flame. Ah! this fooling is lascivious. Retreat, I beseech you. Ah! how you clasp me. I am perfectly devoured!

ANGEL. It would be unreasonable if I did not put in Practice what I teach: After this Manner do they kiss who truly love each other, by amorously darting out their Tongue between the Lips of the beloved Object. For my Part, I find nothing in the World more sweet and delicious, when one does it as one should do; and I never put it in Practice but I am ravished with Ecstacy, and feel all over my Body an extraordinary Titillation, and a certain *Je ne scay quoy* which I am not able otherwise to express, than only by telling thee that it is a Pleasure which pours itself out with a certain sweet Impetuosity over all my secret Parts, which penetrates the most profound Recess of my Soul, and which I have Right to call *The sovereign Pleasure in Epitome*. What, thou sayest nothing? What Sentiments does it cause in thee?

AGNES. Did not I sufficiently declare it to you when I said that you had put me all in a Flame. But whence comes it that you call these Kisses, Kisses *a la Florentine*?

ANGEL. Because amongst the *Italians*, the Ladies of *Florence* are accounted the most amorous and are noted for practicing after this Manner. They find a singular Pleasure in it, and say they do it in Imitation of the Dove, which is an innocent Bird, and that they find in it, I know not what of the *Piquant* and delicious, which they do not otherwise experience. I am astonished that the *Abbé* and the *Feuillant* did not teach it thee while I was in my Retreat, for they have both of them been in *Italy* and undoubtedly have made themselves knowing in all the most secret Practices of Love, which are peculiar to those of that Country.

AGNES. My Mind was too much employed in other Things than those simple Toyings when they came to see me, to remember at present what then passed; but I know very well that there were no Kind of little Wantonnesses and tender Caresses omitted that their Fury would inspire them with; and the Pleasure which I took was so great, and the Ravishments which those Transports caused in me so excessive, that they left me not Judgment enough to reflect upon what was acted.

ANGEL. It is true that the secret Moments in which one tastes that Pleasure, engages us so much, and in such a Manner, that we are not capable to distract ourselves by any Application of our Memory, in order to describe all what passes that Time within us. However, I make no doubt but either the *Abbé* or *Feuillant* pushed their Gallantry to that Point: Besides, as thou hast a Mouth divinely formed, they are perfectly instructed in the most sweet and engaging Manners of Address, as those know, who know how passionately to love.

AGNES. Alas! for Persons consecrated to the Altar, and Vowers of Chastity, they know but too much.

ANGEL. Thou art really very pleasant, and they who did not know thee, would believe that thou speakest seriously. But wilt thou have me tell thee my Thoughts. I believe they cannot know too much, but that they might practice less. For it is certain, that having the Direction of Souls, they ought to have a perfect Knowledge as well of Evil as Good, in order to make a just Discernment; and strenuously to exhort us to the Pursuit and Love of the one, and to preach to us with the same Zeal, to fly from and hate the other. But they do nothing less than this, and the bad Books whence they draw their Light, corrupt their Will, at the same Time that they enlighten their Understanding.

AGNES. I believe you abuse the Terms, and think that with Men of Learning there is no Book which of its own Nature ought to be prohibited, and that the Use only which we make of it, gives it the Quality of good, bad, or indifferent.

ANGEL. Lord! I believe thou ravest to talk after this Manner, and thou oughtest to agree with me that there are some Books which have not one good Line in them, and which contain Instructions essentially opposite to good Morality and the Practice of Virtue. What canst thou say of the *Young Womens School*,[18] and that infamous Philosophy which has nothing in it but what is dull and insipid; and where the Arguments are so sottish that they are persuasive only to low and vulgar Souls, and touch such only who are half corrupted, or who easily suffer themselves to be drawn away by all Sorts of Weakness.

AGNES. It must be owned that that Book should be put into the Catalogue of those that are unprofitable, and indeed, of such as are prohibited. I wish I could redeem the Time I employed in reading it, there was nothing in it [that] pleased me, and which I did not condemn. The *Abbé* who shewed it me, gave me another, which treats much on the same Subject, but the Author has handled it with a great deal more Wit and Address.

ANGEL. I know what it is thou speakest of, as for forming of Peoples Manners, it is not one Jot better than the former; and though the Purity of the Style, and its easy Eloquence have something agreeable in them, it does not hinder their being infinitely dangerous, inasmuch as the Fire and the *Brilliant* which blazes out in a great many Passages, serve only to make the Poison which it is full of, spread with the greater Sweetness, and insinuate itself into such Hearts as are but a little susceptible of it. It has for its Title, *The Ladies Academy; or the seven Dialogues of Aloisia.*[19] I had it eight Days in my Hands, and he who brought it [to] me, explained the most difficult Places, and gave me perfectly to understand all that was mysterious in it, especially these Words in the seventh Dialogue, *Amori vera lux*; and discovered to me the Anagramatical Sense they covered under the simple Appearance of an Inscription of a Medal.[20] I imagine this is the Book thou hadst a Design to speak to me about.

AGNES. Certainly. Ah! Lord! how ingenious is that Author to invent new Pleasures to a Soul all sullied and disgusted! What Provocatives and Incentives does he make Use of to awaken and rouze up the most sleepy and languishing Concupiscence, and even that which is impotent! What extravagant Appetites! What strange Objects! And what unknown dishes does he cook up to debauch us! But I see that I am not yet so knowing as you are.

ANGEL. Alas! my Child, the Knowledge that thou art ambitious of, would lead thee only to what would be very prejudicial to thee. The Pleasures that we propose to ourselves, must be such as are limited by the *Laws*, by *Nature*, and by *Prudence,* and all the Maxims which that Book could teach thee do every one of them contradict all these. Believe me, all Extremes are dangerous, and there is a certain Mean which we may quit, without falling down a Precipice. *Let us love*, it is no where forbidden to do so. *Let us seek for Pleasure,* as far as it is lawful; but let us avoid that which cannot be inspired but by Debauchery, and let us not be seduced by the Persuasion of an Eloquence which only soothes us to our Ruine, and shews itself as a Good, the more easily to tempt us to do Evil.

AGNES. O fine Moralist! And how well do you know how to gild the Pill when you have a Mind to do so: Not that I do not agree with your Reasons, and blame all what you condemn; but I cannot help laughing, when I hear you preach up Reformation with so much Fire, and hear you speak of the Deaf and Blind, such as are our Senses, which will receive no other Rules but what they themselves propose.

ANGEL. It is true, and I own it is ill employing the Time that is unprofitable, in striving to repress Vice, and raise up Virtue, in the Corruption of the Age we live in. The Disease is too great and the Contagion too universal, to prescribe a Remedy by simple Words, and which cannot be cured, but by Medicines operative only on the Mind. It is no Ways my Design, but I have only been glad to let thee know, that I approve not of the Libertinism of those who never taste any perfect Pleasure; they think they shall never find it, unless they seek it in the Lessons of a corrupted Imagination, beyond the most inviolable Bounds of Nature, and even in the most dissolute Licentiousness of Ancient Fables.

I am not an Enemy to Pleasures, nor attached to that uneasy and incommodious Virtue which is not capable of them; and I know, that the most noble Soul cannot be Mistress of her Passions, nor be purified from other humane Infirmities, while she is joined to our Body.

AGNES. Ah! this tacking about pleases me, and this Indulgence may be received. For, what Evil can one find in Pleasure if it be well regulated? One must of Necessity allow something to the Complexion or Temperament of the Body, and bear with the Weakness of our Mind, since we receive them such as Nature gives them to us, and that their Choice does not depend upon us. We are not answerable for the Fancies, Bent, or Inclination she bestows upon us. If they are Faults, it is she that is culpable and ought to be blamed; and one cannot reproach Men for those Vices which are born with them, and which do not proceed but from their Nativity.

ANGEL. Thou are in the Right, my *Mignonne*, and I cannot express to thee the Joy that I feel, when by these Words I see the Progress thou hast made by my Instructions. But let us no longer weary our Minds by finding the Crimes of others, let us bear with what we know not how to reform, and not touch upon those Evils, which would undoubtedly discover the Impotence of our Remedies. Let us live for ourselves, and without making ourselves sick with the Infirmities of other People. Let us establish in our Interiour, that Peace, and that Tranquility, which is the Principle of Joy, and the Beginning of that Happiness which we reasonably desire.

AGNES. For my Part, I am already in that peaceable Enjoyment of Repose and Quietness of Mind, where I must tell you, I should never have arrived, but by your Means. These are the Obligations which I shall never sufficiently acknowledge as I could wish; for you must be contented for all the Pains you have taken to draw me out of the Error I was in with the Friendship I have sworn to you, which must serve instead of all other Recompense.

ANGEL. Alas! my Child, what couldst thou offer to please me more! I prefer thy Caresses to all the Treasures of the World; one Kiss alone of thine charms me, and is the Height of Felicity. But see, somebody is coming this Way. Let us separate, to take away all Suspicion they may have of our Entertainment. Kiss me, my dear Child.

AGNES. I will, and *a la Florentine*.

ANGEL. Ah! thou ravishest me! thou transportest me! I cannot bear it! thou givest me a Thousand Pleasures.

AGNES. There is enough at present, Adieu, *Angelica*, it is Sister *Cornelia*.

ANGEL. I see her. She comes, without doubt, with some Orders from my Lady. Adieu, *Agnes*, Adieu, my Heart, my Delight, my Love.

Dialogue IV.

Sister Agnes, *Sister* Angelica.

AGNES. Ah! Good morrow, *Angelica*, How do you do?[21]

ANGELICA. Very well, my Dear, Heavens be praised: I am glad to see thee: I was just thinking of thee.

AGNES. Very well, and what about?

ANGEL. Enjoying thy dear Company, to tell thee what thou least wouldst expect. Thou knowest Sister *Eugenia*?

AGNES. What, the handsome devout *Novice*!

ANGEL. The very individual Person.

AGNES. Why, What of her?

ANGEL. I'll tell thee; she is no longer a *Novice*, and has actually thrown off the Habit: She passed through the Dormitory this Morning, and paid me a Visit: At first I did not know her: I took her for some Person of Quality, for I saw two Pages (as I imagined) walk after her, and a very fine Gentleman had her by the Hand.

AGNES. Were it not for these Reparations, this Sight would have surprized you.

ANGEL. Very true, but now the Enclosure* is open we must not wonder at these Liberties.

AGNES. But at last you knew her?

ANGEL. Her Voice betrayed her.

AGNES. And who was that Gentleman that was with her?

ANGEL. It was the Marquis *de Grassio*, Native of *Florence*, a Person of a very fine Shape, and very rich in Cloaths.

---

*When there are any Buildings to raise, or Reparations made in Nunneries, the Enclosure of Consequence must be open for the Workman, and anybody may then go in.

AGNES. But tell me, What did *Eugenia* say was the Reason of her quitting the Habit?

ANGEL. Only what we would all quit it for, a handsome young Fellow and one of a good Family.

AGNES. His Name?

ANGEL. 'Tis young *Frederick*, eldest Son to the *Sieur de Vitford*, you do not know him; I would draw you his Picture, but, to tell you the Truth, I had rather draw one of our own Sex.

AGNES. Why so? Is there so vast a Difference between the Men and us?

ANGEL. Most certainly, a very remarkable one; and which thou art very well acquainted with; or the *Abbé* and *Feüillant* have spent their Time but very dryly in their Instructions.

AGNES. You make me laugh. But since you will not give me the Pourtrait of a Man, give me that of Sister *Eugenia*; for it is a good while since I saw her, and I cannot tell whether if I saw her, I should know her.

ANGEL. With all my Heart, my Dear: Thou must know then that she is very tall, and treads extremely well; she is Mistress of a fine Body, and her Flesh is white and delicate, plump, yet as soft as Velvet; she is neither Fat nor Lean; her Breasts regularly divided, round, and not too prominent; she is, however, full chested, and very slender in the Waist; her Face delicately smooth, lovely black large Eyes, her Hair black as Jet, and the loveliest Complexion in the World, her Arms round, her Hands of a moderate Length, but small, her Hips handsomely rising, her Legs beautifully straight, supported with two little Feet, which makes her, altogether, a compleat Beauty. But besides all these Beauties Nature has bestowed upon her, she is Mistress of all those fine Qualities of the Mind, which make a young Lady infinitely agreeable and charming.

AGNES. You may very well say, I do not know her, neither should I if she be thus accomplished as you say, for that little that I remember of her, pointed her out quite the Reverse.

ANGEL. She is indeed much alter'd; I told you I did not know her myself, at first, but you know fine Cloaths and Carriage make a vast Alteration, besides Conversation with the *Beau Monde*, for she has been, it seems, two Months out of the Convent, gives a different polish to what we meet with generally in Religious Houses.

AGNES. There is something in that; but, since you say she is to be married to young *Frederick*, pray inform me, Is not this Gentleman the same Person I told you I saw once at *Paris*, at an Entertainment which the Count *Arnobio*, a *Florentine*, gave to the Gentleman and Ladies on the Grand Duke's Birthday?

ANGEL. The very same; and I am as glad of *Eugenia's* good Fortune as if I were to participate of their first Enjoyments.

AGNES. And I am as glad of the Visit she paid you: It may find subject Matter for Discourse.

ANGEL. That Girl has a great deal of Wit, and knows more than you think of; and tho' thou mayst, I do not wonder at her quitting the Cloister, her Constitution is as amorous as thy own. It is not long since an Affair happened to convince me of this Truth. Thou must know then, that *Frederick* taking the Benefit of our Enclosures being open, got very early into the Convent, disguised like a Workman, and watching his Opportunity, conveyed himself into *Eugenia's* Cell, after her breaking her *Noviceship*, where he found her stark naked, the Weather being very hot; she knew him, and turning about with a Smile, asked him what he wanted? He answered only, my Dear, my Life, my Soul! and could say no more. After these Words, she put on her Smock and came up to him. He immediately put his Hand you may guess where. She, all surprized, asked, if he was not ashamed to treat her after this Manner? All this signified nothing; he embraced her closely in his Arms, and, in a languishing Tone, cried, Kiss me, my Soul, which she had no sooner done, but he threw her upon the Mattress, and run over her Breast and Stomach, and other more secret Parts, with a thousand Kisses, and then proceeded on to Pleasures more particular, which made her, if she was not so before, a perfect Woman.

AGNES. And how came you to know all this?

ANGEL. I'll tell thee: I thought I saw one of the Workmen enter her Cell, and tripping softly along the Dormitory, made up to her Door, which having a large Chink between the Boards, I saw what I tell you. The first Thing I beheld, was *Eugenia* all naked, with *Frederick* sitting by her, holding in his Hand ———— which extremely surprized me, imagining to myself that she could never enjoy that Excess of Pleasure I afterwards found she did.

Said I to myself, Lord! what Pain must poor *Eugenia* undergo? How is it possible he should not tear her to Pieces? These were my Thoughts, but I suppose he treated her very gently on Account of her Youth, for she was but bare Fifteen. While I was thus busied in my Thoughts, I heard *Frederick* say, *Eugenia*, my Dear, turn upon your Back, which after she had done, he got up and put his ———— into her ————. For my Part I was quite frightened when I heard her cry out as if she were in excessive Pain, this gave me, as thou mayest well imagine, a great deal of Uneasiness, for I did not dare to come in for fear of surprizing of them, which might have had perhaps but very ill Consequences. However, a Moment after I saw her move her Legs and embrace her Lover with both her Arms after such an extraordinary Manner as sufficiently expressed the utmost Satisfaction.

Frederick was no less pleas'd with this Encounter. Ha! said he, What Pleasure dost thou give me? In short, after endeavouring to exceed each other in the amorous Combat, they softly sighed, and then for some small Space reposed as in an Ecstasy. And to shew thee what Love *Eugenia* had for her Lover, I must tell thee, that notwithstanding this pleasing Trance, she could not help now and then giving him many a Kiss, nay, I think she kissed him all over, and spoke to him the kindest Things in the World, which sufficiently convinc'd me what Excess of Joy she then received. This raised a Desire in me to taste the same Love Potion, and indeed I even grew distracted with strong unknown Longings and Desires; I could not help thinking of it all Night, and slept not a Moment 'till the Morning, and by a lucky Accident, Fortune, who favored my Desires, gave me some Consolation. It was the Son of the Count *Don Grassio*, who by chance cast his Eyes upon me, and began to fall in Love with me: Every Time I saw him, it was impossible for me not to make a mutual Return. We began both by amorous Looks, Salutes of the Body, then of the Mouth, and after that by sweetest and most particular Testimonies of Love and Friendship. But what gave me some Uneasiness was, that in the height of our Expectations I was obliged to change my Apartment, which gave me the utmost Chagrin; however, this did not hinder him from secretly conveying to my Hands a Letter, in which he assured me that he burned with Excess of Love for me, beseeching me to have Pity on his Sufferings by making suitable Returns to his Flame and Passion. Thou mayest imagine with what Pleasure I read this Letter; I thought I should have fainted away for Joy, and thought of nothing but possessing my dearest *Don Grassio*, and to this End I returned for Answer, that he should come as soon as possible, that I would grant him every Thing that he could desire from a young Woman who loved him more than her own Life; and that he would certainly find me in that Apartment where we first engaged. He no sooner had my Letter but he flew like Lightning, and in the Disguise of a Mason, for that Strategem I learned from *Eugenia*, came to that Place where I was ready to receive him, and where we were to give each other full Proofs of our Affections. It was very happy that he met with Sister *Magdalene*, thou knowest that good-natured Lay-sister, who is my very good Friend and Confidant, from whom I learned what extreme Desire he had to come to the Height of our Wishes, she shewed him up into the old Room through the back Stairs, and placed him in an obscure Hole where we used to put our Wood in, for the Infirmary; which done, she came to me with a great deal of Joy, and told me where she had concealed *Don Grassio*, and that he attended with the utmost Impatience, for my Commands. This Stratagem of poor Sister *Magdalene* was better than I could have hoped for; with her then I went into the Woodhouse, where poor *Magdalene* stood Sentinel, and *Don Grassio* immediately, without any Ceremony, embraced me after such an amorous Manner as gave me just grounds to believe that I should soon be the most happy Creature living. My Modesty, combating with my Passion, made me receive his first Caresses with some Reluctance and inward Shame, but a little after I returned them in so sensible a Manner as he did not expect. Upon which, throwing off his Coat, he gently laid me upon it on the Floor and kissed me a thousand Times, nor were his Hands without Employ. I receiv'd all this like a true Child of *Venus*, and we repeated it more than once, but with a Pleasure still more exquisite. He bestowed on me such Kisses as would raise Jealousy even in the Gods! Ah! how full of Tenderness are these Embraces! how agreeable and delicious his Touches! Let, said he in a trembling Tone, O let me put my Mouth between thy Bubbies, and let this my Hand cover this Mountain sacred to Love and *Venus*, and with this other repose on thy lovely Thighs.

AGNES. And were you often thus happy? Tell me, *Angelica*, and hide nothing from one who loves you as her Soul.

ANGEL. The next Morning we renewed the Battle after the same Manner, though he sweetly told me that our Pleasures would be yet imperfect if I did not contribute a Remedy: But, said I, you have no Manner of Reason to complain against me of any Crime that proceeds only from Ignorance, for I am naturally more inclined to be compassionate than cruel, and insensible in relation to the Pains or Pleasures of other People, and especially of those I love, I beseech you then to pardon my Simplicity; I hope in Time I shall learn how to be provided with every thing that may make us enjoy our Pleasures with the greatest Satisfaction. Having said this, I was going for some Books that treated on these Subjects, and might fully instruct me in my Duty, but he held me by my Petticoat and desired me to stay and return to our Caresses, and to shew each other the Excess of our mutual Passion before we parted; upon this, he laid me down once more, and after swearing that he loved me more than his own Life, and making on each Side Protestations of eternal Friendship, we returned to what ended in each others excessive Satisfaction.

AGNES. And certainly this contented you: Was not your Curiosity fully satisfied to have lost, as I conclude you did from what you say, your Virginity? But tell me, *Angelica*, did not *Don Grassio* run a Risque of falling ill by so much Exercise?

ANGEL. I'll tell thee: Sister *Magdalene*, the next Day, being sent to the Market, accidentally met with *Catharine*, *Don Grassio*'s Maid, who told her the ill Luck which had befallen her Master, who told her with a great deal of Chagrin and Sorrow, that *Don Grassio* had got a violent Fever, which had reduced him to the last Extremity. Thou must easily imagine how much this News afflicted me as well as poor *Magdalene*, to whom I afterwards understood he had been also somewhat lavish of his Favours. She went about her own Affairs, and I was in the greatest Concern in the World, believing I should never be able to retrieve that Loss, for I was told he ran a great Risque of losing his Life, which indeed too truly some Days after Happened, to my no small Affliction.

AGNES. Poor *Angelica*! and so you lost your Play-Thing.

ANGEL. I did so; but it was not long before Fortune provided me with another full as agreeable.

AGNES. And who was this, I beseech you?

ANGEL. No less a Man than *Pierrot*, our young Gardiner.

AGNES. For Shame, *Angelica*, how could you submit to the vile Embraces of such a Fellow?

ANGEL. Poor Fool, thou dost not consider that Love makes no Distinctions, neither shouldst thou judge Things by the External. I tell thee, *Agnes*, under that mean Garb is something more agreeable than under the richest Drapery; besides, he is fresh, of lovely ruddy Complexion, full of Vigour in his Actions and there lies an excessive Charm, simple, artless, and undisguised.

AGNES. Well, you are a mad Creature, but tell me from the Beginning how this Adventure happened.

ANGEL. Thou must know then, that my Lady sent me one Day to carry her Orders to *Pierrot*, concerning the planting of some Roses; when I came to the farther End of the Garden behind the high *Espalier* Hedge of Hornbeam, I saw *Pierrot* musing, as it were in a brown Study, and then starting of a sudden sent out a loud Sigh, and flew immediately into the little House where he lies and keeps his Tools. I followed, moved by a certain Curiosity to see the Cause of this sudden Flight, when coming to the Door, which he only put to, and had forgot to fasten, I saw him throw himself upon the Bed, and handle his Play-Thing with a very deep Sigh or two. Alas, poor Boy! said I to myself, he is without a Woman, as I am without my *Don Grassio*. I perceived, that since he had no other Conveniency, that he was resolved to make Use of what Nature had given him. What! thought I, shall I stand thus, and see that thrown away which may be better elsewhere bestowed; no, no, if he has any Occasion, I'll go and content him after a more agreeable Manner.

AGNES. And you say he is young and handsome?

ANGEL. To a Wonder, he is no more than one and twenty, of a middling Stature, his Hair of light Brown, and the finest in the World, his Eyes very amorous and languishing, his Face unexceptionable, his Lips softer than the softest Velvet, and his Legs admirably turned; but then he kisses, *Agnes*, Oh! I cannot express what ————.

AGNES. No more of your Raptures, but continue your Narration.

ANGEL. Well, to go on regularly, after I had seen what I told you at the Door, all trembling as I was, I resolved to knock, but Love exceeded my Fear, and made me enter boldly without waiting his coming to let me in.

AGNES. Indeed, I think you were very forward to one you have so little Knowledge of.

ANGEL. You are mistaken: I have been acquainted with *Pierrot* these two Years; there have passed indeed some little Liberties between us, but we never came to the grand Point. The poor Boy, in the Condition he was in, was more surprized than I; as not doubting but I had been an Eye-Witness of all the Postures and Gesticulations with which Love had inspired him. I could not help smiling to see how unmovable he sate, not being capable to move a Finger. I came up to the Bed-side, smiling, and he taking my Hand with his Left-Hand, (for his Right-Hand was not quite disengaged) Ah! *Angelica*, said he, my Love, my Heart, what do we do? And then drawing me to him, threw me on the Bed, and viewed my Breasts with Eyes so soft and languishing, that I no Ways doubted of the Consequence; upon which I leaped up, and went to secure the Door, and stop up all the Holes: Then coming back, with somewhat the Air of a Prude, said to *Pierrot*, I took this Precaution to say something in particular to thee. ————— Upon which, interrupting me, he was going to put his Hand ————. Ha! *Pierrot*, said I, what wouldst thou do? Take away thy Hand there. But alas! *Agnes*, all was in vain, the poor Boy, and in my Conscience, I believe it was the first Time by the Awkwardness of his Manner, fell suddenly into a Kind of fainting, which when I perceived, I was frightened; but presently my Fears were over, when I saw, by an involuntary Discharge of his Ammunition before he reached the Counterscarp, his Vigour lost.

AGNES. Terrible Disappointment, indeed, poor *Pierrot*.

ANGEL. Say rather, poor *Angelica*. However, this did not last long, the Champion rallied his Forces, and pushed so furiously in the Attack, that he gained the Fort entirely, though with the Effusion of much Blood.

AGNES. All this I could the better bear with, but with a nasty Gardener Fellow, fogh! I'll no more of it.

ANGEL. I have done, and will change the Subject. Know then, that some Time ago I received a Visit in the Parlour from the *Sieur Rodolphe*, accompanied with a young Person of Quality, whose Name was *Alicia,* who indeed was richly dressed, and in every Respect as beautiful as an Angel. It is impossible to describe her Charms. She sung several fine Songs with those agreeable Rollings of her Eyes, that inspired Love into us both, especially *Rodolphe*, who took this Opportunity to enter into a particular Friendship with her, begging of her, in the most engaging Terms in the World, that she would suffer him to do himself the Honour of sometimes seeing her, hoping that this would not be refused him, as believing it would be a Thing neither disagreeable to her Father's Inclinations, nor her own. He continues his Discourse, by telling her, how charming her Conversation was to him, and that if he dared, he could take, some Day, the Liberty to wait upon her at her Father's Country Seat; in short, he said to her Abundance of other agreeable and tender Things, which I make no doubt had the desired Effect; for he sometime after paid her a Visit, at that Place which he might well have called the *Palace of Pleasure,* not so much on Account of its Regularity of Structure, but because in the Presence of his *Alicia* he enjoyed a thousand unspeakable Pleasures, but dared not farther advance for Fear of her Father, whom he dreaded; but flattered himself, nevertheless, that by some little Artifices and Address, to arrive at the Port of his Happiness.

AGNES. But had he no Amorous Dalliance with her, did he not entertain her with no little Liberties, not talk to her of particular Pleasures? I am afraid, *Angelica*, that you will not tell me all.

ANGEL. I see very well thy Malice; I shall talk to thee another Time of that Affair; every Thing in its Season. I shall now only tell thee, that I heartily pray, that all the Powers Above, who are sensible of his Passion, to be favourable to *Rodolphe* in his Amorous Enterprise.

AGNES. I see *Rodolphe* is one of your good Friends, you wish him so well. I will not tell you what my Thoughts are of *Rodolphe* and you. I shall only say, that I believe he has communicated to you a little of Love's *Elixir Proprietatis*.

ANGEL. I believe in talking this to me, thou hast only a Mind to make thyself merry. But hear what happened to poor *Alicia* afterwards, which I had from her own Mouth.

One Day, above the rest, *Alicia* went with her Father to visit a certain Capucin of this City, called *Pere Theodore*, (or Father *Theodore*) whose Blessing she begged, and whom thou wilt have a perfect Idea of, when I shall have told thee, that he is one of those who affect an Austerity of Life, and a particular Severity: Thou must know, that every Thing preaches up these Fathers, I believe thou understandest these Terms. Mortification, Penance, and their long Beards, which they let grow and nourish with so much Care, which make their Faces look dry and meagre, render in the Minds of the People as so many Mirrours of Sanctity. Well, my Child, said he to

Alicia, you have here a Father, who will spare nothing to make you as perfect as you ought to be. You are to be married in a little Time, as I am informed, to *Rodolphe*. You must therefore cleanse your Soul from all manner of Impurity, to render you worthy of Celestial Grace, which cannot enter into one that is sullied with the least Ordure. You must know, continued he, that if you are pure, the Children produced by this Marriage, and which you shall bring into the World, shall help to supply, one Day, the Places of the fallen Angels; but on the contrary, if you have any evil Quality, they will be infected and go into the Way of Perdition to increase the Number of those miserable Wretches. It is you [who] must choose, my Child, said he, either of these two Conditions, there is no middle State between.

Alicia was so ashamed she knew not how to speak. Speak, speak, said he. I desire, said she, to be purified, and that my Children may be good. There was along with Father *Theodore* a certain Reverend Father *Jesuit*, who having for some time heard this Conversation, went away, which *Alicia* was not sorry at, as having then more Courage to discourse with *Theodore*, to whom, after he entered the Confession-Chair which stood in a dark Corner of the Church, for there it seems was this Entertainment, she confessed all her Sins, even to the least Circumstance of what had passed between herself and *Rodolphe*, her Father staying at some Distance.

When the good Father heard how far she had already advanced in these Love-Affairs, he fell into a violent Heat, and gave her a severe Reprimand, after having told her, she must have all these Kinds of Affections in the utmost Horrour. Then coming towards her Father, gave him a little Bundle of Cords, which he pulled out of his Sleeve with these Words: Go, said he, and do not spare your Daughter, give her an Example your own self, and be not too indulgent. After this, they took their Leave of Father *Theodore*, and went home.

AGNES. Do you not wonder, *Angelica*, how these People abuse our Simplicity? I doubt not but *Alicia*, as well as her Father, believed these Words, as if they proceeded from the Mouth of an Evangelist.

ANGEL. Very probably. However, as soon as they came home, her Father calling her up into her Chamber, shut the Door, and giving her the Bundle of Cords, bid her, with a Smile, untangle them, which she did, and found it to be a Scourge, or Discipline, made up of fine little Cords, knotted with an Infinity of little Knots at some little Distances from each other. Ha! my Child, said he, it is with this Instrument of Piety, as the good Fathers call it, that you must dispose of yourself for the Marriage State, which you desire to enter into, this must serve to purify your Continence. The good Father, continued he, hath commanded us both to make Use of it: I will begin, said he, and you shall follow; but do not let the Vigour with which I treat my Body frighten you; be not afraid, and other think, as well as I do, that during this Holy Exercise, my Mind tastes such Pleasures as I am not able to express.

AGNES. Without doubt *Alicia* trembled to hear her Father talk after this Manner.

ANGEL. No; and I wonder that she had so much Strength as to undergo so rude and painful an Exercise as she did.

AGNES. There is nothing in Reality more constant and courageous than a young Woman when she is resolved to be so; in this Case she will outdo herself to support, with an admirable Firmness of Mind, those Sufferings which would vanquish the most courageous Man in the World: I made no doubt but it was the Love of *Rodolphe* that inspired her to suffer such rude Treatment; but go on with your Relation, I beseech you.

ANGEL. Just in the very Instant, *Alicia* and her Father were going to begin, *Alicia*'s Aunt came into the Room. This Aunt, who is a mighty Bigot, would take her Brother's Place, telling him, It was not usual for Men to Act after this Manner, and that for her Part, it was a great Honour for her to put herself into the Room of another, to execute the Orders of good Father *Theodore*; which she immediately did, by uncloathing herself to her Smock, which she pulled up over her Shoulders; after this she kneeled down, taking into her Hand the Discipline. Look, Niece, and see how you must use this Instrument of Penance, and learn to undergo it by the Example I am going to give you: Scarce had she finished these Words when someone knocked at the Door. Oh! said *Alicia*'s Father, this must be the good Father *Theodore* who is come, no doubt, to assist at this Holy Exercise: He told me, he would not fail of being here, if he could but get Leave of his Superiour to come out of the Convent. He knocked a second Time. It is he, said *Alicia*'s Father to her, go open the Door quickly: What! Sir, said she, would you have him see my Aunt thus naked? You do not know, said her Farther, that this holy Man knows your Aunt to the very Bottom of her Interiour, and that we must conceal nothing from him. Her Aunt, however, pulled down her Smock, while *Alicia* went to open the Door, when immediately Father *Theodore* came in and commended the Aunt for the good Example she gave her Niece; after which he made a Discourse upon that Subject, but with so much Force and Energy, that it had almost made *Alicia* prevent him, by desiring to treat her with greater Vigour, than she might do herself.

AGNES. Lord! Is it possible? Was she such a Fool? So silly, and so much a Bigot!

ANGEL. Had'st thou then been there, thou would'st not have resisted, but have suffered thyself in like Manner to be persuaded. He proved to them, that Virginity, without Mortification and Penance, had no Manner of Merit; that it was a dry and barren Virtue; and, unless accompanied with some voluntary Chastisement, there was nothing more base and despicable. They certainly, continued he, ought to be ashamed and blush, who shew themselves naked before Men, in order to prostitute themselves to their Concupiscence, but on the contrary, others are praise-worthy who do so only out of a Principle of Piety and Penance, and for a holy Zeal to purify their Souls. If you consider the Action of the former, said he, continuing his Discourse, you find nothing in it but what is infamous; and if you cast your Eyes upon the other, you will observe that it contains in it every Thing that is really honest: One can only satisfy men, the other charms, if I may use the Expression, the very Gods. But above all, said he, these Kinds of Correction are of great Use, when they are duly taken; they are like a divine Fountain, the miraculous Waters of which have the Virtue to cleanse the Female Sex from all Impurities they might have contracted; they have no other Way to purge themselves but in suffering with Firmness of Mind and Patience, the Penance that is impos'd upon them, from having tasted, with Sensuality, forbidden Pleasures. In short, he told them, that by this Method their Souls were cleansed from an Infinity of Sins that Shame and Modesty might have often hindered them from revealing in Confession.

AGNES. Pleasant Morality indeed! How engaging are these Precepts! But I suppose he repeats often, to use his own Words, this Holy Exercise.

ANGEL. After these Discourses, he took the Discipline in hand, when *Alicia*'s Aunt fell on her Knees, and *Alicia* retired a little, but still kept her Eyes upon her Aunt. Being then in this Disposition, she entreated Father *Theodore* to begin the Holy Work, as she called it: Scarce had she spoke the last Word, when there fell upon her Postern, which was all naked, a Shower of Stripes as thick as Hail: After which he began to be more gentle, but at length he put her into such a Condition, that her Thighs, which were before very white and smooth, looked as red as Fire, and could not be viewed without Horrour.

AGNES. And did she not complain at all?

ANGEL. Very far from it. She appeared insensible, only gave one Sigh, saying, Ah! Father! But this Executioner of divine Justice, according to him, grew angry; Where is your Courage, then, said he? You shew a fine Example to your Niece indeed: Then commanded her to incline her Head and Body to the very Ground, which she did, which never appeared more beautiful, her Thighs were in such manner exposed to the Stripes of the Discipline, that they did not escape one: This lasted a Quarter of an

Hour or thereabouts. After which the Father told her, it was enough, bid her rise, and that her Mind ought to rest satisfied. She rose up and went to her Niece. Well, Niece, said she, embracing her, it is now your Turn to shew that you have Courage. I hope, said she, that I shall not want it; what must I do, said her Aunt to *Theodore*, prepare your Niece, answered the good Father, I hope she will be stronger and more couragious than you were. In the meanwhile *Alicia* held her Eyes down, without speaking one Word. What! will you not comply with my good Designs, said *Theodore* to her? I will strive to do it, replied *Alicia*.

Her Aunt, during this Discourse, stripped her to her Smock, which she pulled up above her Shoulders. As soon as she saw herself quite naked, Shame and Modesty appeared blushing in her Face. She would have kneeled down. There is no Occasion for that, said her Aunt, stand upright as you are. This said, Father *Theodore* began: Well, *Alicia*, said he, shall I put you into the Way of Paradise? I desire nothing more, said she. After this he gave her a few Strokes, but so gently, that he rather tickled her than made her smart. Could you, my Child, said he, endure it, if I should use you a little more rudely? Her Aunt answered for her, and said, She would not want Courage, that he had nothing to do but pursue this holy Exercise. Immediately he laid on, from Top to Bottom, with such Violence, that she could not help crying out most horribly, It is enough, It is enough, said she, dear Aunt have pity upon me. Take Courage, said she, my dearest Niece. Will you yourself finish that which remains to be done of this Exercise, which is so good and holy as to cleanse our Souls from all Impurity? Very well, said *Theodore*, let us see how she will use it. Take, continued he, this holy Instrument of Penance, and chastise, as you ought, that Part which is the Seat of infamous Pleasure, if I must say so. Her Aunt shewed her with her Hand how she should do it. *Alicia* gave herself five or six Strokes, very rude, but she could not continue it. I cannot, said she to her Aunt, do Justice to myself, if you will, I am ready to suffer it from you. In saying this, she put the Discipline into her Hands, who gave it to Father *Theodore*: Telling her, that it would be more Merit for her to receive it from him than from any other. Who immediately resumed the Exercise, mumbling between his Teeth some certain Prayer. She wept and sighed, and at every Stroke he gave her, moved her Thighs after a very strange Manner: In short, he wearied her so much, she could no longer resist, but scampered from one End of the Room to the other to avoid the Strokes. I can bear it no longer, said she, it surpasses my Strength to undergo it. Say rather, said *Theodore*, that you are a Coward, and have no Heart. Are you not ashamed to be Niece to an Aunt so good and couragious, and you to shew such Weakness? Be obedient, said her Aunt. I consent, replied *Alicia*,

Figure 4.2 Frontispiece and title page of *A Treatise of the Use of Flogging in Venereal Affairs* (1718), another pseudo medical manual produced by Edmund Curll.

to do what you will with me. At these Words her Aunt tied her Hands with a little Cord, because they kept off a great many Strokes from her Thighs: After which they laid her upon the Bed, where she was disciplined very heartily. While Father *Theodore* was whipping her, her Aunt kissed her, saying, Courage my dear Niece, this holy Work will soon be at an End, and the more Strokes you receive, the more Merit you will have. At last, said *Theodore*, This is sufficient: See the poor Victim has spilt enough Blood to make the Sacrifice agreeable.

AGNES. Lord! What Sacrifice! What Butchery! What Execution was here! But where was her Father all the While?

ANGEL. I forgot to tell thee. He went out immediately on *Theodore*'s coming into the Chamber. But, to go on, after this her Aunt untied her, giving her a Thousand Praises for having suffered patiently an Exercise so rude and painful. Father *Theodore* spoke to her a Thousand obliging things as he went away, and gave her his Blessing. As soon as he was gone, her Aunt embraced her with a great deal of Tenderness. You must, dear Niece, said she, feign yourself to be out of Order with a Pain in your Side, that you may take that Repose which is necessary for you. For my Part, continued she, I am used to these Things, and I am not anywise incommoded by them. Adieu 'till tomorrow.

AGNES. And did you hear how she passed the rest of the Day?

ANGEL. She told me after she had reposed a little, that she amused herself with reading these Books, a Catalogue of which she gave me; here, read it.

AGNES. So I will.

> The Religion of Scaramouche.
> The Reformed Prostitute, with Figures.
> The Overthrow of Convents, very curious.
> The Vatican in a Consumption.
> A Dialogue between the Pope and the Devil, in Burlesque
>   Verse
> The Monopoly of Purgatory.
> The Devil disfigured, with Figures.
> The Genealogy of the Marquis de Vitford.
> La Sauce a Robert, a very curious Piece.
> The Politicks of the Jesuits.[22]

ANGEL. Well, What thinkest thou, *Agnes*? These Books, surely, must be very entertaining, if their Insides answer their Titles.

AGNES. Alas! poor Thing, she would have been more agreeably entertained with her dear *Rodolphe*; and I make no Doubt, but had she known where he was, or he her, they had been together and made Use of their Time.

ANGEL. He surmised something, and Fortune was so favourable to him, that at the very Instant her Aunt had left her Father's House, by the Assistance of the Maid, who told him also, that her Master was gone Abroad to Supper, he came into *Alicia's* Chamber, whom he found upon the Bed. Alicia knew who he was, but pretended being asleep, he flung his Arms about her Neck, and kissed her a thousand Times, handling amourously several Parts of her Body. When she who could no longer bear these sweet Caresses with a Transport, took him hold by ———— Ah! Lord, I cannot name it! and then ———— you may imagine what followed. For my Part ———— But hark, I hear somebody coming along the dormitory, let us separate 'till tomorrow.

AGNES. It is fit we should, 'tis now near Supper-time; but you are a terrible Gossip, and love to prattle to your Soul; nor indeed can I be anywise angry with you for affording me so many Hours agreeable Conversation. Adieu.

ANGEL. Adieu, dear *Agnes*, Kiss me, my Soul! Adieu, my Life, Adieu.

Dialogue V.

Sister AGNES, Sister ANGELICA.

ANGEL. I am glad, my dearest *Agnes*, that I have met with you.

AGNES. I have been looking for you a long while, my charming *Angelica*.

ANGEL. Let me kiss thee, my little Puppet.

AGNES. If you continue to caress me, after this manner, you will soon reduce me to Ashes; for I find myself now all on Fire. Truce, I beseech you, with your Embraces, and let us continue our usual Discourse, since we are in so convenient a Place for it.

ANGEL. With all my Heart: I sought thee for that very Purpose; but I must always pay the Tribute of Love and Friendship, kiss me once more.

AGNES. There; but for Heaven's Sake let us lose no Time, lest we should be surprized, or that my Lady, who hath a watchful Eye over every Thing, take Notice of our being so long and frequent together, and for our Penance suffer us to see one another but only at Church and in the Refectory.

ANGEL. I'll answer for her today, for she is gone to visit her Prisoner.

AGNES. What Prisoner?

ANGEL. Poor Soul, Did'st thou hear no Noise on the farther Side of the Dormitory last Night?

AGNES. No indeed.

ANGEL. Thou sleepest very soundly then; but one of the oddest Adventures happened that perhaps the like thou never wilt hear of.

AGNES. Tell it [to] me, dear *Angelica*, and conceal not a Syllable from me.

ANGEL. You know that great two handed Wench that comes sometimes into the convent to help the Lay-Sisters in the most laborious Part of their Work.

AGNES. You do not mean *Franchon*?

ANGEL. No, no, I mean *Marina*, that officious great Thing, who is always ready to do any Thing for us. Now thou must know that this *Marina* is a young Fellow, and it seems well made, who was all on Fire in Love with Sister *Pasythea*, and *Pasythea* loving him likewise to Distraction, he made use of this Disguise of a Female Habit to introduce himself into our Convent, in order to satisfy their Passion. Sometimes, as Business required, he lay in the House, by which Means and by his cunning Address he not only gained *Pasythea*, but several others of the Community; so that I question, besides thyself, whether there are two in the House that he has not had an Affair with. I know by Experience he is a good Musketeer, and discharges his Piece to Admiration, and I never saw either *Abbé* or *Feuillant* that is his Equal in amorous Encounters.

AGNES. You make my Mouth water when you talk so sensibly of these Matters.

ANGEL. I make no doubt but thou wouldst also have thy Share were it not for this unlucky Accident.

AGNES. I pity the poor Wretch, though I do not know why.

ANGEL. Thou should't pity the whole Community, which hath lost a great deal in losing their Champion.

AGNES. To tell you the Truth I pity myself, and I cannot but be very sorry that I have not experienced whether *Marina* was so valiant a Champion as you say he was. You must pardon this Interruption, go on, dear *Angelica*, and tell me how it could be discover'd that *Marina* was a Man disguised in Woman's Cloaths, since all the Nuns had an equal Interest in keeping it a Secret.

ANGEL. I'll tell thee, one Day *Pasythea* having called *Marina* into her Cell to make her Bed, pretending she was very much out of Order, she kept her for one whole Hour, which how they passed you may easily judge. At the same Time Sister *Catherine* popped into the Cell, the Door being half open, and saw a certain Motion of Legs which strangely surprized her; she asked Sister *Pasythea* if it was thus *Marina* helped to make her Bed, and that she saw her in a great deal of Disorder. *Pasythea*, endeavouring to hide her Fault, said, that being lain down to take a little Repose, her Distemper had given her such Uneasiness that she had chang'd her Place above twenty Times, which caused her being in that Disorder she saw her in, and that *Marina*, sympathizing with her in her Distemper, would not quit her till she had found some little Ease. Sister *Catherine* made Shew of believing every Thing that she said, but what she saw with her own Eyes gave her no Room to doubt but *Marina* was a clever young Fellow dressed like a Woman. Ravished with this happy Discovery, she thought of nothing but to make a good Use of the Occasion. However, as I said, she thought fit to dissemble the Matter, and make *Pasythea* believe she fell into her Trap, and that she was her Dupe in this Affair. But *Catherine* had other sentiments, and thought such a handsome Bird should not escape without a Pluck or two at his Pinions; and as she thought so it succeeded. After having told *Marina* that it was proper now to let *Pasythea* sleep, she went out of her Cell, when taking *Marina* by the hand, she led her into her own; where, having shut the Door, she told her she had something for her to do, and desiring her to unlace her, she said the Binding of her Petticoats hurt her very much, which *Marina* having done, Sister *Catherine* told her, that she had a Kind of Itching in several Places of her Body, which she could not so well reach with her own Hand, and therefore desired she would rub her a little, which would be very comfortable and refreshing.

Marina, the officious *Marina* acquitted herself the best in the World to the Satisfaction of her that employed her as well as to herself, who began now to be sensible of a certain Titillation which young women cannot know. Sister *Catherine* perceiving that her Charms began to operate, slid down her Hand, as if by chance, upon a certain Place of *Marina*'s Body; which sufficiently confirmed what she saw in *Pasythea*'s Apartment. Upon this, she fell, as if it were by Accident, backward upon her Mattress; and *Marina*, taking hold of that Opportunity, there passed a Scene no less agreeable than what was acted in *Pasythea*'s Play-house. For besides that Sister *Catherine* was very amiable, you know, that *fresh Meat fresh Appetite*.

AGNES. Certainly *Marina* must have been an incomparable Fellow to please, almost at the same Time, a Brace of Nuns.

ANGEL. She has as well satisfied several others, whom she has served with a great deal of Devotion: But as she could not suffice for all, some grew malcontent, which was the Cause of her present Misfortune, or rather the Misfortune of all these good Nuns whom she served with an indefatigable Care.

AGNES. I own I cannot help interesting myself more for *Marina* than all the Nuns together, and I am sorry that all her Assiduities should be thus rewarded. In short, tho' she has done me no Service, her Misfortune troubles me more than the Loss that all the Sisters sustain.

ANGEL. There is as not so much Reason to complain as thou dost imagine, as thou wilt find after I have finished my Relation. Thou must know that this good Servant was followed by two Nuns, with whom she had last Night made an Assignation, not knowing otherwise how to escape their Importunities, but it was impossible for her to keep her Appointment, because she was with her dear Pasythea longer than she expected. And as nothing is more impatient than Love, the Time of the first Appointment being elapsed, and the Nun who waited for *Marina* not seeing her come, believed that she had forgot her to have an Affair with another, or that she did not think of the Assignation. However, she waited, but with extreme Impatience; 'till finding she could no longer contain herself, she rose out of her Bed like a Fury, and gave two or three Turn round the Convent, to see if she could make any Discovery. This was just at Eleven a'Clock, that is to say, at the appointed Time of the second Assignation, when the other nun waited for her dear *Marina*, with the like Impatience. And as she heard the Noise which the other Nun made in her Walks, she made no doubt that it was her Lover, who was coming to her at the Time appointed. In this sweet Thought she opened the Door of her Cell, which looked into the Gallery where her Rival was walking, as I said, to discover if she could see him who had thus deceived her; so that, seeing the Door open, she believed that it was her faithless *Marina* who was coming out, after having diverted himself with another. She prepared to make bitter Reproaches; but seeing no one come out, she imagined that the Noise she might make in her walking over the Gallery might be the Cause; seeing then the Door still open, she went in, the better to be satisfied of what she apprehended.

The other Nun, who, as I said, waited for *Marina*, seeing one come into her Cell only with a Smock on, made no doubt but that it was *Marina*. She received him, as she thought, with great Transports of Joy, as you may well believe, and threw her Arms about his Neck: When the pretended *Marina* finding herself so closely embraced by her Rival, believed that it was to facilitate the Escape of her Lover, and, disengaging herself from the Arms of that Nun, went about looking if she could find him, but all to no Purpose. Here began now between these two Nuns the most pleasant Scene in the World, each of them asking the other where was *Marina*? The former believed that *Marina* went out of the Cell while her Rival embraced her, and the latter believed, that the other, excited by her

Jealousy, had spoiled the Assignation, and made, by her Presence, *Marina* to retire. But what was most pleasant was, that the poor Nun, who till then had waited for her Man, found only that it was a Woman which she embraced with the same Ardour as if it had been really him she expected.

AGNES. That is to say, that instead of a Dagger she found only a Scabbard; this was a strange *Qui pro quo*.

ANGEL. No one would express it better. Their Dispute at last grew so warm that it awakened my Lady; as she had had a long Experience of Love Intrigues, she doubted not but that this Quarrel, which she had for some Time listened to, proceeded from that Quarter; she then made Sister *Magdalene*, who waits upon her and lay in the next Cell, get up and light a Candle, and rising herself all in her Smock, went to see what was the Outcry. The first Thing she saw was *Marina*, who came at that very Instant from Sister *Pasythea*, who having heard the Noise, and judging it to be upon his Account, went into his own little Room to Bed. He was at a great Distance from the Abbess; who, seeing him appear and disappear in a Moment, could not tell what to think. She judg'd only by the large Strides it took that it must be a Man, but not knowing where to go to look for him, she went to visit the cells of all the Nuns, to see if she could discover any Thing; mean while the two Nuns, who were quarreling about their Disappointment, were surprized by my Lady in the height of their Dispute: And as they had one and the same Interest to conceal the Cause of their Quarrel, that Storm ceased immediately upon the Appearance of the Abbess. But as it was not very easy to make an Excuse that would go down with her, and besides that, these two Nuns appeared somewhat disordered, she judg'd that there was something extraordinary in the Wind, of which she resolved to have an *Eclaircissment*.[22] She did not therefore amuse herself in asking many Questions, nor why they were not in the Cells, nor what was the Fantom that had appeared and disappeared in an Instant; she knew that they would not want Inventions to hide their Follies; she believed the shortest Way would be to hunt about every where, and visit every Bed and Cell. As she had been an old Traveller, she imagined she might discover some Marks that might unfold this Mystery, in which she found a great many Nuns were interested, and especially *Pasythea*, from whose Cell she saw that Fantom retire, and the two malcontent Sisters.

AGNES. Tell me, I beseech you, before you any further, what are their Names.

ANGEL. I wonder thou couldst stay so long without asking me that Question, but, since thou desirest it, know then that I was she who was to have the first Encounter, which makes me better acquainted with every Particular of this Adventure, and Sister *Colete* was the other.

AGNES. And so you were the principal Cause of all this Misfortune.

ANGEL. Say rather that I was the Occasion, which, notwithstanding, would have had no ill Consequence had we had an Abbess of less Penetration, and who made use of Means the most *bizarre* that could ever have entered into the Head of a melancholy old Woman to bring it about.

AGNES. Go on and finish this story, I die with Impatience to hear it out.

ANGEL. The first Thing that the Abbess did, was to secure *Colete* and myself, and command us to be always near her, till she had finished what she went about.

AGNES. Undoubtedly she was afraid that you would have gone and warned all the rest to be upon their Guard.

ANGEL. You may depend upon it; she went then to Sister *Pasythea's* Cell, and knocked two or three Times: *Pasythea*, poor Girl, guessing who it was, counterfeited Sleep, and would not presently answer; but finding the knocking continue, and knowing it certainly to be my Lady's Voice, got up immediately and opened the Door.* The Abbess told her, in a resolute Tone, that she was resolved, at that very Instant, to make a general Visit over all the Convent, and that she was well assured that there was a Man concealed in some Corner or other.

Pasythea was all surprized to hear the Abbess talk after this Manner, she made five or six Signs of the Cross, and said above twenty *Ave Marias*. The Abbess still proceeding in her Journey, was resolved to look into her Bed, and visit *Pasythea* from Head to Foot, which she did so curiously, that looking sometimes upon the Sheets, sometimes upon her Smock, she found at length the fresh Traces of a Man; and having shewed us that fine Furniture, you plainly see, said she, that the Wolf is come into the Sheepfold, and we must find him out. It is impossible he should escape, for I have all the Keys of the House, and the Walls are so high that he cannot get over. This Discourse made us all tremble, and *Pasythea* especially, who had the greatest Reason. However, she endeavoured to put the best Face upon the Matter, and resolutely maintained, that no Man was ever in her Cell. You say then that it was a Woman, I'll warrant, replied the Abbess, for you cannot deny but some body into their Shift came out of your Cell, as it is not a Quarter of an Hour since, and I saw it. It is very true, Madam, said she, but it was *Marina*, who attended me in my last Sickness, and came, as Sister *Catherine* knows very well she has before often done, to ask after my Health, for she heard me frequently groan and bemoan myself.

---

* Tho' the Nuns have nothing but Latches to their Doors, and they may be opened without, yet the Abbess never comes into a Cell before first knocking two or three Times.

227

Well, said the Abbess, I believe what you say, but, however, we will see if this *Marina* be not some *marine* Monster that seeks after human Flesh, like that which put me into such bodily Fear some Nights ago.* These last Words put the finishing Stroke to compleat *Pasythea's* Misfortunes and dreadful Apprehensions, tho' my Lady spoke them by Accident, who never could have it in her Thoughts that *Marina* was a Man. After which, without giving Time to *Pasythea* to put on her Cloaths no more than to us, she commanded her to follow her, and went herself in the Front with *Magdalene*, who held a Taper in her Hand. She went then and knocked at Sister *Catherine's* Apartment, who, having been awaken'd by the Noise which we made, came immediately and opened the Door. The Abbess paid her the same Compliment that she had done to *Pasythea*, and visiting her in her Turn, found her no otherwise than *Pasythea*, only that the Traces were not altogether so fresh. Oh! Oh! said she, the Wolf hath been here too, tho' a few Days ago, and knows the Way to his Quarters; let us continue to follow him by the Mark of his Foot, and we shall take him by and by. After this she went out of Sister *Catherine's* Cell, and made her also follow after us. Going thus from Cell to Cell, our Company increased; and my Lady always found new Traces of this Wolf. Behold, said she, a Beast almost famished, and one who loves to change his Prey! after this she said such Things as we never could have expected from her.

You know, said she, *my Daughters, that Satan changes himself sometimes into an Angel of Light, and that ravening Wolves take great Delight in Mutton, we must consider whether any of us be not that Wolf in Disguise that hath made all this Ravage, of which you have plainly seen the Marks; for if it was not a Wolf in Disguise he could not have the Opportunity to do what he had done.*

In saying this, she pulled up her Smock, and shewed us what God had given her. You see, said she, shewing us a Body as white as snow, that I am an Angel of Light. This done, she made us do the same; there were some who made a Difficulty of so doing: But they could not help passing this Examination. I am very glad, said she at last, that you are what you appear to be; but however, it is certain, that a great many of you have received the Wolf into your Sheep-pen. Let us go, said she, towards the Apartment of the Novices.

AGNES. I expected this, who lie not far off; but tell me how my Lady forgot coming thither.

ANGEL. There was no necessity, as it fell out: Thou know'st, that to go from the Quarter of the professed Nuns to that of the Novices, one must pass by a kind of Garret, which serves for a Lodging-Room for those poor

---

* Meaning the Lobster that, with his Claw, caught hold of her—Vide *Dialogue* III.

Women that come to sweep and wash the Convent. Here *Marina* lay upon a wretched Mattress. The Abbess, who reflected upon what *Pasythea* had told her, I mean, that *Marina* was the only Person that went into her Cell that Night, said to reproach us that we may have nothing, [but] since we are now just come where *Marina* lies, we must see whether she be not that Angel of *Satan* that comes to disturb the Repose of Nuns at Night-time.

Upon which some of those, whose Interest was, that *Marina* should not be known for what he was, represented to the Abbess, that it was very improper to divulge the Secrets of the Cloister; and that a young Woman, who was not of the Community, not even a constant Domestick, should know the Suspicion that they had of a Man's being in the Convent. Be it how it will, said the Abbess, *Marina* shall undergo the Examination as well as others, and with the same Rigour, since as *Pasythea* had told us she was this Night in her Cell.

At these terrible words *Pasythea* was like to sink down in a Swoon at the Abbess's Feet. In short, she went into the Room, but who could express the Surprize of *Marina* when she saw Magdalene with a Taper in her Hand, followed by the Abbess and above twenty Religious, all in their Smocks. This Procession, which portended nothing but what was frightful, put her into the utmost Astonishment and Disorder. Which the Abbess observing, said to her, *Marina*, be not afraid, it is only a Piece of Formality that brings us hither: We look for a Man that is concealed somewhere in the House, and as *all Cats in the Dark are grey*, and that nothing resembles a He-Cat more than a She-Cat, we must see whether thou art Male or Female; for as thou know'st, *The Frock does not make the Frier*, we know very well that thy Cloaths are Feminine, but we will see whether thou art so from Head to Foot.

Marina answered grumbling, That she should let her take her Rest, that having worked very hard all Day, Nature required it; and that she was not in a Humour to hear all this Fiddle-faddle. The Abbess, who would not stop here, gently represented to her, That she must suffer it, that she must undergo the Examination, and that she should not have greater Privileges than the professed Sisters, who had done so.

Some of us then began to say, That they should not be anywise uneasy if *Marina* was let alone; and that she might enjoy that Privilege of not being visited without any Envy. It would be a very fine Pleasure, indeed, said another, for Nuns to look upon the dirty thick Hide of a nasty Servant Wench. But all this served only to increase the Curiosity of the Abbess, and confirm her Suspicions. She observed at the same Time, that *Pasythea* was rather dead than alive, and that *Catherine*, *Colete*, and my self, appeared very uneasy. Well! said she, to spare yourselves the Sight of the

Body of this Wench, you have nothing else to do but to shut your Eyes, and I myself will make the Visit.

Having said this, she took the Taper out of *Magdalene's* Hand, and commanded her to stand to one Side. Poor *Marina* did all she could to hide what Nature had given her, and indeed the Fear she had then upon her, proved of very great Advantage; but Fear may make our Members shrink up, but not annihilate them. In short, she looked like a Dog threatned with a Stick, that hides his Tail between his Legs. I forgot to tell thee that *Marina*, while the Abbess and the Nuns were in this pleasant Contest, took one of her Garters, with which she made a kind of Bridle, and tied about her Play-thing; and bringing it down, made it pass between her Legs; and, with a loose Pin, fastened the End of the Garter behind her Back to the Inside of her Smock. In the mean while, my Lady having un-covered her before saw nothing as yet that might distinguish her from a Woman. She observed, however, that *Marina* crossed her Legs, but in such a Manner as if Shame had made her do so. However, my Lady's Curiosity led her to look much nearer; and as she was extremely short-sighted, she made Use of her Spectacles, which she solemnly adjusted as if she was go-ing to see some Rarity or precious Stones. As she proceeded to a more ample Conviction of the Matter, and as she leaned her Spectacles upon *Marina's* Belly, as if it were her Desk to say her Office upon: While, I say, she was doing all this, that Member which *Marina* had a Mind to hide, with so much care, and which sometimes grows impertinent, when one would not have it so, grew so impudent, in Reality by the Torment my Lady caused it to suffer, that breaking its Shackles all of a sudden, struck with such Violence just upon my Lady's Spectacles, that they flew up to the Bed's Tester, and broke them to Pieces, and with the same Spring ex-tinguished the Taper which she held in her Hand. This good Lady, who knew long since how Men were made, made no Doubt now, but that *Ma-rina* was one; and putting her Hand upon that, which gave such a terrible Stroke, she was so surprized, that instead of a Man, she concluded he was at least a Man and a half.

The Nuns, who were not near enough plainly to distinguish what had passed, and saw the Candle put out, had various Thoughts thereupon. Those who knew *Marina*, guessed at the Matter; the rest believed, that to exempt her from so mournful a Visit, she had put out the Candle, and threw away the Spectacles with her Hand. In short, there were some good Sisters amongst these enlightened ones, who find out miracles in every Thing, [and they] would have it, that it was St. *Ursula*, the Patroness of the Convent, who being not able to suffer that People should suspect of Im-purity, opposed herself visibly to a Visit, which tended to the Dishonour

Figure 4.3   Illustration from *Venus in the Cloister* by Thomas Rowlandson
(c. 1810).

of their Order. The Abbess knew very well what she ought to believe, however, making Semblance of giving into that Sentiment, she said, since this Misfortune had happened of having the Taper put out, and her Spectacles broken without knowing how, she would not pursue her Visit any farther; but that as *Marina* had given Occasion for all that Bustle, by coming, by Night, without any Necessity, into the Cell of Sister *Pasythea*, she should be shut up for some Days in a separate Room, of which she, the Abbess, was to have the Key; so that *Marina* could by no means stir out without her Leave. And in the mean while we were forbidden to speak one word of this Adventure, either to the Novices or Pensioner, or any Person in the World of what had passed between her and us. You may very well guess, my dear *Agnes*, why she commanded us so strictly to keep the Secret, and the Reason that obliged her to confine *Marina* in a Room contiguous to no other.

AGNES. She found that Bird so agreeable to her Humour, that she would put him into a Cage to make use of him in her quaintest Pleasures.

ANGEL. She believed, that Nuns, as we are, did not deserve so sweet a Morsel which was worthy the Mouth of an Abbess. I know not whether *Marina* be contented with her Condition, but I know that she is regretted by more than one Nun.

AGNES. He will not always, surely, be confined.

ANGEL. No; but my Lady's Eyes will carefully watch him.

AGNES. I must own, *Angelica*, that you have done me an exceeding Pleasure in telling me this rare Adventure.

ANGEL. My Dear, I have others yet much more entertaining, perhaps: But hark! The Bell rings to Choir, we must therefore refer all to another Opportunity. Kiss me then, my dearest *Agnes*.

AGNES. There. And *a la Florentine*.

ANGEL. That's well; and, in Return, take this, and this, and this, ah! my dear, dear Soul! Thou killest me with Pleasure! Adieu. I shall think it an Age till we renew our Conversation. Till then, Heavens bless my Dear. Adieu.

FINIS.

5

*A Dialogue Between a
Married Lady and a Maid*
(1740)

A
DIALOGUE
BETWEEN
A MARRIED LADY
AND
A MAID.

DIALOGUE I.

TULLIA *and* OCTAVIA.

TUL. I am extremely well pleased, dear Child, to hear that at last thou art going to be married to young *Philander*, for in his Arms you will find such Pleasures, as thou wilt easily pronounce that Night in which he makes thee a Woman, to be the happiest of thy Life; I only wish *Venus* may be as favourable to thee in the Enjoyment, as she has been in giving thee so much heavenly Beauty to prepare thee for it.[1]

OCT. Indeed my Mother this Morning told me that after To-morrow I must marry *Philander*; and accordingly at Home I see all Things preparing for the Ceremony: my Chamber, my Bed, my Nightcloaths. Every body is busy in something about me; and yet, methinks, all these instead of giving me Joy, fill me with a certain Fear and Apprehension, of which I can give no Account, no more than I am able to understand or conceive with what Pleasure it is you so much talk of.

TUL. I do not wonder at all, that being so young, scarce having passed Fifteen, thou should have no Idea of a Thing, which I myself, being two Years older when I married, had not the least Understanding of: But, prithee, tell me, art thou not sensible, that there is something that *Philander* longs and sighs for? And do'st thou not find in him some Languishings, that express vehement Desires?

OCT. I cannot say that I am altogether ignorant of what his Eyes, his Face, his Person, and all his Actions, tell me every Day; nay, I must own that about a Week ago, while we were free together, he rushed into my Arms and fell a kissing me with such violent Transports, that I could not but wonder, what that Heat and sudden Fury meant.

TUL. Thy Mother was out of the Way, there was no body but yourselves; and I imagine you feared nothing from him—but say, did he ask nothing but Kisses?

OCT. At first, he had even those from me with some Reluctancy; but he gave them with such Ardour that I felt on a sudden, a certain Warmth run thro' my Veins, and a Trembling in all my Limbs, that I was unus'd to; but he saw me blush as red as Fire, which made him hold a little, and take back his Hand, which already he had slipt into my Breasts.

TUL Very well, go on.

OCT. I hate those impudent Hands of his; having observed that, for all my Blushing, I did not much chide him, as indeed I could not, he laid me along upon the Couch upon which I sat, and keeping me down with his Left-hand, as easily he might, in the Disorder I was in, he put his Right-hand under my Coats. I am ashamed to tell you the rest, dear Cousin, excuse me.

TUL. Prithee, Fool, leave off this silly Bashfulness, and think what thou say'st to me, thou say'st to thyself.

OCT. Having turned up my Coats, and my Smock, a little above my Knees, he began to feel my Thighs; and if you had but seen how his Eyes sparkled; then lifting his Hand up, he took hold of that Place which distinguishes us from Men. This, this Place, said he, will make me the happiest Man in the World. Let me alone, my *Octavia*.

TUL. Well said, *Philander*, ha, ha, ha!

OCT. All this while I was out of myself; he put his Finger into the Slit, which is a very little one, and he could hardly get it in, because I felt some little Pain; but at the same Time he cried out, Oh I have a Maid! A Virgin to my Share! And immediately opening my Legs with Force, he threw himself between them flat upon his Face.

TUL. Did you feel nothing else but his Finger?

OCT. I did; But what an Impudence is mine, to relate that which remains!

TUL. Prithee, as if I had not felt the same Thing before. Go on.

OCT. I felt then between my Legs something stiff and warm, endeavouring to force its Passage into me; but I having gathered Strength, turned upon my Side, and threw him out; then clapping my Hand between my Legs, in the Place where the Battery had been erected, I presently felt my Hand and my Belly, as far as my Navel, all wet with a warm Shower which flowed from him: It felt thick and slimy, which made me withdraw my Hand, and he immediately giving my a thousand Kisses, seized both, and wiped them with his Handkerchief.

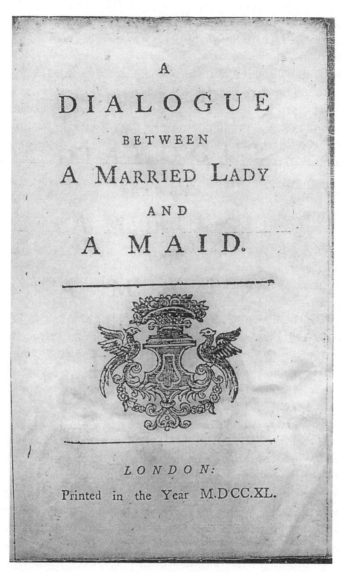

Figure 5.1 The title page of *A Dialogue Between a Married Lady and a Maid* (1740), an abridged translation of Nicolas Chorier's *Satyra sotadica* (1660).

TUL. I see he was very near gaining an entire Victory, but too much Vigour deprived him of it. Say, my pretty *Octavia*, how didst thou like him after this?

OCT. To tell you the Truth, from that Day forwards, he was infinitely more pleasing unto me, and has kindled in me a Desire of something, I know not what it is, which makes me perpetually Restless: I dream of him all Night, and expect from him some great Joy, what it is I cannot tell. I expect and wish for it, and could be content [that] *Philander* had such another Opportunity to try what would come of it.

TUL. What would you do, if he had?

OCT. You may answer yourself, for I cannot; but something more I would do, which would make him more happy, and me more learned. I had scarce put down my Coats, and he put in his Shirt, which hung out of his Breeches, when my Mother came in.

TUL. Woe be to thee, I know her Severity.

OCT. Yet she said nothing harsh, only smiling ask'd, how we both came by such a Colour; then sitting down by *Philander*, told him, within a Day or two, she hoped to make him the happiest Man in the World. He bowed respectful, and being somewhat out of Countenance for me, said, You do not take the Way, Madam, to make *Octavia* lose the Colour you tax her with; For she is so modest, that the least Thought of having a Bedfellow, covers her all over with a deep Vermillion. After some kind Expressions, he went out of the Room and left us.

TUL. What did your Mother say then?

OCT. She began to ask me, what had passed between us, and commanded me to hide nothing from her; I began to excuse myself, and complain'd he had over-power'd me. She ask'd me immediately if he had entred me, I said no; upon which she gave me a Caution, not to let him any more take the same Liberty before Marriage; for, said she, most Men are for that base Principal, that they either never marry those they have enjoyed, or scorn them afterwards when they do: Few are so generous, as to be thankful to their Mistresses for yielding to Love, but had rather owe their Joys to the Formality of a Person, than to the free Concessions of Beauty enflam'd by just Desires; and tho' they have made the same Vows in Private, that they made in Publick, at their Wedding, yet contemn Women for believing them without a Witness. For ever after, she watch'd so narrowly that *Philander* never found me alone.

TUL. Well, my *Octavia*, I love thee for being so sincere in the Account thou hast given me, and to shew thee that I will be so too, I must tell thee, that my own Mother sent me on to pump thee, about what past between you two, and to instruct you against the Wedding-night, to prepare thee, for a better Bedfellow, which thou wilt have To-morrow.

DIALOGUE II.

OCT. Now, my obliging *Tullia,* from whom I am to learn Secrets I cannot yet comprehend, let us lie in one another's Arms, and talk; all the House is asleep, Silence reigns in every Part of it, and we may enjoy ourselves without any Disturbance.

TUL. This Silence and Quiet in the Family, To-morrow Night, would be to thee and thy *Philander* much more welcome; but, instead of that, there will be nothing but Noise about you, till you are both a Bed, and People placed in every Corner, to hear what you do and say; and if the Bed shakes, as certainly it will, upon the first Eagerness of enjoying thee, thou wilt hear them without Laugh and Giggle, to the no small Disappointment of thy Pleasure at first.

OCT. I hope my Mother and you will take care so to clear the Coast, as no Men or Women but yourselves shall be privy to our Endearments, and that at a Distance too.

TUL. I will in that befriend thee, or else thou wilt be exposed next Day to a hundred Railleries from the Men, which will make thee Mad.

OCT. Lord! How much am I to endure, on all Sides, both from *Philander* and his Friends then?

TUL. As for *Philander,* I own thou wilt have something to suffer from him, but he will make thee amends in Time. Now I will tell thee how all will happen.

OCT. Teach me exactly every Thing that is fit for me to know; what Sort of Pain it will be, and how long it will last; I had rather have it sharp and short, than have it last, tho' moderate.

TUL. That Part of thy Body which is under the Belly, between the Thighs, to which Men give so many Names, but is chiefly called by them C—t, and which is so prettily shaded with Hair, is the Field where *Philander* will begin the Fight; you never yet observed the Make of it, and therefore I will describe it unto thee. Without is a long Slit, and which in Women that are most made for Enjoyment, is high and forward upon the Belly, and not low and backward, as some Women have it, more like Cows than Women. The true Proportion is, that when we lie along with our Legs close, two good Fingers Breadth may be seen of the Slit above our Thighs. This Slit is made with two Lips, which being opened gently, discover another inward as red as a Cherry, with two other Lips, which are called Wings, or Nymphs; and under them, about a Finger's Breadth, or more within, are in Virgins, as thou art, four little rising Buds, which, joining together and leaving only a little Hole between, stop up the best Part of the Passage into the Womb, and gives all the Trouble Men meet with in deflouring us, and all the Pain we feel, is upon the breaking thro' them with Violence, for then they fall a Bleeding and smart exceedingly.

OCT. I do foresee, that in the Attempt, there will be a great deal of Pain; for I myself can scarce endure to touch them with my little Finger.

TUL. Let me finish my Description. Just before them, towards the upper Part of the C—t, is a Thing they call *Clitoris*, which, is a little like a Man's P——k, for it will swell and stand like his; and being rubbed gently by his Member, will, with excessive Pleasure, send forth a Liquor, which when it comes away, leaves us in a Trance, as if we were dying, all our Senses being lost, and as it were summed up in that one Place, and our Eyes shut, our Hearts languishing on one Side, our Limbs extended, and, in a Word, there follows a dissolving of our whole Person and melting in such inexpressible Joys, as none but those who feel them can express or comprehend. That which embraces the Man's Member, when it is in, is called the Sheath, and takes such a fast Hold of it in Fruition that it is like a Glove to a Hand, and by its Warmth with the Motion of the Body, makes the Men die with Pleasure, and at last, spend as they call it, a great Quantity of Liquor, which all wets us both within and without.

OCT. You describe Things so exactly, that methinks I see all that is within me.

TUL. In thee, that inward Slit, and the Sheath, are very strait and narrow. Let me see it a little; open your Legs.

OCT. I do; what do you see now?

TUL. Ah! Pretty Creature! How Cherry-red it is! I see all the Flower of thy Virginity, as entire as a Morning Rose-bud, not touch'd by a Traveller's Hand, and sweeter than any Rose in its Enjoyment.

OCT. Oh hold, *Tullia*, you tickle me so that I am not able to endure it; take away that wicked Finger, it hurts me.

TUL. Well, I pity thee strangely; this pretty Shell, prettier than that out of which Venus herself was born, will be sadly torn by *Philander*. Nay, I begin to be concerned for him too; for the Entrance of this Paradise is so narrow, that it will be with great Difficulty, and no small Pain, e'er that he himself will get admittance. Did you ever see the Thing he has between his Legs?

OCT. I never saw it, but felt it hard, big and long.

TUL. Thy Mother is overjoyed with the Reputation he has of being the best provided young Man in all this City, but it will cost thee some tears; yet be not afraid, my Husband had the same Reputation, and with Reason, and yet I am alive and well.

OCT. Prithee, let me see how your C—t is, since it had such a Monster within it.

TUL. Do, my pretty *Octavia*. Here, I open my Legs a-Purpose.

OCT. Lord! What a Gap is here! I can thrust my whole Hand in almost; how strong it smells! Sure the Roses are all gone here, which you find in mine.

TUL. You are very pleasant, but when once you have had a Child, you will be as I am, for this is a necessary Consequence of Marriage.

OCT. Well, go on, and tell me how first I shall be made a Woman from a Maid that now I am.

TUL. First, I will describe unto thee, the Man's Member, and then I will tell you the Use thereof. There is between the Thighs, just at the Bottom of the Belly, a Piece of Flesh, which, when it is not employed for our Pleasure, hangs loose, bobbing here and there; but when our Beauty excites it, stands hard and firm, and grows at least as long, and as thick again, as at any other Time. In ordinary Men, 'tis about seven or eight of their own Thumbs Breadth long, when it stands, and about four of their Thumbs in Compass: But, in those whom Nature has favoured, 'tis about ten or eleven of their Thumbs Breadth long, and six or more in Compass, as I have seen my Husband measure his, and make me do it in wanton Humour. The Head of it is of a fine Carnation, and over it is a loose Skin which they draw backwards and forwards, and which contributes something to our Pleasure in its Motion: The Flesh of it is soft and firm, and of a delicate Sense, so as they feel us when we spend upon it: All round about the Root of it, is a great deal of fine short Hair, generally more than with us; underneath, hangs in a Bag, or Purse, two little Balls, pretty hard, and the harder the better, they call them Stones, and in them is contained that white thick Liquor, which comes out from them with such Transports to make us Mothers; they call it Sperm and Seed, and when their Vessels are full of it, they come often to us, and charge us Home, till all their Power be spent.

OCT. I believe *Philander* has a good Stock of it, for he wet all my Belly and my Shift, with that warm Shower.

TUL. You will like him much better, when it is shot into you; for it comes out with that Force, that it leaps two Foot or more from 'em upon spending; and then a Woman must be very insensible, that is not pleased to see the Joys she gives 'em, which they express by a thousand Murmurs, and kind dying Words; and now I will tell thee all, how it pass'd between me and *Horatio*, when I was first married unto him.

OCT. I long to hear that, because an Example, is always more full of Instruction, than any bare Advice.

TUL. As soon as my Mother had put me to Bed, she gently put a fine Handkerchief under my Pillow, and bid me use it when I wanted to wipe myself or my Husband: then, [having] given me and *Horatio* kind Kisses, she withdrew, and carried with her all the Company, except *Pomponia*, who had hid herself so slyly, that she did not perceive her. She had been married about two Months, and I had received from her kind Instructions, the good Office I now do thee, and 'twas out of Desire to see how I could behave myself, that she lurked behind the Hangings, in a Corner of the Room. As soon as the Company was gone, and the Room still and quiet, 'tho lighted with a Flambeaux at a Distance, which made it very clear, *Horatio*, turning towards me, and taking me in his Arms, with sparkling Eyes first gave me a Kiss; then untying with one Hand my Smock, he viewed my Breasts, which were white, round and firm, upon which he bestowed as many Kisses, as if they had been the only Objects of his Desires, sucking my Nipples, and then squeezing and pressing them with his Hand. But this Time I felt something thro' his Shirt very pressing against my Thigh, which when, by my Blushing, he found I had perceived, he threw off the Cloaths, and taking up his own Linnen, shewed me a long stiff-headed P—ck; his Skin and Shape were admirable, the one being clean and well proportion'd, the other white as Snow, and only here and there, upon the Breast and Belly, shaded with some light brown Hair. I turned away my Eyes, being all covered with red: Upon that he threw all the Cloaths from me, and whilst I innocently endeavoured, with my Hands, to hide that which I thought was a Shame to have exposed to his View, he fed his Eyes with the Prospect of the rest of my Person, kissing my Breasts, my Belly, my Thighs, in a Word, all that he could come at; then taking away my Hand, which hid from him the Place of his Joys, he gently put his Forefinger into my C—t, and thrust it a little Way up, till he met with a Stop, and I complained he hurt me. This he did on Purpose, to be satisfied whether I was a Maid or not, as afterwards he himself confided.

OCT. See the Cunning of these Men!

TUL. A true Maid, as thou art, and I was, is so far from taking it ill at their Hands, that she is extremely pleased to give them Proof of her Intireness, and 'tis most certain, that in those that are so, the Marks of it are plain, and easily discoverable, at least till twenty Years old. When *Horatio* was satisfied, that none had been there before him, he began to use the kindest amorous Words in the World to me, calling me his Soul, his Life, his Joy, and to desire me, as I lov'd him, to lie still and to let him do what he had a Mind to, without any Hindrance.

OCT. And did you?

TUL. I was so beside myself that I knew not what to do; his Person appeared most lovely in my Arms, and I could not, methoughts, find [it] in my Heart to thrust him away from my Embraces. He saw I began to be moved, and presently opening my Legs as wide as he could, he got between them upon his Knees; then turning my Smock up under my Chin, and slipping both his Hands under my Buttocks, he pull'd my Head quite from the Pillow, that my Body might lie high, and be the more exposed to View. Then gently setting himself down, he with one Hand softly opened the outward Lips of my Slit, and introduced the Head of his Yard into it.

OCT. Were you dumb all this while?

TUL. My Sighs and Blushes were all the Interruptions I gave him, longing I must confess, as much to see what would come of his Endeavours, as he could to perform them.

OCT. Now I tremble for thee.

TUL. Having placed himself in this Posture, he bid me take fast hold of him about the Middle, and thrusting with all his Force towards me, he endeavoured, but in vain, to open himself a Way into those secret Parts; for he had not thrust above one or twice, in which Time he did not advance an Inch, but I felt his Member grow lank and soft, and found myself all over wet. I presently reach'd the Handkerchief behind the Pillow, and went to wipe myself, but he took the Office from me, and did it for us both, bestowing on me, at the same Time, many burning Kisses and languishing Looks. This first Attack was not without some Pain when he pressed very hard, but not enough to make me cry out, for it was but just a beginning, when it ended. After this, he rested a little, and lying by me, he took one of my Hands, and putting it to his Mouth, kissed it; then looking kindly upon me, Let me die, my dearest *Tullia*, but I love thee more than my Eyes; my Life, nothing can be handsomer than thou art! How prettily thy Breasts lie panting! How hard they are! How sound! How handsomely parted one from another! Saying this, he kissed my Nipples, sucked them, and fooled with me a hundred Ways: I began to find myself warmed by I know not what Desires; and turning towards him, I repaid his Kisses with Interest. Then he slipt his Hands between my Legs, and playing gently with the light brown Hair about my Belly, of which I have a great Deal, he admired the pretty Effects of its Shade upon a white Skin: Then opening softly the Lips of my C—t, and putting in now one Finger, then another, made me almost Mad. Put away that vexatious Hand, said I, why do you torment me? He began to Laugh, finding he had stirred me, and taking his Left-hand, and putting his Member into it, Take, my dearest *Tullia*, said he, a better and pleasanter Instrument, and fit it thyself to the Place of my Joys.

I being grown bolder, because I was more desirous to see the End, took it and 'twas as much as my Hand could well grasp. Courage, said he, my pretty Rogue. Let us try once more that thy Mother may not find thee a Maid To-morrow, to my Shame. I answered, I never can endure it, it will split me in two, you'll kill me, if all this must go into my Body. Do thou guide it, said he, and be sure you do not let it slip aside. I obeyed him, and once more, with all his Force he thrust at me; but finding it advance but little, he made me lift up one of my Thighs, which he embraced with one of his Arms. I suffered some Thrusts, even very strong ones, very patiently. At last he began to drive it in with such Fury that I was not able to endure the Pain any longer, and gave a great Shriek, and let go my Hold, crying, Oh! You kill me, dear *Horatio*, I am not able to bear it, and withal some Tears fell from my Eyes such was the Smartness of the Pain. In the mean Time, he had got in about two Fingers Breadth, when I felt myself wet with another warm Shower, as I had been at first. In all this I felt no Pleasure, only a small Tickling, which did a little mitigate the Sharpness of what I endured. *Horatio* being got off me again, began to complain of my Unkindness, in the Disturbance I gave him in those Joys that he designed to make me taste; and said, if thou dost love me, *Tullia*, thou wouldst never deny me to gather the true Fruit of thy Enjoyment. I love thee, said I, my dearest *Horatio*, with all my Soul; but what wouldst thou have me to do in this miserable Pain that I endure? I am sure, if thou didst know the Sharpness of it, you would have Compassion of your poor *Tullia*; but I will not dispute any longer, said I, but shew the Obedience of a Wife, if you'll take upon you once more the Authority of a Husband. He smiled at my Application of those Things, and bid me prepare for a new Attack; for by this Time, the terrible Foe began to raise his Head, and threaten my Fort with a new Assault. Hold me fast about the Middle, said he, and when I faint away upon thy lovely Breasts, forsake not thy Hold, if thou intended to have me for a kind Husband. I promised to do all he desired of me.[2]

OCT. And you kept your Promise?

TUL. You shall see. He first shut my Mouth with Kisses; then placing himself between my Legs, which he made me clap about his Back, as high as we could, he opened with one Hand the Lips of my C—t, and with the same Hand gently put in the Head of his Member: I felt it go in about two Fingers Breadth without any great Difficulty; but then, upon a strong Thrust, I cried out, that he tore me in Pieces. He, little minding my Cries, put his Tongue in my Mouth to stop it, and moving still strongly on, he at Length broke thro' and got the whole Length of his Yard into me. I roared then, and Tears came in my Eyes, but he wiping them and repeating his Kisses, bid me hold him fast and not stir my Legs from about his

Buttocks; and beginning to move gently to and fro in my C—t, he asked me if I did not begin to feel something that made me some amends for all my Pain. I said, as it was true, that besides a small Tickling, I had no other Sense of any great Pleasure. Immediately after, he stirring quicker and stronger, expres'd the inconceivable Delight which he took now he was enter'd, and in the same Moment, fell languishing and dying upon my Breasts, giving me a thousand Kisses. He did not after this, as he had done before, leave me and lie still, but keeping his Hold and Place, Now, my *Tullia*, said he, that I have taken Possession as a Conqueror, I will not so soon leave it; and since it has cost me so much Pain and thee such Blood (looking upon the Sheets, which were all stained with the Marks of my Virginity), I will run one Race more in Course of Love. Having said this, I felt his P—ck swell within me. Now, saith he, I will make thee share with me in this Pleasure if thou wilt be ruled by me: as I thrust forward, do thou, just upon my going back to make another Thrust, follow me with thy Buttocks, from the Bed, towards me, and then fall again, as I come with my Buttocks forward to thee. This Motion, at first, will seem strange to thee, but a little Practice will make it easy, and exceedingly pleasant. I am sure thy Youth and Dexterity, at all other Exercises, must make thee no Dunce at this. I refused, at first, to try so odd a Motion, but he so intreated me, I did it once, and then repeated it upon a second and third Intreaty; and, in a Word, after that, I commanded it for my own Pleasure very nimbly; for I began to feel something so unusual within me, that I was almost transported. We had not long continued, when he cried out, Oh! My *Tullia*! Oh my dear! And I, immediately finding something come from me, with inexpressible Delight, held him fast in my Arms, and with a kind Murmur and broken Words, cried, Oh! Oh! ———— My *Horatio*! My Soul! Melt! Oh, what it is to feel my Love! My *Horatio*!

He embraced me still harder, and thrusting his Member up as high as it would go, after two or three more Motions, die'd in my Arms, with infinite Pleasure, just as I had made an End of mine; so both languishing, and almost weary, we lay in one another's Arms, when from behind a Hanging, *Pomponia*, who had over-heard and seen a great Part of our Engagements, came running to me, and catching me naked, as I was, in her Arms, began to kiss me with great Joy, telling me how she pitied me when she heard me cry out, but that since a kinder Sound and softer Expressions of my Joy, had assured her of my Felicity, she was now at Ease. *Horatio* was about to put in with some roguish Compliment, when he found himself seized by another Hand and kissed as earnestly; it was my Mother, who gave him a thousand Thanks, for having behaved himself so bravely. Thy Victory, said she, was made known to me by *Tullia*'s Cries, but I make no

Question, they will hence forward be turned into kind Expressions between you for ever. I was so ashamed to hear my Mother's Voice so near, that I endeavoured to cover *Horatio* (who was almost naked) with the Bed-Cloaths, and turn myself under 'em, not being able to look my Mother in the Face, but she laughing, bid *Pomponia* pull me out; and so having set before us some excellent Wine and Sweetmeats, she made us take some of them to refresh our Spirits. After a little Stay, taking *Pomponia* by the Hand, she was leading her to the Door, saying, Now we both might well need Sleep; But *Horatio*, who had been hindered from speaking roguishly to *Pomponia*, resolved she should not go so; therefore calling her hastily from the Door, to the Bedside, he immediately got a-top of me, and his Member now knowing the Way, had already entered me as *Pomponia* came to the Bedside. His going in so quick hurt me so, my Wounds being yet fresh, that I cried out, Ah! My dear *Pomponia*, come and deliver me from the murdering Man. My Mother and she only answered me with Laughing as loud as they could, and so went out, and *Horatio* kept jogging in. After a while, I felt no Pain, but in its Place, a sweet Tickling, and in the End, a Seizure in every Joint and Limb, which made me languishing lay my Head on one Side, and in Sighs and short Breathing, express the inconceivable Pleasure of all my Senses. This Bout was something longer than the rest, but infinitely more pleasant; for in this Exercise, the last Bouts are always the most delightful. And whether it be that the Sense grows more refined with the Action, or that the latter Flowings of the heavenly Liquor that comes from us, are of a more exquisite Nature, 'tis certain that the Extasy, at last, is such, that in some it comes near Pain, by being so ravishingly delightful. *Horatio*, overjoyed to see me so delighted, said a hundred kind Things to me in that Instant, calling me his Life, his Soul, and answering all my broken Murmurs with his, he at last died too in my Arms. After this, we both in a short Time fell asleep and lay till late in the Morning.

OCT. Thou hast sufficiently painted to me, all that will befall me in the Battle of Love, where my Virginity is to be the Prize of the Conqueror; and, if I am not mistaken, I have something more to endure than thou didst, by how much *Philander* has the Reputation of being better provided for than any Man, and he will, I am afraid, meet in me the least C—t that ever was; which, as it is likely to increase my Pain, so I hope, in Time, it will my Pleasures. However, I am resolved to bear all patiently that is to lead me to this Paradise.

TUL. I cannot wish thee, my dear *Octavia*, a better Fate than mine, who now enjoy a perfect Felicity with my lovely *Horatio*. Let us rise now, my pretty Maid. To-morrow thou wilt lose that Name for a better. I think thou art sufficiently prepared for the Engagement.

DIALOGUE III.

TUL. No Day was ever more agreeable than this Night will be, my dearest *Octavia*; for I shall not only enjoy thy Company, but a Part of thy Pleasures, by the Repetition thou wilt make of them to me.

OCT. I came on Purpose to give my kind Instructor an Account, how I had observed her Rules, and what Pleasure I had found in her Doctrine, by the Use and Applications of it. In a Word, all the Joy which you foretold me, comes short of what I really felt, and I attained to that Bliss which equals us with Angels, with less Trouble much than I expected from your Description.

TUL. Prithee, good *Octavia*, begin then with all that happened to thee on thy Wedding-Night.

OCT. You must take something that happened in the Day-time too; for *Philander* was so eager, that he did not stay till Night, to have his Body wearied with Dancing and Drinking, and his Fancy pall'd with the bawdy Jests of a publick Wedding. No sooner we were come from the Church, but pretending a Business with my Mother in Private, he went up Stairs into her Closet, not being willing to use her Bed-chamber, lest it should raise too much Suspicion; there he entreated her to send for me, saying he had something to communicate to us both, which highly concerned his present Joy, and future Quiet. My Mother did, and order'd me to come up a back Pair of Stairs, which she had for her own Privacy. I entered the Room, blushing so soon as I saw *Philander*, for I fancied 'twas not without Design I was carried that private Way. As soon as he saw me, he ran and catch'd me in his Arms, giving me a thousand Kisses, with sparkling Eyes and close Embraces, so that I scarce knew where I was. Then, turning to my Mother, Madam, said he, I beg your Pardon for this unmannerly Cheat of making you do, in an unusual Time of the Day, that which you would not scruple by Candle-light, with a much less troublesome Ceremony; but since I have my *Octavia* in my Arms, the only Kindness you can do me, is to go and entertain the Company, while I go and receive the first Joys of Love. Your Desires, *Philander*, said my Mother, are very unreasonable, and I should think, that the very Expectation of it should increase the Joys at Night. Oh, Madam, said he, I die, I languish; and if you did but know the Pain I suffer, you would pity me. Will you pity *Octavia*, said my Mother, and not use her with that Roughness, which the Vehemence of young Men makes them think a Piece of Courtship? However, said she, whispering unto him, and drawing him aside, I am content she shall be kind for once, tho' I believe it will be to little Purpose on her Side. Then calling on me, Daughter, said she, you are now your Husband's. Do what he will have once, but no more.

247

After that, come away, or I shall be very angry. This said, she clapt to the Door and took the Key with her. *Philander* immediately taking me in his Arms, set me upon a Table, before a great Looking-Glass, and taking up my Coats, he set two low Stools under each Foot; then coming between my Legs with his Breeches and Drawers down, and his Thing stiff and red, he was just going to try to enter me, when we heard the Key turn in the Door, and saw my Mother enter the Room. I was naked up to the Navel, and *Philander's* Linnen was well tuck'd up under his Coat, to give him the more Liberty of his Hands. I presently leap'd from my Place, and put down my Coats; but *Philander* turning hastily about, shewed his Weapon naked. My Mother, taking Notice of the Bigness of it. Gemini! said she, what a Monster is this! But be not daunted, Daughter, it will be so much the more pleasant to you in Time. I came in, said she, to take off thy upper Petticoat, lest by its being rumpled, the Guests of the Wedding should perceive that you have been at it already. This said, she undid my upper Petticoat, and laid it by; then turning to *Philander*, Be merciful, said she, to poor *Octavia*, for my Sake. He, putting her out of Doors, made no Reply, but running to me, set me in the same Posture I was in before, then putting one of his Hands upon my Buttocks, which he gently thrust toward him with the other, he opened the Slit of my Commodity, and conveyed the Head of his Engine to it. Now, said he, my dear *Octavia*, embrace me with both Arms, and meet with a Thrust, when I make one towards thee. I do not know what you mean, said I, nor what you would have me to do. He made no more Words, but began to thrust at first gently, but then a little harder, and at last so strongly, that I made no Question but my Maidenhead was in extream Danger. His Member was stiff and hard as a Horn, and hurt me so, that I thought he would split me in two: But he little minding me, gave such a home Thrust, as made me cry out as if I had been killed. He followed it close with a great many more, begging me to hold still, and not disappoint his first Joys. As he said this, I saw his Eyes turn in his Head, and all his Body fainting, fall upon me, and breathing out his Soul in amorous Kisses, cry, My dearest Dear, how infinite is my Pleasure! Just as he had finished, my Mother, who had heard me shrick, came into the Room. Oh! said she, *Philander*, you forgot your Promise. I, at that Instant felt something extraordinary come from me, and closing my Eyes, and taking fast hold of *Philander*, I laid my languishing Head in his Arms, and upon his neck, and cried, Oh! I feel some thing so sweet that it kills me! He embraced me kindly, and seeking my Lips to lay his to them, made me all in a Transport, that I never felt before or imagined.

TUL. Thou describest it rarely well; but I wonder thou shouldst have so much Pleasure the first Time, for that seldom happens to Maids.

OCT. Venus was kind unto me, and had, it seems, prepared a Liquor, which flowed from me in such Abundance, as *Philander* himself felt it, and cried, Oh! What Joys do effect us both, with such a Stock of this heavenly Nectar, as we are each of us provided with!

TUL. Well, go on.

OCT. As soon as I had done, *Philander* took out his Thing, which was now grown soft and humble, from threatening and proud that it was before: So then I asked him if he would have any Thing more with me; and being ashamed of my Patience in letting him do so much already, desired him to let me go: My Mother seconded me, and whilst she pulled me away with one Hand, and he strove to keep [me] still in his Arms, I threw down one of the Stools that my Feet were upon. My Mother cry'd out that the Noise would alarm the Wedding-Guests, who were underneath, and so carried me away into her Bed-Chamber. There, immediately, having kissed me tenderly, she began to question me, how it was with me? Bidding me tell her all the Particulars without Shame, for now she was more my Companion than any Thing else. I obey'd; and as I made the Description her Eyes sparkled, her Veins swelled, and embracing me she almost fell away in my Arms with the Sense of my Pleasures; and no Wonder, for she is not yet above nine and twenty Years old. My dearest *Octavia*, said she, thou art now born to a new Life; and this Night will make an End of shewing you that which the Light of a thousand Days would never do without thy dear *Philander*. Thy Wit and Understanding will clear up with thy Enjoyments, for that very Engine that opens our Bodies, will do the same to our Minds; and make us despise all childish Sports and Amusements, to give our Hearts up to this one heavenly Pleasure, the greatest of all mortal Delights. Having said this, she bid me shew her my Smock, which when she saw, all wet, and almost stiff with *Philander*'s Liquor, Oh! What a happy Girl are you! Said she, and what a Fountain of Joys has this Husband of thine in Store for thee! Pluck off this Smock, which I will keep for a Relick, since it is stained with thy Virgin's Blood. She helpt me off with it, and dressed me all a new, setting my curls afresh, and ordering my Hair and Knots so that nobody might suspect what we had been doing. So I then boldly ventured down; and what blushes appeared now and then in my Cheeks, were taken more for the Effects of my Modesty, than of my Guilt.

TUL. Do not trouble yourself, no more, with the Description of your Dinner, your Dancing, nor your putting to bed; I know enough of that foolish Ceremony: Come to the Point of fresh Enjoyment between *Philander* and you.

OCT. When I was in Bed, my Mother asked me if I were afraid. I asked her of what! At which she smiled and added, If you will, I will desire *Philander* to use you kindly, and not to put you to such pain as he did in the Morning. I answered that any Pain which would procure him Pleasure, would be a Delight to me. He was just then come to Bed and overheard me: Where, catching me about the Neck, My dearest Love, said he, how beholding am I to thee for that pretty Thought! They all, seeing us in close Embraces, withdrew; and *Philander*, leaping out of Bed, locking all the Doors after 'em, and viewing every Corner of the Room, after he had found all safe, came to Bed again. There were four great Wax Candles in the Room, all which he drew near, and set them upon Stands, by the Bed-Side, so that it was a Light as Noon-day, within my Curtains; then, taking me in his Arms, he began to give most amourous Kisses, not only to my Lips, but to my Breasts, Arms, Belly, and almost every Part about me, which he viewed with great Curiosity, one after another, saying, at every one, that it was impossible to see a greater Beauty in the World; and that I had the Proportions and Graces, which could be desired in a Woman. At last he came to the secret Paradise of his Joys, and begging of me to hold still, and let him view it, he gently opened its Lips, which he said was as red as a Rose-bud: I put my Hand once or twice to put away his, which hurt me, and he, laughing said, I confess I ought to put something else there more pleasing. With this he got upon me, and having found me so straight in the Morning, that he not only hurt me, but himself also, he had furnished himself with a Bottle of most delicate Essence; with this he rubbed himself, and me, in those Parts, which were to encounter each other: And I cannot imagine, *Tullia*, what a Secret that is: for after a Thrust or two, with much less Pain than in the Morning, I felt his Member above half in, and he had scarce stirred in my Arms, but, Oh! my Dear, said he, I die! Embrace me! Hold me close! I did so, and in that Instant such a Shower of Seed fell into my Womb, that I was wet all over. Part of it coming back again, his P—ck fell upon this, and he took it out half languishing, wet and frothy. I have done, my Angel! said he, let us rest a little in each other's Arms.

TUL. Ah! Dear Cousin, had you no Pleasure this Time?

OCT. You shall hear a pleasant Thing. No sooner was he off me, but I began to be tickled with a certain Itching in those Parts, that I catch'd fast hold of him in my Arms, and, with Sighs and Kisses, demanded, as it were, that he should help me: He could not do it with the proper Instrument, it was not then in a Condition to obey his Desires, therefore, putting his Finger into my C—t, and stirring gently up and down towards the upper Part of it, he made me spend so pleasantly, such a quantity of the delicious Nectar, that it flew about his Hand, and all wetted him. I beg thy Pardon, my lovely *Octavia*, [said he,] for not expecting thy Pleasure; for

Nature in us Men is something so eager that we cannot withstand its first Impetousities. I was struck with a mighty Confusion at my own Lust, and blushing and hiding my Face, I said that if he felt any Moisture, it was that which he had put into me, and not any that I had sent out. Deny it not, my Love, said he, for I adore thee so much the more, being able to give me such infinite Pleasure as I see thou wilt. Most Women are in that Error that they think they ought to hide their Joys from us, but it is the greatest Mistake in the World, for our Pleasures consist more in theirs, than our own. These Delights in Men of Wit and Understanding, please not only the Body, but charm the Mind, and so our whole Enjoyment is made up of being pleas'd in pleasing, and none but Brutes can be delighted only with that unusual Evacuation of easing themselves: But to see a delicate Creature, whose Modesty struggles with her very Senses, be forced, in our Arms, to give up all her Reserve, and to abandon herself to the Joy we give her, is, at the same Time, paying back to us a more infinite Pleasure, who cannot but imagine that we are infinitely lov'd by a Thing, which seems pleased without Measure by us. After this, we lay still in one another's Arms, he ever and anon, mingling his amorous Kisses, with some Expressions and dying Looks, till within a little while, he found his Member stiff for another Engagement. Now, said he, my Dear, you must be complaisant, and put yourself intirely into my Management. Have not I already done that sufficiently? said I. No! said he, you must learn another Lesson you have not yet try'd. Then throwing off the Sheet, and turning up my Smock, above my Breasts, up to my very Chin, he put his P—ck into my Left hand, desiring me to hold it fast, and convey it to its beloved Place. I did, and it entered about Halfway. Now, said he, I would have thee tell all the Thrusts I make, which I promised, but he, by half a Dozen strong Thrusts, broke it up to the very Stones, which pained me so much that I gave over keeping Account, crying out I was split in two. Now, said *Philander*, thou art a Woman, and that silly Thing called a Maidenhead is gone to all Intents and Purposes. Now, the Field of Delight is opened unto thee for ever. Take it out, said I, it hurts me cruelly. Rather, said he, I would thrust it farther in, and so lying close upon me, he seem'd, if he could, to thrust his whole Body into me. Our Bellies were so joined that the Hair of both our secret parts lay close to each other. He began then to thrust again, and after about Half a Score he cry'd, he was going to sp—d. I, who was just as near it, catch'd fast hold of him about the Middle, and raising myself towards him, I fell away in Joys just as he express'd his by swooning in my Arms! And this was much the pleasantest Bout I had yet. He remained upon me a while, after both our Pleasures were over, delighting himself to view me in that Posture, and see, as he said, so great Raptures of Joy. After this, we lay still and fell into Discourse of a great many past Things of our Love and other Matters. I, who had observed him to be a great Judge of Beauty and an excellent Critick in the Charms which make a Woman lovely, had a great Mind to make him describe unto me how a Woman must be, to arrive to that Perfection of Beauty; and so I desired him to make me a Description of an exact one, such as none could with more exact words; hoping, I must confess, to find myself a great part, if not all, that should make up such an excellent Composure.

TUL. I love thy Curiosity. Most Women love to hear of no other Body's Beauty but their own, and very few, abating some Charms of a Face, know where the rest that pleases lies. I long to hear what Description he made.

OCT. He told me, at first, my Request was unanswerable; for some Men loved the Fair, others Brown, many Black, and not a few the red-hair'd Women, tho' generally not so esteemed as formerly; so that to fix a Description would be a hard Thing. Ah, but, said I, there are in all these a Contexture of Parts and proportion of Shapes and Limbs that make them beautiful in their kind.

In my Opinion, said he, a Woman that would pretend to Perfection, ought to be of a middle Size, neither of the tallest or the least; her Skin ought to be white and smooth, without any Speckles or Roughness. Her Flesh firm, neither too fat nor too lean, but so as to have but few Bones seen any where about her; her Breasts little, and prettily parted from one another, but standing firm and round; her Belly smooth and a little standing out, not flat and falling in; her Arms turned, as if they were of Ivory; her Hands long and dapled, with Holes at the Joints; her Thighs plump, white and lessening by Degrees; her Knees round, little and smooth; her Legs straight, with the Calf of it rising gently, and not of a sudden, into a thick Bulk; the Small of her Leg little, and wrought, as it were, slender to the Proportion of her Foot, which ought to be white, plump and little; her Buttocks ought to be round, firm and white; and, last of all, her C—t, with plump Lips forward, and shaded above with hair; but free from it below and on the Sides. It was with great Pleasure, I must confess, that I heard this Description; for, as he went on, I full viewing myself, and making Reflections upon every Part, found that I had most, if not all these Perfections mentioned; but still not thinking this enough, and being desirous to see the Bottom of his Thoughts, asked him, Whether or no, it might not be possible, that a Woman, with all that Beauty, might still be very disagreeable, for some other Reason? He said, Yes. For, if with all these Perfections, she had not white Teeth, a sweet Breath, and no ill smells about her, she would be far from an agreeable Creature; but, above all, her Carriage would be that

which would most enchant a Man. I desired him, since we were upon that
Subject, and that in Part of Agreeableness, it might lie in my Power, to add
something to that little Nature had favoured me with, and that I resolved
to make him the only Object of my Desires, and place my Felicity in pleasing him, that he would instruct me which Way to do it.

Thou art, said he, my dearest *Octavia*, so sweet natur'd, and of thyself
so inclin'd to all that is gentle and virtuous, that I need not give thee any
Caution about thy Behaviour; but since I have begun thy Picture (for I believe thou wilt answer all the Strokes of it) I will, for thy Sake, give it the
last finishing, by describing what Humour I would have a perfect beauty
be of.

A chearful Behaviour, without Giddiness or Frolick, is the most lasting Pleasure. Pleasant Thoughts limited by modest Expressions, that make
one think more than they declare, are the most acceptable in Conversa- *Companion*
tion; but, above all Things, she must avoid injurious Reflections and jealous Repinings at other Women's Beauty and Conduct. I need not recommend Reading, without which a Woman is absolutely unsociable and can
never captivate the Heart, nor amaze the Mind of a Man of Sense. Lying
is to be avoided, as the Rock upon which all the rest of her good Qualities will miscarry, since it will certainly lessen the Esteem of her Lover, and,
by little and little, create in him a Distrust of her Conduct: And when in
private with her Lover, she abandons herself to his Desires, it must not be *want it / to*
with Impudence, nor yet with Reservedness and peevish Shyness; but she *be pleased*
must yield to him as to a Thing she loves, and to whom she sacrificeth all
her Scruples, embracing him tenderly, and accepting with modest and
inviting Reluctancies, all his Caresses and Kindness.

TUL. I see *Philander* is one of those Men, who being great Observers,
and having a refined Imagination, manage the Pleasure of Enjoyment with
extreem Niceties, and are in that (when they meet with a Woman in their
Mind) most infinitely happy, and as much surpassing the ordinary Rate of
Men, who do only brutishly satisfy their own Lusts in us, as other Men
think themselves above Beasts. But withal, these nice Men are easily displeased, and when their Imagination is once struck, tho' but with little Offence, it works with them till it grows a kind of nauseating, if not quickly
perceived and remedied.

OCT. For that, I suppose, we must blame none but ourselves, if it
come to pass; for what have we to do, being delivered up to those Enjoyments, but to mind the Improvements of 'em, and by the Neatness of our
Persons, the Sweetness of our Temper, and the Pliableness of our Humour,
keep them so enchanted, that they shall never be clogged with our Embraces?

TUL. You are in the right, *Octavia*, for Men have a thousand Businesses and Crosses in their Heads, and they often come Home full of them, and little in a Condition to oblige us, if we by our Softness do not first make them forget their Cares, and then by our Pleasantness tempt them to our Joys. —But tell me, *Octavia*, did *Philander* content himself with the Enjoyment of so heavenly a Creature; if he did, I shall have an ill Opinion of his Metal, and think that those monstrous P—cks are to be raised only with Machines, when once they are fallen.

OCT. When I have told you all, you will have a better Opinion of my dear *Philander*; for no sooner were his Descriptions and Reflections ended, but of a sudden, throwing off the Cloaths from himself, he shewed me his Member stiff and red; this, said he, my *Octavia*, after all, is the best Instructor, and as long as you take Lessons from him, you will never fail to please. I believe it, said I, but asking him (smiling, and half hiding my Face) whether he would always be in a Condition to teach when I had a Mind to learn? He laugh'd heartily at my Question and returned it with taking me in his Arms, and giving me a hundred passionate Kisses, pulled the Cloaths from off me; then he bid me put my Hands above my Head, and not stir them from thence, while he viewed with curious Eyes, the Shape of all my hidden Parts; how did he commend the white Smoothness of my Belly, the Situation of my C—t, the Cherriness of its Lips, the Frizing of the Hair about it! He made me draw my Legs up, and bend them backwards almost to my Breech, so that I shewed all to the greatest Advantage. This Sight so enflamed him, that, leaping upon me, he entered me briskly, before I expected it. It began now to be very pleasing, and methinks, the going in was so agreeable, when I considered how it filled me now, without much hurting me, and what kind Effect it would have for the Future, I embraced him about the Middle, which he has white and finely shaped; and he, bearing himself upon his Hands, pressed upon no Part, but that which he could now no longer injure: His Eyes were intent upon me, and I, sometimes shutting, then opening mine, to look upon him, lay panting under him with great Content. Our Motions were now pretty even; he had taught me to answer his so, that, in a very little Time, I felt the extreamest Pleasure, which, seizing all my Limbs, made me abandon my Head upon the Pillow in dying Sighs and Murmurs. Oh! My lovely *Octavia*, said he, how dost thou delight me with thy Joys, and how infinite is my Pleasure in seeing thine? As he said this, I felt the very utmost Parts of my Body contract themselves with convulsive Pleasures, and at last, I lay unmoved as a Stone, as dissolved in Joys.

TUL. Thou makes me mad with thy Descriptions, they are so natural, and the Image of thy Pleasures create such in me, as comes very near thy own.

OCT. He took his P—k out, finding it all wet with sp—ding, and having wip'd it and me, he immediately put it in again, and began to thrust with great Vigour. I was some Time before I could recover my Strength, enough to answer him; but, after a while, finding the pleasing Tickling began to be renewed, as I vigorously pursued the Motions, he had so instructed me, that my Back was as supple as an Eel's. He bade me raise my Legs, and clap them about his Buttocks, as high as I could. Upon this I found he enter'd much better. He then putting one Hand under my Head, and another under my Buttocks, laid himself gently down upon me, and so we continued in a regular Motion, in one anothers Arms, till I finding the highest Joys to be coming on again, called to him to make an End too, for I was going to die; but he only minded my Extasy, which was followed, as before, with a Fainting of my whole Person in his Arms. Being a little come to myself, I begged of him to give over, else he would kill me. He said he intended to die first himself, and begged of me to do it once more, in which Time, he would endeavour so to nick it that we should both die together. I obeyed, and having wiped himself, and me, put it in again, and you cannot imagine with what Pleasure it comes in after an Enjoyment, in order to begin another. After a little stirring, I observed he now shut his Eyes and began to breathe shorter, which I perceiving and finding I was not ready to die with him, could not forbear saying, Gently, my lovely *Philander*, gently, that I may meet thee in my Joys. He took the Hint, and moving very slowly, laid his Lips close to mine, and putting his Tongue into my Mouth, met with mine, and whilst they both managed a new Combat, all my Person was seized with a strange, and not before felt Extasy, for I was almost out of myself; and he seeing it, renewed his Endeavours with so good Success that, at one and the same Time, we both cried out, Oh, *Philander*! Oh, *Octavia*! My Dear, my Soul! My Life! I die! I am kill'd! Ah! What shall I do! And so in confused Murmurs, and half Words, we finished our Felicities.

TUL. Sure this Bout had something in it Divine, for you are transported even at the Remembrance of it, and make me ready to die with the Description.

OCT. So it had; and I have observed ever since, that the last Bouts are the best, and chiefly those which are the longest. So, *Philander* getting off me, we both lay extended by each other, Breathless; like a Hare and Greyhound, that have, upon a strong Course, just tired one another; so that the one cannot run, nor the other follow a Step further. I, after a little Time, first came to myself; and pulling the Cloaths on us both, and making the bed a little, I kept close to *Philander*, who receiving me in his Arms we both fell into the most lovely Sleep that can be imagin'd, in which we continued till very late the next Morning.

TUL. Ah! *Octavia*, how happily have you begun to run this Career of Love's Enjoyment, and under what a fortunate Constellation were you born! That have, in the Flower of your Youth, the Embraces of the most lovely and vigorous of his Sex; long may they continue so! But I think it is now high Time to give ourselves up to Rest, and therefore, my dearest *Octavia*, good Night.

FINIS.

6

A New Description of Merryland
(1741)

A NEW DESCRIPTION OF MERRYLAND.

Containing, A TOPOGRAPHICAL, GEOGRAPHICAL, AND NATURAL HISTORY of That COUNTRY.

Define [quapropter] *Novitate* exterritus ipsa
Expuere ex Animo Rationem; sed magis acri
Judicio, perpende, &, si tibi vera videtur,
Dede Manus; aut, si falsa est, accingere contra.
LUCRET. *Lib. 2.*

Fly no *Opinion*, Friend, because 'tis *New;*
But strictly search, and after careful View,
Reject it *False, embrace* it, if 'tis *True.*
CREECH's *Translat.*[1]

CHAP. I.

Of the NAME *of* MERRYLAND, *and whence it is* so called.

THE *Names* of most Countries have been much altered from those they were formerly known by; and even at this Day, different Nations, nay, People of the same Country, give different Names to the same Place. MERRYLAND, like other Countries, has been known under great Variety of Names, and perhaps now has as various Appellations as any Part of the Creation: It is not my Purpose to trouble the Reader with a long Recital of them, nor to dispute which is the most proper; let it suffice in these Pages to call it MERRYLAND, so named (as the learned Antiquarians inform us) from the *Greek* Word μυρίζω, i.e. *Unguentis inungo,*[2] alluding to the unctuous Nature of the Soil, or perhaps to the Practice of some People in that Country, of whom the Historians say, *In Lætitiâ Unguentis utebantur* erantque, μεμί ρίσμένοι, i.e. *Unguentis & Oleo delibuti,* from the transporting Delight that it gives.[3] By the *French* it is called *Terre-Gaillarde,* from the *Greek* ἀγαΜιάώ, *Lætitiâ exulto,* or from γαίγ *Lætor .*[4]

Either of these Derivations seem to me very plausible, and have very significant Reference to the wonderful Delight People enjoy in MERRY-LAND, as will be more fully related in the succeeding Chapters: However, far be it from me to presume absolutely to fix this Derivation as infallible; it being a Matter of great Consequence to the learned World, I shall with all Humility submit it to the more judicious Determination of the learned and useful SOCIETY of ANTIQUARIANS: In the mean-while I am pretty much confirmed in the Justness of this Etymology by the *High-German* and *Dutch* Names of MERRYLAND, the first calling it *Frolich-landt*, and the other *Vrolick-landt*,[5] both which agree in the same Signification, and in my humble Opinion clear up the Matter almost beyond Dispute.

CHAP. II.

Of the Situation of MERRYLAND.

MERRYLAND is a Part of that vast Continent called by the *Dutch* Geographers, the *Vroislandtscap*; it is situate in a *low* Part of the Continent, bounded on the upper Side, or to the Northward, by the little Mountain called MNSVNRS, on the East and West by COXASIN and COX-ADEXT, and on the South or lower Part it lies open to the TERRA-FIRMA.[6]

There is something very remarkable and surprising as to the *Longitude* and *Latitude* of this Country, neither of which could ever yet be fixed to any certain Degree; and it is pretty evident, however strange it may seem, that there are as great *Variations* both of the Latitude and Longitude in MERRYLAND, as of the Mariner's Compass in other Parts of the World: To confirm this, I beg leave to assure the Reader of a Matter of Fact, which, if he be an entire Stranger to MERRYLAND, he will perhaps scarce have Faith to believe; but they who have any tolerable Experience and Knowledge of the Country, will be so far from discrediting, that I do not doubt but they will be ready to confirm it by their own Observation.*

Know then, courteous Reader, soon after my first Entrance into this wonderful and delightful Country (having as prying a Curiosity as most Men) I endeavoured to get the best Insight that was possible in every Thing relating to the State of MERRYLAND, observing with diligent Attention every thing the Country afforded that was remarkable either in *Art*

---

* But now attend; I'll teach thee something *new*,
'Tis *strange*, but yet 'tis Reason, and 'tis *true*.

or *Nature*, all which I intend to communicate to the Publick in the following Sheets. Among other things I made very accurate Observations
both of the *Latitude* and *Longitude*, and may venture to say, there could be
no considerable Mistake in my Observations, as they were made with a
proper Instrument, of a large Radius, and in perfect good Order; nay, I have
been assured, when I was in MERRYLAND, that my Instrument was inferior to none: But some years after, happening to be there again, and repeating the Experiment, I found both Latitude and Longitude increased
many Degrees, tho' I tried in the same Spot, and with the same Instrument
as before. It may, perhaps, be suspected, that my Instrument might have
suffered since the first Experiment was made, (as it is well known the best
are liable to Damage by Time and frequent Use) but that was not the
Case; for tho' mine had, I must confess, been often used, yet it was with
such prudent Care and Caution, that it was in as great Perfection as ever;
and even at this Day I could venture to recommend it as a tolerable good
one, tho' I have had it above these 30 Years, and used it pretty freely, and
with great Satisfaction to myself and others.*

That the Latitude and Longitude then were evidently and considerably increased, is Matter of Fact beyond Dispute; but how to account for
so wonderful a Phenomenon I must leave to others, and should think it
well worthy the Consideration of that curious and learned Body, the *Royal
Society*:

> *Felix, qui potuit rerum cognoscere Causas.*
> —VIRGIL.[7]

That they may have all the Hints and Information towards it, which
my Experience can afford, I must acquaint them, that this surprising Increase of Latitude and Longitude in MERRYLAND, seldom fails to happen, after having a *fruitful* Season in that Country (as had been the Case
when my Experiment was last made) so much does it increase, that after
a few Years one would scarce believe he was in the same Part of the World;
nor is its Fruitfulness the only Cause of this Variation; frequent tilling the
Soil, tho' it should prove utterly barren, or no Seed be sown in it, is observed in some measure to produce the same Effect.

This extraordinary Alteration of the Latitude is not at all agreeable,

---

* Ev'n what we now with greatest Ease receive,
 Seem'd strange at first, and we could scarce believe:
 And what we wonder at, as Years increase,
 Will seem more plain, and all our Wonders cease.
  CREECH's Lucret. B.II.

but the greater Degree it extends to, the less delightful is the Country to its Inhabitants: on which Consideration some Projectors have been induced to try several Methods (and as they pretend with Success) for reducing the Latitude, when too much augmented, and by that means restore MERRYLAND, at least in Appearance, to its primitive State; but they must be ignorant People indeed, who can be imposed on by such Practices; yet such it seems there have been, but they are justly laughed at for their Credulity, and by no-body more, than by the very Persons who so easily deceived them.

I need say no more of the Situation of this Country, but after the Example of that excellent Geographer Mr. *Patrick Gordon* (who in his *Geographical Grammar* tells us what Place is the *Antipodes*, or opposite Part of the Globe to the several Countries he treats of)[8] I shall conclude this Chapter by informing the curious Reader, that the *Antipodes* to MERRYLAND is by some said to be that prominent Part of the Continent called PDX, known in *High Dutch* by the Name of *der Arsz-back*;[9] others affirm the *Antipodes* to be in the very uttermost Point of the Promontory CPT; but as it is not my Intention to concern myself in these Disputes, but stick as close as may be to my Subject, I shall leave the Affair of the *Antipodes* to those who have a *Taste* that Way; only shall observe, there are some People who very preposterously (as I think) give the Preference to the PDX: the *Italian* Geographers are pretty much inclined that Way; some of the *Dutch* have likewise come into it, and of late Years a few in *Great-Britain* have appeared not altogether averse to it.

CHAP. III.

Of the AIR, SOIL, RIVERS, CANALS, *&c.*

The Air in MERRYLAND is very different, being in some Provinces perfectly pure and healthy, in others extreamly gross and pestilential; for the most part it may be said to be like the Air in *Holland*, "*generally thick and moist, by reason of the frequent Fogs which arise from its Lakes and Canals,*" yet it is mostly very pleasant and agreeable to the Inhabitants, tho' it cannot always be said to be wholesome. In the most healthful Provinces it agrees well with young and vigorous Constitutions; but for old Men, or those who are consumptive, this Country is at best esteemed very pernicious, especially if they enjoy it too much, which many are tempted to, by the bewitching Pleasantness of the Place, of which we may say with *Solomon*, "*How fair and how pleasant art Thou, O Love, for Delights!*"[10]

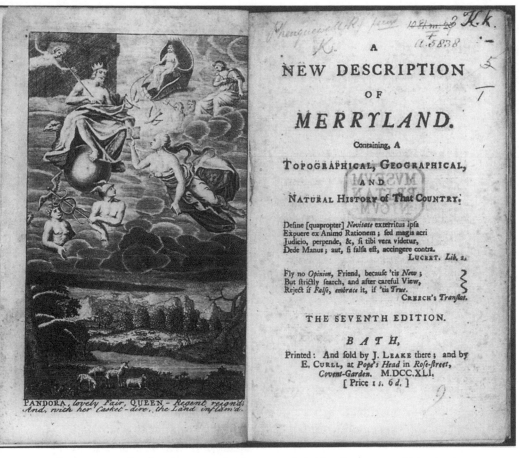

A

NEW DESCRIPTION

OF

MERRYLAND.

Containing, A

TOPOGRAPHICAL, GEOGRAPHICAL,

AND

NATURAL HISTORY of That COUNTRY.

Define [quapropter] *Novitate* exterritus ipsa
Expuere ex Animo Rationem; sed magis acri
Judicio, perpende, &c, si tibi vera videtur,
Dede Manus; aut, si falsa est, accingere contra.
LUCRET. *Lib.* 2.

Fly no *Opinion*, Friend, because 'tis *New*;
But strictly search, and after careful View,
Reject if *False*, embrace it, if 'tis *True*.
CREECH's *Translat.*

THE SEVENTH EDITION.

BATH,

Printed: And sold by J. LEAKE there; and by
E. CURLL, at *Pope's Head* in *Rose-street*,
Covent-Garden. M.DCC.XLI.
[Price 1 s. 6 d.]

PANDORA, *lovely Fair*, QUEEN—*Regent reign'd;*
And, with her Casket-dire, the Land inflam'd.

Figure 6.1 The frontispiece and title page of *A New Description of Merryland* (1741).

The Climate is generally warm, and sometimes so very hot, that Strangers inconsiderately coming into it, have suffered exceedingly; many have lost their Lives by it, some break out into Sores and Ulcers difficult to be cured; and others, if they escape with their Lives, have lost a Member. It is certain there can be no Distemper more to be dreaded than this, occasioned by the Heat of the Climate in MERRYLAND; the Curious may see it particularly described, with all its hideous Symptoms, by our Countryman *Bartholomew Glanville* (who flourished about the Year 1360) in his Book *De Proprietatibus Rerum*, translated by *John Trevisa*, Vicar of *Barkeley*, in 1398.[11] But notwithstanding this Inconvenience is so well known, so bewitchingly tempting is the Country, that People will too frequently rush into it without Caution, or Consideration of their Danger; even those who know the ill Consequence, from dear-bought Experience, are not always deterred from precipitantly repeating the same Folly; nay, so remarkable is this Rashness in the Inhabitants of MERRYLAND, that it is become a common Proverb to say *they have no Forecast*. But this dangerous Heat of the Climate, with all its dreadful Concomitants, is not so very terrible, but it may be guarded against by taking proper Precautions, and People might venture into it without much Hazard, even at the worst Seasons, and in the most unhealthy Provinces; they need no more to avoid the Danger, but be careful always to wear *proper Cloathing*, of which they have a Sort that is very commodious, and peculiarly adapted to this Country; it is made of an extraordinary fine thin Substance, and contrived so as to be all of one Piece, and without a Seam, only about the Bottom it is generally bound round with a scarlet Ribbon for Ornament. This *Cloathing* has been found so useful, that a modern Bard thought fit to write a Poem in its Commendation, and has most elegantly celebrated its Praises in Blank Verse.[12]

Sometimes the Climate is as much on the other Extreme, *cold*, to a great Degree; but this rarely happens, nor has it any bad Effect on the Inhabitants, otherwise than by being disagreeable and uncomfortable to live in.

In general the Country is warm enough, and so exceedingly delightful, that every Man at first coming into it is transported with Pleasure; the very sight of MERRYLAND, or any near Approach to it, puts one in strange Raptures, and even in dreaming of it, People have enjoyed a most pleasing kind of Delirium: In short, it is the loveliest and sweetest Region of the World, and is thus painted by the Poet:

> *Quas neq, concutiunt Venti, neq; Nubilæ Nimbis*
> *Aspergunt, neq; Nix acri concreta Pruinâ*

Cana cadens violat, semperq; innubilus Æther
Contigit & latè diffuso Lumine ridet.

Which, Winds nor ruffle, nor the humid Train
Of gathering Clouds e'er deluge o'er with Rain;
Nor fleecy Snow, nor Frosts deform the Soil,
Or frustrate, or suspend the Lab'rour's Toil;
Perpetual Spring smiles on the fertile Ground,
And genial Suns diffuse their Influence round.[13]

However, I must own, the Poet seems to have been a little too bold
and hyperbolical in this Description; and fond as I am of the Country, I am
not so partial as to think this poetic Flight strictly justifiable, notwithstanding all the learned Commentators have wrote to reconcile it to
Truth:

Crescit in immensum facunda Licentia Vatum.
Poets claim Licence that will know no Bounds.[14]

The Country lying very low (as Mr. *Gordon* says of *Holland) its Soil is naturally very wet and fenny,*[15] the Parts that are best inhabited are generally the
moistest; and Naturalists tell us, this Moisture contributes much to its
Fruitfulness; where it is dry, it seldom proves fruitful, nor agreeable to the
Tiller: The Parts which have never been broke up, nor had Spade or
Plough in them, are most esteemed; and so fond are People of having the
first Tilling of a fresh Spot, that I have known some Hundreds of Pounds
given to obtain that Pleasure.

MERRYLAND is well water'd by a River, which takes its Rise from
a large Reservoir or Lake in the Neighbourhood called VSCA, and discharges itself with a most impetuous Current and fearful Cataract towards
the *Terra-Firma* near the Entry of the Great Gulph; of this River I shall
treat more particularly in another Chapter.[16]

There is a spacious CANAL runs through the midst of this Country,
from one End almost to the other; it is so deep that Authors affirm it has
no Bottom. I have often sounded it in many Parts, and tho' I don't doubt
but it has a Bottom, I must own I never could reach it; perhaps, had my
Sounding-line been a *few Fathoms* longer, it might have reached the Bottom.

We are told of *Solomon's Wells* or Cisterns at a Place the *Turks* call *Rose-
layne,* which, like this Canal, are reputed to be unfathomable; and the current Tradition is, that they are filled from a subterraneous River, which

that wise King, by his great Sagacity, knew to run under-ground in that Place. Vide *De Bruyn. Voyag. au Levant.*[17] Whether this might not as properly be called *Solomon's Canal,* I leave to the Reader's Judgment; it is certain, that wise King was no Stranger to this Country, but spent a great deal in Improvements he made in several Provinces of it.

All the superfluous Moisture of the Country is drained off through this Canal, and it is likewise the Conveyance of all Provisions to the upper Part of MERRYLAND; all the Seed sowed in that Country is conveyed this Way to the *Great Storehouse* at the upper End of it; and in short, there is no Commodity imported into MERRYLAND, but by this Road; so that you may easily conceive it to be a Place of *great Traffic.* We may say of this Canal, as the learned Doctor *Cheyne* says of the *alimentary Tube,* "that it is, as it were, a *Common-Sewer,* which may be fouled or cleaned in various Manners, and with great Facility; it is *wide, open,* and *reasonably strong.*"[18]

The Country is generally fertile enough, where duly manured; and some Parts are so exceedingly fruitful as to bear two or three Crops at a time; a *Dutch* Traveller tells us, there was once known to be as many Crops as Days in the Year; but this I look upon as apocryphal. Other Provinces are so utterly barren, that tho' a Man should leave no Stone unturned but labour and toil for ever, no Seed will take Root in them; yet so whimsical are many of the Inhabitants, that they would chuse one of these barren Spots, rather than the more fertile ones; and indeed there is some Reason for it, People having found by Experience several great Inconveniencies by too fruitful a Crop. 'Tis a lamentable Thing for a Man to have a large Crop, when his Circumstances can't afford Houses to keep it in, or Thatch to cover it; to let it perish would be infamous, and what can a poor Man do? For he can't dispose of it immediately, it must be kept several Years at great Expence to him, before it is fit for the Market, or capable of making the least Return for his Labour and Expence. These are melancholy Circumstances for the poor Farmers:

> *Quæque ipse miserrima vidi,*
> *Et Quorum pars magna fui.*

> ———— Which I, alas! have seen,
> And deeply felt.[19]

This Peculiarity has put some People on inventing Means to prevent the Seed taking Root, or to destroy it before it comes to Maturity; but such Practices are only used by Stealth, and not openly approved of; it is looked on as a bad Practice, and we are told it was formerly punished with Death.

It sounds odd, but it is no less true than strange, that many have been ruined and forced to run away, by the Greatness of their Crop; and on the other hand, many are in a manner miserable and never satisfied, because their Spots prove barren. Strange Contradiction in People's Tempers! that what would be one Man's Delight, should be another Man's Torment!

men produce yet don't want the weapons.

We are told by *Kercher* of a Mountain at *Chekian*, whose Soil is of that Quality, that it *tames Tygers*, &c. This Mountain, I presume, must be of the same Kind of Soil as MERRYLAND, which in some Degree has the Power of *taming* the wildest Creatures; nay, it will first make them in a manner *mad*, and *tame* them afterwards.[20]

I shall conclude this Chapter on the Soil of MERRYLAND, by saying, "her Vallies are like *Eden*, her Hills like *Lebanon*, her Springs as *Pisgah*, and her Rivers as *Jordan*; that she is a *Paradise* of Pleasure, and *Garden* of Delight."[21]

CHAP. IV.

Of the vast Extent of MERRYLAND, *its Divisions and principal Places of Note.*

The *Arabian* Geographical Lexicographer cited by *Schultens* in his Geographical Commentary at the End of his Edition of *Soltan Salah'addin's* Life, very justly observes, that the exact Limits of this vast Country are entirely unknown, the greatest Traveller having never been able to discover its utmost Bounds; and whoever attempts such a Discovery, may properly enough be said to grope in the dark.[22]

Besides those Parts which are well known, and have been described by Travellers, there are others of which we know but little, tho' some Authors have pretended to be very exact and particular in their Descriptions of them, for which they have no better Authority than their own Fancy and Invention; and there are other Parts of this Country still unknown to us. It would swell this Work too much, and be of little Use to the Reader, to take notice of every Particular; I shall therefore content myself with mentioning such Parts as are of most Note, which are these:

1*st*, At the End of the great Canal toward the *Terra Firma*, are two Forts called LBA, between which every one must necessarily pass, that goes up the Country, there being no other Road. The Fortifications are not very strong, tho' they have *Curtains*, *Hornworks*, and *Ramparts*; they have indeed sometimes defended the Pass a pretty while, but were seldom or never known to hold out long against a close and vigorous Attack.

2*nd*, Near these Forts is the Metropolis, called CLTRS; it is a pleasant Place, much delighted in by the Queens of MERRYLAND, and is their chief Palace, or rather *Pleasure Seat*; it was at first but small, but the Pleasure some of the Queens have found in it, has occasion'd their extending its Bounds considerably.

3*rd*, A little farther up the Country are two other Fortresses, called NMPH, seated near the Banks of the great River. These have sometimes made a stout Resistance, against strong Attacks and skillful Engineers, and have endured a great deal of Hardship in the Assault, so that Instances might be given of the most vigorous Assailants being repulsed with great Loss and Confusion. On the other hand, they have often been known to give way upon the first slight Attack, and admit the Assailants without any Opposition.

4*th*, At the upper End of the great Canal, mentioned in the former Chapter, is the great Treasury or Store-house called UTRS, of which *Plautus* gives this Description,

> —*Item esse reor*
> *Mare ut est; quod das devorat, nunquam abundat,*
> *Des quantum vis.*—

> ——Semblance meet
> Of the wide Ocean, which ingulfs whate'er
> Within its Circuits falls; in its Abyss
> Absorbing Great, or Little, as it chances:
> Gorge it to the Brim, strait it All devours!
> And craves for more.[23]

This *Store-house* is of a particular Structure; in Shape it somewhat resembles one of our common Pint-Bottles, with the Neck downwards. It is so admirably well contrived, that its Dimension are always adapted to its Contents; for as the Store contain'd in it increases, so the Bounds are extended in Proportion; and when it is quite empty, or but little in it, it contracts or diminishes proportionably, and that without any Art or Assistance.

5*th*, Another Part of the Country, often mentioned by Authors, is HMN, about which there have been great Controversies and Disputes among the Learned, some denying there ever was such a Place, others positively affirming to have seen it: For my part, after the nicest Inquiry I could make, I never could discover any thing satisfactory about it; and most Travelers now agree, that if it ever did exist, it is utterly defaced by

Time or Accident, so that in these latter Ages, no Footstep of it is to be found; agreeable to that saying of the Poet,

—*Etiam ipsæ periere Ruinæ.*
—No Mark of such a Thing now seen.[24]

6th, Here I must not omit to mention a famous pleasant Mount called MNSVNRS, which overlooks the whole Country; and, lastly, round the Borders of MERRYLAND is a spacious Forest, which (as Mr. *Chamberlayne* says of the Forests in *England*) "*seems to have been preserved for the Pleasure of Variety, and the Diversion of Hunting.*"[25]

These are the principal Places observed by Travellers; and to give a more compleat Geographical Description of this Country, I intended to have added a Map of it, but recollecting it would considerably enhance the Price of the Book, I chose rather to refer the curious Reader to a Map of MERRYLAND, curiously engraven on Copper plate, and published some Years ago by the Learned Mr. *Moriceau,* who was a great Traveller in that Country, and surveyed it with tolerable Exactness.[26] There the Reader may see all the noted Places and Divisions laid down exactly as they are situated; and here I must in Justice to the Learned Sir *R.M.* acknowledge, that his late contrived *Model* or *Machine* is a very ingenious Invention, which gives a better Idea of MERRYLAND than can possibly be done by the best Maps, or any written Description.

CHAP. V.

Of the Ancient and Modern Inhabitants, their Manners, Customs, &c.

MERRYLAND is well known to have been inhabited soon after the Fall, and *Adam* was the first Adventurer who planted a Colony in this fruitful and delicious Country. After him the *Patriarchs* were industrious Tillers of the Soil. *David* and *Solomon* were often there, and many modern Kings and Princes have honour'd this Country with their Royal Presence and Protection. King *Charles* II. in particular was in close Alliance with it, and it flourished exceedingly in his Days. Nor has it been slighted by his Royal Successors, some of whom have taken great Delight in it, and their Councils have sometimes been influenced by the Situation of Affairs in MERRYLAND. We have had *Ministers,* who preferred its Welfare to that of their own Country, and Bishops who would not be displeased to have a small *Bishoprick* in MERRYLAND. At present, the Inhabitants of

[handwritten margin note: original sin]

this Country are very numerous, and composed of all Degrees, all Religions, and of all Nations.

As to the Manners of the Inhabitants, tho' they are sometimes very low and despicable, being soon dispirited and dejected by violent Exercise; yet, when in good Spirit, they are very strong and vigorous, and when bent upon their Pleasure, are very bold and daring. They are much addicted to Pleasure and Diversion *in private*, notwithstanding they affect great Gravity and Restraint in public.

They are vastly *ticklish*, and so fond of it, that when they can get nobody to please them that way, they will *tickle themselves*. They are naturally given to love Freedom and Liberty, prone to Change and Variety, much given to Dissembling and Flattery, and greatly addicted to Venery; they have little Esteem of Frugality or Oeconomy, but *spend all they can*, and glory who *spends most*. They pride themselves much in their stiff and stately Carriage, and cannot have a greater Compliment paid them, than by comparing them to the *Behemoth*, of whom it is said in *Job*, that *his Strength is in his Loins, and he moveth his Tail like a Cedar*.[27]

Homer gives a beautiful Description of their Boldness and Bravery in an Engagement, and with what Intrepidity they make an Attack; which Mr. *Pope* has translated thus—

> *He foams, he glares, he bounds against them all;*
> *And if he falls, his* Courage *makes him fall*.[28]

One remarkable Custom of the Natives is, that the Moment they come into the World, they leave the particular Spot they were born in, and never after return to it, but wander about till they are 14 or 15 Years old, at which Age they generally look out for some other Spot of MERRY-LAND, and take Possession of it the first Opportunity; but to enter again in that Part they were born in, is looked on as an infamous Crime, and severely punishable by Law; yet some have been hardy enough to do it.

There are some whimsical Ceremonies commonly observed by People when they take Possession of any Part of this Country, such as prostrating themselves on their Faces, and muttering many Ejaculations in praise of the Spot they have chosen; then laying their Hand on it by way of *taking Seisin*; then he sticks his Plough in it, and falls to labouring the Soil with all his Might, the Labourer being generally on his Knees: Some indeed work standing; but the other way is the most common.

Another thing very remarkable is, the Custom observed commonly at all Merry-makings among the Men when over a Bottle; instead of toasting their Mistresses, they begin with drinking a Health to MERRYLAND;

and it is a known Rule, that this must be always drank in a *Bumper.* If any one refuses, he is looked on as a sneaking Fellow. To keep them in mind of this Duty, I have seen the following Verses inscribed on their Cups and Glasses under the Word MERRYLAND:

Hic quicunque legis nomen Amabile
Pleno lætoque Cyatho salutem libes,
Sic tibi res amatoriæ prospere cedant,
Tua sic coronet vota Cupido.

Whoever takes this Glass in Hand,
And reads thereon dear MERRYLAND,
Fill it sparkling to the Top,
Toast the Health, and tope it up;
So may all thy Vows be heard,
When at VENUS' Shrine preferr'd;
So may thy Fair One gentle prove,
And CUPID ever crown thy Love.[29]

As to the *Genius* of the Inhabitants it may be observed, the *Liberal Arts* are here in the greatest repute; here *Experimental Philosophy* has been improved to a wonder; *Physic* and *Surgery* have flourished exceedingly; and no Country is better stock'd with *Divines.* And for *Merchandizing,* the great Wealth arising from Trade in some Provinces is a plain Proof and Demonstration that *Traffick* is carried on in MERRYLAND with great Success.

Here I must not omit taking notice, that this Country has produced and inspired great numbers of excellent *Poets,* and in return, they have in many of their Works expressed their great Regard for the Country, and celebrated its Praises with the utmost Gratitude and Affection. One of them says,

Hic ætatis nostræ primordia novit,
            Annos fælices, lætitiæque dies:
Hic locus ingenuus pueriles imbuit annos
            Artibus, & nostræ laudis origo fuit.

Here my first Breath with happy Stars was drawn;
            Here my glad Years and all my joys began:
In gradual Knowledge, here my Mind increast;
            Here the first Sparks of Glory fir'd my Breast.[30]

CHAP. VI.

Of the Product and Commodities, such as
Fish, Fowls, Beasts, Plants, &c.

Tho' this Country is so plentifully watered, by so fine a River and
Canal, it is but indifferently stored with *Fish*; yet when a Stranger comes
to MERRYLAND he would imagine by the Smell of the Air, that the
Country abounded with *Ling* or *Red-Herrings*; as we are told the River
Tyssa in *Hungary* smells of *Fish*; so strong is this Smell sometimes, that it is
very offensive; but here are no such Fish to be seen. *Cod* indeed are often
found about the lower end of the great Canal, and *Crabs* in plenty on its
Banks. I never heard of any other Fish in MERRYLAND, except *Muscles*, *Gudgeons* in abundance, some *Dabs*, and a few *Maids*; these last are
rarely met with, and it is the Difficulty of catching them, I suppose, makes
them much valued by Persons of *nice Taste*. I have indeed heard of a *Mackeral* being found here by Mr. *R* a Surgeon of *Plymouth*; but this was purely
accidental, it being only one single *Mackeral*, brought to MERRYLAND
by a young Woman merely for the sake of *trying an Experiment*. However,
this scarcity of Fish is the less to be lamented, as in this Country a *Flesh*
Diet is most delighted in, and with that they generally are pretty well sup-
plied.

For *Fowls*, here are *Cocks*, *Wagtails*, *Buzzards*, *Widgeons* and *Gulls*, besides *Tomtits*, which being small insignificant Creatures are of no Esteem,
and *Capons*, which are likewise held in great Disrepute.

Of Beasts, here are plenty of *Asses*, some *Bears*, *Dromedaries* and *Mules*,
and many sly old *Foxes*. I have heard likewise of *Baboons*, *Monkeys*, and
Spaniels; but as it is unnatural to find them here, I believe it is likewise more
uncommon than is reported. I know it has been strongly insisted on by
several learned Men (some of them great Travellers in MERRYLAND)
that Rabbits have been bred in that Country, and they expected great
Profits from a Warren they pretended to have lately discovered; but, after
a great Noise made about it, All came to nothing.[31]

As for the Commodities of the *mineral* and *vegetable* Kind, here are a
few of each which I shall take notice of, as far as my Observation and
Memory serve me.

Of the *mineral Kind*, the *Blue* or *Roman Vitriol* (which is of great Use
to eat away proud Flesh) is often found on the Borders of this Country;
and it is observed the Provinces, where this is found, are generally un-
wholesome.

There have been Instances of *Gold* and *Silver* discovered here, nor is

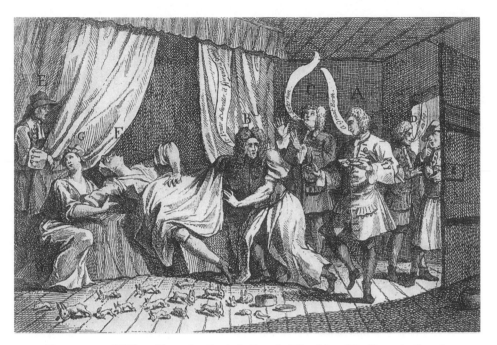

Figure 6.2 William Hogarth, *Cunicularii, or the Wise Men of Godlimen in Consultation* (1726).

the Country destitute of *precious Stones*, here being a Kind very much esteemed, tho' very common to be met with on the Surface; so fond are they of them, that a Man would be look'd on with Contempt in MERRY-LAND, if he had not at least two of them, which they always carry about them in a Purse; they contribute very much to the Fruitfulness of the Soil.

Of the vegetable Kind, here is *Rue* in great Plenty; *Carrots* are no ~~Strangers to this Soil,~~ but are much used; here is some *True-love* and *Sweet-Marjoram*, and the Plant call'd *Maiden-hair*; but the last is very scarce. Here is no Scarcity of several kinds of *Simples*, of which they make great Profit. *[margin: masturbation]*

There is a Plant of the submarine Kind, which delights much in this Soil; the End of it resembles the *red Coral*, and partakes much of its Virtue; it is highly esteemed in MERRYLAND, and is undoubtedly a great Sweetener; it being frequently applied very successfully to cure *sharp* and *sour Humours.* This Plant yields a *whitish viscid Juice*, which, when taken inwardly, has a bad Effect on some People, causing a large Tumour in the Umbilical Regions, which is not got rid of again without great Pain. But there are many on whom it never has that Effect, let them take ever so great a Quantity of it. It is generally reckoned an excellent Cosmetic, "giving a most inexpressible Countenance, and causes sparkling Life, Spirit, and *[margin: ?]*

juvenile Bloom to reign in every Feature." It may properly enough be called the *Coral-plant*, as it resembles it in several Particulars. Mr. *Boyle* affirms of the Nature and Generation of *Coral*, that whilst it grows, it is often soft and succulent, and propagates its Species: And *Kircher* was informed by the Divers, that the Coral would sometimes let fall a spermatic Juice, which lighting on a proper Body produced another *Coral*.[32] The same may be said of the Plant above mentioned.

Another submarine Plant is said to be found in MERRYLAND, of the *Sponge-kind*, the Name of which I have forgot. They use it not only as a *Cleanser*, but also as an Antidote against the bad Effects of the Juice above mentioned.

Here are *Flowers* in great Plenty, but not much to be commended, either for Fragrancy or Beauty. They are not variegated, nor is there any great Diversity of Colours; *Red* and *White* are most common. Some Naturalists have imagined these Flowers to be of a poisonous Quality; but that Notion is now sufficiently exploded, and it is observed, if they happen not to spring in their due Season, the Country generally proves unhealthy and barren.

As for *Manufactures*, I never heard of any in MERRYLAND worth mentioning, except those for *Pins* and *Needles*, which are made in great Plenty in some of the most trading Provinces, and are famous for their *exquisite Sharpness*.

CHAP. VII.

Of the Rarities, Curiosities, *&c.*

The great RIVER mentioned in the 3rd Chapter is very remarkable; the Water is *warm* and *brackish*, and does not run in a constant Stream like other Rivers, but the Current stops every Day for Hours together; and without observing any regular Period, it all on a sudden falls a running again with great Rapidity. This River (like the River NESS in *Scotland*, and the Lake of DRONTHEIM in *Norway*) never freezes in the hardest Frosts, but always retains its natural Heat; and has another remarkable Quality, like that of the River *Adonis* near *Byblus* in *Phœnicia*, which at certain Seasons *appears bloody*, as we are told in *Maundrel's* Journey from *Aleppo* to *Jerusalem*.[33]

The CANAL, before taken notice of in the 3rd Chapter, deserves to be ranked among the Curiosities of this Country, not only for its *wonderful Depth*, which is said to be *unfathomable*; but for another extraordinary

Quality, no less surprising; for as it is reported of some Lakes in *China*, that the throwing any thing into them causes a Storm, so on the contrary many violent Storms have been appeased, if not entirely laid, by throwing into this Canal a handsome Sprig of the *Coral-plant* mentioned in the 6th Chapter. This famous Canal answers the Description given in the *Atlas*, of a Lake near LE BESSE in *Brittany*, which is so deep, it never could be sounded; and in a hollow Place near it, a Noise is heard like Thunder.

Among the Rarities may likewise justly be reckoned that wonderful Mountain on the Confines of MERRYLAND, which at some Seasons begins to extend its Dimensions both in Height and Bigness, and increases its Bulk so considerably, that it is esteem's one of the most admirable Works of Nature; after it has continued swelling thus gradually for some Months, it will fall again all at once, and be reduced to its former Compass. This Swelling is generally the Fore-runner of a *dear Year*; and therefore some of the poorer Sort, who are not bound to their Farms by Lease, take the Alarm at this ominous Swelling, and fly the Country, as soon as they perceive it.

There are two other pleasant little Mountains called BBY, which tho' at some Distance from MERRYLAND, have great Affinity with that Country, and are properly reckoned as an Appendage to it. These little Mountains are exactly alike, and not far from each other, having a pleasant Valley between them; on the Top of each is a fine *Fountain*, that yields a very wholesome Liquor much esteemed, especially by the younger sort of People. These Fountains are often quite dry; but it is observed, they seldom fail to run plentifully after the Swelling of the other Mountain beforementioned, and they have in some degree the same Faculty of rising and falling; so that it is not without good Reason, Philosophers have imagined there is a secret Communication between these Places.

But of all the Curiosities, nothing deserves our Notice so much as a small Animal, somewhat of the serpentine Kind, known by the Name of PNTL;[34] it is often found plunging about in the great Canal, which is the Place it most delights in; so wonderful is this Creature, that it deserves a particular Description in this Place, and tho' it be but small, I may say of it, as is said of the *Leviathan*, "I will not conceal his Parts, nor his Power, nor his comely Proportion; he maketh the Deep to boil like a Pot; he is King over all the Children of Pride."[35] This Animal has neither Legs or Feet, but, by the vast Strength of its Muscles, has a Power of erecting itself, so as to stand almost upright. That learned Physician and Philosopher Dr. *Cheyne* seems to have had this in his View, when he said, "The *animal* Body is nothing but a *Compages* or Contexture of Pipes; an *hydraulick Machine*, filled with a Liquor of such a Nature as was transfused into it by its

Parents, or is changed into by the Nature of the *Food* it is nourished with, and is ever afterwards *good*, *bad*, or *indifferent*, as these two Sources have sent it forth."36 They are only of the Male-kind, and yet propagate their Species very plentifully. This may seem very strange, at first sight, to those *who have not thrown off the material* INCRUSTATION, *that entangles and fetters the full Exercise and Penetration of their natural Powers, which are tied down, sopited, and fettered, by the Manner of our* ORIGINATION;37 but any one, who will consult the learned Author before-mentioned, will find he very logically proves, that in all Animals "originally, there must have been no *Difference of Sexes*, BECAUSE at last in their restored State there will be none. And that it is highly probable, the *Female* was but a *secundary* Intention, or a *Buttress* to a falling Edifice."

They are of different Sizes, from six to seven or eight Inches in Height, when full grown, and from four to six in Circumference; there are some indeed of much larger Dimensions, but very rarely to be met with; and there are others much less, but they are of little or no Value; those of a middling Size are observed to be more lively and vigorous than the larger Sort, who like the Grenadiers in a Regiment, are not able to make so long and frequent Marches as the Battalion Men, the latter being for the most part better set and nimbler, as being furnished with a greater plenty of Spirits. One thing is very remarkable of these Animals, that either sleeping or waking, when they lie down, they immediately contract themselves to one third of their Length and Bigness, and grow so flagged and limber, one would scarce think they had ever been enabled to stand; but when they are roused up and in full Vigour, they are very stately, and much admired for their portly Mien. Here I must beg leave to refer once more to the above quoted Author, who tells us, "This *spiritual animal* Body, at first divinely organized, may be *rolled up, folded together*, and *contracted* in this State of its Duration, into an infinitely small *Punctum Saliens*, into a *Miniature of Miniature in infinitum*, and proceeding in a *diverging Series*, and progressive Gradation, that in due time it may be fit to be *nourished* and *increased* by the Juices of the proper *Female*." In pursuit of their Prey, no Creature can be more keen, and they rush on it with great Eagerness. Their Skin is of a swarthy Complexion, and hangs so loose about their Shoulders, that it frequently serves as a Hood to draw up quite over its Head and Face, or rather the Head shrinks into the Skin as a Snail pulls in his Horns and Head into his Shell. The Face of this Creature is of a reddish Complexion, and most delicately soft to the Touch; they are flat nosed, and have no Eyes, but find their Way by Instinct: They have no Bones, but are all Muscles and Flesh, which properly prepared and taken inwardly, is very refreshing and nourishing. It is reckoned a Specifick for

the Green-sickness, and many other feminine Disorders; "and is a Medicine so wonderfully pleasant, and easy in its Operation, that the nicest
Palate or weakest Constitution may take it with Delight, and so innocent,
that it is administered to Women with Child with great Safety." *[? even during pregnancy]*

CHAP. VIII.

Of the Government *of* MERRYLAND.

THE Government of this Country is *Monarchial*, and absolute in the
highest Degree. As the *French* have their *Salique-Law*, by which all Females
are excluded from the Throne, so on the contrary, MERRYLAND may
be said to be entirely under *Female Government*, there being an absolute *[female reign]*
Queen over each particular Province, whose Power is unlimited; no
Tyrants having ever required a more servile and blind Submission than the
Queens of MERRYLAND. *Herodianus*, Lib. 4. Cap. 3. says, "They treated
their Subjects as the meanest of Slaves, and scarce as Men, while they put
themselves on a Level with the immortal Gods." There are numberless Instances of the vast Power of these Queens, the Conquests they have made,
and the many cunning and crafty Methods they have used to obtain their
Ends; but as I do not intend to write their History, I must not here enlarge
on that Subject. Few of these Queens but have some Favourite or prime
Minister, and when they are well satisfied with his Abilities and Behaviour,
they will suffer themselves to be governed in a great measure by his Advice; but alas! there are some, who, tho' they have abundance of able Ministers, will never be ruled by any of them, are always varying and changing, turning out their greatest Favourites, for no other Reason in the
World, but to shew their Power, and gratify their inconstant Tempers; ad-
mitting a new Favourite every Day, as if *Variety* was their greatest Delight.
Such are the Caprices of these Queens, and so uncertain the Prosperity
of their *ablest* Ministers. Besides their Capriciousness, many of them are
also justly accused for their greedy and insatiable Tempers, forcing their *[their desires in exchange]*
Subjects to labour, drudge and toil without ceasing, to satisfy their vora-
cious Appetites. Some few able-bodied Men have indeed made shift to do
their Work, and these, it must be owned, meet with good Encouragement;
tho' they are kept to hard Labour, they get a comfortable Subsistence as
their Reward. I have known some of them well-cloathed and fed, and in
a very thriving Way; but it is not every one is qualified by Nature to go
through so much Fatigue.

Some of these Queens have deserved the worst of Characters, and are recorded for their Infamy in the Works of the *Greek* and *Roman* Satyrists. But our BRITISH JUVENAL, in an excellent *Latin* Satyr, lately published, has given us so lively a Picture of one of them, that I cannot forebear transcribing four Lines, which excel all I have ever met with, either in the Ancients or Moderns:

> *Saga petit Juvenes, petit innuptasque Puellas;*
> *Vel Taurum peteret, Veneris quoque mille Figuras,*
> *Mille modos meditans, Ætas in Crimina Vires,*
> *Datque Animos: crescunt anni, crescitque Libido.*
> SCAMNUM

> The Witch seduces Youth and Virgins pure,
> And would a Bull, could she the Weight endure;
> She tries all Postures Lust has e'er contriv'd,
> And of her own adds many more beside;
> Her Crimes, by Age, have Strength and Courage found,
> And as her Years increase, her Lust abounds.[38]

As to the MILITARY GOVERNMENT in this Country, I cannot pretend to say much, as I am not acquainted with their several Rules; but I have observed in general, that Soldiers are well esteemed and encouraged, and there are no Complaints against *Red Coats* in MERRYLAND, however they may be disapproved of in other Countries. Their *Naval* Forces are likewise very considerable, and of great Service to the Country, being a Set of lusty Fellows, always willing to work when ashore, and never backward in *spending their all*, for the Service of the particular Queen under whose Jurisdiction they live.

It would no doubt be very acceptable to the Reader, if after the *Civil* and *Military*, I could give him any particular Account of the *Ecclesiastical Government* of this Country; and it is with the greatest Concern that I am not able to gratify his Curiosity; for the Clergy endeavour to keep it a secret as much as possible among themselves, being a *Mystery* they think improper to be divulged among the Laity; and tho' I could mention some particulars on this Subject, which have accidentally come to my Knowledge, I must desire to be excused, being very unwilling to give Offence to a Body of Men, for whom I have the greatest Veneration, and to some of whom I am particularly obliged for their kind Assistance and Recommendation, which contributed much to the Pleasure I have enjoyed in MERRYLAND. I shall therefore say no more of the Ecclesiastical Government, but only observe in general (and I hope without Offence) that there are many *Bishopricks* in this Country, the exact Number I cannot pretend to guess at, nor how far their several Jurisdictions reach. Of the *inferior Clergy* here are such abundance, that they may, on a modest Computation, be reckoned to enjoy more than the *Tythe* of all MERRYLAND.

CHAP. IX.

Of the Religion *in* MERRYLAND.

Christianity was first planted here, in all probability, in the earliest Ages of the Church; at present no Country can boast of more Religions, and yet no Part of Christendom may be truly said to be less religious than this. Here we may see all Sects and Parties (all Religions being embraced) and yet that which the Apostle calls *the pure and undefiled Religion before God and the Father*,[39] is as little, if not less thought on here, that in any Christian Country whatsoever.

IMAGE WORSHIP (to the Shame of the Country be it spoken) is a Vice they are not entirely free of: for it is well known, too many of the Queens of MERRYLAND have a particular Veneration for a certain *Image*, made in Resemblance of the *Coral-plant* mentioned in the 6th Chapter; to this they often pay their Devotions, with the greatest Privacy; the Ceremony consists of various Emotions and Agitations of the Body, and Manual Performances, which my Abhorrence of the *idolatrous Custom* forbids me to describe more particularly: 'Tis much better my Readers should by kept in Ignorance of such shameful Actions, which all Men must detest, than by any further Description be informed how to practice them.

Here are Popish Missionaries in great Plenty, and by that means the *Roman* Catholick Religion is pretty much propagated, they being very laborious and indefatigable; *Quakers, Presbyterians, Independents*, and of late the *Methodists*, have been great Labourers in these Parts, 'tho not so professedly and openly perhaps as some others. It is to be lamented that so many Sects are tolerated, especially considering the dangerous Heats and Flames that are kindled in the Country by the intemperate Zeal of so many different Sects. In short, there is no Sect whatever, but has found footing in MERRYLAND; and it is hard to say, which of them all is the most established. One Thing is pretty remarkable, in which they all agree with that excellent *Litany* of our Church, all of them joining in that Prayer, *to strengthen such as do stand, to comfort and help the weak, and raise up those that fall.*

CHAP. X.

Of the Language.

The same may be said of the Language used in MERRYLAND, as Mr. *Gordon* says of the *Japanese Tongue;* "It is very polite and copious, abounding with many synonymous Words, which are commonly used according to the Nature of the Subject, as also the Quality, Age, and Sex, both of the Speaker, and the Person to whom the Discourse is directed."[40] There is something very sweet and emphatick in the Language, and at the same time it may be said, they have the least need of it of any People, for they have the Art of communicating their Sentiments very plainly by their *Eyes and Actions*, so that mute Persons can (if I may be allowed the Expression) speak intelligibly by their Eyes; and this Kind is often used with better Success than the finest Speeches.

To confirm this I beg leave to refer the curious Reader to the following Quotation from a learned Author, who says, "Mirantur OCULI, adamant, concupiscunt, Amoris, Iræ, Furoris, Misericordiæ, Ultionis Indices sunt; in Audacia prosiliunt, in Reverentia subsident, in Amore blandiuntur, in Dio efferantur, gaudente animo hilares subsident, in Cogitatione ac Cura quiescunt, quasi cum Mente simul intenti, *&c.*" —LAUR. *Lib de Sens. Org.* II. *Cap.* 3. The EYES may properly be term'd the Index of the Soul, inasmuch as they discover her various Passions of Admiration, Fondness, Desire, Love, Anger, Fury, Pity, and Revenge; when daring, they dart forth; when obsequious, they submissively recline; when enamour'd, they sooth; when at Liberty, they roam; plainly demonstrating when the Mind is exhilarated, and when overwhelmed with Anxiety and Care, *&c.*

They have likewise some *particular Motions* of the *Tongue*, which very emphatically express their Meaning, without uttering any articulate Sound, and is frequently more successful than the finest Flowers of Elocution.

It is much to be lamented, that no-body has given us a *Grammar* of the MERRYLAND Language; it would by very useful to the World, and I do not despair of prevailing on the Modesty of a *learned Orator* to undertake it, who has already obliged the World with *half a Score* other Grammars, and is universally allowed to be as well qualified for compiling *this*, as he was for *those*.

CHAP. XI.

Of the several Tenures, *&c.*

There are perhaps as many Kinds of Tenures in MERRYLAND as in any Country whatever, and it would be as difficult as it is needless to enumerate them all: Some holding by *Tail-special*, some by *Tail-general*, some by *Knights-service*, some in *Fee-simple*, others only *during Pleasure*, and others by *Lease for Life*. This last is pretty common, and 'tho not perhaps the *best* Tenure, is the *most encouraged by Law*, and therefore shall first be treated of. The Circumstances attending it are very singular, and worth Observation.

When a Man resolves to take a Spot in MERRYLAND by this Tenure, he makes the best Agreement he can with the Proprietor of the Farm, and the Terms being concluded on, publick Notice is given, that he designs speedily to enter into Possession, that any Person, who has just Objection to it, may forbid it before it is too late. You must know, there are several lawful Objections, such as the Farm being engaged before to another, or the Man having already another Farm on his Hands (for none are allowed to hold two at a time by this Tenure) his being any ways pre-engaged, or having any Incapacity to manure his Farm, *&c.* If no Objection be made, (to avoid which, they sometimes purchase a License, which dispenses with the Ceremony of giving publick Notice) then the Lease for Life is executed in this manner: The Officer, whose Business it is (and of which there is one in each Parish) reads a short Panegyrick on Farming, setting forth its original Institution and Use, the great *Importance* and *Honour* of that State, with proper Precautions not to take it in hand unadvisedly, lightly or wantonly, and requires the Man (as he shall answer at the dreadful Day of Judgment) to confess freely, if he knows any lawful Impediment, why he should not proceed in taking his Lease. — Then the Man makes a solemn Promise, that he will take the Farm according to Law, that he will keep it whether it prove good or bad, and forsaking all others keep only unto that for Life; the Officer then gives his Blessing to the Undertaking, prays for the Success, and then sings a Song, setting forth the happiness of Farming, and great Promises of Fruitfulness. The Ceremony being ended, the Man takes Possession of his Lot, and commonly begins to till it before he sleeps; and whatever Season of the Year it be, he generally continues tilling and labouring hard for the first few Days, till he is tired, and forced to take some Respite.

These long Leases have been the Ruin of many a substantial Farmer, for People are too apt to engage in a hurry, without due Consideration of the Consequence, or competent Knowledge of the Goodness of the Farm, which frequently proves to be a stubborn Soil, and makes the poor Farmer soon repent his Bargain; but there is no Remedy, the Man is bound, and must drudge on for Life. This Inconvenience has deterred many from ever taking Leases; and others, who have rashly been bound to a hard Bargain, when they find there is no Remedy, have been so discouraged, that they become ill Husbands, growing quite indolent and negligent of their Farm; and tho' they cannot throw up their Leases, they will let their Farms lie fallow, and clandestinely take another that is more agreeable to them.

There are many People who never will venture to take a Farm by the Tenure before-mentioned, but chuse rather to hold as *Tenants at Will* or *during Pleasure*, and tho' they pay a *dear Rate*, they have this Advantage, that whenever they do not like their Farm, they can immediately quit it and take another; there is little Danger of one of these Farms lying long unoccupied, for if one Man leave it To-day, another takes it To-morrow.

Those who hold by *Knights-Service* in the Courtesy of MERRY-LAND, thrive generally well, and reap good Profit by their Labour, especially if they be able, pains taking Men; let the Soil be ever so long worn, and out of heart, yet they will make something of it.

There is a great deal of Ground in MERRYLAND, which lies *Common*, and this is so bad, that let a Man sow ever so much Seed in it, it seldom produces any thing better than Briars and Thorns. — This Ground is not worth enclosing, tho' some People have been Fools enough to attempt it.

There is one Inconvenience [that] attends most of the Farms in MERRYLAND, for it is a difficult Matter to fence or enclose them so securely, but the neighbours, who are very apt to watch all Opportunities, may easily break into them; and it is surprising, where there is so much *Common*, and a great deal of good Pasture to be got at easy Rates, that People should be so fond of breaking into their Neighbours' Inclosures, where if they are catched, and prosecuted, they run a Risque of paying very severely, the Law being very strict in these Cases; and Juries are so apt to give the Plaintiff immoderate Damages, that I have known a Man cast in several *thousand Pounds* Damages, for a small Trespass on a Farm, which was little better than *Common*, and which the Owner would gladly have sold the *Fee simple* of for a *hundredth Part* of the Money.

CHAP. XII.

Of the Harbours, Bays, Creeks, Sands, Rocks, *and other dangerous* Places; *with the* Settings *and* Flowings *of the* Tides *and* Currents; *also* Directions *for* Strangers *steering safe into* MERRYLAND.

To recite all the *Bays, Creeks,* &c. would be an endless Piece of Work; and it is as impossible to point out all the *Rocks,* which People have split on, when bound for MERRYLAND: But I shall here give the Reader the best Directions I can to pilot him safe to this charming Country, by describing the Two Courses that are most commonly steered, and leave it to every one to chuse which suits best with his Inclination or Convenience.

They who go by the *upper Course,* make first for that Part of the Continent called LPS, where they generally *bring to,* and salute the Fort; and sometimes it is required that they *pay the Customs* and *Duties* here, before they are allowed to proceed further; but this is not always demanded. Then if you find the Wind favourable, steer along the Shore to the *Bby-Mountains,* where there is *good Riding;* and if you meet with no Storm, but find it calm and quiet, you may thence safely venture to run on with the Tide, and push in boldly for the Harbour: But if you find rough and tempestuous Weather, as sometimes happens at touching at *Bby,* and the Tide strong against you, it is best to *lie-by,* till the Storm is appeased, and a fairer Prospect offers of a prosperous Voyage; nor should you be discouraged by every little *Squall* which you may meet with at this Place, for generally these Squalls, tho' they seem violent at first, soon blow over without much Damage.

Some People prefer the *lower Course,* which is, at once to run in boldly up *the Straits of Tibia,* with the *Coxadext* bearing close on the Larboard-Bow, and so run a-head, directly as the Current carries you, into the Harbour; and indeed when the *Trade-winds* set in, this Course cannot fail.

In either of these Courses, it is best to be provided with a good *Forestaff,* kept in such Order, as to be always ready for Use at a Moment's Warning. I have known some People, for want of this Instrument being in Readiness, make a very unsuccessful Voyage, and been put back again, to their great Disappointment, when they were just at the Entry of the Harbour. It is also proper to make frequent *Observations* and *Soundings;* but, as Mr. *Collin* says in his *Coasting Pilot,* "the Thing principally to be observed, is the *Setting of the Tide,* which often alters the Course, to the Disappointment of the Mariner; for when you fail close upon a Wind, if the Tide takes you on the Weather-bough, you will fall too much to Leeward of your Expectation, and if on the Lee-bough, it carries you too much to Windward." The same Author very justly observes, "There is generally so great an *Indraught* of the Tide, that in little Wind, or a Calm, you will *be drawn in*, to Admiration."[41]

Tho' the Tide is generally very favourable, and sets into the Harbour, it is to be noted, that at the Time of *Spring-Tides*, which only flow for four or five Days, once in a Month, the Current then runs *strong out*, and it is best to *lie-by* til the Spring is over, tho' some People make no Scruple of going in when the Spring-Tides are at the Height.

There are People who, instead of steering either of these Courses, incline sometimes to go about by the *Windward-Passage*, but this I do not so well approve; in some Circumstances indeed it may be convenient, but I believe it is commonly done more for the sake of Variety than Conveniency.

Different Pilots have given us Variety of Directions, and shewed many Ways of steering safely to MERRYLAND; among others, that ingenious Pilot M. *Aratine* has published several *Charts*, with the different Bearings, &c. to which I refer the curious Reader, rather than swell this Chapter any more;[42] and indeed I do not see any great Necessity for many Directions, the Voyage not being so difficult, but what a blind Man may almost find his Way thither, by one Course or another; or should any one be at a loss, when he comes to the Coast of MERRYLAND, it's ten to one but he will find a Pilot to help him into Harbour, they being ready enough to oblige Strangers in that Way, as I myself found in my first Voyage, when I was very young and not expert in these Matters. It is remarkable, that when our Mariners come near the Coast in other Parts of the World, they wish for light Nights, that they may see the Shore, &c. but in the Voyages to MER-RYLAND, they meet with no inconvenience from the Dark, but find it generally favours them, and helps into Harbour with less Trouble than broad Day-light.

After you are fairly entered the Mouth of the Harbour, go up as far as you can, and come to an Anchor, *veering* out as much Cable as possible; the more you *veer*, the better you will ride. The chief Thing is, to beware of anchoring in *foul Ground*; for here is some much *gruffer* than others, and a great deal so bad, that it will soon spoil the best of Cables; the *sandy* or *grey Ground* are not good to anchor in, the *brown* is best, in my Opinion: But as People cannot always have their Choice, they must be contented with such as they can get.

Now, having brought my Reader to Anchor in this pleasant Harbour, I conclude with wishing him all the Delight MERRYLAND can afford:

I have endeavoured to conduct him safe, and give him a full View of this delicious Country, without the Danger of *Waves*, *Tempests*, or *Shipwreck*; and if he reaps either Pleasure or Profit from my Labour, I shall think the Pains I have taken to compile this short Treatise, very well rewarded.

FINIS.

7

The Female Husband
(1746)

The

Female Husband:

Or, the Surprising History

of

Mrs. *Mary*, Alias Mr. George Hamilton,

Who was convicted of having married a Young
Woman of WELLS and lived with her as her
Husband.
TAKEN FROM
Her own MOUTH since her Confinement.

———Quodque id mirum magis esset in illo;
Faemina natus erat. Monstri novitate moventur,
Quisquis adest: narretque rogant.———
Ovid Metam. Lib. 12.[1]

That propense inclination which is for very wise purposes implanted
in the one sex for the other, is not only necessary for the continuance of
the human species; but is, at the same time, when govern'd and directed by
virtue and religion, productive not only of corporeal delight, but of the
most rational felicity.

But if once our carnal appetites are let loose, without those prudent
and secure guides, there is no excess and disorder which they are not liable
to commit, even while they pursue their natural satisfaction; and, which
may seem still more strange, there is nothing monstrous and unnatural,
which they are not capable of inventing, nothing so brutal and shocking
which they have not actually committed.

Of these unnatural lusts, all ages and countries have afforded us too
many instances; but none I think more surprising than what will be found
in the history of Mrs. *Mary*, otherwise Mr. *George Hamilton*.

This heroine in iniquity was born in the Isle of *Man*, on the 16th Day
of *August*, 1721. Her father was formerly a serjeant of grenadiers in the

Foot-Guards, who having the good fortune to marry a widow of some estate in that island, purchased his discharge from the army, and retired thither with his wife.

He had not been long arrived there before he died, and left his wife with child of this *Mary*; but her mother, tho' she had not two months to reckon, could not stay till she was delivered, before she took a third husband.

As her mother, tho' she had three husbands, never had any other child, she always express'd an extraordinary affection for this daughter, to whom she gave as good an education as the island afforded; and tho' she used her with much tenderness, yet was the girl brought up in the strictest principles or virtue and religion; nor did she in her younger years discover the least proneness to any kind of vice, much less give cause of suspicion that she would one day disgrace her sex by the most abominable and unnatural pollutions. And indeed she hath often declared from her conscience, that no irregular passion ever had any place in her mind, till she was first seduced by one *Anne Johnson,* a neighbour of hers, with whom she had been acquainted from her childhood; but not with such intimacy as afterwards grew between them.

This *Anne Johnson* going on some business to *Bristol*, which detained her there near half a year, became acquainted with some of the people called *Methodists*, and was by them persuaded to embrace their sect.

At her return to the Isle of *Man*, she soon made an easy convert of *Molly Hamilton*, the warmth of whose disposition rendered her susceptible enough of Enthusiasm, and ready to receive all those impressions which her friend the *Methodist* endeavored to make on her mind.

These two young women became now inseparable companions, and at length bed-fellows: For *Molly Hamilton* was prevail'd on to leave her mother's house, and to reside entirely with Mrs. *Johnson*, whose fortune was not thought inconsiderable in that cheap country.

Young Mrs. *Hamilton* began to conceive a very great affection for her friend, which perhaps was not returned with equal faith by the other. However Mrs. *Hamilton* declares her love, or rather friendship, was totally innocent, till the temptations of *Johnson* first led her astray. This latter was, it seems, no novice in impurity, which, as she confess'd, she had learnt and often practiced at *Bristol* with her methodistical sisters.[2]

As *Molly Hamilton* was extremely warm in her inclinations, and as those inclinations were so violently attached to Mrs. *Johnson*, it would not have been difficult for a less artful woman, in the most private hours, to turn the ardour of enthusiastic devotion into a different kind of flame.

Their conversation, therefore, soon became in the highest manner criminal, and transactions not fit to be mention'd past between them.

They had not long carried on this wicked crime before Mrs. *Johnson* was again called by her affairs to visit *Bristol*, and her friend was prevail'd on to accompany her thither.

Here when they arrived, they took up their lodgings together, and lived in the same detestable manner as before; till an end was put to their vile amours, by the means of one *Rogers*, a young fellow, who by his extraordinary devotion (for he was a very zealous *Methodist*) or by some other charms, (for he was very jolly and handsome) gained the heart of Mrs. *Johnson*, and married her.

This amour, which was not of any long continuance before it was brought to a conclusion, was kept an entire secret from Mrs. *Hamilton*; but she was no sooner informed of it, than she became almost frantic, she tore her hair, beat her breasts, and behaved in as outrageous a manner as the fondest husband could, who had unexpectedly discovered the infidelity of a beloved wife.

In the midst of these agonies she received a letter from Mrs. *Johnson*, in the following words, or as near them as she can possibly remember:

Dear Molly,
I know you will condemn what I have now done; but I condemn myself much more for what I have done formerly: For I take the whole shame and guilt of what hath passed between us on myself. I was indeed the first seducer of your innocence, for which I ask GOD's pardon and yours. All the amends I can make you, is earnestly to beseech you, in the name of the Lord, to forsake all such evil courses, and to follow my example now, as you before did my temptation, and enter as soon as you can into that holy state into which I was yesterday called. In which, tho' I am yet but a novice, believe me, there are delights infinitely surpassing the faint endearments we have experienced together. I shall always pray for you, and continue your friend.[3]

This letter rather increased than abated her rage, and she resolved to go immediately and upbraid her false friend; but while she was taking this resolution, she was informed that Mr. *Rogers* and his bride were departed from *Bristol* by a messenger, who brought her a second short note, and a bill for some money from Mrs. *Rogers*.

As soon as the first violence of her passion subsided, she began to consult what course to take, when the strangest thought imaginable suggested itself to her fancy. This was to dress herself in men's cloaths, to embarque for *Ireland*, and commence Methodist teach[ing].

Nothing remarkable happened to her during the rest of her stay at

Bristol, which adverse winds occasioned to be a whole week, after she had provided herself with her dress; but at last having procured a passage, and the wind becoming favourable, she set sail for *Dublin*.

As she was a very pretty woman, she now appeared a most beautiful youth. A circumstance which had its consequences aboard the ship, and had like to have discovered her, in the very beginning of her adventures.

There happened to be in the same vessel with this adventurer, a Methodist, who was bound to the same place, on the same design with herself.

These two being alone in the cabin together, and both at their devotions, the man in the extasy of his enthusiasm, thrust one of his hands into the other's bosom. Upon which, in her surprize, she gave so effeminate a squawl, that it reached the Captain's ears, as he was smoking his pipe upon deck. Hey day, says he, what have we a woman in the ship! and immediately descended into the cabin, where he found the two Methodists on their knees.

Pox on't, says the Captain, I thought you had had a woman with you here; I could have sworn I had heard one cry out as if she had been ravishing, and yet the Devil must have been in you, if you could convey her in here without my knowledge.

I defy the Devil and all his works, answered the He Methodist. He has no power but over the wicked; and if he be in the ship, thy oaths must have brought him hither: for I have heard thee pronounce more than twenty since I came on board; and we should have been at the bottom before this, had not my prayers prevented it.

Don't abuse my vessel, cried the Captain, she is a safe a vessel, and as good a sailer as ever floated, and if you had been afraid of going to the bottom, you might have stay'd on shore and been damn'd.

The Methodist made no answer, but fell a groaning, and that so loud, that the Captain giving him a hearty curse or two, quitted the cabbin, and resumed his pipe.

He was no sooner gone, than the Methodist gave farther tokens of brotherly love to his companion, which soon became so importunate and troublesome to her, that after having gently rejected his hands several times, she at last recollected the sex she had assumed, and gave him so violent a blow in the nostrils, that the blood issued from them with great Impetuosity.

Whether fighting be opposite to the tenets of this sect (for I have not the honour to be deeply read in their doctrines) or from what other motive it proceeded, I will not determine; but the Methodist made no other return to this rough treatment, than by many groans, and prayed heartily

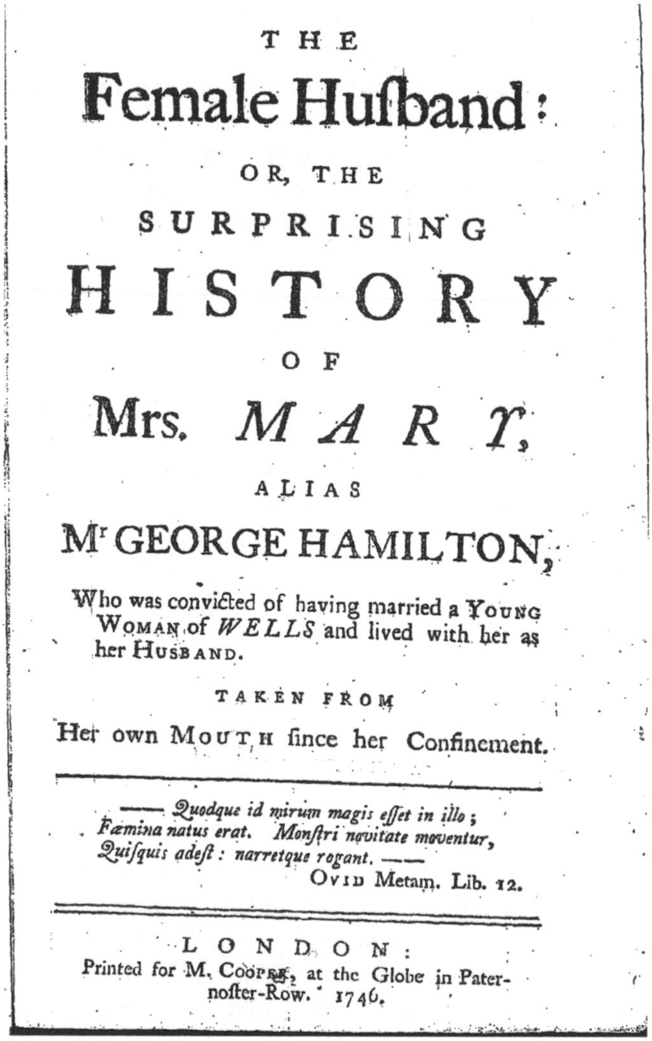

THE
Female Hufband:
OR, THE
SURPRISING
HISTORY
OF
Mrs. *MARY*,
ALIAS
Mr GEORGE HAMILTON,

Who was convicted of having married a YOUNG
WOMAN of *WELLS* and lived with her as
her HUSBAND.

TAKEN FROM

Her own MOUTH fince her Confinement.

———— *Quodque id mirum magis effet in illo ;*
Fæmina natus erat. Monftri novitate moventur,
Quifquis adeft : narretque rogant. ————
OVID Metam. Lib. 12.

LONDON:
Printed for M. COOPER, at the Globe in Pater-
nofter-Row. 1746.

Figure 7.1 The title page of Henry Fielding, *The Female Husband* (1746).

to be delivered soon from the conversation of the wicked; which prayers were at length so successful, that together with a very brisk gale, they brought the vessel into *Dublin* harbour.

Here our adventurer took a lodging in a back-street near *St. Stephen's Green*, at which place she intended to preach the next day; but had got a cold in the voyage, which occasioned such a hoarseness that made it impossible to put that design in practice.

There lodged in the same house with her, a brisk widow of near 40 Years of age, who had buried two husbands, and seemed by her behaviour to be far from having determined against a third expedition to the land of matrimony.

To this widow our adventurer began presently to make addresses, and as he at present wanted tongue to express the ardency of his flame, he was obliged to make use of actions of endearment, such as squeezing, kissing, toying, &c.

These were received in such a manner by the fair widow, that her lover thought he had sufficient encouragement to proceed to a formal declaration of his passion. And this she chose to do by letter, as her voice still continued too hoarse for uttering the soft accents of love.

A letter therefore was penned accordingly in the usual stile, which, to prevent any miscarriages, Mrs. *Hamilton* thought proper to deliver with her own hands; and immediately retired to give the adored lady an opportunity of digesting the contents alone, little doubting of an answer agreeable to her wishes, or at least such a one as the coyness of the sex generally dictates in the beginning of an amour, and which lovers, by long experience, know pretty well how to interpret.

But what was the gallant's surprize, when in return to an amorous epistle, she read the following sarcasms, which it was impossible for the most sanguine temper to misunderstand, or construe favourably.

S I R,
I was greatly astonished at what you put into my hands. I indeed thought, when I took it, it might have been an Opera song, and which for certain reasons I should think, when your cold is gone, you might sing as well as *Farinelli*, from the great resemblance there is between your persons.[4] I know not what you mean by encouragement to your hopes; if I could have conceived my innocent freedoms could have been so misrepresented, I should have been more upon my guard: but you have taught me how to watch my actions for the future, and to preserve myself even from any suspicion of forfeiting the regard I owe to the memory of the best of men, by any future choice. The remembrance of that dear person makes me incapable of proceeding farther.————

And so firm was this resolution, that she would never afterwards admit of the least familiarity with the despairing Mrs. *Hamilton*; but perhaps that destiny which is remarked to interpose in all matrimonial things, had taken the widow into her protection: for in a few days afterwards, she was married to one *Jack Strong*, a cadet in an *Irish* regiment.

Our adventurer being thus disappointed in her love, and what is worse, her money drawing towards an end, began to have some thoughts of returning home, when fortune seemed inclined to make her amends for the tricks she had hitherto played her, and accordingly now threw another Mistress in her way, whose fortune was much superior to the former widow, and who received Mrs. *Hamilton's* addresses with all the complaisance she could wish.

This Lady, whose name was *Rushford*, was the widow of a rich cheesemonger, who left her all he had, and only one great grand-child to take care of, whom, at her death, he recommended to be her Heir; but wholly at her own power and discretion.

She was now in the sixty eighth year of her age, and had not, it seems, entirely abandoned all thoughts of the pleasures of this world: for she was no sooner acquainted with Mrs. *Hamilton*, but, taking her for a beautiful lad of about eighteen, she cast the eyes of affection on her, and having pretty well outlived the bashfulness of her youth, made little scruple of giving hints of her passion of her own accord.

It has been observed that women know more of one another than the wisest men (if ever such have been employed in the study) have with all their art been capable of discovering. It is therefore no wonder that these hints were quickly perceived and understood by the female gallant, who animadverting on the conveniency which the old gentlewoman's fortune would produce in her present situation, very gladly embraced the opportunity, and advancing with great warmth of love to the attack, in which she was received almost with open arms, by the tottering citadel, which presently offered to throw open the gates, and surrender at discretion.

In her amour with the former widow, Mrs. *Hamilton* had never any other design than of gaining the lady's affection, and then discovering herself to her, hoping to have had the same success which Mrs. *Johnson* had found with her: but with this old lady, whose fortune only she was desirous to possess, such views would have afforded very little gratification. After some reflection, therefore, a device entered into her head, as strange and surprizing, as it was wicked and vile; and this was actually to marry the old woman, and to deceive her, by means which decency forbids me even to mention.

The wedding was accordingly celebrated in the most public manner, and with all kind of gaiety, the old woman greatly triumphing in her shame, and instead of hiding her own head for fear of infamy, was actually proud of the beauty of her new husband, for whose sake she intended to disinherit her poor great-grandson, tho' she had derived her riches from her husband's family, who had always intended this boy as his heir. Nay, what may seem very remarkable, she insisted on the parson's not omitting the prayer in the matrimonial service for fruitfulness; drest herself as airy as a girl of eighteen, concealed twenty years of her age, and laughed and promoted all the jokes which are usual at weddings; but she was not so well pleased with a repartee of her great-grandson, a pretty and a smart lad, who, when somebody jested on the bridegroom because he had no beard, answered smartly, There should never be a beard on both-sides. For indeed the old lady's chin was pretty well stocked with bristles.

Nor was this bride contented with displaying her shame by a public wedding dinner, she would have the whole ceremony compleated, and the stocking was accordingly thrown with the usual sport and merriment.

During the three first days of the marriage, the bride expressed herself so well satisfied with her choice, that being in company with another old lady, she exulted so much in her happiness, that her friend began to envy her, and could not forbear inveighing against effeminacy in men; upon which a discourse arose between the two ladies, not proper to be repeated, if I knew every particular; but ended at the last, in the unmarried lady's declaring to the bride, that she thought her husband looked more like a woman than a man. To which the other replied in triumph, he was the best man in *Ireland*.

This and the rest which past, was faithfully recounted to Mrs. *Hamilton* by her wife, at their next meeting, and occasioned our young bridegroom to blush, which the old lady perceiving and regarding as an effect of youth, fell upon her in a rage of love like a tygress, and almost murdered her with kisses.

One of our *English* Poets* remarks in the case of a more able husband than Mrs. *Hamilton* was, when his wife grew amorous in an unseasonable time.

> *The doctor understood the call,*
> *But had not always wherewithal.*[5]

So it happened to our poor bridegroom, who having not at that time *the wherewithal* about her, was obliged to remain merely passive, under all this torrent of kindness of his wife; but this did not discourage her, who was an experienced woman, and thought she had a cure for this coldness in her husband, the efficacy of which, she might perhaps have essayed formerly. Saying therefore with a tender smile to her husband, I believe you are a woman, her hands began to move in such direction that the discovery

---

* Prior.

would absolutely have been made, had not the arrival of dinner, at that very instant, prevented it.

However, as there is but one way of laying the spirit of curiosity, when once raised in a woman, *viz.* by satisfying it, so that discovery, though delayed, could not now be long prevented. And accordingly the very next night, the husband and wife had not been long in bed together, before a storm arose, as if drums, guns, wind and thunder were all roaring together. Villain, rogue, whore, beast, cheat, all resounded at the same instant, and were followed by curses, imprecations and threats, which soon waked the poor great-grandson in the garret; who immediately ran down stairs into his great-grandmother's room. He found her in the midst of it in her shift, with a handful of shirt in one hand, and a handful of hair in the other, stamping and crying, I am undone, cheated, abused, ruined, robbed by a vile jade, imposter, whore. ——What is the matter, dear Madam, answered the youth; O child, replied she, undone! I am married to one who is no man. My husband? a woman, a woman, a woman. Ay, said the grandson, where is she? —— Run away, gone, said the great-grandmother, and indeed so she was: For no sooner was the fatal discovery made, than the poor female bridegroom, whipt on her breeches, in the pockets of which, she had stowed all the money she could, and slipping on her shoes, with her coat, waist-coat and stockings in her hands, had made the best of her way into the street, leaving almost one half of her shirt behind, which the enraged wife had tore from her back.

As Mrs. *Hamilton* well knew that an adventure of that kind would soon fill all *Dublin*, and that it was impossible for her to remain there undiscovered, she hastened away to the Key, where by good fortune, she met with a ship just bound to *Dartmouth*, on board which she immediately went, and sailed out of the harbour, before her pursuers could find out or overtake her.

She was a full fortnight in her passage, during which time, no adventure occurred worthy [of] remembrance. At length she landed at *Dartmouth*, where she soon provided herself with linen, and thence went to *Totness*, where she assumed the title of a doctor of physic, and took lodgings in the house of one Mrs. *Baytree*.

Here she soon became acquainted with a young girl, the daughter of one Mr. *Ivythorn*, who had the green sickness; a distemper which the doctor gave out he could cure by an infallible *nostrum.*[6]

The doctor had not been long intrusted with the care of this young patient before he began to make love to her: for though her complexion was somewhat faded with her distemper, she was otherwise extreamly pretty.

This Girl became an easy conquest to the doctor, and the day of their marriage was appointed, without the knowledge, or even suspicion of her father, or of an old aunt who was very fond of her, and would neither of them have easily given their consent to the match, had the doctor been as good a Man as the niece thought him.

At the day appointed, the doctor and his mistress found means to escape very early in the morning from *Totness*, and went to a town called *Ashburton* in *Devonshire*, where they were married by a regular Licence which the doctor had previously obtained.

Here they staid two days at a public house, during which time the Doctor so well acted his part, that his bride had not the least suspicion of the legality of her marriage, or that she had not got a husband for life. The third day they returned to *Totness*, where they both threw themselves at Mr. *Ivythorn's* feet, who was highly rejoic'd at finding his daughter restor'd to him, and that she was not debauched, as he had suspected of her. And being a very worthy good-natur'd man, and regarding the true interest and happiness of his daughter more than the satisfying his own pride, ambition, or obstinacy, he was prevailed on to forgive her, and to receive her and her husband into his house, as his children, notwithstanding the opposition of the old aunt, who declared she would never forgive the wanton slut, and immediately quitted the house, as soon as the young couple were admitted into it.

The Doctor and his wife lived together above a fortnight, without the least doubt conceived either by the wife, or by any other person of the Doctor's being what he appeared; till one evening the Doctor having drank a little too much punch, slept somewhat longer than usual, and when he waked, he found his wife in tears, who asked her husband, amidst many sobs, how he could be so barbarous to have taken such advantage of her ignorance and innocence, and to ruin her in such a manner? The Doctor being surprized and scarce awake, asked her what he had done. Done, says she, have you not married me a poor young girl, when you know, you have not ——————— you have not ——————— what you ought to have. I always thought indeed your shape was something odd, and have often wondred that you had not the least bit of beard; but I thought you had been a man for all that, or I am sure I would not have been so wicked as to marry you for the world. The Doctor endeavoured to pacify her, by every kind of promise, and telling her she would have all the pleasures of marriage without the inconveniences. No, no, said she, you shall not persuade me to that, nor will I be guilty of so much wickedness on any account. I will tell my Papa of you as soon as I am up; for you are no husband of mine, nor will I ever have any thing to say to you. Which resolution the Doctor finding himself unable to alter, she put on her cloaths with all the haste she could, and taking a horse, which she had bought a few days before, hastened instantly out of the town, and made the best of her way, thro' bye-roads and across the country, into *Somersetshire*, missing *Exeter*, and every other great town which lay in the road.

And well it was for her, that she used both this haste and precaution: for Mr *Ivythorn* having heard his daughter's story, immediately obtained a warrant from a justice of the peace, with which he presently dispatch'd the proper officers; and not only so, but set forward himself to *Exeter*, in order to try if he could learn any news of his son-in-law, or apprehend her there; till after much search being unable to hear any tidings of her, he was obliged to set down contented with his misfortune, as was his poor daughter to submit to all the ill-natured sneers of her own sex, who were often witty at her expence, and at the expence of their own decency.

The Doctor having escaped, arrived safe at *Wells* in *Somersetshire*, where thinking herself at a safe distance from her pursuers, she again sat herself down in a quest of new adventures.

She had not been long in this city, before she became acquainted with one *Mary Price*, a girl of about eighteen years of age, and of extraordinary beauty. With this girl, hath this wicked woman since her confinement declared, she was really as much in love, as it was possible for a man ever to be with one of her own sex.

The first opportunity our Doctor obtain'd of conversing closely with this new mistress, was at a dancing among the inferior sort of people, in contriving which the Doctor had herself the principal share. At that meeting the two lovers had an occasion of dancing all night together; and the Doctor lost no opportunity of shewing his fondness, as well as by his tongue as by his hands, whispering many soft things in her ears, and squeezing as many soft things into her hands, which, together with a good number of kisses, &c. so pleased and warmed this poor girl, who never before had felt any of those tender sensations which we call love, that she retired from the dancing in a flutter of spirts, which her youth and ignorance could not well account for; but which did not suffer her to close her eyes, either that morning or the next night.

The Day after that the Doctor sent her the following letter.

My Dearest Molly,
Excuse the fondness of that expression; for I assure you, my angel, all I write to you proceeds only from my heart, which you have so entirely conquered, and made your own, that nothing else has any share in it; and, my angel, could you know what I feel

when I am writing to you, nay even at every thought of my *Molly*, I know I should gain your pity if not your love; if I am so happy to have already succeeded in raising the former, do let me have once more an opportunity of seeing you, and that soon, that I may breathe forth my soul at those dear feet, where I would willingly die, if I am not suffer'd to lie there and live. My sweetest creature, give me leave to subscribe myself

Your fond, doating,

Undone S L A V E.

This letter added much to the disquietude which before began to torment poor *Molly's* breast. She read it over twenty times, and, at last, having carefully survey'd every part of the room, that no body was present, she kissed it eagerly. However, as she was perfectly modest, and afraid of appearing too forward, she resolved not to answer this first letter; and if she met the Doctor, to behave with great coldness towards him.

Her mother being ill, prevented her going out that day; and the next morning she received a second letter from the Doctor, in terms more warm and endearing than before, and which made so absolute a conquest over the unexperienc'd and tender heart of this poor girl, that she suffered herself to be prevailed on, by the intreaties of her lover, to write an answer, which nevertheless she determin'd should be so distant and cool, that the woman of the strictest virtue and modesty in *England* might have no reason to be asham'd of having writ it; of which letter the reader hath here an exact copy:

SUR,

I haf recevd boath your too litters, and sur I ham much surprise hat the loafe you priten to haf for so pur a garl as mee. I kan nut beleef you wul desgrace yourself by marring sutch a yf as mee, and Sur I wool not be thee hore of the gratest man in the kuntry. For thos mi vartu has all I haf, yit hit is a petion I ham rissolv to kare to my housband, soe noe moor at preseant, from your umble savant to cummand.[7]

The Doctor received this letter with all the ecstasies any lover could be inspired with, and, as Mr. *Congreve* says in his *Old Batchelor*, thought there was more eloquence in the false spellings, with which it abounded, than in all *Aristotle*.[8] She now resolved to be no longer contented with this distant kind of conversation, but to meet her mistress face to face. Accordingly that very afternoon she went to her mother's house, and enquired for her poor *Molly*, who no sooner heard her lover's voice than she fell a trembling in the most violent manner. Her sister who opened the door informed the Doctor she was at home, and let the imposter in; but Molly being then in dishabille, would not see him till she had put on clean linen, and was arrayed from head to foot in as neat, tho' not in so fine a manner, as the highest court lady in the kingdom could attire herself in, to receive her embroider'd lover.

Very tender and delicate was the interview of this pair, and if any corner of *Molly's* heart remain'd untaken, it was now totally subdued. She would willingly have postponed the match somewhat longer, from her strict regard to decency; but the earnestness and ardour of her lover would not suffer her, and she was at last obliged to consent to be married within two days.

Her sister, who was older than herself, and had over-heard all that had past, no sooner perceiv'd the Doctor gone, than she came to her, and wishing her joy with a sneer, said much good may it do her with such a husband; for that, for her own part, she would almost as willingly be married to one of her own sex, and made some remarks not so proper to be here inserted. This was resented by the other with much warmth. She said she had chosen for herself only, and that if she was pleased, it did not become people to trouble their heads with what was none of their business. She was indeed so extremely enamoured, that I question whether she would have exchanged the Doctor for the greatest and richest match in the world.

And had not her affections been fixed in this strong manner, it is possible that an accident which happened the very next night might have altered her mind: for being at another dancing with her lover, a quarrel arose between the Doctor and a man there present, upon which the other seizing the former violently by the collar, tore open her wastecoat, and rent her shirt, so that all her breast was discovered, which, tho' beyond expression beautiful in a woman, were of so different a kind from the bosom of a man, that the married women there set up a great titter; and tho' it did not bring the Doctor's sex into a absolute suspicion, yet caused some whispers, which perhaps might have spoiled the match with a less innocent and less enamoured virgin.

It had however no such effect on poor *Molly*. As her fond heart was free from any deceit, so was it entirely free from suspicion; and accordingly, at the fixed time she met the Doctor, and their nuptials were celebrated in the usual form.

The mother was extremely pleased at this preferment (as she thought it) of her daughter. The joy of it did indeed contribute to restore her perfectly to health, and nothing but mirth and happiness appeared in the faces of the whole family.

The new married couple not only continued, but greatly increased the fondness which they had conceived for each other, and poor *Molly*, from some stories she told among her acquaintance, the other young married women of the town, was received as a great fibber, and was at last universally laughed at as such among them all.

Three months past in this manner, when the Doctor was sent for to *Glastonbury* to a patient (for the fame of our adventurer's knowledge in physic began now to spread) when a person of *Totness* being accidently present, happened to see and know her, and having heard upon enquiry, that the Doctor was married at *Wells*, as we have above mentioned, related the whole story of Mr. *Ivythorn's* daughter, and the whole adventure at *Totness*.

News of this kind seldom wants wings; it reached *Wells*, and the ears of the Doctor's mother before her return from *Glastonbury*. Upon this the old woman immediately sent for her daughter, and very strictly examined her, telling her the great sin she would be guilty of, if she concealed a fact of this kind, and the great disgrace she would bring on her own family, and even on her whole sex, by living quietly and contentedly with a husband who was in any degree less a man than the rest of his neighbours.

Molly assured her mother of the falsehood of this report; and as it is usual for persons who are too eager in any cause, to prove too much, she asserted some things which staggered her mother's belief, and made her cry out, O child, there is no such thing in human nature.

Such was the progress this story had made in *Wells*, that before the Doctor arrived there, it was in every body's mouth; and as the Doctor rode through the streets, the mob, especially the women, all paid their compliments of congratulation. Some laughed at her, others threw dirt at her, and others made use of terms of reproach not fit to be commemorated. When she came to her own house, she found her wife in tears, and having asked her the cause, was informed of the dialogue which had past between her and her mother. Upon which the Doctor, tho' he knew not yet by what means the discovery had been made, yet too well knowing the truth, began to think of using the same method, which she had heard before put in practice, of delivering herself from any impertinence; for as to danger, she was not sufficiently versed in the laws to apprehend any.

In the mean time, the mother, at the solicitation of some of her relations, who, notwithstanding the stout denial of the wife, had given credit to the story, had applied herself to a magistrate, before whom the *Totness* man appeard, and gave evidence as is before mentioned. Upon this a warrant was granted to apprehend the Doctor, with which the constable arrived at her house, just as she was meditating her escape.

The husband was no sooner seized, but the wife threw herself into the greatest agonies of rage and grief, vowing that he was injured, and that the information was false and malicious, and that she was resolved to attend her husband wherever they conveyed him.

And now they all proceeded before the Justice, where a strict examination being made into the affair, the whole happened to be true, to the great shock and astonishment of every body; but more especially of the poor wife, who fell into fits, out of which she was with great difficulty recovered.

The whole truth having been disclosed before the Justice, and something of too vile, wicked and scandalous a nature, which was found in the Doctor's trunk, having been produced in evidence against her, she was committed to *Bridewell*, and Mr. *Gold,* an eminent and learned counselor at law, who lives in those parts, was consulted with upon the occasion, who gave his advice that she should be prosecuted at the next sessions, on a cause in the vagrant act, *for having by false and deceitful practices endeavoured to impose on some of his Majesty's subjects.*

As the Doctor was conveyed to *Bridewell*, she was attended by many insults from the mob; but what was more unjustifiable, was the cruel treatment which the poor innocent wife received from her own sex, upon the extraordinary accounts which she had formerly given of her husband.

Accordingly at the ensuing sessions of the peace for the county of *Somerset*, the Doctor was indicted for the abovementioned diabolical fact, and after a fair trial convicted, to the entire satisfaction of the whole court.

At the trial the said *Mary Price* the wife, was produced as a witness, and being asked by the council, whether she had ever any suspicion of the Doctor's sex during the whole time of the courtship, she answered positively in the negative. She was then asked how long they had been married, to which she answered three moths; and whether they had cohabited the whole time together? to which her reply was in the affirmative. Then the council asked her, whether during the time of this cohabitation, she imagined the Doctor had behaved to her as a husband ought to his wife? Her modesty confounded her a little at this question; but she at last answered she did imagine so. Lastly, she was asked when it was that she first harboured any suspicion of her being imposed upon? To which she answered, she had not the least suspicion till her husband was carried before a magistrate, and there discovered, as hath been said above.

The prisoner having been convicted of this base and scandalous crime, was by the court sentenced to be publickly and severely whipt four [separate] times, in four market towns within the county of *Somerset*, to wit, once in each market town, and to be imprisoned, &c.

These whippings she has accordingly undergone, and very severely have they been inflicted, insomuch, that those persons who have more regard to beauty than to justice, could not refrain from exerting some pity toward her, when they saw so lovely a skin scarified with rods, in such a manner that her back was almost flayed: yet so little effect had the smart or shame of this punishment on the person who underwent it, that the very evening she had suffered the first whipping, she offered the goaler money, to procure her a young girl to satisfy her most monstrous and unnatural desires.

But it is to be hoped that this example will be sufficient to deter all others from the commission of any such foul and unnatural crimes: for which, if they should escape the shame and ruin which they so well deserve in this world, they will be most certain of meeting with their full punishment in the next: for unnatural affections are equally vicious and equally detestable in both sexes, nay, if modesty be the peculiar characteristick of the fair sex, it is in them most shocking and odious to prostitute and debase it.

In order to caution therefore that lovely sex, which, while they preserve their natural innocence and purity, will still look most lovely in the eyes of men, the above pages have been written, which, that they might be worthy of their perusal, such strict regard hath been had to the utmost decency, that notwithstanding the subject of this narrative be of a nature so difficult to be handled inoffensively, not a single word occurs through the whole, which might shock the most delicate ear, or give offence to the purest chastity.

FINIS.

NOTES

PREFACE

1. MacKinnon, in addition to her legal work on sexual harassment and pornography, is the author of *Feminism Unmodified* (Cambridge: Harvard University Press, 1987) and *Pornography and Civil Rights* (Minneapolis: OAP Press, 1988).

2. See Dworkin, *Intercourse* (New York: Free Press, 1987) and Kappeler, *The Pornography of Representation* (Minneapolis: University of Minnesota Press, 1986).

3. For Sprinkle, see *Angry Women* (San Francisco: Re/Search, 1991); and Linda Williams, *Dirty Looks: Women, Pornography, Power* (London: BFI, 1993). For Bright, see *Herotica* (New York: Plume, 1990) and *Susie Bright's Sexual State of the Union* (New York: Simon and Schuster, 1997). For Califia, see *Macho Sluts* (Boston: Alyson, 1988) and *Public Sex: The Culture of Radical Sex* (San Francisco: Cleis Press, 1994). For Paglia, see *Sexual Personae* (New Haven: Yale University Press, 1990) and *Vamps and Tramps* (New York: Vintage, 1994).

4. See Mudge, *The Whore's Story.*

5. The diary tells the well-known story. Entries for January 13 and February 8 and 9 detail his purchase, his reading, and his destruction of the French edition.

6. British libertine literature of the eighteenth century has recently become available in two noteworthy "library" editions. The first, edited by Alexander Pettit and Patrick Spedding, is a five-volume set, *Eighteenth-Century British Erotica*, and the second, my own microfilm edition of the Private Case Collection at the British Library, *Sex and Sexuality, Parts Three and Four*. Although both are extremely valuable resources, neither is a convenient option for the reader wishing to use the material outside the library.

INTRODUCTION

1. April 11, 1779. Quoted in *Memoirs of a Woman of Pleasure*, edited by Peter Sabor (New York: Oxford University Press, 1985), p. xii.

2. Walter Kendrick, *The Secret Museum*, pp. 1–32. See also Lynn Hunt, *The Invention of Pornography*, pp. 9–45.

3. See, for example, Nancy Armstrong, *Desire and Domestic Fiction* (New York: Oxford University Press, 1987); Rosalind Ballaster, *Seductive Forms* (Oxford: Oxford University Press, 1992); Catherine Gallagher, *Nobody's Story* (Berkeley: University of California Press, 1994); Terry Lovell, *Consuming Fiction* (London, Verso, 1987); Michael McKeon, *The Origins of the English Novel* (Baltimore: Johns Hopkins University Press, 1987); Dale Spender, *Mothers of the Novel* (London: Pandora,

1986); William Warner, *Licensing Entertainment* (Berkeley: University of California Press, 1998); and Ian Watt, *The Rise of the Novel* (Berkeley: University of California Press, 1957).

4. *School of Venus* (London 1680), pp. 107–8.

5. Cleland, *Memoirs of a Woman of Pleasure* edited by Peter Wagner (New York: Penguin, 1985), p. 1.

CHAPTER 1

1. Valeria Messalina (d. A.D. 48) was the third wife of Claudius I. She was 16 and he was 50 when they married. Her name has become synonymous with greed and lust because she openly abused her position for individual gain and because she dared to marry her lover, Caius Silius, in public ceremony while Claudius was away from Rome. He had her executed upon his return. Juvenal (c. A.D. 60–c.136), the Roman satirist, relates that Messalina, in search of sexual satisfaction, masqueraded as a whore in a brothel (*Satire 6*).

2. The word "pintle" derives from the German word "pint" and means "penis."

3. "Sophy" or "supreme ruler" is a title most frequently associated with the rulers of ancient Persian, The reference here is to Timur. Timur (c.1336–1405), better known at Timur Leng or Timur the lame or Tamerlane, was a fierce, ruthless Scythian shepherd-robber who conquered Persia and claimed to be a descendant of Genghis Khan. He was the subject of Christopher Marlowe's play *Tamburlaine the Great* (1590), which luridly recounts his conquests. Timur was an especially cruel conqueror. After capturing large cities he routinely slaughtered thousands of the inhabitants and built pyramids of their skulls.

4. Priapus, the son of Aphrodite and Dionysus, was, in the ancient Greek religion, a fertility god of gardens and herds. He was frequently depicted as short and unattractive and with enlarged genitalia. His name was used for the title of a well-known tenth-century collection of ancient obscene satire, the *Priapea*. The most famous eighteenth-century treatment of Priapus is Richard Payne Knight, *An Account of the Remains of the Worship of Priapus, Lately Existing at Isernia, in the Kingdom of Naples* (1786).

5. The word "congee" means "the taking of one's leave" or "a retiring bow."

6. Sex is frequently used in early eighteenth-century French and British erotic texts as the great leveler, that which—regardless of class differences—makes us all the same. In keeping with its connections to satire, this material targets hypocrisy and pretense as it establishes sexuality as a natural, materialistic "real" against which we are to measure social and cultural restriction. Sexually explicit material has thus been used—from Ovid to Nicholas Chorier, from Juvenal to the Marquis de Sade—as an extremely effective political weapon. For a detailed account of the political and philosophical roles played by French protopornography, see Darnton, *The Forbidden Best-Sellers*, pp. 3–114.

7. Frances here confirms what historians of medicine call the "one-sex model"

of human biology; that is, an understanding of the reproductive systems of men and women based on similarity rather than difference. Anatomists, physicians, and philosophers from Aristotle and Galen to Leonardo da Vinci believed in a "homology," a visual and structural likeness, between make and female reproductive organs. See Laqueur, *Making Sex*, pp. 25–62; and chapter 3 hereafter.

8. This preoccupation with sexual positions establishes a direct connection between *The School of Venus* and what has become known as *Aretino's Postures*, a series of engravings and accompanying sonnets that is arguably the first "pornographic" work in western culture. The original designs were executed by Guilio Romano and engraved by Marcantonio Raimondi in 1524. Pietro Aretino, inspired by engravings, wrote sonnets for each in 1525. Sometime in the following years, the original number of engravings, sixteen, was expanded to twenty. *Aretino's Postures* became a well-known curiosity and existed in many different forms throughout the seventeenth and eighteenth centuries. See, for example, Foxon, *Libertine Literature in England,* pp. 5, 19–20.

9. "Jante mien," that is, a "jaunty air or appearance."

10. What earlier appeared as a kind of sexually inspired challenge to class hierarchy, here becomes clearly antipatriarchal. The real question, however, is the degree to which the passage names an authentic female subjectivity or in fact creates the appearance of that subjectivity to better serve the interests of men. See Darnton, *The Forbidden Best-Sellers*, pp. 111–112; and Manuela Mourao, "The Representation of Female Desire in Early Modern Pornographic Texts, 1660–1745," *Signs* 24 (1999): 573–593.

11. The word "glister" means "to sparkle or glitter" but in archaic usage is also a synonym for "clyster," which is another word for "enema."

12. "Curveted," from Old Italian, meaning "to prance or frolic."

13. "Hypocras" is a cordial drink made of wine and flavored with spices.

14. There appears to be some confusion here as to the identity of Frances's lover. She says earlier that the account describes her husband, and yet here seems to refer to a man with whom she is having a secret affair.

15. "Aloisia" is the supposed author of Nicholas Chorier's *Satyra Sotadica* (c. 1660). The first French edition, *L'Academie des dames,* appeared in 1680, with English editions following in 1688, 1707, and 1740. The latter, an English abridgement, is reprinted here. See chapter 5. See also Foxon, *Libertine Literature in England,* pp. 38–43. Juvenal (c. A.D. 60– c.136) was the Roman author of sixteen biting satires of contemporary Roman life, one of which, (*Satire 6*), addresses "The Ways of Women." Therein Messalina figures prominently. Martial (c. A.D. 40–104), the Roman epigrammatist of Spanish origin, wrote of—among other things—sodomy, pederasty, fellatio, and cunnilingus. The latter two writers would have been familiar to anyone with even a cursory knowledge of Greek and Latin.

16. In contrast to that earlier statement that celebrated sex as a great leveler of class privilege, Katy here appears to link sexual knowledge to class difference: the king knows more about sex than his lowly subjects. The two passages are not, however, necessarily contradictory.

17. "Pomatum," or "pomade," is a scented ointment for skin or hair, originally made from apples.

18. "Glib" in the older sense of "slick" or "slippery."

19. This passage illustrates another common belief of the "one sex model" of reproductive biology: that women had a "seed" like men. See chapter 3.

20. This passage clearly illustrates the philosophical materialism that informs much of the erotic/protopornographic writing of the period. Unlike Christian idealism, which begins with the celebration of the spirit over the body, erotic writings of the late seventeenth and early eighteenth century enact a subversive reversal and celebrate the primacy of the body and its "natural" functions. See Darnton, *The Forbidden Beset-Sellers,* pp. 85–114.

21. "Busque," or busk," is another word for "corset."

22. One popular subgenre of the salacious medical manual dealt exclusively with the evils of masturbation. See Wagner, *Eros Revived,* pp. 16–20.

23. Midwifery manuals of the seventeenth and eighteenth centuries confirm a commonly held belief that simultaneous orgasm was required for conception. See Laqueur, *Making Sex,* pp. 43–52.

24. This question is a commonplace in philosophical, medical, and literary texts from ancient times to the present. One of the most famous early examples is from the third book of Ovid's *Metamorphoses,* where he relates the story of Tiresias, who, having experienced both male and female, confirms that women have the greater sexual pleasure. Juno, irritated by this answer, blinded Tiresias.

25. Love defined as one soul seeking its missing other half originates with Plato. See Plato's *Symposium* (c. 360 B.C.) and *Phaedrus* (c. 360 B.C.).

26. This is one of several instances in which the writer of *The School of Venus* recognizes the importance of the erotic imagination.

27. "I know not where the fates draw me."

CHAPTER 2

The Pleasures of a Single Life

1. "Grutch'd" is an obsolete word for "grudged."

2. Unidentified. Possibly Artaxerxes II (405–359 B.C.); possibly Nimrod (*Gen.* 10. 8–12).

3. Alexander III (356–323 B.C.), the king of Macedon better known as Alexander the Great, was the son of Philip II of Macedon and Olympias. Alexander had Aristotle as his tutor and was given a classical education. After the death of his father, Alexander united Greece and defeated Persia. These events brought the Persian empire to an end and marked the beginning of the Hellenistic period. Buceph'lus was Alexander the Great's favorite horse. Like his master, Buceph'lus was exceptionally strong, fast, and brave. After he died in 326 B.C. at a battle on the Hydaspes River, Alexander founded the city of Bucephala there in his honor.

4. Fabricius (d. 250 B.C.) was a Roman general and statesman renowned for his simplicity of habit and his integrity. He resisted bribes on several occasions and became famous for his scrupulous honesty.

5. Alexander the Great. Plutarch gives the following account: Alexander "fell again to sacrificing and drinking; and having given Nearchus a splendid entertainment, after he had bathed, as was his custom, just as he was going to bed, at Medius's request he went to supper with him. Here he drank all the next day, and was attacked with a fever, which seized him, not as some write, after he had drunk of the bowl of Hercules, nor was he taken with any sudden pain in his back, as if he had been struck with a lance, for these are the inventions of some authors who thought it their duty to make the last scene of so great an action as tragical and moving as they could. Aristobulus tells us, that in the rage of his fever and a violent thirst, he took a draught of wine, upon which he fell into delirium, and died on the thirtieth day of the month Daesius." *Lives,* vol. 14, *Great Books of the Western World,* edited by Robert Hutchins (Chicago: University of Chicago Press, 1952), pp. 575–76.

6. Valeria Messalina (d. A.D. 48), the third wife of Claudius I, was known for her unbridled lust and for being disparaged by Juvenal in his sixth Satire. See chapter 1, note 1.

7. "Mein," that is, her "appearance" or "aspect."

8. "Linick" is not listed in the *Oxford English Dictionary.* Possibly a variant of "linnet," a songbird.

9. "Ignis Fatuus": "foolish fire."

10. Bedlam, refers to the Hospital of St. Mary of Bethlehem, the oldest institution for the care and confinement of the mentally ill in England. It was founded as a priory in 1247. The word "bedlam" has come to mean "wild confusion" or "riot."

11. Gordius, the King of Phrygia, tied a knot so complex that no one could untie it. The local oracle then decreed that the one to untie it would be a leader great enough to unite all of Asia. Folk lore has it that when Alexander the Great went to view the knot, he studied it only briefly before slicing it in half with his sword. A "Gordian knot" thus signifies a perplexing problem that requires a bold and unexpected solution.

12. "Shrow": "shrew."

13. "Freeks," a varient of "frecks," meaning "spots, marks, or freckles."

14. "Drisled": "sprinkled, spotted, or flecked."

15. "Stote": the obsolete form of "stoat" or "weasel."

16. "Varges": the obsolete form of "verjuice," which means "the acid juice of unripe grapes."

17. "Truckled": "to be servile or submissive."

18. "Juggle" here means "a conjurer's trick" or "an imposture, cheat, or fraud."

The Fifteen Comforts of Cuckoldom

1. "Cornuted": having horns, or cuckolded. The word "cuckold" includes an allusion to the "cuckoo" bird, the female of which lays its eggs in the nests of other

birds, leaving them to be cared for by the resident nesters. This parasitic tendency has given the female bird a reputation for unfaithfulness. Traditionally, antlers or horns are the sign of a cuckold.

2. "Muscadine," a rich, sweet wine made from muscat grapes.

3. "Doxie," possibly derived from "docks," means either "an unmarried mistress of a beggar or rogue" or simply "prostitute."

4. "Hap": "luck."

5. "Prest": "forcibly enlisted."

6. "Banned," means "to call forth" or "summon" or "curse."

7. "Pet," that is, "petulance." "Strait": short for "straight away."

8. "Chapman," means "peddler, dealer, or merchant," while "dun" means "to demand payment on a loan."

9. "Rubber": "a predetermined set of card games, usually three or five." Not meant in the modern usage as slang for "condom." In the eighteenth century, the analogous term for condom was "skin." In this passage, "rubber" becomes a euphemism for sexual intercourse, while "Powd'ring Tub" refers to the powder administered by a physician to cure a venereal disorder.

10. "Frail": another word for "whip."

11. "Peck: slang for "food."

12. "Stews": slang for "brothel."

13. "Trull": "prostitute."

14. "Tick," shortened from "ticket" to mean "run into debt" or "buy on credit."

The Fifteen Plagues of a Maiden-Head

1. Obsolete spelling of "lancet," a small spear-like medical instrument used for opening boils, veins, and festering wounds.

2. An "anchorite" is a religious hermit.

3. "Moap'd" is the obsolete form of "moped," which could mean here either "stupefied or bewildered" or "dejected or melancholy."

4. "Wem" is a bodily blemish, disfigurement, or defect.

5. In addition to "twistings, coils, or convolutions," "twines" can also mean "embraces."

6. "Clip" is slang for "embrace."

7. "Green-sickness," or the physical trials and tribulations of unsatisfied lust, is described in detail in "The Seventh Plague." See also chapter 5.

8. "Tripes," that is, "intestines."

9. "Stews" is slang for "brothel."

10. "Kit" could be either slang for "fiddle," "dab," or "smear," connoting masturbation, or an errant spelling of "knit."

11. "Bauble," that is, "a child's toy."

CHAPTER 3

1. As the phrase "Secret Infirmities" suggests, Marten makes the most of his role as the disseminator of forbidden knowledge. At once scientific and salacious, Marten vacillates between doctorly objectivity and voyeuristic titillation. Like other forms of early eighteenth-century protopornography, Marten's medical manual relishes the book's ability to make the private public. A significant portion of Marten's *Venereal Disease* (1708), for example, includes letters from his patients in which they disclose their medical hardships. Thus, there is an important connection between Marten's narrative and the epistolary realisms of Defoe and Richardson.

2. "Gleets," a medical term meaning "slimy discharge" or "filth."

3. Nicolas Venette (1632–98) was the author of *De la generation de l'homme, ou tableau de l'amour conjugal* (Amsterdam, 1687), which appeared in English in 1703 as *Mysteries of Conjugal Love Reveal'd* and was reprinted throughout the century. Like *Aristotle's Masterpiece* and Albertus Magnus's *Secrets of Women*, Venette's work was derived from the writings of Aristotle, Hippocrates, and Galen. Although he disagreed occasionally, Marten was knowledgeable of and indebted to this tradition. See notes 4, 6, and 14 hereafter. See also Roy Porter, "Spreading Carnal Knowledge or Selling Dirt Cheap? Nicholas Venette's *Tableau de l'amour conjugal* in Eighteenth-Century England," *Journal of European Studies* 14 (1984): 233–255.

4. Of these, *Aristotle's Masterpiece* was the most well known and influential medical manual of the eighteenth century. Alternately objective and voyeuristic, informed and speculative, the *Masterpiece* was loosely derived from the *Problemata* but remained largely a creation of English hack writers. It appeared in more than thirty editions throughout the century, borrowed heavily from its predecessors, and indulged a penchant for what has been termed "folklore medicine"—that is, a reliance on anecdote as a substitute for scientific evidence. See Roy Porter, "The Secrets of Generation Display'd: *Aristotle's Masterpiece* in Eighteenth-Century England," *Eighteenth Century Life* 11 (1985): 1–21. See also Wagner, *Eros Revived*, pp. 8–21; and Laqueur, *Making Sex*, p. 150.

5. Possibly either Rodrigo Sanchez de Arevalo (1404–70), author of *Speculum vita humanae* (1468), or Francisco Sanchez de Oropesa, author of *Discurso para averiguar, que male de urina sea* (1594).

6. Peter Magnus is the supposed author of the twelfth-century text *De secretis mulierum; or, Secrets of Women*, which appeared regularly in England until the middle of the eighteenth century. Magnus, like Nicholas Vanette, is heavily indebted to the Galenic tradition. See note 15 hereafter.

7. William Cowper was the author of *The Anatomy of Human Bodies* (1697), which included separate drawings of the various parts of female genitalia. See Laqueur, *Making Sex*, pp. 159–160.

8. Ambroise Pare, a famous French surgeon of the sixteenth century, published his *Oeuvres* in 1579; they were translated into English by Thomas Johnson in 1634

and reprinted several times over the course of the century. I have not been able to locate Chamberlain's edition.

9. For a discussion of quacks in the early eighteenth century, see Wagner, *Eros Revived,* pp. 41–46; and Roy Porter, "Medicine and the Enlightenment in Eighteenth-Century England, " *Bulletin for the Society for the Social History of Medicine* 25 (1979): 27–40.

10. "To salivate"; to produce "an excessive flow of saliva by administering mercury" as a cure for venereal disease.

11. Dr. Fitcherton did not, evidently, complete his treatise, but the "quack" to whom Marten refers was most likely John Sintelaer, who later in 1709 published *The scourge of Venus and Mercury: represented in a treatise of the venereal disease, giving a succinct, but most exact account of the nature, causes, signs, degrees, and symptoms of that dreadful distemper: and the fatal consequences arising from mercurial cures, with the several ways of taking that infection: of the virulent gonorrhoea, the caruncula or excrescences in the urinal passage, the phymosis and paraphymosis, the tumours of the scrotum and testicles, the venereal bubo, warts, &c. . . . : unto which is added, the true way of curing, not only the consummate and inveterate, but also the mercurial pox, found to be more dangerous that the pox itself. . . .* Appended to the work is a small section entitled, "An answer to John Marten's personal invectives, malicious reflections, and false aspersions, contain'd as well in his last sixth edition of his treatise of the venereal disease, and in his late appendix to the said treatise."

12. "Emulgents," that is "emulgent vessels," the body's veins or arteries.

13. Nicholas Culpepper, the seventeenth-century writer and publisher, agitated against the medical establishment and disseminated information in the vernacular. He was the author of *Directory of Midwives* and the publisher of *Bartholinus' Anatomy* (1668). See Charles Webster, *The Great Instauration: Science, Medicine, and Reform, 1626–1660* (London: Holmes and Meier, 1975).

14. "Dropsie," any bodily distemper characterized by the retention of fluid and swelling.

15. Hippocrates (460?–377? B.C.), the most famous physician of antiquity, is remembered not only for the oath but also for the *Hippocratic Collection,* some seventy different texts only six or seven of which are actually by Hippocrates. Generally considered the father of modern medicine, Hippocrates nevertheless believed in the ancient theory of the humors: an imbalance among the four (blood, phlegm, black bile, and yellow bile) caused ill health, while good health resulted from their harmonious balance. Galen (129–99?), along with Aristotle and Hippocrates the third most influential of the ancient medical philosophers, elaborated on the theory of the humors by introducing four corresponding temperaments: the sanguine, buoyant type; the phlegmatic, sluggish type; the choleric, quick-tempered type; and the melancholic, dejected type.

16. William Harvey, more famous for his arguments about the human circulatory system in *An Anatomical Study of the Motion of the Heart and of the Blood in Animals* (1628), was also the author of *Essays on the Generation of Animals* (1651), and in it, as Marten points out, a case is made for women producing eggs, not seed.

See Walter Pagel, *New Light on William Harvey* (Basel: Karger, 1976); and Laqueur, *Making Sex,* pp. 142–148.

17. Regnier de Graaf (1641–1673), the German physician, is generally acclaimed as the discoverer of the mammalian egg. He had his collected works published in 1677, 1678, and 1705. Marten have also have been familiar with a 1701 French edition of his work on generation, *Nouvelles decouvertes, sur les parties de l'homme et de la femme, qui servent a la generation: avec la deffense des parties genitales, contre les sentimens de quelques anatomistes; un traité du pucelage, du pancreas, de l'usage du siphon, & des clysteres.*

18. The "same-sex model" model of human biology continued to be important to medical science throughout the eighteenth century. See Laqueur, *Making Sex,* pp. 1–113.

19. Marten is obviously reliant on the theory of the humors. Of particular importance to him are the corresponding characteristics of hot, cold, wet, and dry. Men were thought to be hot and dry, women cold and wet. Conception can only occur when women "warm" to the act of intercourse.

20. "Whites," taking its name from the color of discharge, is a catchall term that refers to various kinds of vaginal infections.

21. Proverbs 30:18–19: "There be three things which are too wonderful for me, yea, four which I know not: The way of an eagle in the air; the way of a serpent upon a rock; the way of a ship in the midst of the sea; and the way of a man with a maid."

22. Realdus Columbus was a lecturer in surgery at Padua and, in his *De re anatomica* (1559), claimed to have discovered the clitoris.

23. See note 8.

24. Johann Weyer (1515–88) published *De praestigiis daemonum, et incantationibus, ac veneficiis, libri V* in 1563. Numerous editions appeared throughout the sixteenth and seventeenth centuries. See a recent translation of the work *Witches, devils, and doctors in the Renaissance* (Binghamton, N.Y. : Medieval and Renaissance Texts and Studies, 1991). See also Stephens, *Demon Lovers.*

25. Avicenna (980–1037), Islamic philosopher and physician, was the most influential name in medicine from 1100 to 1500. He was the author of *The Canon of Medicine* and *The Book of Healing*, both of which were strongly influenced by Aristotle. Avicenna believed the female seed was a kind of menstrual blood, and his writings were reprinted continually throughout the sixteenth and seventeenth centuries.

26. *Almansor* was the title of a textbook of medicine by Rasis (860–932), a Persian physician. Working in Baghdad, he distinguished smallpox from measles and was the author of *Liber de pestilentia* and *Liber continens.*

27. Dr. James Drake (1667–1707) translated Daniel Le Clerc's *History of Physic* (1699) and was the author of *Anthropologia nova: or, A New System of Anatomy* (1707)

28. St. Augustine (354–430) believed in the idea of original sin, and in his treatise *The City of God* (415) he argues that when individuals feel sexual excitement, they are corporeally reenacting Adam and Eve's fall. For a detailed account of St.

Augustine and human sexuality, see Elaine Pagels, *Adam, Eve, and the Serpent* (New York: Random House, 1988).

29. Joannes Leo Africanus published *Africae descriptio IX. lib. absoluta . . .* in 1632.

30. Hermaphrodites were of great interest to readers of the seventeenth and eighteenth centuries, a staple in medical and libertine literature alike. Edmund Curll, for example, publisher of *Venus in the Cloister*, included *A Treatise of Hermaphrodites* as an appendix to his *Treatise of the Use of Flogging in Venereal Affairs* (1718). See Wagner, *Eros Revived*, pp. 21–36; and Ruth Gilbert, *Early Modern Hermaphrodites: Sex and Other Stories* (New York: Palgrave Press, 2002).

31. Felix Platter (1536–1614) was a doctor, scientist, and prolific author. Marten may have known the Latin originals but most likely read Platter in Nicholas Culpepper's *Experimental physick; or, Seven hundred famous and rare cures. Being part of the physitian's library. Containing a collection of the most useful parts of the works of M. Ruland, L. Riverius, D. Sennertus, and F. Plater* (1662).

32. There Marten writes: "In some Women, especially those that are very Lustful, [the clitoris] is so vastly extended, that it hangs out of the Passage externally, and so much resembles the Yard of a Man, that by some they have been called *Fricatrices*, and accounted *Hermaphrodites*, and we have read that such have been able to perform the Actions of a Man, in accompanying with other Women: But however it is, this is certain, that the bigger the *Clitoris* is in Women, the more Lustful they are, and even so Salacious, at sometimes especially, as scarcely to be satisfy'd by several Men" (374).

33. "Vegete," obsolete, meaning "active and flourishing in respect to bodily health."

34. These men are "rare birds in the world."

35. Pliny (Caius Plinius Secundus), A.D. 23–79, the Roman naturalist, died of asphyxiation near Vesuvius, having gone there to investigate the eruption. He is famous for an encyclopedia of natural science, entitled *Historia naturalis*. It is divided into thirty-seven books, and although his industry was immense and his knowledge of extensive, his information is mostly secondhand and more folklore than science. Marten could have read an English translation of 1634 or Latin edition of 1635 or 1668.

36. Valescus de Tarenta, or Henricus Valesius (1603–76), was one of four contributors to *Lexikon ton deka retoron Lexicon decem oratorum* (1683).

37. Averroes (1126–98), the twelfth-century Arabic physician, was the author of a popular medical encyclopedia that was reprinted throughout the seventeenth century. The story that Marten refers to, that of a woman conceiving in the bath, was well known and frequently cited in medical literature of the period.

38. Sir Thomas Browne published *Pseudodoxia Epidemica: or, Enquiries into Vulgar and Common Errors* in 1646.

39. For Hippocrates, see note 15.

40. Following Pare, Marten is here recommending the efficacy of medically supervised masturbation.

41. For Ambrose Parry, see note 8.

42. Hesiod, the eighth-century Greek poet, is known for his poem *Works and Days*, an epic of Greek rural life, which served as a model for Virgil's *Georgics*.

CHAPTER 4

1. Sir Samuel Garth (1661–1719), the English poet and physician, studied medicine at Cambridge. He is remembered for his satirical poem *The Dispensary* (1699).

2. Francisco de Quevedo y Villegas (1580–1645), the Spanish satirist, novelist, and wit, wrote *Los sueños, or The Visions* in 1627. Following Dante, it is a bitterly satiric account of the inhabitants of hell. Richard Crashaw translated it from the French in 1640, and Sir Roger L'Estrange followed with another edition in 1667. Quevedo is also known for his picaresque novel *La vida del Buscón* (1626), which appeared in English as *The Life and Adventures of Buscon* (1657). The reference to Quevedo and the insistence that *Venus in the Cloister* has a moral purpose serves as a reminder that modern pornography is a descendent of obscene satire and that the sexual transgressions of *Venus* are inextricable from a larger philosophical attack on the Catholic Church and its teachings.

3. On the private being made public, compare Marten's discussion of "Secret Infirmities" in chapter 3.

4. Sir Roger L'Estrange (1616–1704) was well known as a journalist and pamphleteer in service of the royalist cause. He translated *The Visions of Quevedo* in 1667.

5. "Bagatelle," an unimportant, insignificant thing, a trifle; or a short, light piece of verse or music.

6. "Mignonne" means "one who is highly esteemed or favored," a "darling."

7. "Devoir": "duty."

8. It translates as "A Sweet and Easy Remedy for the Dangerous Plumpness," where the latter phrase refers to pregnancy.

9. The translation is "Hail law, justice, and love."

10. Again, "dangerous plumpness" or pregnancy.

11. The titles on this list are fictitious.

12. St. Alexis, according to Greek legend, which antedates the ninth century and is the basis of all later versions, was the son of a distinguished Roman. The night of his intended marriage he secretly left his father's house and journeyed to Edessa in the Syrian Orient where, for seventeen years, he led the life of a pious ascetic. He then left Edessa and returned to Rome, where he dwelt as a beggar under the stairs of his father's palace.

13. "Syncope": "fainting fit."

14. "My sweet Jesus, send me your thanks."

15. "Whoever fools with children, with children she will find herself."

16. Castiglione (1478–1529), the Italian soldier, author, and statesman, was attached to the court of the duke of Milan and later in the service of the duke of

Urbino. He is famous for *Libro del cortegiano* (*The Courtier*), a treatise on etiquette, society, and the intellect that gives a vivid and elegant picture of fifteenth- and sixteenth-century court life. It had enormous influence as far away as England, where it contributed to an ideal of aristocracy celebrated by Sir Philip Sidney. That Edmund Curll should mention that the book is available at his shop is characteristic of his aggressive self-promotion. In fact, the translator of the 1724 edition of *The Courtier* was none other than Robert Samber, the man who translated *Venus in the Cloister* (1725) and who earlier had translated *Eunuchism Displayed* (1718). All three translations were commissioned by Curll.

17. See Song of Solomon 1: 2.

18. I.e., *L'Academie des Dames* (1680), a French translation by Jean Nicolas of Nicolas Chorier's Latin *Satyra Sotadica* (1660); included here (see chapter 5) is the English edition of 1740, *A Married Lady and a Maid*, which is abridged.

19. This English title perhaps refers to an 1707 edition by John Marshall. See Foxon, *Libertine Literature in England,* p. 42.

20. Dialogue 7, which is referred to, was omitted from the 1740 edition. The translation reads: "True light of love."

21. Dialogues IV and V of Curll's 1725 edition were added to the three of Barrin's 1683 original. As a result, there is a significant shift in tone and in subject matter, due, no doubt, to the material having been borrowed from other sources. The episode in Dialogue V that involves the unmasking of Marina, for example, was borrowed from Jean de La Fontaine's *Nouveau contes* (Paris 1675). For a modern translation, see *La Fontaine's Bawdy,* trans. Norman Shapiro (Princeton: Princeton University Press, 1992), pp. 201–13.

22. These titles are fictitious.

23. A "clearing up," or "clarification."

CHAPTER 5

1. Centering as it does on Octavia's wedding night and the loss of her virginity, *A Married Lady and a Maid* uses graphic descriptions of sexual intercourse to maintain the legitimacy of marriage while at the same time using the legitimacy of marriage to justify the graphic descriptions of sexual intercourse. Unlike *The School of Venus*, which encourages affairs and infidelity and uses sexual freedom as a weapon against the status quo, this dialogue does not consider sex out of wedlock, nor does it wield sexual liberation as a political weapon. As Foxon mentions, the abridgement carefully omits both the lesbian interactions of chapters 2 and 3 of the original and the Tullia's speeches in favor of a variety of sexual partners from chapter 4.

2. The martial metaphors of this passage hark back to Ovid's *Art of Love* (c. 4 A.D.) and anticipate Cleland's *Memoirs of a Woman of Pleasure* (1749). In the case of the former, the metaphors are a reminder of the *Art of Love*'s self-conscious pos-

NOTES TO PAGES 259–264

turing as a satiric "antiepic," a parody of the classic tales that chooses for its subject the clever maneuverings of infidelity instead of the grand battles between the Greeks and the Trojans. In the case of the latter, the metaphors obscure the coarse language of anatomy while they at once indulge and satirize the early eighteenth-century preoccupation with female chastity and its loss. Much more so than either *The School of Venus* or *Venus in the Cloister*, *A Married Lady and a Maid* centers on the loss of female chastity. The narrative is clearly built around the defloration of Tullia in the second dialogue and the defloration of Octavia in the third. Unlike *The Memoirs of a Woman of Pleasure*, however, which includes Mr. Norbert as a way of questioning the male obsession with female chastity, *A Married Lady and a Maid* indulges that obsession uncritically. In addition, although the abridgement does omit the more sadistic details of the original, *A Married Lady and a Maid* reproduces nonetheless the ongoing tension between pleasure and pain that characterizes many such defloration scenes.

CHAPTER 6

1. Lucretius Carus (99–55 B.C.), the epicurean philosopher and poet, is known for his masterwork *De rerum natura*. This passage, from book 2.1040–1043, can be translated literally as follows:

> Cease to eject reason from your mind,
> Having been terrified by novelty;
> But rather weigh it carefully with a sharp judgment,
> And if it seems true to you, throw in your hand;
> Or if it is false, gird yourself against it.

The translation by Thomas Creech was published originally in 1682 and reprinted in 1699 and 1700.

2. "Unguentis inungo": "anointed with perfumes."

3. "In Laetitia . . .": "they possessed and used perfumes in gladness." "*Unguentis & Oleo delibuti*": "I smell of anointed things and perfumes."

4. "Terre-Gaillarde": "merry land." "Laetor": "I rejoice" or "I am merry."

5. "Frohlich" is German for "merry." "Vrolick" means the same in Dutch.

6. "Vrouw" means "woman" in Dutch. "MNSVNRS" is an acronym for "mons veneris" or "mound of venus."

7. Virgil's *Georgics* (2.490): "Fortunate is he who has been able to learn the reason of things."

8. Patrick Gordon was the author of *Geography anatomiz'd, or, The geographical grammar. being a short and exact analysis of the whole body of modern geography, after a new and curious method*. The seventeenth edition was published in London in 1741.

9. "Podex" is the Latin word for "anus." "Caput" is the Latin word for "head."

10. Song of Solomon 4:1.

11. Bartholomew de Glanville, or Anglicus Bartholomaeus, was the author of

De proprietatibus rerum (*On the Properties of Things*; first published c.1470), a famous medieval encyclopedia of natural history.

12. The poem is possibly "A Panegyrick upon Cundums," which was included in a 1774 edition of Rochester's poems. John O'Neill, to whom I am grateful for the reference, believes that the poem is not by Rochester and that it dates from well before 1774, possibly around 1702 or 1703, just after the publication of another poem in imitation of Milton, "The Splendid Shilling." The opening lines of the "Panegyrick" are as follows:

> O all ye Nymphs, in lawless Love's Disport
> Assiduous! whose ever open Arms
> Both Day and Night stand ready to receive
> The fierce Assaults of Britain's am'rous Sons!
> Whether with Golden Watch, or stiff Brocade
> You shine in Playhouse or the Drawing-room.
> Whores thrice magnificent! Delight of Kings,
> And Lords of goodliest Note; or in mean Stuffs
> Ply ev'ry Evening near St. Clement's Pile,
> Or Church of fam'd St. Dunstan, or in Lane,
> Or Alley's dark Recess, or open Street,
> Known by white Apron, bart'ring Love with Cit,
> Or strolling Lawyer's Clerk at cheapest Rate;
> Whether of Needham's or of Jordan's Train,
> Hear, and attend: In Cundum's mighty Praise
> I sing, for sure 'tis worthy of a Song.
> Venus, assist my Lays, thou who presid'st
> In City Ball or Courtly Masquerade,
> Goddess supreme! sole Authoress of our Loves
> Pure and impure! whose Province 'tis to rule
> Not only o'er the chaster Marriage Bed,
> But filthiest Stews, and Houses of kept Dames!
> To thee I call, and with a friendly Voice,
> Cundum I sing — by Cundum now I cure
> Boldly the willing Maid, by Fear a while
> Kept virtuous, owns thy Pow'r, and takes thy Joys
> Tumultuous; Joys untasted but by them.
> Unknown big Belly, and squawling Brat,
> Best Guard of Modesty! She riots now
> Thy Vo'try, in the Fulness of thy Bliss.
> "Happy the Man, who in his Pocket keeps,
> Whether with green or scarlet Ribband bound,
> A well made Cundum — He, nor dreads the Ills
> Of Shankers or Cordee, or Bubos dire!"

13. Lucretius, *De rerum natura* 3.19-22.

14. Ovid, *Amores* Book 3.12.41.

15. "Fenny," that is, "marshy."

16. "Vesica" is the Latin word for "bladder." Other parts of the anatomy will be similarly abbreviated, including "labia," "clitoris," "hymen," and "uterus."

17. Kornelis Philander de Bruyn was the author of *Voyage au Levant. c'est-a-dire dans les principaux endroits de l'Asie Mineure, dans les isles de Chio, Rhodes, Chypre &c. de meme que dans les plus considerables villes d'Egypte, Syrie & Terre Sainte* (1725).

18. George Cheyne (1671–1743), Scottish physician, vegetarian, and diet guru, was the author of *An Essay on Health and Long Life* (1725) and *The English Malady; or, A treatise of nervous diseases of all kinds, as spleen, vapours, lowness of spirits, hypochondriacal, and hysterical distempers, &c. In three parts.* (1733).

19. Virgil, *Aeneid* 2.5–6.

20. Athanasius Kircher (1601?–1680), the German archaeologist, mathematician, philologist, and musicologist, was a well-known polymath and prolific author. His writings fill over forty volumes, and all were in Latin. He was noted for, among other things, his understanding of volcanos. *The vulcano's: or, Burning and fire-vomiting mountains, famous in the world: with their remarkables : Collected for the most part out of Kircher's Subterraneous world: and expos'd to more general view in English, upon the relation of the late wonderful and prodigious eruptions of Aetna.* was published in 1669.

21. This passage remains unidentified. It is not, I believe, from Kircher.

22. Albert Schultens (1686–1750), the well-known biblical scholar and Orientalist, provided notes to a 1732 edition of Baha'al-Din Shaddad's *Vita et res gesæ sultani, Almalichi Alnasiri, Saladini.* Saladin (1137–1193) was the sultan of Egypt, and this edition does include a "Geographical Commentary." There is a copy of the book at the Bodleian Library, Oxford.

23. T. Maccius Plautus, *Truculentus*, act 2, scene 7, lines 568–571. The passage, when translated by Henry Thomas Riley, reads: "I take a harlot to be just like what the sea is; what you give her she swallows down, and yet never overflows. But this at least the sea does preserve; what's in it is seen. Give her as much as ever you please, it's never seen either by the giver or the acceptor."

24. Lucan, *Pharsalia* 9.969.

25. Edward Chamberlayne's *Magna Britannia Notitia, or the Present State of Great Britain, with divers remarks upon the antient state thereof.* (1669) was revised by John Chamberlayne in 1716 and frequently reprinted. The last edition, the thirty-sixth, appeared in 1755.

26. Unidentified, but not to be confused with Jean Michel Moreau (1741–1814), a popular engraver who also did erotic prints. See Wagner, *Eros Revived,* p. 271.

27. Job 40:15–19.

28. Alexander Pope (1688–1744) published his six-volume translation of the *Iliad* between 1715 and 1720. These lines—book 12, lines 53–54—describe Hector fighting at the gates of Troy.

29. The translation is freely rendered. More literally: "Here, whoever reads the

delightful name, drink a toast with a happy, full pint, thus may your love affairs fall out luckily for you and may Cupid reward your vows." Unidentified source.

30. Unidentified source.

31. "Warren" is an obsolete form of "warrant." The reference is to Mary Toſt, who in November 1726 claimed, along with her man-midwife John Howard, to have been delivered of fourteen rabbits. Hogarth celebrated the hoax with a December print entitled *Cuniculari, or the Wise Men of Godlimen in Consultation*. See figure 6.2.

32. "Mr. *Boyle*" is most likely Robert Boyle (1627–91), the Anglo-Irish physicist and chemist, who late in life wrote several treatises on natural history. For Kircher, see note 20.

33. Henry Maundrell, *A Journey from Aleppo to Jerusalem at Easter* (1697).

34. "Pintle," middle English for "penis."

35. Job 41:1.

36. George Cheyne (1671–1743). See note 18.

37. "Sopited": "to render dull or sluggish," "to put to sleep," or "to end."

38. Unidentified. "SCAMNUM" means "bench" or "stool" in Latin.

39. James 1:27.

40. For Patrick Gordon, see note 8.

41. Greenvile Collins, *Great Britain's Coasting-Pilot. The first part. Being a new and exact survey of the sea-coast of England, from the River of Thames to the Westward, with the Islands of Scilly, and from thence to Carlile.* (London, 1738).

42. Pietro Aretino (1492–1556), the Italian satirist, is generally known as the first European "pornographer." He was responsible for what has become known as *Aretino's Postures*, a series of engravings and accompanying sonnets. The original designs were executed by Guilio Romano and engraved by Marcantonio Raimondi in 1524. Pietro Aretino, inspired by engravings, wrote a sonnet for each of the plates in 1525. Sometime in the following years, the original number of engravings, sixteen, was expanded to twenty. *Aretino's Postures* became a well-known curiosity and existed in many different forms throughout the seventeenth and eighteenth centuries. Aretino was also responsible for the *Ragionamenti* (1534–36), the first of the "whore dialogues." See Foxon, *Libertine Literature in England*, pp. 5, 19–20.

CHAPTER 7

1. Fielding's epigraph is taken from book 12.174–176, where Nestor explains how the warrior Caeneus was originally the nymph Caenis, who was raped by Neptune and then transformed into a man and made invulnerable in warfare. The passage reads:

> But what did most his martial deeds adorn,
> (Though since he changed his sex) a woman born.
> A novelty so strange, and full of fate,
> They asked him to relate. —Bryden et al. (London, 1717)

Coming at the beginning of Nestor's story, this passage asks us to consider Fielding as another Nestor compelled to relate "A novelty so strange, and full of fate." It is important to note that while Fielding is writing *The Female Husband*, he is also translating Ovid's *Art of Love*, which appeared in February 1747, and working on his masterwork *Tom Jones*. Central to all three is the problem of sexual identity and its various instabilities. See Paulson, *Henry Fielding*, pp. 232–234.

2. Fielding's attack on Methodism is curiously intertwined with his attack on lesbianism. From his perspective, the religious enthusiasms of the former are directly responsible for the perversions of the latter.

3. Fielding is clearly having fun with this letter and, in particular, with both the speed with which Mrs. Johnson's transformation occurred and the interplay between religious and sexual pleasure. In this regard, the letter is reminiscent of the prefatory letters of *Shamela* (1741), in which Parson Tickletext becomes excited by the vision of Pamela with "all the Pride of Ornament cast off."

4. Carlo Broschi Farinelli (1705–82) was a famous Italian male soprano and the greatest of the castrati. He was a pupil of Niccolò Porpora, in whose operas he sang in London during the 1730s. After leaving London, Farinelli became the official singer for Philip V of Spain and renounced his public career. Fielding's joke lies in the widow's insistence that there is some resemblance between Farinelli, the famous castrato, and Mr. George Hamilton.

5. Matthew Prior (1664–1721), the poet and diplomat, was the author of *The Country Mouse and the City Mouse* (1687), a satire on Dryden's poem *The Hind and the Panther* (1687), and several other volumes of light verse.

6. "Green sickness" referred to a distemper common to female virgins. Symptoms varied but included irritability, sleeplessness, and fainting, all of which resulted from unsatisfied lust. See chapter 2, *The Fifteen Plagues of a Maiden-Head*, stanza 7, and chapter 3, *Gonosologium Novum*.

7. Fielding here exhibits the same kind of orthographic gamesmanship that characterizes *Shamela* (1741). Indications of his irony are to be found in the sentence that introduces the letter.

8. William Congreve (1670–1729) was the author of the novel *Incognita* (1691) and numerous plays, the most famous of which is *The Way of the World* (1700), generally considered a masterpiece of restoration drama. Congreve's play *The Old Bachelor* (1693) was the first to bring him critical acclaim.

BIBLIOGRAPHY

Ballaster, Rosalind. *Seductive Forms: Women's Amatory Fiction, 1684–1740*. New York: Oxford University Press, 1992.

Bold, Alan, ed. *The Sexual Dimension in Literature*. New York: Barnes and Noble, 1982.

Bouce, Paul-Gabriel, ed. *Sexuality in Eighteenth-Century Britain*. Manchester: Manchester University Press, 1982.

Brewer, John. *The Pleasures of the Imagination: English Culture in the Eighteenth Century*. New York: Farrar Straus Giroux, 1997.

Butler, Judith. *Gender Trouble: Feminism and the Subversion of Identity*. New York: Routledge, 1990.

Castle, Terry. *The Female Thermometer: Eighteenth-Century Culture and the Invention of the Uncanny*. New York: Oxford University Press, 1995.

———. *Masquerade and Civilization: The Carnivalesque in Eighteenth-Century English Culture and Fiction*. Stanford: Stanford University Press, 1986.

Darnton, Robert. *The Forbidden Best-Sellers of Pre-Revolutionary France*. New York: Norton, 1995.

Dollimore, Jonathan. *Sexual Dissidence: Augustine to Wilde, Freud to Foucault*. Oxford: Oxford University Press, 1991.

Donoghue, Emma. *Passions between Women: British Lesbian Culture 1668–1801*. New York: Harper Perennial, 1993.

Fort, Bernadette, and Angela Rosenthal, eds. *The Other Hogarth: Aesthetics of Difference*. Princeton: Princeton University Press, 2001.

Foucault, Michel. *The History of Sexuality: An Introduction*. New York: Vintage Books, 1980.

Foxon, David. *Libertine Literature in England, 1660–1745*. New York: University Books, 1965.

Gallagher, Catherine. *Nobody's Story: The Vanishing Acts of Women Writers in the Marketplace, 1670–1820*. Berkeley: University of California Press, 1994.

Gilbert, Ruth. *Early Modern Hermaphrodites: Sex and Other Stories*. New York: Palgrave Press, 2002.

Hitchcock, Tim. *English Sexualities, 1700–1800*. New York: St. Martin's Press, 1997.

Hunt, Lynn, ed. *Eroticism and the Body Politic*. Baltimore: Johns Hopkins University Press, 1991.

———. *The Invention of Pornography: Obscenity and the Origins of Modernity, 1500–1800*. New York: Zone Books, 1996.

Hunter, J. Paul. *Before Novels: The Cultural Contexts of Eighteenth-Century English Fiction*. New York: W. W. Norton, 1990.

Jordanova, Ludmilla. *Sexual Visions: Images of Gender in Science and Medicine between the Eighteenth and Twentieth Centuries*. Madison: University of Wisconsin Press, 1989.

Kahn, Madeline. *Narrative Transvestism: Rhetoric and Gender in the Eighteenth-Century Novel*. Ithaca: Cornell University Press, 1991.

Kendrick, Walter. *The Secret Museum: Pornography in Modern Culture*. New York: Penguin Books, 1987.

Laqueur, Thomas. *Making Sex: Body and Gender from the Greeks to Freud*. Cambridge: Harvard University Press, 1990.

Lewes, Darby. *Nudes from Nowhere: Utopian Sexual Landscapes*. New York: Rowman and Littlefield Publishers, 2000.

Loth, David. *The Erotic in Literature*. New York: Dorset Press, 1961.

Marcus, Steven. *The Other Victorians: A Study of Sexuality and Pornography in Mid-Nineteenth-Century England*. New York: Norton, 1964.

McCalman, Ian. *Radical Underworld: Prophets, Revolutionaries, and Pornographers in London, 1795–1840*. Cambridge, England: Cambridge University Press, 1988.

McKeon, Michael. *The Origins of the English Novel, 1600–1740*. Baltimore: Johns Hopkins University Press, 1987.

Moore, Lisa. *Dangerous Intimacies: Toward a Sapphic History of the British Novel*. Durham: Duke University Press, 1997.

Moulton, Ian. *Before Pornography: Erotic Writing in Early Modern England*. New York: Oxford University Press, 2000.

Mudge, Bradford K. *Sex and Sexuality. Parts Three and Four. Erotica, 1650–1900, from the Private Case Collection at the British Library, London*. London: Adam Matthew, 2003.

———. *The Whore's Story: Women, Pornography, and the British Novel, 1684–1830*. New York: Oxford University Press, 2000.

Nussbaum, Felicity. *Torrid Zones: Maternity, Sexuality, and Empire in Eighteenth-Century English Narratives*. Baltimore: Johns Hopkins University Press, 1995.

Paster, Gail Kern. *The Body Embarrassed: Drama and the Disciplines of Shame in Early Modern England*. Ithaca, N.Y.: Cornell University Press, 1993.

Paulson, Ronald. *The Life of Henry Fielding: A Critical Biography*. London: Blackwell, 2000.

———. *Popular and Polite Art in the Age of Hogarth and Fielding*. Notre Dame, Ind.: University of Notre Dame Press, 1979.

Peakman, Julie. *Mighty Lewd Books*. New York: Palgrave, 2003.

Pease, Allison. *Modernism, Mass Culture, and the Aesthetics of Obscenity*. Cambridge, England: Cambridge University Press, 2000.

Pettit, Alexander, and Patrick Spedding, eds. *Eighteenth-Century British Erotica*. 5 vols. London: Pickering and Chatto, 2002.

Phillips, Kim, and Barry Reay, eds. *Sexualities in History: A Reader*. New York: Routledge, 2002.

Porter, Dorothy, and Roy Porter. *Patient's Progress: Doctors and Doctoring in Eighteenth-Century England*. Stanford: Stanford University Press, 1989.

Porter, Roy, and Mulvey-Roberts, Marie eds. *Pleasure in the Eighteenth Century*. New York: New York University Press, 1996.

Rembar, Charles. *The End of Obscenity:* The Trials of *Lady Chatterley, Tropic of Cancer,* and *Fanny Hill*. New York: Random House, 1968.

Richlin, Amy, ed. *Pornography and Representation in Greece and Rome*. New York: Oxford, 1992.

Shattuck, Roger. *Forbidden Knowledge: From Prometheus to Pornography*. New York: St. Martin's Press, 1996.

Stanton, Domna. *Discourses of Sexuality: From Aristotle to AIDS*. Ann Arbor: University of Michigan Press, 1992.

Stephens, Walter. *Demon Lovers: Witchcraft, Sex, and the Crisis of Belief*. Chicago: University of Chicago Press, 2002.

Straus, Ralph. *The Unspeakable Curll, Being Some Account of Edmund Curll, Bookseller; to Which Is Added a Full List of His Books*. London: Chapman and Hall, 1927.

Thomas, Donald. *A Long Time Burning: The History of Literary Censorship in England*. New York: Praeger, 1969.

Trumbach, Randolph. *Sex and the Gender Revolution*. Chicago: University of Chicago Press, 1999.

Wagner, Peter. *Eros Revived: Erotica of the Enlightenment in England and America*. London: Secker and Warburg, 1988.

Warner, William. *Licensing Entertainment: The Elevation of Novel Reading in Britain, 1684–1750*. Berkeley: University of California Press, 1998.

Watt, Ian. *The Rise of the Novel. Studies in Defoe, Richardson, and Fielding*. Berkeley: University of California Press, 1957.

Williams, Linda. *Hard Core: Power, Pleasure, and the "Frenzy of the Visible."* Berkeley: University of California Press, 1989.

Yeazeall, Ruth Bernard. *Fictions of Modesty: Women and Courtship in the English Novel*. University of Chicago Press, 1991.

INDEX